THE
ALADDIN TRIAL

THE
ALADDIN
TRIAL

ABI SILVER

Lightning
Books

Published in 2018
by Lightning Books Ltd
Imprint of EyeStorm Media
312 Uxbridge Road
Rickmansworth
Hertfordshire
WD3 8YL

www.lightning-books.com

ISBN: 9781785630750

Cover by Shona Andrew/www.spikyshooz.com
Typesetting and design by Clio Mitchell

British Library Cataloguing in Publication Data
A catalogue record for this book is available from the British Library.

Printed by CPI Group (UK) Ltd, Croydon CR0 4YY

This one's for you, Mum

PART ONE

PART ONE

1

THE BODY LAY unnoticed for hours. This was not startling; the area behind St Mark's Hospital was hardly a magnet for revellers or a main thoroughfare, and it had been night time when she had fallen. But it might have surprised the corpse – before she died, of course – given the manner of her launch from the platform above and the spectacular splintering of her skull against an exposed tree stump.

As a young art student, she had tried many times to imitate Picasso's style in his Cubist period, before tiring of painting portraits in vibrant colours with one eye bigger than the other. It might have been comforting to her to imagine her own face appearing that way now, one side swollen and disfigured, the eye bulging, out of proportion, a mass of yellow and purple, rather than the more gruesome reality of her situation.

And if she had had time to reflect on things, the deceased might have conceived of her plunge as a glorious swan song, a piece of intense performance art to herald her departure from this world and her arrival in the next, worthy of a standing ovation.

But in truth, there was almost nothing of any note; the crack of her head's destruction, the snap of her neck and then her body listing to one side before settling quickly into the undergrowth, its flamboyant fall a distant memory. And then silence. No trumpets or fanfares, no applause, no rush to her aid. Barbara Hennessy's life came to an end much as she had lived: erratically and with a burst of great drama.

This was how she was found by a walker around 5.30am, his dog first romping towards her crumpled body then pausing, its head turning one way and the other, enveloped in sensory confusion. Now the area was a hive of activity; forensics and police and local people, including hospital employees and workers, trying to get a glimpse on their way into work.

Barbara was still wearing her nightdress and hospital wrist tag. If she had been allowed to choose her own attire for such an occasion, she would have preferred the Stella McCartney number she had picked up from a car boot sale in Tring, and her Boho bangle. Sadly, those items were languishing in the bedroom of her modest flat in Primrose Hill (closer to Chalk Farm but she had persisted with the Primrose Hill tag), the dress hanging in the wardrobe, the bracelet in the drawer by her bed.

Perhaps, if considering the matter objectively (which was not actually Barbara's forte) she would have appreciated the aesthetics of the scene: her forget-me-not blue nightgown complemented the rose bay willow herb and set off the last of the bluebells. And her fiery orange Vivienne Westwood rinse blended in with the carpet of crisp, fallen oak leaves she lay upon.

Chief Inspector Dawson lifted the flap of the makeshift tent erected over the dead woman. He was no art-lover and paid no attention to the colours or hues or shapes of what he saw. 'Cause of death' was what interested him first and foremost, and whether, as a result of what he could glean from the body and the attending pathologist, he would be heading up another murder enquiry.

Later, after a few direct questions to the pathologist, Dawson would go into the hospital, ride the crowded lift, and stand with furrowed brow at the place from which the deceased had perhaps plunged to her death. She had fallen – or been pushed (no conclusions had yet been drawn; all options were being assessed and weighed up) – not from her allotted bedroom but a staff room at the end of the corridor. So, for all Dawson's complaints about 'contamination', in truth there was no way to secure this crime scene. This was a hospital. It was impossible to move any other patients out from their rooms. Even if he could negotiate the administrative minefield of where to relocate private patients in an NHS hospital, there weren't any spare beds. And the staff needed somewhere to go, or they'd be changing in the corridor.

He would sniff the air in the woman's room and smell only disinfectant and a mild, sweet scent from the roses next to her hospital bed. But here, again, the evidence was damaged. When the nurses had been alerted to the grisly discovery eleven floors below, they had rushed into Mrs Hennessy's room (he knew her name now, although while he was outside and she was spread on the ground in front of him, she had been very much 'the woman' or 'the body'), tweaking the bed and its covers, opening and closing doors.

One nurse admitted later on that she had crawled underneath the bed; ridiculous given Mrs Hennessy's age and the fact that the gap beneath the bed was visible from the door. But perhaps the nurses had needed corroboration of what they had been told?

How could effusive Barbara Hennessy, who had chatted to them animatedly about the effective use of elephant dung in paintings (they had been rather disgusted), and sitting as a model for Lucian Freud (they had pretended to know who he was, but it made her sound eminent in any event), really be lying dead on the ground below?

It was much simpler to imagine the former inhabitant of room 3 as having been discharged a little earlier than expected; all that remained was for a relative to return to pick up her things.

Inspector Dawson would placate himself with the conclusion that there was little of note in Mrs Hennessy's room to assist his investigation: three pillows at the head of the bed, suggesting her last position had been fairly upright; the bed covers turned back as if she had exited in a hurry. A paperback book, *The Arabian Nights*, lay on the table, a bookmark showing limited progress through its pages.

And when Dawson exited, he would notice the blinds were closed across the glass-panelled door. For a second, he had a vision of a man with gloved hands, wearing a surgical mask, creeping in during the hours of darkness, sliding the blinds closed and rushing forward to strike the helpless woman as she lay asleep in bed. Dawson shook his head. He should stick to the facts and where they led him, and avoid extrapolation. He reached out to touch the glass and then hurried off to give express instructions for fingerprinting to dust that area down thoroughly when they arrived.

'What can you tell me?' he asked the pathologist, gruffly, acutely aware of the staleness in the air beneath the canvas. 'And don't hold back, I've already been put off my lunch.'

2

CONSTANCE Lamb was basking in the delightful aroma of her newly brewed coffee when her mobile rang. She toyed with ignoring it but then snatched it up on the last ring before it transferred to voicemail. Thirty seconds later she was considering how best to broach, with Mike, the subject of yet another early morning summons to the cells.

Mike lay on his side in the bed they shared, with his eyes closed. Constance hovered in the doorway, cup in hand, preparing herself to speak but, at the same time, certain that he had heard the ringtone and the snatched conversation which followed and knew what it heralded. This feeling that Mike was 'all-knowing' was borne out by prior experience.

Mike had that impact on other people too; after meeting him for the first time, her mother had remarked that he had 'a presence.' There were other things she had wanted to say to her daughter about Mike but she had held back.

It was hard to explain why he commanded such authority. He

wasn't enormously tall or dazzlingly handsome, and his voice was not piercing or resonant. Perhaps it was the opposite: his ability to focus long and hard on the task in hand, engendering the belief that he was a deep thinker, that nothing, however insignificant, would pass him by. This single-mindedness was what had attracted Constance to him that very first time she had spied him in Sammy's bar, two years earlier.

He had been drinking a beer with ferocious intensity, and she had found herself peering at him over and over again. When he had drained it to the bottom, he had placed the bottle down deliberately in the centre of the table, lifted his eyes and smiled at her. Although now she knew him better, she sometimes doubted if that absorbed, intense personality was 'the real Mike' or only the image he had wanted to portray.

Constance crossed the room and retrieved her black trousers from the chair in the corner. They had almost made it back into the wardrobe the previous night, but Mike had interrupted her to ask if they had run out of cereal for his late-night snack and she had forgotten to put them away. She heard Mike's breath leave his body in a short burst. She interpreted this as a sign of annoyance, but she wasn't sure; she had finally taken a day's holiday, they had planned to spend the day together, finishing up with the press night of a new play. Mike's friend – well, rival might be a better description, as they had both auditioned for this part – had bagged the lead, and had graciously handed out tickets.

'Mike,' she whispered, receiving no response. 'I've got to go out. I'll probably only be an hour.'

Now Mike twitched his head away from her and lay still again. This time all traces of breathing stopped. He had performed this respiratory deception before and she wondered if it were a party trick he had used to impress previous girlfriends: 'play dead' so they would make a fuss of him. But she didn't have time for his games this morning.

She pulled a white shirt from the wardrobe, tugged it over her head and buttoned it up. Then she sat down next to him, kissing his exposed neck above the covers. Mike remained unnaturally still but, unperturbed, she kissed him a second time and ran two fingers down his cheek ending on his lips, then returning them to her own. She shook her head almost imperceptibly. *God he was stubborn.*

'Don't go anywhere. When I get back I'll fix you a huge breakfast. OK?' she tried a final time.

When he failed to respond, Constance stood up and slipped her feet into her shoes before twisting her hair around into a tight bun and securing it with a hair pin. Five minutes later she was striding out into the cool air of the May morning, wondering how long she would have to wait for a train.

3

AHMAD QABBANI removed his jacket and hung it in the staff cupboard. The day was warm but, after three years in England, he knew better than to place any trust in the weather. He had learned the hard way that even the brightest start could be smothered and drenched in the time it took to unwrap his lunch, leaving him shivering and damp on his journey home.

He opened his locker and extracted his white apron, replacing it with the one he had carried home two nights before. His third and final apron had been delivered to Aisha, his wife, for washing only last night. He repeated this process every day to ensure he was always wearing a clean uniform. Not that he got really dirty, not often anyway, but you couldn't see most germs and he had always had a spotless uniform in his previous life, before coming to England, so why should he change things now?

Aisha didn't complain about the washing, she didn't complain about anything at all. She accepted Ahmad's apron each evening, or sometimes in the mornings when he worked nights, and there

15

was always a clean replacement folded by the front door, together with a homemade meal for every day he went to work.

Maia, the other hospital cleaner, had worked through the night; not on this floor – they didn't clean the private rooms during the night unless they received a special instruction – but they both had their lockers up here and their cleaning materials in the store room. She had left him a note on top of the bucket; she did that sometimes, scribbled on the back of a Tesco receipt. It read 'Mr D room 6 very sick.' And she had drawn a sad face with its tongue sticking out.

Ahmad grinned. Some days he and Maia worked at the same times and took breaks together. She was only twenty and from Romania, and had big dreams of marrying a doctor and living in a mansion overlooking the heath. Then she would have her own cleaner. He interpreted her note as a warning both to be prepared for whatever he may have to clean up in room 6, and also to enter quietly. Ahmad always did this anyway. He had learned the hard way that English patients really don't like to be woken up when they have 'just got off to sleep' even if, in reality, they spend most of the day and night snoozing.

He checked his phone for messages. Only last week the school had called to say that Shaza, his daughter, was ill and he had had to return home almost as soon as he arrived, although it was still early – not time yet for school. He switched the phone to silent; he was not allowed to take calls on the ward.

Ahmad unpacked the pie Aisha had baked for his lunch and took a moment to savour the pungent aroma of *zaatar* before placing it in the staff fridge. The day she had visited the local shops and bought thyme and sumac and ground up her own *zaatar*, he had begun to hope she had turned a corner, that things might return to some semblance of how they used to be. But even though he had *zaatar* pie for his lunch, with olives and a pot of *fatoush* salad, little else of the joy of their former life had returned. How could it?

As he placed the apron over his head, he became aware of pounding footsteps in the corridor and raised voices speaking over each other. Ahmad peered out to see the cause of the commotion. Three nurses were standing outside Mrs Hennessy's room talking in an animated way. One of them reached her hand out to touch the door handle and then withdrew it. Then a second nurse did the same. Ahmad watched them huddled together stepping forwards and back, stretching out and retracting their arms, rather like a bizarre form of dance. Maia would have thought it funny. She would have copied them, turning it into a loud, raucous Eastern European version of the hokey-cokey.

Ahmad considered offering to help but decided against it. Sometimes the nurses were friendly but not all of them and not always. He would wait to be asked.

He collected his bucket, mop and trolley from the cupboard and checked that all his cleaning materials were intact. But then heavier steps thundered past him and he heard a deep voice he recognised as Dr Mahmood, one of the senior consultants, delivering orders. Ahmad had little direct interaction with Dr Mahmood, although he frequently saw him on the wards and corridors. On the first occasion they had come across each other, he had nodded politely. On the second, Ahmad had tried to make eye contact, had tentatively craved recognition or kinship, from this English-adopted countryman of his.

But Dr Mahmood had merely reflected Ahmad's bow of their first encounter and averted his eyes, and Ahmad had chewed his lower lip and chastised himself for his impertinence. After that, when he saw Dr Mahmood heading in his direction he stepped back and busied himself with something else. It was better that way.

4

Tracy Jones removed a KitKat from the cupboard and unwrapped it hurriedly, snapping the bar in two cleanly along its perforation. She almost shoved the first piece in her mouth then and there but suddenly remembered those 'tips for dieting' which recommended that you always sit down before eating, and assess clinically and rationally if you really want to consume something unhealthy before doing so. Huffing, she sat down at the table, held the KitKat under her nose for five seconds then, muttering 'oh sod it' under her breath, she ate both halves simultaneously.

Reaching forward, she grabbed the pile of letters which had accrued through the week, and began to leaf through them. Eventually she stopped and opened one brown envelope. She read its contents and scowled before moving on to the next one. She continued the shuffling and selection exercise, followed by opening, reading and a grimace, until all had been examined, the ripped envelopes forming an impromptu fan on the table top.

Then she read through each one again, placing them in a pile in her own order, at times holding one next to another to compare and contrast, all the time her tongue working around her mouth for the last vestiges of the chocolate she had just consumed.

The final item of post was a laminated, double-sided flyer for a cruise: 'Aegean Odyssey', it was called, and the sea in the picture was the blue of Vermeer, the ultramarine he loved to spread around so generously. She held the card up to her face, allowing it to touch her cheek. One small tear squeezed out of the corner of her right eye.

She pulled a magnet from the fridge in the shape of a Cornish pasty, from their holiday of sorts last summer – seven nights in Bude. It had rained for five of the days; the kids hadn't minded but she had sat in the car, propped up with a flask of coffee, watching them cavorting in the spray, calculating whether there was enough radiator space in the cottage to dry everything off later. She couldn't allow herself to dwell on holidays past: Barbados, The Maldives, Dubai. It was simply too painful.

She stuck the photo in the middle of the fridge and sighed before extracting a pile of green, dog-eared exercise books from her bag. She had an hour to spare before her own boys emerged from their beds, demanding breakfast, and another half hour before the school run.

Then she had promised her mother to be at the hospital by twelve, which she could manage if her colleague covered her afternoon lessons. God, she hoped Barbara wouldn't make too many demands, as she wanted to get back to school in time for pick-up. She would make sure she took in some fresh food tomorrow, and the boys could visit too. That would be a daughterly thing to offer. But there was no way Barbara was convalescing at her house. There wasn't the space, and Tracy wouldn't survive twelve hours of her mother's reflections on life and on what she should be doing to 'lose that spare tyre.' That had been the topic Barbara had helpfully canvassed with her at least three times over Christmas lunch.

Tracy focused again on the book in front of her, and her eyes glazed over. How many days were left till the end of the school term? But glancing across at the new addition to the fridge display, at least now she could dream.

Halfway through marking the third book, her mobile phone rang.

5

CHIEF INSPECTOR Dawson was leaning against the glass wall of the interview room in Hampstead police station when Constance arrived, and he greeted her with a tired smile and a perfunctory shake of her hand.

'You're a long way from home?' he said.

'Not so far. And you called me. But what are *you* doing here?'

'The Chief here had to take some leave. I'm told it's not terminal but I don't like to ask. And I fancied a change – see how the other half lives, you know. NW3 postcode is a nice addition to my portfolio. I'm here for six months probably. See how it goes. It's an older station though, over one hundred years. The lads swear it's haunted.'

Constance peered through the glass. The man she could see was sitting alone, his hands resting on his thighs and his head bowed. He was in his early thirties, hair receding at the temples, with a neat beard, and he was dressed in jeans and a casual shirt.

'This is your guy. We've only got a few questions for him but he demanded a lawyer.'

'Who is he?'

'Cleaner at St Mark's Hospital. We found a body there a few hours ago…well, I should say, outside there. A woman, Barbara Hennessy, seventies, injuries consistent with a fall from a height, probably from her ward on the eleventh floor. No idea if she fell or jumped or was pushed, provisional time of death between seven and midnight last night, so we're talking first to everyone who was in the ward then, and that includes this guy.'

'What's his name?'

'Ahmad Qabbani.'

'English?'

'No. From Syria.'

Constance's lips parted slowly but no sound came out. She examined Ahmad again through the glass.

'He's not a suspect?'

'No. Not at the moment. We asked him and a few others to come here to help us with enquiries, to see if we could begin to work out timings better. He's the only one who requested a lawyer. D'you think he has something to hide?'

Constance frowned.

'Not necessarily,' she replied. 'Maybe that's how they do things in Syria.'

Dawson guffawed.

'Come on. You think you get a lawyer at a Syrian police station? Not sure if he'll talk to you though, you being a woman.'

Constance bit her lip.

'We were going to send him home,' Dawson continued, 'when he started the lawyer nonsense, but you have to be thorough these days. We're even going to question the doctors. 'Course we couldn't get them to come here. Something about sick patients... but I'm heading over there this afternoon to interview Dr Wolf, Mrs Hennessy's doctor, at the hospital. To get the full picture.'

'Was she very ill?'

'Who, Mrs Hennessy? No. She only went in to have her bunions done. Had the operation yesterday. She was going home today.'

'She might have fallen?'

'Might have. And the most likely place, given the location of the body, was from a fire escape right at the end of the corridor, if she was able to get herself down there. Or silly old bat might have got it into her head that she fancied a night out in Camden Town and didn't want to take the lift. But we're keeping an open mind.'

***

'Mr Qabbani?'

'Yes.' Ahmad's voice was imbued with concern.

'I'm Constance Lamb. I'm a solicitor, a lawyer. You asked for me.' She stretched out her hand and he eyed her suspiciously before taking it, his long, elegant fingers curling and uncurling themselves gently around the palm of her hand.

'I have waited more than an hour and I need to return to my work now please,' he replied, his fluid English augmented with a heavily accented 'k' sound which split the sentence unevenly.

'I'm sorry. I came as quickly as I could but I live some distance away. This won't take long now I'm here. The police just want to ask a few questions. They're trying to piece together what happened. Then you can go. Can I check some personal details first? Your full name is Ahmad Qabbani and your address is 33 Braham Terrace, London W3?'

'That is correct.'

Constance pulled a business card from her pocket and offered it to him.

'This is my card, with my details, phone number, email. Just in case, well, just in case you need me afterwards. And the police will take your fingerprints and a sample of saliva after you've answered their questions.'

'Am I being arrested?'

'No. Nothing like that. It's just routine. An elderly lady, a Mrs Hennessy, was found dead this morning, outside the hospital.'

Ahmad sat in silence.

'Did you know Mrs Hennessy had died?'

'Yes. I heard about it. That's why I'm here.'

When Ahmad made no sign of interest in her offering or in providing any further response, Constance placed her card down on the table in front of him. He picked it up and put it in his pocket without reading it.

'Did you know Mrs Hennessy?'

'Yes. I cleaned in her room.'

'When did you last see her?'

'Yesterday in the morning.' Ahmad was gazing somewhere over Constance's left shoulder.

'What time was that?'

He hesitated then continued, 'Maybe around eleven o'clock. I am not sure.'

'And when did you leave the hospital?'

'I finish at eight o'clock.'

'Did anyone see you leave?'

'I don't think so.'

'Do you know why Mrs Hennessy was in hospital?'

A flicker of hesitation. 'I'm just the cleaner,' he said, his eyes finally settling on hers, but only fleetingly. They were black and probing, keen and searching. Constance cleared her throat.

'Did you see her walking after her operation?'

'I only saw Mrs Hennessy in the morning. Then I clean the rest of the hospital. Can you see if we can do the questions with the police now? I don't want to lose more pay.'

'You've lost your pay?'

'If I'm not working I don't get paid,' he replied simply, his eyes wandering off again.

'They'll be in soon. Why did you ask for a lawyer?' Constance watched Ahmad intently. He moistened his lips twice before answering.

'I have read stories, in the newspapers, about what happens sometimes to people in police stations,' he said.

'I wouldn't let Inspector Dawson hear you say that,' Constance said. 'He would be very offended.' She attempted a smile. 'How long have you been in England?'

'Three years.'

'Your English is very good.'

'Like I was saying, I read the newspapers.'

'And your family?'

Ahmad closed his mouth. Constance was not sure if he was preparing himself to stonewall her question but then the door opened and Inspector Dawson entered.

6

'Hi Shadya, are you there?

'Ah. You are. I thought you might have been sleeping. I haven't slept a wink all night. No. Really I wasn't.

'When Baba came in this morning I was only pretending to be asleep. He had that "hard day at work" serious look on his face.

'No. I was going to ask him but he got home so late and I was already in bed. And then, this morning, like I said, he had *the serious* look.

'Anyway, I don't want to talk about Baba. What shall we do today when I get back from school? Let's go outside and play elastics.

'Oh you sound just like Mama. She's always saying that.

'That the street "isn't safe". She says there are bigger children who will hurt me but I'm not scared. And anyway, I'd be with you.

'No. I don't tell her about you.

'You know why?

'She's been OK, I think. Taking her tablets. Not crying too

much although I made her cry last night.

'I didn't mean to.

'She prepared kebab but she made so much. I said to her "Mama. You forget it's just me. I can't eat all this." That's when she cried.

'No I wasn't being mean. I just couldn't eat it all.

'Yes. But honestly, why do I always have to say things differently? Why can't I just say what I think? Grown-ups are so weird, pretending they're the ones who do everything and understand everything. We do too. Especially you and me together.

'What's that? OK. We still have time before breakfast. Let's play Aladdin. I'll be Princess Jasmine and you can be Aladdin. OK, OK. I'll be Aladdin and you can be Princess Jasmine, just this once. But I'll be the Genie too.

'Shadya. If you had three wishes, three real wishes and they were going to come true, what would you wish for? I know already what mine would be.'

7.

'HEY, YOU'RE UP? I can still cook you some eggs if you like?'

Constance dropped her keys back into her handbag and swung it over the back of the chair. It was only just after eleven; she had been out longer than expected but the day was still young.

Mike was sitting at the table in his pyjama trousers, finishing off some toast, thick rolls of butter floating like rafts on the bread. He rose, without speaking to Constance, and slid the remains into the bin, before depositing his plate in the sink. Then, still mute, he marched towards the bathroom.

'Mike, what's up?' Constance didn't want to apologise. She had hurried back and, from what she could ascertain of Mike's usual daily routine, he was hardly ever out of bed before 10:30 during the week in any event.

Mike stalled outside the bathroom, his fingers strumming the door frame. He didn't turn around.

'Is it because you had to make your own breakfast? We've still got the whole day,' she said, shuffling her feet out of her shoes.

When he remained motionless she sashayed up to him, slid her arms around his waist and pressed her face against his back, basking in the warmth of his body. Mike removed her hands, albeit gently, continued inside the bathroom and closed the door behind him. She heard him switch on the shower.

Constance retreated to the table.

Mike wasn't being fair. It wasn't fair that he was cross when she had no choice about her work. Did he really think she enjoyed trekking half way across London to a police station instead of enjoying a rare lie in? And she was always there for him, at endless rehearsals and 'after parties' with producers and actors who never remembered her name, helping him learn his lines, standing in for various other characters and props. If Mike had only evaluated things logically, as she did, he might have viewed things the same way. Granted he would still have been cross, but he would have recognised he had no right to be cross. And slowly, slowly he would have come around.

But Mike wasn't like that. He enjoyed the theatricality of it all; inhabiting the skin of the wronged partner, the abandoned, lonely homemaker, the down-on-his-luck actor waiting for his big break.

For a second she thought about Ahmad Qabbani, his reticence, the way he had shrunk in his seat when Dawson arrived, had answered Dawson's questions in clipped and hushed tones and, at one point, had steadied his right leg with his hand when it began to tremble. How she had concealed herself nearby and watched him leave the police station; first his lurch out onto the street, then his stagger to a shop doorway where he had crouched shivering for some minutes before standing up stiffly and heading down the hill towards the hospital.

Suddenly Mike reappeared, the patter of the shower his cue, inscrutable, his head tipped to one side, his hand outstretched, and he wasn't wearing his pyjamas or his towel.

'Would mademoiselle care for some brunch?' he asked in an exaggerated French accent.

'You are an unreasonable pig, do you know that?' Constance replied.

'Yes, but totally irresistible all the same.'

Constance unbuttoned her shirt as she went to take his hand.

8

TRACY JONES was upset. Since Dawson had called her, first thing that morning, to tell her that her mother was dead, she hadn't known what to think or feel. His words were still ricocheting around her skull, and the two paracetamol she had taken had not made any dent in the wall of pain which traversed her forehead. She hadn't called Pete, her husband – he had left early to visit a potential development site in the Midlands with his brother – and she had not been able to face telling the boys. So, she had dropped them off at school, pretending everything was fine and then emailed in a message that she had a migraine and would not be coming to work. She had hoped to have some time alone. But now her brother, Joe, had arrived without warning.

Tracy took refuge in the kitchen on the pretext of making some coffee. She filled the kettle and switched it on, pressing the palms of her hands onto the cool worktop to calm her nerves. She could hear Joe whistling to himself in the lounge, a trait he had had since childhood, and usually reserved for the most stressful of moments.

'I brought some biscuits anyway,' she mumbled, re-entering the room with two mugs and a packet of chocolate digestives, her voice quivering as Joe scowled from his vantage point by the window. 'Joe, come and sit down. I know you're upset…'

'Too right I'm upset. Mum isn't even in the ground and they're asking all these questions. At ten o'clock they arrived at the showroom, put all the customers off.'

Tracy's hands trembled as she balanced the biscuits on the arm of the sofa and sat down herself. She should have known that Joe wasn't just here to commiserate.

'Who's asking questions?'

'The police. They think I don't know what they're after. They came around pretending they were sorry; "bereavement counselling", they called it. But then they started asking all this stuff. Have they been here yet?'

'No. Someone's coming this evening, I think.'

'Well, be prepared for the third degree, I'm warning you.'

'What did they ask you?'

'First they asked about when I last visited. And how Mum was before? All that kind of thing.'

'Well that should have been easy enough for you to answer. It's months since you saw her and you wouldn't have had a clue how she was.'

Tracy took a sip from her coffee. She really wanted a biscuit but forced herself to focus on Joe.

'Then they asked all this other stuff: who were Mum's friends? Did she have enemies? Even, did she have debts? I mean, she was in hospital, wasn't she? She was ill. And then she died.'

'She wasn't ill. She had had her feet done, and she didn't exactly die in her bed. They think someone pushed her out of a window. That was what the policeman told me.' Tracy's lip started to wobble and tears began to course down her cheeks.

Joe headed towards her, but stopped short and leaned against the back of the sofa.

'They don't know that, do they?'

'What? You think she just fell out? One minute she was propped up in her hospital bed watching *Britain's Got Talent*, the next she decided to see if she could fly?' Tracy wiped away her tears.

'I don't know, do I? Last time I saw her she was being, well, a bit irrational.'

'Irrational. I can't believe you're saying that. Of course she was irrational. The whole world knew that. Miles worked that one out after eighteen months; that's why he never hung around very long. But if the police are asking about "enemies", they must think someone pushed her. Why's that got you so wound up? Don't you want to find out what happened to her?'

'Would it change anything?' Joe said. 'She'd still be dead. And I doubt she would be doing much investigating if either of us had pegged it.'

'Don't say that. She was our mother.'

'Maybe someone should have told her that, explained to her what the word meant. I'd rather we could just have the funeral and move on.'

'Hang on, Joe. Mum is hardly cold yet. I haven't even had time to tell anyone she's dead and you want to "move on". I know you didn't get on – not since, well never mind that now. But you're wrong about her. The last year or so she had been more interested in us – all of us, including you – always asking how you were, and Janice. And she was so positive when I saw her at the hospital, like a new woman. She talked about painting again. Said she had an unfinished one of me. Asked me if I would sit for her again, like in the old days.'

'You used to hate it, said it was boring.'

'And she said she wanted to paint Pete, too. And the kids.'

Joe bit the side of his thumb, the tips of his ears flushing bright red.

'She was a self-centred bitch and I don't want people sniffing around us – our family – because of her. I don't like it. First it'll be the police and then the newspapers too.'

'What is it you're worried about exactly?' Tracy finally succumbed and took a biscuit, waving it around as she spoke, and the relief associated with the sugar rush of that first bite was palpable. 'That's it, isn't it?' Now she felt capable of going on the offensive. 'You're worried about them finding out what you got up to at Mackenzies. They let you go without any fuss. That's just like you. Mum's dead, maybe murdered, and you're just thinking about yourself.'

'No!' He roared out the word and it reverberated off the bare walls. 'No one cares about that stuff now. I'm thinking about all of us, Trace, including you. That's why I came here, to tell you what to expect when the police come around. I could've just called, or not bothered.' Joe stood up straight. 'I'm off now. Another stupid bloody idea that Janice had.'

'When did you last see Mum?' Tracy sat quietly, hunched over, her back to her brother.

'None of your business,' he replied.

'Or even speak to her? She asked me, you know, "Is Joe going to come and visit, do you think?" That's what she asked me, pretending she didn't care too much. She even checked over my shoulder when I arrived, as if you might be waiting outside in the corridor and I was just the warm-up act.'

'Shut up Trace. You don't know what you're talking about. You're just trying to make me feel bad. Well it won't work. She never wanted to see me. Or if she did, it was only to remind me of how I disappointed her. Well, now I don't have to hear it from her any more.'

Joe exited the room swiftly, and Tracy heard the front door bang in his wake.

AHMAD FINISHED his shift at 5pm and hurried home. It had been a difficult few hours. All the time he had been thinking about Mrs Hennessy. He tried not to imagine her lying dead on the cold, hard ground, but when he had passed the police tent on his way in and on leaving, and had seen the people wearing white suits hovering around, it was hard to block it out.

The nurses had congregated in the corridor over lunch, as the staff room was 'off limits', and all they had spoken about was *Mrs Hennessy* and *how awful* and *who had been the last one to give her her meds* and *who had been the last to take her blood pressure*, shaking their heads and clicking their tongues. He had shrunk back, stumbled his way up the corridor, and sat down on the floor of the toilet cubicle to escape it all.

When he closed his eyes and concentrated, he could hear Barbara's voice. 'Ahmad,' she was whispering in his ear. 'This is such a treat. I don't have a cleaner at home.' She had imparted the information proudly.

'You do yourself?' he had replied. 'Oh no. I just don't clean. My apartment is very dirty.' And she had laughed, a high girlish laugh like the trilling of a bird, and he had laughed too, a genuine laugh, not the one he put on so often for politeness.

It was just before he got off the train at Acton Central that Ahmad remembered he had left his apron behind in the hospital. He could picture it lying folded on the seat of the chair in the corridor, and imagined it scrunched up and discarded or, worse still, confiscated overnight for incineration. Then he'd have to go cap in hand to Sinead in Supplies to ask for another one, and he could imagine the disdainful response he would receive. He almost headed back to retrieve it, but Shaza would be waiting by Suzy's door, brimming full of her day at school, and Aisha would worry if he was late. And, anyway, Mrs Hennessy was dead, so what importance did a dirty apron have in comparison?

Ahmad stood at the bottom of the staircase leading up from the platform to the outside world, as the other disembarking passengers streamed past him. Suddenly, for some reason he couldn't articulate, it was as high and impassable as the Berlin Wall. He retreated to a nearby bench and placed his bag down between his legs on the smooth concrete. *Did you know Mrs Barbara Hennessy?* the policeman had asked him. And *when did you clean her room?* And *did you notice anything unusual?* And he had heard his answers – *yes, yesterday* and *no* – echo loudly in his head, even though in reality he had spoken feebly.

He disliked police officers and the lawyer he'd requested had been next to useless. She had just sat there and allowed the policeman to ask all his questions in his slow-witted manner. Still, at least he had walked out in one piece. Ahmad shivered. All this stuff with Mrs Hennessy, it had made him forget his apron. *You've lost another one?* He could hear the disgust in Sinead's voice and the way she would tut and glower at him until he stammered out an apology.

He stared blankly at his hands, turning them palm up and then palm down before clenching them into fists. But they rotated before his eyes as if through a mist, and within seconds he felt unnaturally cold. It began at his toes and spread rapidly along the length of his feet, hovering around his ankles to sear into his flesh before worming up his calves. He had to stop it early on; he knew that from past experience. Otherwise it would overwhelm him – that slithering, scrambling, clambering cold.

He stamped his feet repeatedly, one after the other, and rolled his shoulders back. Then he inhaled and exhaled deeply and tried to clear his mind. That was what the psychiatrist had taught him; to help him relax, to make it go away.

There. He was beginning to get the measure of it. As he brought his breathing under control and wriggled his toes inside his boots, the cold began to recede. By the time he felt able to stand, it was retreating along each foot, driven away by his efforts. He dabbed at his forehead with his handkerchief; despite feeling cold himself, he was aware he had been sweating profusely. He shouldered his bag and climbed the steps away from the platform, two at a time.

Five minutes later, Ahmad and Shaza were walking alongside each other. She was chattering away about Mrs Crane and Mr Martin and what they said today in assembly and how Mrs Crane had said her Maths was very neat. Usually Ahmad would ask a question or two and provide some encouragement, but not today. Today he was moving quickly and focusing all his energy on getting home. Shaza had to skip her fastest skipping, with her hugest giant-step leaps, to keep up with her father's strides, her attempts to grab his hand being rejected without explanation.

10

DR DAVID WOLF was a slim, slight man, around five foot seven in height, although he identified with five foot nine. He was an orthopaedic surgeon of considerable skill and some years' experience. But Inspector Dawson's visit to the hospital that afternoon, and his blunt, trampling questions about Barbara Hennessy, had left him anxious and bruised, and he hovered, tapping papers on his desk ineffectually and tweaking the ends of his burgeoning moustache, until he was certain the police officer had left the hospital.

His wife, Jane, had suggested he grow the facial hair, and he was now attached to it; she propounded a theory that his lack of promotion to the highest echelons was the result of his youthful appearance. He thought it was more likely the work of senior doctors who refused to retire despite less-than-optimum working conditions, so that it was truly 'dead men's shoes'. And he wasn't a 'team player' according to Hani Mahmood, his immediate boss, in his last appraisal. That was rich, coming from a man who was head of the team but had never attended one of its Christmas parties, forever pulling the religion card.

And it was Dr Wolf's chance meeting in the corridor with Hani, just an hour earlier, that had made him even more jumpy when Dawson called in.

'David. Any update on how she died, the Hennessy woman?' Hani had begun.

Dr Wolf had stammered over the words.

'No. It's nothing to do with me. It's hardly a medically related death. I'm letting the police get on with it.'

Hani had fixed him with a hard stare.

'She was your patient, David. I think you need to take an interest. We wouldn't want anyone pointing the finger at our team – unfairly, of course.'

Dr Wolf had opened his mouth to protest at how ludicrous that sounded but thought better of it.

'We'll have to add it to our list for the monthly review, so be prepared,' Hani had said.

'Why would we do that? She didn't die as a result of her treatment.'

'We don't know that yet, do we?' Hani had said. And he had marched off leaving Dr Wolf open-mouthed in his wake.

Dr Wolf pulled his mobile from his pocket and paused with his fingers hovering above the screen. It had started off innocently enough with Dawson. *Who carried out the operation?* Dawson had asked. But instead of providing a couple of job titles or simply referring to 'the usual team' he had found himself reeling off names and embellishing. 'Myself, Dr Bridges was the anaesthetist; she's very experienced, our 'go to' person for tricky operations – not that there was anything remotely complex about this one –

41

Nurse Li, another key member of our nursing staff, Steven King, a highly able specialist registrar.'

'The team you mentioned – they work together on many operations?' Dawson had asked.

'Yes. But I don't see that any of this is relevant.'

'Just part of our enquiries. Gathering all the facts. I may need to speak to the others in the team who operated on Mrs Hennessy.'

'If you want to waste your time, of course, go ahead,' Dr Wolf had said. 'Anyway, we'll have our own internal review of procedures.'

'Will you?'

'Yes, our head of department, Dr Mahmood, is going to examine all aspects of Mrs Hennessy's care at our monthly meeting; it's standard when we have a death in the hospital. Nothing sinister, or anything like that.'

'There'll be a note of this meeting?'

'There'll be a report.'

Then Dawson had asked how Mrs Hennessy was after her operation, in his slow way. And Dr Wolf had reported she was 'fine' and the officer had left shortly afterwards.

Dr Wolf made his call.

'Hi. It's me. I know you're busy, so just listen; you don't have to speak,' he barked into the phone.

A pause.

'The police were here asking questions about Barbara Hennessy. It's possible they'll come to find you and Steven and Nurse Li. They asked about the team involved in the operation.

'I just said you were the anaesthetist; that's all. He made a note of your name.

'Yes I know. Crazy isn't it? Although Hani seemed to think it was perfectly normal.

'I saw him just before. He told me I had to *protect the team* – as if I would do anything else.'

Another pause.

'Hani says he wants to review the procedure in the monthly meeting next week.

'I know, it's pointless, but he wants to. So we'll need to be prepared, with our version of events. Will you speak to the other two? And the police want to see the report.

'It just kind of slipped out.

'No, I wasn't trying to drop anyone in it. Why would I do that?

'No. I'm fine. I just don't like being interrogated, that's all. It's not a pleasant experience. Speak later.

'No, I don't think I should see a solicitor.

'I'm not talking to a solicitor about this and neither should you. I've told the police we'll follow usual procedures and there'll be a report at the monthly meeting.

'Yes. I'll remember. Don't worry about me.'

11

'SHADYA? BABA was a bit weird today don't you think?' Shaza was sitting cross-legged on her bed with a selection of toys surrounding her.

'No. Like I think he had been crying but when I asked him he said it was dusty at work – *working in a hospital was a dusty job,* he said – and that made his eyes sore.

'Well, Mrs Crane showed us a programme once about miners digging for coal in somewhere called New Castle and she asked if we knew what happened to them. Then Jamie Green said their eyes got sore. And Jamal Khan said they got lung cancer. Then Mrs Crane told us they took yellow birds down under the ground to check for gas. We all laughed then. Although afterwards I didn't think it was very funny because the birds couldn't fly away and they died.

'But there must be a lot more dust under the ground for the miners than there is at the hospital and it was the morning, so I said to Baba that he'd had all night to get rid of the dust.

'No, me neither. Maybe someone was mean to him, like that lady that time, and he'd been thinking about it.

'You remember. When she said "all migrants are thieves". I asked Dad "What are migrants?" but he didn't reply. Then she said "I think you'd better leave" in a funny voice, staring out into the street, as if she had been waiting years to say it.' Shaza giggled.

'You do. That time dad took me for a new dress. He saved up, too. I'd seen him counting the money in his wallet when I was sitting on the stairs.

'I told you about it. He chose a blue one but he *said* it was purple. Then he said it was "perfect" and it would suit me. But I still said it was blue. So Dad said if we took it near the door we could see the colour better. Then the alarm went off. That's when she said it. And she folded her arms, but only after she called a guard, too.

'And I said, "No, we have the money, lady; show her, Dad. My dad has the money. He's saved it all up. It's just because the dress is blue", and then his eyes went all red and he pushed me out of the shop and he didn't speak again until we got all the way home. And he did that scary stamping thing with his feet.

'It wasn't my fault. I don't like blue.

'Suzy let me borrow one. She said her daughter only wore it once but it smelled of dogs and it was too long because Suzy's daughter is the tallest girl in the class, almost as tall as Mrs Crane.

'It was OK 'cos mama washed it for me. Then I wore it. You remember?

'Yes. It was blue, but I didn't say anything this time.

'Maybe it was just the dust.'

12

CHIEF INSPECTOR Dawson arrived at Tracy's house around lunchtime on Saturday. He had postponed seeing her the previous evening, as a number of other matters had kicked off and he would have preferred some developments to report on his visit. He brought with him Mrs Hennessy's bag with her clothes and personal items from the hospital.

Tracy was alone in the house and her eyes were red and puffy. Her hair was tied back in a neat ponytail but the bottom of each leg of her jeans was frayed and they pulled tight across her stomach as she sat down on the sofa. Inspector Dawson remained standing for a few moments and then sat too.

'Mrs Jones. I know this must be a very difficult time for you. I'm so sorry for your loss.' His grandmother had repeatedly reminded him that on occasions like this you had to say something friendly and empathetic to the relative of a victim. It didn't come naturally to him.

Tracy sniffed her appreciation. Dawson took out his notepad

and pen and laid it down on his lap.

'I have a few questions to ask you. Just a bit of background about you and your mum; when you last saw her, that kind of thing. Is that all right?'

She stared out towards a family photo on the window ledge.

'What do you do for a living?'

'I'm a teacher.'

'High school?'

'I teach at the local primary. I've been there for ten years off and on. Years 3 and 4, usually.'

'Off and on.'

'In between having my own kids; full time for the last year.'

'And your husband?'

'Pete? He's not working at the moment.'

'He's unemployed?'

'Yes.'

'And before that?'

'He had a successful business – property developer. But he had an accident, hurt his back. He's not able to work at the moment.'

'And your children?'

'Pete's taken them out, thank goodness.'

'How old are they?'

'Oh. Eleven and nine.'

'Your mother went into hospital on Tuesday?'

'Yes, that's what's so crazy. She wasn't ill; just her feet.'

'Did you see the doctor with your mother?'

'No. She was very independent. And I am busy with work and the kids. The first thing I knew was she called me the night before, on Monday. Said she was going into St Marks the next day, not to worry but it would be nice if I visited.'

'And when did you visit?'

'On the Wednesday. I couldn't make it on Thursday. I had, well, I had something planned all afternoon, but I was going to pick her up, drive her home yesterday.'

'Was she worried about anything?'

'No. Well, of course, she did the usual, like I said, told me the anaesthetic was a risk and all that. She was a bit like that, Mum. She wanted me to know it was nothing but then she couldn't resist adding that bit, so it sounded dangerous.' Tracy sighed; the irony was not lost on her.

'Was she in good health generally?'

'I think so. Oh, she was forgetful; we joked, Joe, my brother and me, that she was in the early stages of some kind of dementia. But I didn't really think that. She had always been, well, a bit detached from reality. She was an artist. Not a great one but she had a studio when we were young and sold a few paintings. She'd shifted everything to her flat about five years ago.'

'And your father?'

'Miles? He left when Joe was a baby. He used to visit, but Mum brought us up.'

'Did he provide financial support?'

'Yes. I mean, I don't know how much, but he put money in Mum's account every month. Otherwise we wouldn't have eaten. Mum didn't sell that many paintings.'

'Is your father still alive?'

'Well I haven't heard he isn't. I had a Christmas card. The last one was from California.'

'Have you told him about your mother?'

'No. Do I need to?'

Inspector Dawson closed his notebook.

'That's really up to you, but I think you should probably try. Or give us his contact details and we can do it if you prefer. He may want to attend the funeral.'

Tracy shrugged, evidently thinking on the question, staring out past Dawson at the photo again.

'Do you know any reason why anyone might have wanted your mother dead?'

Tracy shook her head slowly.

'No. She was just an ordinary woman. OK, she lived an unconventional life when she was younger, but there was nothing dodgy going on. God! I sound like the mother of one of those kids who gets killed in a knife fight, don't I? And when I read it I always think there *must* have been something going on. But this is my mother.'

'No other men on the scene?'

'Noooo. I think she scared the men off. She was a bit uninhibited. Said what she thought. But we weren't that close. I don't know much about her friends.'

'Is there any reason why she might have wanted to harm herself?'

Tracy swallowed hard. 'Is that what you think?'

'We're not ruling anything out yet.'

'Not Mum. Never. And if you wanted to kill yourself, why on earth would you do it in a place full of people, when you live on your own?'

'Where were you on Thursday night? We have to ask – apologies.'

'I was at home, with the kids.'

'And your husband was at home?'

'Yes. All evening.'

Inspector Dawson stood up, walked to the window and picked up the photo Tracy had been studying during their talk. It showed a woman holding a baby in her arms and a slimmer Tracy standing behind. Dawson could only assume the woman was Barbara, her red hair was the only way to connect the corpse he had viewed with this image of the woman she had been.

'That was just after Luke was born. She did come and help me, for a day or two. I think she wanted to be a bit more hands-on, you know, a better grandmother than she'd been a mother.' Tracy stopped abruptly. She really shouldn't be sharing confidences with a police officer. But his silences made her gabble.

Inspector Dawson returned the photo to its place on the window ledge. He noticed how sparsely furnished the room was, no rug, no coffee table, no ornaments of any kind. And while there was a curtain rail above the bay window, there were no curtains.

'Just moved in?'

'A year.' Tracy opened her eyes wide. 'It's just temporary, till Pete gets back on his feet. I haven't really bothered much with the furnishings.'

Dawson bowed solemnly. 'OK, thank you. I'll be in touch if we have any further information. There are one or two items we have kept hold of, but everything else should be in your mum's bag. Actually, I do have one more question. There was a bunch of red roses in a vase by your mum's bed. Did you bring them?'

'No... And I don't remember seeing them.'

'So probably someone who visited after you then?'

'Yes.'

Dawson tapped the end of his pen against his lip. 'She didn't say she was expecting more visitors, when you saw her, on Wednesday?'

'No. But like I said she was a bit forgetful.'

'Well, it's probably nothing. The nurses could have transferred them from another patient, rather than throw them away. Your brother, Joseph. Were he and your mum close?'

'No.' Tracy wouldn't drop Joe in it, but she was also keen not to lie when this was so serious a matter. 'They didn't get on very well. Just usual stuff. But you probably asked Joe about that, didn't you?'

Dawson turned to go.

'Can we organise the funeral?' Tracy asked, standing up herself. The mention of flowers had turned her attention to more practical things.

Dawson attempted a reassuring smile.

'Not yet. But soon, I hope.'

'Will there be, well, a lot of publicity? We, Pete and I, we're private people. I don't even have a Facebook account. Lots of teachers don't, in case the pupils see stuff, you know.'

Dawson examined Tracy's face as a flush swept over it from the tip of her nose outward. What was she hiding? Then he chastised himself; her mother had just died, after all.

'There might be,' he said. 'But if we find out there was no foul play, then things will die down quickly enough.'

'And when will that be?' Tracy was trying to repress the choking feeling which was seeking to overwhelm her. Maybe Joe had been right and this would be all over the papers. The sympathetic glances of parents at the school gates would rapidly transpose into suspicious murmurings, and she wouldn't be allowed to help with breakfast club any more.

'A few days. I can't be more precise than that for now. You have my number. You're not on your own all day, are you?'

'No. Thank you. Pete'll be back soon with the boys. You've been very kind. I know Joe appreciated it too. And I may not take any more time off work. It's a busy time of year, and no point just sitting here moping around, is there?'

13

DAVID WOLF sat at home with a brimming cup of coffee at his side. He was reviewing documents on his laptop, switching backwards and forwards, tutting, muttering under his breath and occasionally talking aloud. Once or twice he rotated a document or blew it up to larger than normal size. Then he made a couple of calls, checking up on lab results, clarifying information.

Jane returned home with a clatter, towing bags of shopping from the car. He glanced up in her direction and then closed his documents and laptop.

'Hi,' he called out with feigned enthusiasm. 'You're home early.'

'Yes. My last operation was cancelled and I thought I would catch up on the paperwork at home. I bought some of that fresh pasta you like and a bottle of Prosecco. Thought we might even make it into the garden, pretend we're on holiday?'

'Sure,' he replied, noticing for the first time what a bright afternoon it was.

'Phew. Have you been sitting here all this time with the

windows closed? It's boiling.'

She pulled back the sliding door leading out onto the patio.

'Maybe we should spend a few minutes running through what we'll tell Hani next week about Mrs Hennessy's operation,' David said.

'I'd rather not do it now. It's been a long week.'

'I just think we need to plan what we say carefully. Is Steven on board?'

Jane began to unpack the shopping bags.

'I really don't want to talk now.'

'Can't you just tell me what Steven said?'

'He said he's happy to confirm that it was all straightforward. I don't know why you're getting so stressed. He said he can even talk about post-op if you want.'

'No. It's OK. You can tell him I'll cover that. But you didn't see Hani's face. He's dying to trip me up, to find something I did wrong. Even though the woman fell from the top floor. Sometimes I think he hates the fact my record is so good.'

Jane shrugged.

'I'm sorry if I'm annoying you but it's not just me, you have a promotion coming up,' he continued. 'You don't want suspicions hanging over you either. None of us will be off the hook till the police find the killer. And don't assume Hani will stand up for you; if push comes to shove he'll look after number one.'

'You are being ridiculous. No one is accusing either of us of being involved in that woman's death, including Hani, who is simply trying to protect us by making sure we follow the right procedures. So stop fussing, or people will be suspicious. And patients die every day, no matter how hard we try or how well we do our jobs. I have to remind myself of that or I would spend sleepless nights questioning my own ability, and that wouldn't help anyone, let alone my "promotion" prospects.'

She took an apple from the fruit bowl and washed it under the tap.

'Look, I thought we could try to have a relaxing evening together, just for once. So, can we make a deal? I cook the pasta and make a sauce and you stop talking about Mrs Hennessy. Deal?'

'Deal. Sure, deal.'

14

JOE HENNESSY sat at his desk, sliding his hands over the glossy surface in circular motion. Eventually he stopped and then stretched his arms out wide until his fingertips glanced its bevelled edges.

'Mine. All mine,' he murmured, giggling to himself, shifting his head from side to side to double-check that no one was watching or within earshot. But he had taken care of that; his new desk was at the far end of the gleaming showroom, in splendid isolation, just how he liked it. From his vantage point he could see everything that was going on, both inside and outside on the forecourt.

Joe enjoyed keeping tabs on the newbies; Kyla, only twenty-one and beginning to learn the ropes, and Simon, a decade older but still 'wet behind the ears'. Kyla didn't know much about cars but she made up for it with looks and enthusiasm. And Joe had already provided her with lots of information on the history of the BMW, and a guide to all the latest models, and she was catching on quick. He would have to be careful with Kyla. She was just his type: big boobs, tight arse and long, glossy hair. But he had vowed to keep things strictly professional after Debi (with one 'b'), his last dalliance. That had almost ended in disaster.

Debi had finally come to accept (via Joe, delivered in a suitably contrite and panicked voice) that were Janice (his long-term partner) to discover the existence of their relationship, her wrath was likely to be of unearthly dimensions. Joe had conjured up images of Janice at the keyhole, stalking them day and night, hacking their social media accounts, even poisoning their food. Of course, Janice was at home watching *EastEnders*, oblivious to all these tall tales. But Debi had not been completely taken in. She had her price for relinquishing the love of her life; a 'shoe in' at the Beaconsfield branch, frequented by wealthier clientele than theirs, and a £5,000 'relocation allowance'. No doubt, Debi was already spreading her many talents among Buckinghamshire's finest. No, he wouldn't even dip his toe in the water surrounding Kyla Roberts. But her attributes would help draw in the customers.

Simon liked to be called 'Si' but Joe secretly called him 'Si-co', given his quick temper and the fact that he still lived with his mother. Joe had given himself a mental pat on the back when he had thought up that one. There were a couple of others who worked part-time but those two, Kyla and Simon, were his protégés, the ones who craved his approval and their bonus confirmation at the end of each month.

Joe was going to have to be very careful training them, to make sure they knew his way of doing things, and understood all the hurdles it was necessary to negotiate to make a success of the role. Sometimes unusual things happened, he had warned them. But they always had a sensible explanation. You just had to search for it; conversely, sometimes it was better not to look.

Kyla's education had started yesterday when an old guy had come in, wanting to trade in his 2012 5 series for a newer, sportier model. Joe had thought he was too old to be driving a convertible, but hadn't said that to the customer. He had learned that honest opinions were not always welcome – better to give customers what they thought they wanted – and he had passed the old man to Kyla, with a steer in the direction of a 2015 6 series model in midnight blue with only 11,000 on the clock, or at least that was what the clock said now. Kyla – *not stupid that girl; head screwed on straight* – had queried it with him. 'That's very low mileage,' she'd said, calling up the details on her iPad.

'Yeah. Geezer owned it got ill. It stood outside his house for months,' Joe had replied.

This rehearsed line sounded plausible. In reality, Joe had accepted the car, after hours, last Sunday, so no one had seen the young and healthy owner arrive, springing out of the vehicle, gym bag in hand. And Joe had been cautious when he reduced the mileage. Everything was tracked on computer these days. And no one would believe that the car had only covered 500 miles since its last service, however ill the owner was. Still, winding it back 10,000 miles was probably worth four grand to him.

But then he heard Kyla providing her own, fabricated explanation to this elderly potential buyer. 'Yes,' she had said, beaming widely. 'You have such good taste, Mr Carter. A man bought it for his wife but she didn't like the colour. He kept it for ages to try to persuade her, but she refused to drive it and he had his own BMW; couldn't justify driving two.'

When the customer went outside to phone his own wife, Joe had called her over. 'Why did you give him all that bullshit about a wife?'

'I thought it sounded better than what you said. No one wants a car that some invalid's been driving!' And he had to admit, it had worked. The guy, Anthony Carter, had bought it, almost straight away, joking with Kyla about how he would never even buy a handkerchief without consulting his wife on the colour or pattern.

Simon had made another good sale too, of a 2012 X5 for a cool £23,000. He had talked relentlessly at the customer, bamboozling him so much with all the specifications that he'd forgotten to ask for the log book.

'I'm sorry Joe,' Simon had lamented. 'You rang me about my holiday just when I was closing the sale. I clean forgot to get the book for the guy and he never asked.'

'Don't worry, Si,' Joe had replied with a smirk. 'We've all done it. I once sold a car and forgot to get the guy to sign the V5 transfer form. If this guy makes a fuss just put him through to me; no problem.'

When he'd arrived home later than usual that evening, after two celebratory rounds of drinks, Janice had been cold and cutting, not appreciative of his tremendous business acumen and achievements. He kept to himself that Kyla had given him two sympathetic 'how awful about your dear mum' hugs, one on arrival at the pub and the second, rather more all-embracing, in the alleyway leading to the car park. Even Si had managed a pat on his back and a 'We'll cover for you, if you need some time out, mate.'

'What'll people say? Your mother's not buried yet and you're out bingeing.' Janice had turned her head away with a moan when he went to kiss her.

'What d'ya mean?' he replied. Janice didn't understand him. 'What about me? I'm an orphan now. If I want to go for a drink with my team, I bloody will.'

Janice concluded sensibly that this was not an appropriate time to remind him that Miles, his father, was still alive, albeit a few thousand miles away. She kept her counsel. Part way through his sausage and chips, Joe stopped eating.

'You'll always stick by me, won't you?' he asked.

She lifted her head from her magazine and tousled his hair. He might be more upset by his mother's death than he let on; that wouldn't surprise her. He didn't find it easy to share things. It hadn't been great having Barbara as his mum but the way she had departed had shocked them all.

'Course I will. I'll always be here,' she replied.

15

'Inspector Dawson?'

'Yes.'

Dawson stood back from the flow of bodies on Haverstock Hill, into the shadow of the shop awning, and tucked his phone close into his ear. He wasn't used to Hampstead with its constant stream of beautiful people up and down the street: mothers with babies in elaborate prams or strapped to their fronts in myriad different positions; older, coiffured, manicured women savouring long coffees; men in polo shirts doing business deals over lunch.

'It's Tracy Jones, Barbara Hennessy's daughter.'

'Yes, hello.'

'It's a silly thing really. And I don't want you to think I care about this now. But just in case it's important.'

'Yes.'

'Well. Mum had these rings. Really big and loud they were. One with a huge green stone, the other a big gold knot.'

'Yes, go on.'

'She had them at the hospital. But they weren't in her things you brought over and they weren't on the list of items you kept.'

'Are you sure?'

'Yes. I was cross when I found out she had them in hospital. We had a bit of a row about it. I wanted to take them home for safekeeping, but she insisted she was going to keep them. In the end, I didn't push it any further. She could be a bit stubborn.'

Dawson had to step forward as a customer prodded him from behind to exit the shop. He hoped Tracy was mistaken. He really didn't want to think that any of his team had taken anything from Mrs Hennessy's affairs. More likely one of the nurses or...

'I don't remember hearing anything about any rings in her possessions,' he said.

'She always told us they were valuable,' Tracy continued, 'but I'm not sure they were. I just thought it might be important, you know, for the investigation.'

Dawson scratched at his stubble. He hadn't shaved this morning and now it was bothering him.

'Is there anything else missing?'

'I can't say. I've no idea what she packed. Her handbag seemed to have the usual things; money, credit card. Mum only had one.'

'OK. I appreciate you calling, Mrs Jones. Can you give me a full description of each ring again?'

16

CONSTANCE walked haltingly along Braham Terrace. She had no idea how her visit would be received, especially given Ahmad's indifference to her efforts last time they had met. And Acton, where he lived, was not a familiar part of London.

Ahmad's house was towards the end of the street. A barrier made it effectively a dead end. And, although the kerb was set out in a circular shape, to allow unsuspecting motorists to turn around without too much angst, it had become, instead, the dumping ground for unwanted items of furniture, left in sprawling piles on either side of the street.

Constance stopped abruptly. She had seen the downstairs curtain twitch at no 33, Ahmad's house, she was certain, but there was no one visible at the window now. She approached and knocked at the door, all the time keeping one eye out for further signs of movement from inside. She waited and tried a second time.

After another minute of silence, she pondered shouting through the letterbox, but her own sense of decorum prevented it. She stepped back into the street and gazed at the upstairs windows. Then she approached the bay window, grasped the peeling ledge with both hands and pressed her face up close to the glass. The room was in darkness, but she made out some chairs and a TV in the far corner. She knocked at the door one more time, before taking out another business card, writing *Ahmad. Please call me urgently, Constance* on the back, posting it through the letterbox and heading off up the street.

Two houses down, the door opened and a lady beckoned Constance over.

'You looking for Mrs Qabbani?' she asked.

'Yes.'

'What's she done?'

'Nothing.'

'So why're you looking for her then?'

'I need to speak to Mr Qabbani.'

'He works at the hospital; Hampstead it is. Sometimes, he's there days, sometimes nights. You should try there.'

'Yes, thank you. But I thought Mrs Qabbani might have been at home?'

'Oh, she's at home all right.'

'Oh?'

'She's always at home. Never goes anywhere, that one.'

'Is she ill?'

The woman tapped her fingers lightly to the side of her head.

'Only in there, I reckon. And she won't let you in, not if she don't know who you are. Come back later when the husband's home. He's very nice, polite, and the little girl's sweet. Over there at number thirty-two – Suzy Douglas – she keeps the girl till he gets home, most days.'

'Thank you. Maybe I'll talk to Mrs Douglas then.'

'You can try but she'll be at work herself now. Back around four o'clock. Come back then.'

Constance was disappointed and now she was unsure what to do next. She didn't really want to wait around but Dawson's call of two hours ago had made her anxious. 'Had the forensic report back on Mrs Hennessy. Might put your man, Qabbani, in the frame. I'll send it through. Have you heard from him at all?' he'd asked cryptically.

She had said something anodyne in response, something stupid like 'It's good of you to call me.' Dawson had waited for her to say more and then, when she hadn't – in truth, only because she was struggling with a response that would make her sound experienced – he added, 'You might want to speak to him again, just to make sure he's told you everything.'

'You're certain Mrs Hennessy was killed then? She didn't jump?' was all she could muster. And Dawson had countered with a snappy 'looks that way' before hanging up. Then Constance had read the forensic report, three times. That was why she had come today. Trouble was heading Ahmad's way and she wanted to ward it off as best she could.

'Is there somewhere I can get a cup of tea?' she enquired gently of Ahmad's neighbour. 'A café, I mean,' just to make sure the woman didn't think she was expecting hospitality.

'End of the street, back the way you came. Turn right. It's called Sultan's. If you get any nonsense, tell them Cath sent you.'

***

Constance settled herself down with a mug of tea in the café and waited. It was already 3:30. She would have preferred to talk to Mrs Qabbani first without Ahmad, just to see what titbits she could pick up, even down to the very obvious, what time he had come home last Thursday night; now that was not going to be possible.

It was close to 5:45 when she saw Ahmad emerge. He was striding out of the station with a bag over his shoulder. She stood up and stretched out her stiff back. Once he was at least a hundred metres ahead, she exited the café and followed him, keeping a safe distance behind.

He stopped a few doors short of his own house on the opposite side of the street and a young girl with long black hair came running out to meet him. He crouched down and she wrapped her arms around his neck and planted a kiss firmly on his cheek, before the two of them continued down the street, hand in hand.

Constance hesitated. The sight of the little girl made her more anxious. It was one thing to offer Ahmad advice when he was seated in a police station, but quite another to arrive uninvited at his house and invade his personal space. What was she going to say to him? That she was worried he may be implicated in Barbara Hennessy's murder, that he might be called back for questioning?

Why was she so interested in Ahmad anyway? He had hardly been engaging when they had met; quite the opposite. But something about his manner had captured her interest: the contrast of his large bulk and intense stare with his slender hands and judicious choice of words; his veneer of deference, when faced with Dawson, which reminded her of her mother's own manner, adopted when coping with formal events in a country far away from her birth. That might explain things: yet another opportunity for Constance to try to put the world to rights, but with a more worthy victim than usual.

She knocked gingerly this time, and heard voices before the little girl opened the door.

'Hello. Can you tell your daddy I'm here please?' Constance asked.

The girl stood in silence for a moment, unblinking. Then she sped off into the house, leaving the door open. Constance stepped inside, searching around on the floor for the business card she had posted through earlier, but it was nowhere in sight.

'Baba. There's a lady here to see you.' She heard the girl speaking and the noise of a chair being scraped along the floor.

Then Ahmad was striding towards her purposefully. He closed the front door behind her, frowning all the time.

'You're the lawyer. From the police. What do you want?' His manner was hardly welcoming.

'Mr Qabbani. You don't have to talk to me, but I need to advise you of some developments in the case of Mrs Hennessy. Can you spare me a few minutes, please?'

Ahmad's frown deepened but he nodded once and then led the way into the dingy lounge. He shouted a few guttural words out into the echoing space of the hallway, to whomever might have been listening. The smell of food wafted in from the kitchen and Constance guessed she had interrupted a family meal.

She sat down on the threadbare sofa, but immediately found herself in the firing line of the draught streaming in through the cracked, wooden window frame. She shifted to her left and drew her coat tightly around her.

'I have been sent a copy of a report into Mrs Hennessy's death. I wanted to talk to you about it.'

'Why talk to me?'

'There are some things in the report which could link you to Mrs Hennessy's death.'

'What things?'

'Your fingerprints were on the door of the staff room; the one leading out on to the balcony.'

'I use that room, so does everyone else. We were allowed back in today, just like before.'

'Yours were near the top of all the prints, suggesting you had recently opened or closed the door.'

Ahmad shook his head.

'I went out there, maybe that evening before I went home.'

'Some of your hair was found on Mrs Hennessy's clothing, wound around one of the buttons of her nightgown. Can you explain why your hair was on her nightgown?'

Ahmad gazed out into the distance.

'Ahmad?'

'Why would I want to hurt Mrs Hennessy?' He folded his arms defiantly, but it was not lost on Constance that his hands were shaking.

A noise at the door startled them both. The little girl was standing there, peering around the frame. Her face seemed very narrow and drawn, her eyes wide and bottomless, a carbon copy of her father's. Neither of them could be sure how long she had been watching or listening. Ahmad straightened up and smiled reassuringly at her. He spoke to her softly in a language Constance didn't understand and she withdrew. Constance heard her feet padding up the stairs and then a door close.

'Miss Lamb, I need this job, at the hospital. It took me one year to find work after we came here. One year living off charity. I wanted to work…but no one would have me. Do you understand how important this job is for me, for us? So you need to sort this out for me. To tell them I know nothing about how Mrs Hennessy is dead.'

'I will, of course. But you won't help yourself by keeping quiet about things you know. You and all the other staff who were in the hospital that night are under suspicion. Did you see anything strange that night? Anything at all? Was there someone around who was new, a technician, a new nurse, a new delivery man?'

'There are always new nurses – they are all agency. But I don't think so. I will try to remember. It was just a normal night. I did my shift and went home.'

His face lit up for a moment. 'I use Oyster. That will tell you when I went home. You can check?'

Constance attempted to appear encouraged. It would be helpful, of course, if Ahmad's Oyster card corroborated his story that he headed home at the end of his shift, but not conclusive.

The doorbell rang again. Ahmad jumped up. He was unused to any visitors, and twice in ten minutes was fraying his nerves. He called out an acknowledgement and, this time, answered the front door himself. Constance checked her phone messages and emailed her office to say she would not be back that evening. Ahmad was talking loudly but haltingly in the hallway.

'Excuse me please, sir, one moment. My lawyer is here. I will speak to her,' she heard him say.

'His lawyer, do you hear that?' The man outside the door had a deep, resounding voice and a Cockney accent.

Constance slipped her phone back in her bag and joined Ahmad by the front door, where she was surprised to find a burly police officer filling the door frame. The grin on the police officer's face was replaced by an expression of bemusement.

'Blimey. I'm PC Brown.' He flashed his police ID. 'Mr Qabbani was telling the truth. You're the lawyer, are you? Is that a guilty conscience then? Can I come in, love, save all this stuff on the doorstep, just a spectacle for the neighbours?' PC Brown shouldered his way past them both and stepped inside, closely followed by a young woman colleague.

'Mr Qabbani. As I was saying, I have a warrant here to search your property. This is on account of a suspicion that certain items belonging to a Mrs Hennessy, now deceased, may be in your property. Me and Richards here, we'll do our best to do this without messing things up too much, but we do have to search in drawers and cupboards and things. Do you understand what we're saying?'

Ahmad half turned his head towards the kitchen and did not reply.

'Can I see the warrant, please?' Constance asked, her pulse suddenly racing. Dawson had mentioned the DNA evidence to her but this must be something new.

'You can have your own personal copy. Here you go.' PC Brown handed it over. She read it through quickly and handed it on to Ahmad.

'Can you tell us specifically what the items are?' she asked, knowing as she spoke that it would make little difference now to know the answer. 'It only says jewellery.'

'It's set out clearly in the warrant. We'll start upstairs I think. Anyone up there?'

PC Brown placed his size twelves on the bottom step but Ahmad flung himself forward to bar the policeman's way, his eyes aflame. PC Brown raised his eyebrows as Constance rushed to

Ahmad's side, tapping his arm gently, her gaze never leaving the policeman, willing him not to take any precipitative action. At Constance's touch, Ahmad gathered himself.

'My daughter is upstairs, please. One moment. Please not to scare her,' he said.

Ahmad bounded up the stairs and knocked on the nearest bedroom door. The same little girl who had opened the front door and eavesdropped on their conversation peered out, then descended the stairs with a Barbie doll clutched tightly in one hand. Ahmad propelled her into the kitchen and, scowling, closed the door behind them.

'Tell your client to watch himself,' PC Brown cautioned Constance. 'He's lucky you were here,' he continued, as the two officers trudged upstairs, leaving Constance alone in the hallway.

She stood for some moments, surveying the dreary space. The wallpaper was yellow and peeling by the front door, the skirting was cracked and chipped. There were marks from a long-gone coat hook and the carpet was worn from the tread of many feet. Restless and ill at ease, she wandered into the living room. Should she call Dawson and ask him what this jewellery was? What would she say? Did she have the right to ask for more information?

Upstairs she could hear loud footsteps and talking, the occasional interruption of PC Brown speaking abruptly into his radio and the low responses of his colleague. There was no noise from the kitchen. Constance crept up close to the door and knocked before entering.

Ahmad, his wife and daughter were seated around the table, a plastic square with an embroidered cloth draped over it. The little girl was writing with a focused expression in an exercise book, Ahmad and his wife sat opposite each other, quiet and still.

71

Ahmad half rose and offered Constance his seat.

'This is my wife, Aisha, and my daughter, Shaza.' He introduced them to Constance as if this were a social occasion, and then suddenly he asked Constance, 'What do they want?'

'It says jewellery on the warrant. I could call the Inspector but...'

Constance's voice tailed off. Although she had done nothing wrong by coming to Ahmad's house, she didn't particularly want to admit to Dawson that she had. If Ahmad ended up in trouble, she wanted to be able to maintain that there was nothing worrying in the forensic report but her very presence in his house gave it credence. She was cross Dawson hadn't mentioned the warrant though; it must have already been in hand when they spoke. Then she thought back to the interview at the police station. Perhaps Dawson had been right, and Ahmad had asked for a lawyer in the first place because he knew he had something to worry about.

She took the place at the table Ahmad had offered her. He went to the sink, poured himself a glass of water and downed it in one. Shaza glanced up at him and then returned to her maths.

'Have you lived here long?' Constance turned to Aisha.

'My wife doesn't speak,' Ahmad replied, filling his glass a second time. Shaza frowned, opened her mouth then closed it.

Aisha Qabbani sat perfectly still, hands folded on the table, watching her daughter at work. She exuded tranquillity. Her composed expression was in contrast to her husband, who was agitation personified. Aisha turned her head away, but not before Constance had seen how unusual her sad eyes were; petrol blue flecked with gold, around the blackest pupil, her headscarf grey, setting them off to perfection. They reminded her of sunflowers set against a thunderous sky.

But gradually, observing his wife and daughter, Ahmad, too, calmed himself. He stopped half way through his second glass of water, placing it down on the table top.

'She understands you perfectly,' he added.

'When did…'

'Since we came here,' Ahmad's eyes flitted to the tiny back window overlooking the squalid yard. There was a plastic play kitchen outside, leaning against the wall for support, adorned with plates and cups, one of them tipped on its side, half filled with water, the colour washed out by endless days of rain.

Constance wondered how she would explain this to Mike in the evening over dinner. He wouldn't understand it, why she was 'getting so involved,' what had drawn her to spend her afternoon sitting in the damp, dingy end-of-terrace, with a murder suspect and his mute wife, while the police rampaged around upstairs.

The banging and scraping and furniture-shifting continued, interspersed with low chatter and PC Brown's honeyed tones permeating the ceiling. At one point, Shaza ceased her work and stared hard at Constance till Constance looked away, and at one particularly loud bang, Mrs Qabbani placed her hand over her face but then recovered and smiled encouragingly at her daughter.

Suddenly, the noise overhead changed. The thudding of furniture being heaved around morphed into that of enthusiastic voices, and PC Brown could be heard talking into his radio again. Constance strained to hear what he was saying.

'What is happening?' Ahmad asked, and Constance seized the moment to go and see.

The two officers were in Shaza's bedroom. Constance gasped to see the chaos they had generated. The bedding was heaped in a pile on the floor and all the clothes had been removed from the wardrobe. Games in boxes had been opened and their contents, too, were spilling out randomly. PC Brown noticed Constance but continued his conversation without breaking breath.

'Yep. It's the one the daughter described. Yep. As big as the Taj Mahal. And the other one too. In the bedroom. Yep. We'll take him in.'

Constance's mouth opened. The officer was holding a gaudy ring in his gloved hand between thumb and forefinger. It contained an enormous green stone. He dropped it into an exhibit bag and handed it to the female officer.

'No, you don't need to do that. She's here. I think so.' And to Constance. 'Are you Lamb?'

Constance nodded slowly. 'Yes, that's her. Yes, I'll tell her.' He returned his radio to his top pocket.

'They always stash 'em in the kids' rooms,' he advised her, knowledgeably. 'Inspector Dawson says good job you were passing by for a cuppa,' he continued. 'We'd better go downstairs I think. Your client's nicked.'

17.

'IT'S BEEN A BIT busy today.' Shaza stood on the threshold of her decimated room, the door half open, talking quietly.

'First the lady with the black hair came. Did you see her?

'Well you should've been. Then two policemen came, well, a policeman and a police lady, and they made such a mess. Just look! And they didn't even wipe their feet.

'Suzy said "power goes to their head".

'No. I'm not sure what it means either. They still made a mess!' she lamented, hands on hips.

'I can see lots of things I thought were missing, though.

'That pink t-shirt I got for my birthday last year. And the lego car – yuch.

'No. I'm not sure who she was either. Said her name was Contents and her second name was an animal but I'm not sure which now. She tried to be nice, all friendly, but she couldn't help Daddy.

'Yes I asked. She said just to the police station like that's somewhere we go all the time, like just to the shops or just to school.

'I don't know. Mama doesn't know either. Contents said she would visit him later and tell us what was happening. She asked if we had a phone and Mama wrote down the number, although I don't know why, as no one will answer if Baba's not here.

'No. I know. Baba could have explained but he was already in the police car.

'I thought the policeman was nice at first, even though he had dirty shoes, because he sort of smiled. But I don't think it was real smiling 'cos when Contents said Baba didn't need the handcuffs he carried on smiling and put them on Baba anyway. Then Baba told Mama to take me into the kitchen.

'Yes lots of them did, I know. I suppose because they were all home from work and "had nothing better to do".

'Then Contents got in a taxi and I heard her say "Hampstead", and that's where Daddy works.

'I think I'll start to fold up my clothes again. I don't want to ask Mama. She's crying too hard anyway, although she thinks I don't know. Will you help me? Let's do the t-shirts first. You can borrow any you really like. Except for the pink one from my birthday.

'No. I don't know what they found.

'I told you, I don't know. I don't want to talk any more.

'Mrs Crane says you get a lot more work done when you stop chatting, that's why.

'I'm not cross. I just think we should do the tidying now and talk later.'

PART TWO

18

CONSTANCE sat outside the Starbucks on Paternoster Square sipping a latte, the sun warming her back.

'Ah. You've found a table already. Well done. More coffee?'

Constance marvelled at how Judith Burton swept past her and into the café, without waiting for her response, accidentally pushed to the front of the queue, apologised profusely in convincing style and was then served first anyway. She was back with her coffee almost by return.

'Well, what was so urgent you had to see me today?' Judith enquired, sitting down and unbuttoning her jacket, her red silk shirt peeping through to accentuate the pallor of her skin.

'This isn't your usual haunt,' Constance remarked, deliberately avoiding the direct question.

'No? Well, that shows that you're not up to date, Connie. But that's my fault I suppose. I've been a bit cloak-and-dagger recently.' She leaned in close and whispered. 'I'm on a mediators' course; don't tell anyone.'

Constance covered her mouth with her hand. 'Mediator. You?'

'Well it's not so surprising, is it? Many lawyers do it.' Judith appeared mildly hurt.

'Yes, they do but they're not all you. You spend your time scaring people half to death with ferocious cross-examination. Isn't mediation all about reconciliation?'

'I'm telling you, I'm a natural. Jeremy, the course leader, has already praised my "ability to combine persuasiveness with subtlety" or some such nonsense.'

'Are you sure he doesn't fancy you?'

Judith ignored the jibe and continued to sip at her coffee.

'Anyway, it's just a hobby, to stop me from being bored. Greg suggested it, actually. I think it was because I offered to iron one of his shirts. He knew then something drastic had to be done. You haven't sent me anything in a while so you can hardly complain.'

Constance noticed, but decided to file away, Judith's reference to Greg. She had heard a rumour that Judith was seeing Dr Gregory Winter, their expert witness from their first case together but, during their sporadic conversations over the past year, Judith had not confirmed this to her. Perhaps this was her preferred way of telling Constance she and Greg were an item.

'That's not true. You're too fussy,' she replied. 'But I have something for you now, and you're going to be very interested.'

'OK. Spill the beans. Not another fifteen-year-old boy?'

'No. Did you see the story at the weekend about the woman who fell out of the eleventh floor of St Mark's Hospital?'

Judith's eyes widened.

'Yes. But that's Hampstead. More upmarket than your regular stamping ground?'

'Dawson is spending six months over there. Helping out. He

called me when he needed someone.'

'And what's *our* involvement?'

Constance grinned. Judith already wanted a piece of the action.

'I'm representing the hospital cleaner, Ahmad Qabbani. They're holding him pending further enquiries, but I think they'll be charging him later today.'

'Hmm. What did he do to court all this interest, Mr Qabbani? Other than the obvious.'

'He was on duty around the time of death.'

'But presumably so were a thousand other hospital employees.'

'Yes. Although he was near her room and he'd been in there, to clean.'

'Go on.'

'There's DNA linking him to the deceased, and he had some of her expensive jewellery at his house.'

'Hmm. Not great but not insurmountable. Background?'

Constance was used to Judith's quick-fire questions and replied without drawing breath, although she reflected on how clients requiring a swift but amicable resolution of their dispute through mediation might feel differently when faced with Judith's lashing tongue.

'The family are refugees from Syria. Him, his wife and daughter.'

'The deceased?'

'Barbara Hennessy. English woman, early seventies, two children, used to be an artist, bit flighty, went in to have her bunions treated, privately, stayed in for a few days and then, as you know, fell, or was pushed, out of the window.'

'Yes, I didn't quite understand the description of where she fell from?'

'They can't be certain but there's this staff room at the end of the corridor and it has a sort of balcony above a fire escape. They go outside and get a breath of fresh air.'

'You mean have a cigarette – or perhaps I should say "vape" these days.'

'That too, yes.'

'And it's not locked?'

'No. Has to remain open because of fire regulations.'

'So the deceased walked down the corridor, into this staff room, opened the door to the balcony and fell over or was pushed to the ground below. Or jumped. Hmm. What injuries did she sustain?'

'Well her skull was completely shattered. It's woodland out the back and her head hit a tree-stump. But there were not many other injuries, I don't think. I haven't seen the final pathology report, just some provisional conclusions.'

'And no one saw or heard anything?'

'No. Or they're not saying.'

Judith sat back and folded her arms, then unfolded them and stood up. She marched to the centre of the square, oblivious to the fact that she was obscuring a screen which had been erected for passers-by to watch international athletics with their lunch. After some pacing backwards and forwards, she returned and sat down.

'What's our client, Ahmad, say about all this?'

'Well, if I believe him, and I think I do, he's as confused as we are. He says he did his job and went home.'

'You mentioned jewellery? At his house?'

'The police found it upstairs.'

'Could they have planted it?'

'I suppose so. But, well, I was there when they did the search. Seemed genuine to me.'

Judith raised her eyebrows high but kept silent. Constance's devotion to duty knew no bounds.

'I've suggested to Ahmad that he admit the theft at least.'

'What did he say?'

'He was really angry, said he wasn't a thief.'

'So how did he explain the rings being in his house?'

'He said he didn't know how they got there.'

'Hmm. We'll need to work on that one. Any other suspects?'

'The children, a son and daughter. Dawson hasn't given much else away yet but I'll work on him. The newspapers say her ex-husband was wealthy, could be an inheritance issue.'

'Could be. OK. Send me everything you've got straight away, but we should probably start at the "scene of the crime". I finish this ghastly course tomorrow and I'm dying for something really meaty to get my teeth into. And to stop having to be nice to people. Agh! If I smile any more times my face will remain stuck with that vile expression for ever more. Now I remember why I abandoned commercial law and turned to a life of crime. Ha!' Judith laughed at her own joke. Then she took a swig of coffee and grimaced.

'God I hate decaf. It's like drinking mud.'

19

'WHEN DID YOU last see your mother?' The man asking the question was attempting small talk, biding his time until his other appointed visitor arrived.

Brian Bateman applied pressure to his hexagonal tortoise-shell glasses, to ensure they didn't roll off the end of his nose. He had worn a suit for this auspicious occasion, but most of the time nowadays his clients were happy with a shirt and a pair of chinos. Marks & Spencer made a great range in different lengths in a variety of colours, and they emerged crease-free from the washing machine too. He had lived the past thirty-five years alone, apart from a short dalliance with a hamster; he hadn't been sorry when this was short-lived, its nocturnal rustlings had disturbed his sleep patterns.

'A few months ago?' Joe replied, running a finger around the inside of his collar. Joe, too, was used to wearing a shirt for work but Janice had suggested a tie this time and, struggling to fasten the top button earlier, he had managed to burst it off. He had then dispensed with the tie, with a few choice words which, fortunately, had been directed at the mirror in the bathroom rather than at Janice, but the collar was still troubling him.

'So, in March then?'

Joe shrugged. 'It might have been a bit longer. You know how quickly time goes when you're busy.'

Brian had no children of his own but he felt sure that, if he had, he would have expected more regular visits. He kept his voice even, apart from the slight elevation in pitch of the penultimate word which could not be avoided when formulating his question.

'Yes. It does. I make lists to help keep track of things,' he said. 'Do you ever make lists, Joseph?'

'No.' Joe shook his head. 'I keep it all up here.' He tapped the side of his head and sniggered. When would Tracy arrive? The sooner they could hear what the old guy had to say and get out of here the better.

Joe resembled his mother, if you took the time to scrutinise his face closely, as Brian was now doing. He had inherited her features, all of them individually, but his colouring was quite different; his skin was dark and his hair almost black. Barbara had been fair-skinned with a few stray freckles adorning her nose and hair, which had run the gauntlet from orange to yellow and back to orange again. If Barbara had been reproduced in an Andy Warhol Pop Art print, her face appearing in myriad different shades, then the resemblance between mother and son would have been more apparent.

'We had an argument about something – something stupid. I was planning to go. But now…' Joe was speaking.

'Now it's too late.' Brian completed his sentence for him.

Joe tugged at his collar again. God he wished Janice hadn't

gone on about the tie.

When Barbara had first visited Brian, she had been distracted, not desperate, but clearly anxious at how she would manage with two young children and an erratic income. Brian had brought the divorce papers over to her house, to save her travelling back to his office. He remembered the generous welcome she had given him, thanking him for taking the trouble, and how she had offered him a glass of wine and a tour of her studio.

'Well, we'll just wait for your sister to arrive and then I can read the will,' he said.

Tracy had also dressed up for the occasion. She wore a navy suit and bright red lipstick, although it was pasted so thickly across her mouth that a layer had rubbed off on her front teeth, giving her a ghoulish expression. Her hair was tidied up into a neat ponytail but the taupe face make-up she had applied, to cover the grey shadows which had overtaken her face since her mother's death, lent her an unnatural hue.

'Hello Joe, Mr Bateman. Sorry I'm a few minutes late.'

'Pete not coming?' Joe coughed out the question, with a pointedness heightened by his own discomfort.

'I didn't think it right. Janice not coming then?'

'No.'

Brian rustled some papers on his desk and waited. Then, when he had their attention, he reached into his drawer and removed a large white envelope.

'So, Tracy, Joseph, let's begin. Your mother made a will five years ago. Your father had suggested it many times.'

'Have you been in touch with Miles?' Tracy asked, still catching her breath from the stairs.

Joe shot her a look of pure disdain.

'I've tried to contact him this week but without success. But on the basis of the contents of the will and my instructions from your mother, there is no need for him to be here today.'

Tracy glared back at Joe. She would not let him dominate her today. But Joe was pleased with Brian's reply. It didn't sound like his crazy mother had left anything to Miles, and quite right too. Brian extracted some A4 paper, unfolded it with a dramatic flourish and began to read.

'Here we are then. The reason you are both here today. This is the last will and testament of Barbara Hennessy, née Tennyson, made this… I don't need to read you all this preamble,' he said. 'I'll stick to the important stuff or we'll be here all day. And I will send you each a copy by email so you can read it yourselves afterwards, in case anything is not clear.'

Tracy shuffled in her seat; Joe folded his arms.

'The bequests provided in this will are subject to some caveats which can be found at the end at paragraph 6. So starting with paragraph 1. Bequests,' Brian continued.

'To each of my grandchildren, currently Luke Jones and Taylor Jones, the sum of £300.'

Joe's mind wandered to his mother's face. It wasn't a recent memory. It was the only time she had come to see him participate in anything at school. He had won the sprint at sports day, when he was eight years old. Barbara had been late – timekeeping was not one of her best attributes – and then, as he had been lining up, he had spotted her, sauntering towards the crowd of parents in a see-through, floaty dress with dangly earrings and sandals, caught up in her own thoughts. A couple of the other mums had noticed Barbara's arrival too, but returned to their conversations. She wasn't part of their crowd; they feared her bare legs and

Bohemian tendencies.

But as Joe ran, he had kept his mother in his sights, his body pulsing forward, his breath coming thick and fast, and just as he broke through the tape, and maybe because in addition to running he had been screaming 'look at me, look at me' inside his head the whole time, Barbara had turned at the last possible moment and seen him crossing the line, first by a mile. Her expression? Recognition, followed by surprise which quickly became pride, unadulterated pride, without any of the usual qualifications or admonishments she often attached to her interactions with him.

'To each of my children, Tracy Jones née Hennessy and Joseph Hennessy, half my remaining estate in equal shares.'

Now Joe shifted noisily in his seat. Tracy remained still, her eyes fixed on Brian.

'Sorry, Brian. Can you say that again please?' Joe asked.

'Yes. Certainly. To each of my children, Tracy Jones née Hennessy and Joseph Hennessy, half my remaining estate in equal shares.'

'How much is that then, her estate?' he asked, swallowing his surprise.

Brian glanced up from the text and Tracy rolled her eyes, although she had wanted to ask the same question herself.

'I will get to that in a moment,' he said. 'Let me read the remainder.'

Brian continued to read, words with little meaning, occasionally skipping parts and referring each of them again to the copy he would provide. Then he stopped.

'Is everything clear so far?' he asked.

'She's left Tracy's kids three hundred quid each and the rest is split between me and Trace. That's it, isn't it?'

Brian nodded. 'That's exactly it. But the next bit is crucial. It's the qualifications your mother has added. Then we can get on to the value of your mother's estate.'

'Can't we do the value bit first?'

Brian raised his eyebrows, his head moving from Joe to Tracy, his glasses slipping floorwards dangerously until he pressed them back up his nose.

'Oh come on, Trace. Stop pretending that isn't what all this is about,' Joe said. And to Brian: 'We don't expect Mum to have left us much, Mr Bateman, before you think we're just money grabbing. But we do want to know how much.'

Brian allowed his eyes to rest on Tracy's face, awaiting her answer.

'It's fine,' she mumbled. 'I don't mind what order we do things in.'

'All right. I don't have power over your mother's investments or her bank account, but last year she provided me with a summary of her assets. At that time, they were worth just short of £1.9 million.'

Tracy leaned forwards, eyes wide. The corners of Joe's mouth twitched up and down.

'Did you say £1.9 million?' Tracy asked.

'Yes.'

'But where did she get it from?'

'I understand some of her paintings sold well through the 1970s and '80s, and my contact, Mr Williams, invested the money for her.'

'We always thought Mum's paintings were rubbish,' Joe said.

'Oh, no.' Brian was quick to jump in. 'She had some successful exhibitions; you were probably both too young to remember.

She was very modest about her work, that's all. And that's not including the house in Spain,' Brian added, his cheeks suddenly tinged with pink. He had remembered the time his holiday to Fuengirola had coincided, coincidentally of course, with Barbara's trip to her place in Marbella and she had invited him to join her on her veranda for some Sangria. It had been such a lovely evening.

'She owns that place? I thought she just went there on package holidays.'

'No. Miles bought it when they were first married, but he gave it to her as part of the divorce settlement. It is rented out much of the year and provides a steady income. And, like you say, Barbara stayed there from time to time when it was available.'

Joe laughed out loud.

'What's so funny?' Tracy asked.

'Well I can't believe she kept all of this secret for all these years.'

'I'm sure things would have been different if your father had been at home. You might have lived more, well, in a more materialistic way. Like I say, she was modest about her achievements.'

Tracy sat back in her chair and crossed and re-crossed her legs.

'This is mad,' she said, when she found both the men looking in her direction. 'I kept worrying about how much to put away to care for Mum, in case she lived another twenty years. And all the time she could look after herself and the rest of us. Why didn't she move, re-decorate, travel?'

'You know your mother,' Brian replied, questioning, as he spoke, if this was an accurate conclusion to draw. 'She was happy with what she had. I am sure if she'd wanted those other things she would have done them. And I think, in part, once the money had been invested, she considered it gone. Waiting to be passed on to the next generation.

'I'll be able to provide you with more details, like I said, but we had better move on to those caveats I mentioned earlier. They are important.' He cleared his throat.

Joe smirked knowingly at Tracy, who coloured and turned away. *He's probably planning how to spend his share already*, she thought. *And none of it on Janice.* Then she thought of Pete, sitting at home watching TV with the boys in that bare room in that soulless house. This was a chance to change their lives forever, not just going back to what they had before Pete's accident.

'These are qualifications which apply to the bequests to my children, Tracy and Joseph, at paragraph 1b above; namely:' – Brian paused dramatically – '1, if Tracy or Joseph does not visit me within six months of my death (not including the day of my death)…'

Brian halted again to draw breath. He had included the words in parentheses on the second re-write. He had started to explain to Barbara how important it was to make these kinds of things clear, whether days were included or not in the period of calculation, but she had waved him on with a 'you're better at dealing with these things than little old me' expression and he had not bothered to complete the explanation.

'…then their share will vest in my grandchildren. 2…'

'Wait a minute.' Joe's hand was in the air and he let it hang there until he had Brian and Tracy's attention. 'So, as long as Trace and I visited Mum in the last six months we get our share.'

'Yes. But there are some other conditions too, if I can read on.'

'But if, for example, Joe *hadn't* visited Mum then his share goes to Luke and Taylor?' Tracy added loudly, with a touch of superiority. Joe tipped his head back and scowled at the ceiling.

'Or any other grandchildren,' Brian countered.

'My boys *are* the only grandchildren,' Tracy said.

'At the moment, yes, but let me get on to that a little later.'

'Is this legal?' Joe asked, suddenly agitated, leaping up and crossing the room to the window where he leaned one hand against the pane.

'Absolutely.'

'Trace. You see what she's done. She always preferred you.'

'Mr Hennessy, there is no favouritism here. The provision applies equally to you and your sister. Barbara…your mother, didn't want you, either of you, to be strangers from her, that's all. That's understandable, isn't it?'

Joe glared at Brian. 'That's why you asked me.'

'I'm sorry.'

'You tricked me, asking me how long it was since I saw her. Before Tracy arrived.'

'I wasn't intending to trick you. I was just chatting. It is some time since I assisted your mother with her will and I do have many clients. This provision was not at the forefront of my mind.'

'Mr Bateman. How do we show you when we last saw Mum?' Tracy willed her brother to keep quiet. It wasn't lost on her that Brian was in control of their cool nearly two million pounds, and that it might be prudent to keep him sweet. She tried to remember if her mother had ever spoken of him.

'It's not too onerous. If you went out somewhere together you could show a receipt, for a restaurant or theatre and make a declaration on oath that you were together.'

'What if we just went to her flat, or she came to us?'

'Someone else, over eighteen, should be prepared to sign and say that's where you were that evening. They'll need to come in here and sign in front of me, or another solicitor; that's all.'

Joe's mind was racing as he thought back to his last visit to Barbara's flat. It might have been March or April but it could have been before Christmas. How could he check?

'Mum had a calendar on her wall,' he blurted out before he could stop himself.

'That's right, she did.'

'So that may help, I was just thinking. She put appointments on there.'

'Yes.' Now Brian was smiling. This was all going swimmingly.

'Mr Bateman. Is there something else in the will? You were beginning a "2" when Joe interrupted.'

'Yes. I'll read on. Two and three are crucial. They override the first caveat. So I am afraid that if *either* of these two conditions are satisfied your bequest is forfeited in its entirety. There is no fallback onto grandchildren.'

He paused, and both Tracy and Joe viewed him suspiciously.

'2, if either Tracy or Joseph or their spouse has been convicted of a criminal offence during the relevant period they shall forfeit their share of the bequest.'

'Ha!' Joe shouted. 'And what was she after with that one then?'

'Not rewarding the undeserving?' Brian ventured, but worried he may have gone too far when Joe, who had only just returned to his chair, squeezed the arms until his knuckles turned white.

'What is she talking about "during the relevant period"?'

'It's in the Definitions section again.'

'I don't care where it is. What does it mean?'

'Relevant period ends on the day your mother's estate is distributed and it begins five years before that date.'

'So any conviction older than five years doesn't count then?'

'That's right. And 3,' Brian collected himself and continued with a little less confidence than before. He sensed Tracy would try to restrain her brother if necessary, but Joe was seated closer to him than Tracy and she was a little, well, even delicately, one must admit, 'on the large side' and may not move quickly enough to blunt any blows. He took a deep breath and gripped his spectacles with one hand.

'And 3, if either Tracy or Joseph or their spouse is in debt during the relevant period, then they shall not receive my bequest unless such debt is cleared by the time the money is distributed. Debt will include having any overdrafts, unpaid credit card balances more than one month old or mortgage or rent arrears. There, that's it.'

Tracy's mouth fell open.

'She always wanted you both to be independent financially, to make your own way in the world,' Brian added, by way of further assistance, 'but in a prudent, far-sighted manner.'

'This is bullshit!' Joe shouted and Brian flinched and dropped the will. 'First you tell us we're getting Mum's money and then we find out that we have to open ourselves up to all this snooping before we get any of it. God, it's so like her. Didn't care about us when she was alive but determined to ruin things for us now she's dead. I bet you've never had anyone else write a will like this. Or was this *your* bloody idea?'

Brian shrank back from the table, picked up the will and folded it neatly, quickly placing it back in its envelope.

'I can't possibly discuss other clients with you, and whatever advice your mother sought from me will stay with me until my own death! But I can assure you that your mother was only thinking of each of you and what she wanted from you as members of society when she set out those stipulations.'

'Bullshit!' Joe repeated, 'And it's Tracy's kids who get everything if we can't satisfy you.'

'Well, perhaps not.' Brian spoke hesitantly now. He had not anticipated quite so much antagonism, and Tracy had not moved since he had read out the third condition.

'What do you mean "perhaps not"?' Joe clenched his fists tight to his sides.

'It's in the Definitions section. "Grandchildren" includes any children living today (like Tracy's boys) but also any children born before your mother's assets are distributed, as long as they are born within matrimony.'

'Matrimony?'

'Yes. Marriage. They have to be born within marriage and before the money is distributed.'

Joe unclenched his fists but his fingers continued to move. Tracy stood up, unsteadily. She suddenly needed to be gone, out of this oppressive room with her mother's judgement of her life, the life she shared with Pete, hanging all around her.

'What happens now?' she asked Brian, who was hoping, but not certain, that the worst of the storm had passed.

'Well, I submit all the papers to Probate, which should take a month or two. Then I will liaise with Mr Williams to collect together and liquidate, to the extent possible, all the assets, although he will advise on whether that is sensible in this economic climate. And finally, there will be the distribution, so you have plenty of time to get together for me the very basic evidence I will need to satisfy those conditions.'

'And the distribution itself?'

'It will be some months, assuming none of the bequests are forfeited. And I suppose if you don't agree on the liquidation of the assets, that may hold things up. Once Mr Williams has done his bit it will be up to you two how quickly things move.'

'What does "forfeited" mean? Where does the money go if we don't get it?' Tracy asked.

Brian cleared his throat. 'It goes to a charitable trust which is registered offshore, in the Cayman Islands, very tax-efficient, to be used for charitable purposes.'

Joe was hovering near the door but he turned around, his eyes dancing crazily in his head.

'No!' he bellowed. 'I will only say this once, Brian. Our mum's money is not going to the frigging Cayman Islands, do you understand?'

Without another word, Joe marched out of the room. Tracy offered Brian her hand and then followed him.

JUDITH AND Constance arrived at St Marks armed with a prearranged plan in case of challenge; Constance had found out the name of a long-term patient from Ahmad but, ultimately, when they burst through the swing doors at the entrance to the eleventh-floor private ward, they found the reception desk and surrounding area empty. Grinning at each other conspiratorially, they strode on to the ward, Judith heeding the signs to hand-sanitise on her way, muttering 'clean is best' under her breath as she went.

Mrs Hennessy's room, two down, on the right, was still cordoned off but the door was open. They each peered in and noted the layout; metal-frame bed, bedside cabinet on wheels, all set against a large window but without any mechanism for opening. Nevertheless, Judith craned her neck and peered in for an age, then gazed back up the corridor towards the swing doors, and down the corridor, towards the room where, reportedly, Mrs Hennessy had headed on that fateful night.

She counted the number of rooms and made a note in her book, asking Constance to photograph the room and its surroundings from various angles. 'Do it quickly and quietly,' she said. Constance raised an eyebrow but said nothing in response.

She noted the top part of each door was made of glass and that Mrs Hennessy's door had a slatted blind which was currently closed. There was no CCTV as far as she could see. At the end, also on the right, was the staff room, which Constance entered, while Judith wandered off to survey the rest of the ward.

'Can I help you?' the young male nurse seated in the staff room, drinking from a steaming mug, asked Constance, with a touch of annoyance.

'I hope so. I'm Miss Lamb. I represent Ahmad Qabbani.'

She was rewarded with a blank expression.

'Ahmad. He's one of the hospital cleaners.'

'Ahmad's not in today.'

'Yes I know. I'm, well, as I said, I represent him. I'm a lawyer. Do you work with Ahmad? You obviously know him.'

'I've been here three months but I'm only up here one day a week. I see Ahmad sometimes.'

'I'm here to find out about Mrs Hennessy, the lady who died?'

'Oh. Mrs Hennessy. I saw her just one time. We have a rota.'

'What was she like?'

'A nice lady. I did her blood pressure. She liked to talk. She had an operation, on her foot.'

'Could she walk alone after her operation?'

'I didn't see her after. You should speak to the physio.'

'And Ahmad. Did you talk to him?'

'We said hello. He used to talk to the patients more, I think. Ask Lottie, Nurse Li. She's permanent on this ward. She knows Ahmad much better. She has holiday today but she's back tomorrow.'

'Yes, I will, thank you.' Constance gestured over to the door leading outside, noticing it was newly installed, with a combination code. 'Is that where...?'

'Yes. Now they're saying we should lock it. See the numbers? They put in the new door – said they need the old one for fingerprints. It's open, though. We all complained, so it's open. You don't close all staircases down, just in case someone, some day, decides to jump off one of them.'

Judith wandered in, grinned at the two of them and marched straight out onto the balcony. Constance joined her and the two of them stood shoulder to shoulder in the cramped space. They were standing on a metal grate which allowed tantalising glimpses of the ground, one hundred feet below. A few stray cigarette ends, no doubt smoked since the murder, littered the floor. The railing was low, finishing around mid-thigh on Constance, at a convenient hand-height for ascending or descending the stairs, but not suitable for any serious leaning; it would be easy enough to push someone over, more difficult to fall unintentionally.

'What did he say?' Judith asked.

'He doesn't know Ahmad well. Said to come back tomorrow to talk to another nurse.'

'Ah.'

'And the door's new. They've kept the other one.'

'Gosh. They are taking this enquiry seriously then.'

Judith surveyed the expanse of overgrown woodland below. The area where Mrs Hennessy had been found was still cordoned off, although her body was long gone, and a lone officer remained stationed below.

'I find the lack of any security here staggering,' Judith began.

'We've just walked in, straight off the street, and no one has challenged us. I mean, I know we appear fairly respectable, well, I do anyway, but that's really not the point, is it?'

'No.' Constance ignored Judith's attempt at humour.

'The people in here are sick and vulnerable and no one checks who comes and goes.'

'It'd be expensive I s'pose,' Constance replied. 'To have security. And inconvenient. You come to visit someone. You don't expect to be subjected to the third degree.'

'What about the doctors?'

'How do you mean?'

'Well, Dawson's been oh so interested in the nurses and other staff, but just because they've taken the Hippocratic oath doesn't mean we should ignore the doctors in our evidence gathering. I mean, Harold Shipman clearly forgot his responsibilities.'

'Yes. Dawson said that the patients see lots of different doctors up here on the private ward.'

'OK. That may be. But there must be someone in charge. Find out who that was and let's also examine her medical records. I want a list of every person who saw Mrs Hennessy, and what they prescribed from the time she arrived until she ended up down there on the ground.'

***

'Can I help you, ladies?' a slim doctor in a white coat, with the beginning of a grey moustache, opened the door to the balcony and leaned out. The nurse stood, red-cheeked, behind him; he had probably alerted the doctor to their presence.

'Oh, thank you. No. We were just admiring the view from up

here. And you are?'

Constance had to hand it to Judith. They were the ones who were trespassing and she was giving the doctor the third degree.

'I'm Doctor Wolf. Who are you?'

'I am Judith Burton and this is Constance Lamb. We are lawyers in the case involving the late Mrs Hennessy. Chief Inspector Dawson sent us. It helps with our preparation of the case. You know, sometimes even judges and juries visit the crime scene these days.'

Doctor Wolf folded his arms.

'If you say so. But you should have told us you were coming. We can't just have people wandering in here any time of day or night.'

'Just what I was saying to Constance...'

'It's been almost impossible to look after my patients since, well, since Mrs Hennessy died. Do you know when we will get her bed back? We are very short of space.'

'I have been reassured it will be very soon, doctor,' Judith cooed sympathetically. 'And I can only imagine what it must have been like for you; and that's before the media circus begins.'

'Media circus?'

'Oh yes. There'll be lots of speculation about how Mrs Hennessy met her end – conspiracy theories, that kind of thing, I'm afraid. Think of Kennedy or Marilyn Monroe. Was she one of your patients?'

'She was, yes.'

'Did you prescribe any medication for her?'

'It's all in the statement I gave to Inspector Dawson and in her log if I did.'

'Did you see her the night she died?'

'Like I said…'

'Humour me, Dr Wolf,' Judith said. 'I have other clients too, and Inspector Dawson is busy fighting crime.'

Dr Wolf took a deep breath and his shoulders relaxed. He stepped back into the staff room and Judith and Constance followed. The nurse scuttled off in a hurry.

'Her wound was healing well, her blood pressure was normal.'

'And how was she?'

'I am a surgeon not a therapist but she seemed perfectly fine.'

'She had just had an operation, presumably she had some pain?'

'She was prescribed pain relief.'

'And were you in the hospital that night?'

'Yes. I was here till around midnight. Then I went home.'

'Thank you. We won't take up any more of your time. Come on Constance. Let's fly.'

21

JOE WAS WAITING for Tracy as she reached the bottom of the stairs.

'Bitch,' Joe muttered as he grabbed her arm.

'Joe, stop it. I'm cross too, but we shouldn't let him see us like this.'

He tightened his grip. 'You don't care. You're in the money and if you're not, your kids are, which is just the same thing. For one moment there I thought she was treating us the same.'

Tracy gave a deliberate and anxious glance back up the echoing staircase.

'Let's go and calm down and talk somewhere else.'

Joe followed her gaze. Upstairs a door clanged in the distance. He released her arm, slammed the flat of his hand against the door onto the street, which swung open obligingly, and exited into the welcome fresh air. Tracy followed.

'I walked past a Nero on my way. Let's sit down and talk about it there,' she suggested.

They staggered along in silence, Joe's anger failing to abate, so that he attacked the pavement at each step, chin thrust forward, arms swinging.

Seated at a table near the back of the café, Tracy began her campaign to keep Joe on side. 'What were you thinking about going off on one in front of Mr Bateman?'

'Trace. The guy's a complete tosser. Mum didn't think up that stuff on her own. You know as well as I do that she wasn't capable of that kind of…well…logical thinking. And all that jargon: "bequest", "forfeit". He put her up to it. What's his game then?'

Tracy bit her lip, and then remembered her lipstick too late. She ran her tongue over her teeth to try to remove it and then gave up and rubbed at them with her index finger.

'I don't know, but I know that we need him sweet so we can get our money. He's the executor. He will decide if we can have it. That's why it was stupid to get angry in front of him. If we've got nothing to hide, we wouldn't be bothered by Mum's ridiculous conditions, would we?'

Joe stared at his sister and his anger began to subside. He ordered two black coffees and returned to his seat.

'Listen, if anything, I'm the one in the shit, not you,' Tracy began, 'assuming you can show you saw Mum since Christmas?' she said pointedly. 'What did you tell the police?'

'I can't remember now. I said a few months, I think.'

'Well I can't see Brian talking to the police to check up. He's a strange one. Do you remember Mum ever mentioning him?'

'No. But it's not the kind of stuff she would tell me about, is it? *By the way, my solicitor is helping me make a will and if you get into any more trouble you don't get a penny.*'

'Didn't you hear? He said in the last five years. Unless there's something else you've been nicked for that I don't know about, then you're in the clear.'

Joe collected the drinks and returned to the table.

'No, Trace. I'm completely clean,' he replied. 'And Janice will remember when I last saw Mum.'

'There you are then. We just need to keep calm and not shout at Brian again, just to make sure.'

'But you saw her at the hospital. And you and Pete, you fixed everything you owed and you don't even cheat at cards, so why aren't you on the phone now telling dear Peter that he's finally hit the jackpot? That our side of the family is the one with the money, for once.'

Tracy covered her face and sat very still. When she finally removed her hands and blinked, Joe was staring at her.

'What's up, Trace? Is it something bad?'

Tracy couldn't help but wonder if his question was tinged with secret pleasure at her discomfort. She stifled a sob.

'We're in debt,' she said.

'You were, I know. But you sold everything, to pay it off?'

'We did. The house, the car. Bastards at the school insisted on keeping a whole term's money because we didn't give them "sufficient notice" but our lawyer said we wouldn't win that one. Stupid cow of a secretary enjoyed telling me that. Sold those gorgeous sofas, the Italian ones, the curtains from Florence. Pete had borrowed so much. He was expanding.'

'But he had insurance?'

'It's not come through yet. They said it will take a few more months *if* they agree to cover him. You remember he went up that ladder to unblock the drainpipe and they snapped him. Now he's paranoid. He hardly goes out, unless it's very early or very late. He thinks they're watching him all the time, through binoculars. He's become obsessed.'

Joe stifled a giggle. He had never liked his brother-in-law much. Such a big shot with his Gucci shoes and Patek Philippe watch. He doubted *that* had been relinquished.

'How much?' he asked.

'Our credit card debts are about three thousand, still. Business debts much more – Pete won't even say, although he gave personal guarantees, too, all over the place, and you heard what Brian said: the debt condition includes "spouse". I'll have to get some more advice on what the will means. God, more lawyer's fees.'

She swirled her coffee in its cup. She really wanted milk and two sugars but she wasn't going to ask. 'Maybe you could give me the money, the three thousand. That may be all I need to get my share from the will. Then I can give you it straight back.'

Joe regarded Tracy carefully. She had been good to him when they were kids. She had been the one who had reminded Mum to buy his uniform, on occasion had taken him shopping for clothes herself with money from Mum's purse. She had tried, with limited success, to help him with his maths homework so he could pass his GCSE, and had even cajoled one of Mum's boyfriends to give him some impromptu coaching. And she had intervened when Mum had wanted to throw him out after the Mackenzies' business. But recently, well, for the last twenty years, what had she done for him?

'It'll probably come good for us both. You heard – he said it might take months for the distribution. I'm sure you'll be fine by then. But I'll talk to Janice and see what we can spare.'

'Nooooo!' Tracy shrieked out her response. 'Please don't tell Janice about...well...Pete would be so embarrassed.'

'So you'll take her money but you don't want her to know

where it's going.'

'That's not fair. And unless you've changed a lot I doubt you two have a joint account.'

Joe stood up and fixed the lid on his coffee, ready to go. Tracy could always see through him. She was cleverer, always had been. The brains had gone to the girl. Still, he had the gift of the gab and the better looks by far. And at the moment, he held all the cards.

'All right. I won't tell Janice if you don't want me to. Did he say he was sending us the will?'

'Yes, by email.'

'We can speak again when we've received it and talked to the man with all the money.'

22

CONSTANCE approached her own front door on tiptoe, turning the key in the lock in super slow motion to avoid the mandatory click when the levers finally released their hold. She had even dawdled as she descended the steps to the Underground platform, missing an earlier train, delaying her by an additional six minutes, so as to increase the chances of Mike being asleep.

But he was propped up in bed with a can of beer next to him on the bedside table.

'You're up late,' she called to him through the open door, peeling off her jacket and dropping it by the door.

'You too.' He didn't move and Constance decided to attempt a joke.

'At least you have a beer,' she said.

Mike's eyes flitted to his right. He picked up the can, drank from it and returned it to the table where it nestled in a pool of liquid. Constance undressed quickly, splashed her face in the bathroom, cleaned her teeth and hurried to bed.

'How was your day?' she tried cheerily, the image of Judith rubbing disinfectant over her hands and forearms as they left the hospital indelibly imprinted on her mind.

Mike drank some more beer as Constance burrowed her way into his armpit.

'What's wrong?' She sat up and stroked his shoulder.

'I was worried,' he said. 'You didn't say you'd be late.'

'No. I got delayed and I forgot the time. You could have called me.'

'I did. Twice.'

'Oh. Sorry. I didn't notice. I was so busy.'

'Then I called your office. They said you'd been at St Marks Hospital but that was hours ago.'

Constance shifted her weight away from him.

'I was. I went there with Judith earlier today, on a case.'

'The Syrian cleaner.' Mike spat out Ahmad's title with a curled lip.

'Yes.' Constance was on her guard now. 'How do you know that?'

'I saw it in the paper. You're not defending him are you?'

'Maybe.'

'You can't tell me?'

'Everyone has the right to legal representation.' Constance stuck out her chin.

'That's just words to make you feel like it's all worthwhile.'

'Important words.'

'Really? Even if he's a terrorist.'

'Ahmad's not a terrorist.'

'You're already on first name terms? Take a look at tonight's *Standard* then. I left it for you, on the table.'

Constance scrambled out of bed, located the *Evening Standard* and turned its pages furiously. She found the article and read through it hurriedly, following the text with her finger. Then she remembered Mike and returned to the bedroom with the paper clasped tightly in her hand.

'Did you see what it says?' he challenged her. 'You're defending a killer, a person who kills indiscriminately – this time an old lady, next time maybe a school full of children.'

'I need to call Judith.'

'Go ahead. Call Judith. Tell her the Syrian cleaner's a terrorist. I bet she'll drop him like a stone. She won't want her career ruined by association.'

'There's nothing in the article of any substance. It just says that "an unnamed source" said his brother was an ISIL commander and that he and his brother were close. It's almost certainly not true.'

Mike took a deep breath and pulled off the covers. He walked around the bed, went to Constance and put his hands gently on her shoulders.

'You are such a good person,' he said, 'and you always try to do what's right. And I love you for it. But some of the people you defend, they don't deserve you or your time or your efforts. You must see that. You need to be a bit less charitable and a bit more hard-nosed.'

Constance pushed him away and hunted for her mobile in her bag.

'Now you're being selfish,' she said.

'Really? I'm being selfish in not wanting you to associate with this low life? You've got sucked in, Con, but you can't see it.' Now he was waving his arms around. 'And, OK, maybe I am being selfish, because you're never here and the whole point of us being together is so that we can be together, at least some of the time. And if I thought you were doing something really worthwhile then I might understand more.'

'And your job is so worthy.'

'I'm an actor. That's what I do. I entertain people, for fun. I'm not…Martin Luther King, OK?'

Constance's eyes narrowed.

'Sorry.' Mike realised his mistake. 'I didn't mean…I just meant I'm not someone on a personal crusade all the time. And maybe you shouldn't be, either.'

'Wow!' Constance spoke quietly, finding her phone but laying it down on the bedside table. 'Well, I appreciate you getting all of this off your chest. How long have you been feeling like this?'

'Oh come on. You've known I was pissed for a while now. You missed my first night in *Macbeth* when that fight kicked off in Newham.'

Now Mike crushed the can to a pulp before throwing it across the room to land with a clang in the bin in the far corner.

'I'm not going to change what I do.' Constance spoke softly.

'Other stuff I can deal with. But this Syrian terrorist is one step too far. You must be able to see that?'

'I'll assess the case in the normal way, but I won't drop Ahmad just because a newspaper, which may not have done its homework, doesn't like him. That wouldn't be right.'

'Even if he's a terrorist?'

Constance turned her head away and bit her lip.

'OK. I get the message. Here's what I think,' Mike said blandly, grabbing a blanket out of the top of the wardrobe and flinging it from the doorway across the living room on to the sofa. 'You're right that I can't tell you what to do. And I don't want it to be like that.' He picked up his pillow and tucked it under his arm.

Constance sat down on the bed. Was the fight over? A message beeped on her phone and she struggled not to acknowledge it. Mike gathered the crumpled copy of the *Standard* and scanned the article again. Then he folded it up and dropped it into the bin, hovering by the door with his back to her for a few seconds. When he turned around his expression was sad.

'This isn't working for me any more,' he said. 'You're hardly ever here, and when you are, you're totally preoccupied with work. We don't have any fun together. I'll move in with my brother for a few weeks from tomorrow. We can make arrangements to see each other like before. See how things go.'

Constance hadn't expected this from Mike, not this depth of feeling or the willingness to act on it. A muscle in his left cheek along the jawline pulsed once and was still. She imagined him practising his lines and his facial expressions over and over before the mirror, like he did before an audition, while she was running around the hospital, holding her breath to stave off the smell of death.

'I see. You've told Nick before me.'

Mike shrugged.

'I asked if his spare room was free, that's all. I'll pack in the morning. We'll see how things go. Maybe it will be better if we have to make a date. Maybe we'll make more effort with each other.'

'Maybe,' Constance replied inside her head, but she doubted it very much.

23

DAVID WOLF was loitering in the corridor for what seemed like an age. Finally, Dr Mahmood appeared from his ward round, holding a paper file under his arm. David fell into step beside him as naturally as he could manage, trying not to appear agitated or anxious.

'Hi Hani,' he said lightly, the older man returning the greeting by increasing his speed one notch. David chastised himself for his own reserve; he had known Hani for ten years, worked with him closely for almost as long, but he still felt a distance between them. Perhaps it was a cultural thing, Hani not trusting people who were not of his faith. But Jane had always disagreed. She claimed she found Hani 'warm and supportive' and argued that his distant manner was misunderstood.

'Do you have a moment? There's something I need to talk to you about.'

'I can't stop, David. My ward round overran; nurse got something wrong and it needed sorting. Really behind schedule now, sadly.' He headed towards the lift. 'We can talk on my way to my next appointment if you like.'

David gave a cursory glance over his shoulder before continuing.

'It's about tomorrow's mortality review meeting and Mrs Hennessy's death.'

'Yes.'

'Is there anything in particular you wanted to focus on? I thought it might be useful to know in advance.'

'No. Why do you ask?'

'Well, I'm worried about Jane to tell the truth.'

'Really?'

'And I talked to the police, like you suggested, reassured them about the operation. But they want to see a copy of the report, so we want to make sure it's…well…accurate.'

'Are you meaning to imply that my reports are inaccurate?'

'No. Of course not. But we usually prepare them for an internal audience. We should probably be more careful if the police are going to be reading it.'

'Your comments are noted, David. I'm not an imbecile. Is that all?'

'I would really appreciate it if nothing bad is said about Jane because of this. It's a critical time for her career. There's the head of department post coming up, you know.'

Hani entered the lift and stuck out his arm to bar David's way.

'We'll have the review tomorrow. If Jane has something she's worried about she knows my door is always open.'

'I didn't mean that,' David called out, as the lift doors closed and Hani disappeared from view.

24

KYLA ROBERTS had sold a 4 series coupé that morning and had two customers booked in for test drives in the afternoon. Simon was busy clambering in and out of a Touring 5 Series with a family of four. The phone was ringing every ten minutes or so, just as Joe liked it, busy but not hectic, demanding but manageable. Having said that, he thrived on the crazy days too. It gave him a buzz to pick up call after call, show two or sometimes three customers around simultaneously, flitting seamlessly from one to the other, ensuring that he kept his voice low enough that the selling points he emphasised to one customer were not overheard by another.

There was only one stage in the day when he had to take Kyla to one side. He waited till her customer had left and Simon was deep in conversation with the family, having just prevented their toddler from crawling underneath an X5. He had thought about intervening but decided Simon could handle it. His sister was heavily pregnant so he needed the practice.

Kyla was filling her water bottle from the cooler and he

marched over to join her.

'Having fun today?'

'Yes,' she replied. 'The guy this morning was such a gentleman. I think we could have got another two grand from him if we'd really wanted.'

'Well, I'm not sure. Sometimes these older guys are cleverer than we think and they've done their homework before they come in. Anyway, better he's satisfied and recommends us to someone else.'

'Well that's what he did. His son is coming in tomorrow. I've arranged to show him the 7 series.'

'Which one?'

'He says he'll like the blue one, the 2014.'

'Ah.' Joe had to think quickly. There were reasons why he should not sell the blue 2014 model to the son of the man who had just bought the coupé. 'That might be sold already,' he said.

'Oh?' Kyla strode back to her laptop. 'It didn't say on the computer.'

Joe took a deep breath. Of course it didn't because he was making things up. There was a – how could he put it? – 'issue' with the mileage on the car Kyla had just sold. He couldn't risk selling a similarly 'issue-concerned' beamer to his son. That might be pushing their luck too far.

'My mistake,' he said. 'I've been so busy I haven't completed the paperwork. But I can get a couple of other similar cars over. What time will he be in?'

'Eleven.'

'No problem then. Listen, Kyla. If you have someone come in again in the future, who's a friend or a family member of another customer, let me know.'

115

'Sure. Why?'

'Well. I want to make sure we charge them consistently or I make a note on the computer so that, maybe we offer the first customer money off next time; that kind of thing. Sort of thank you for recommending us.'

Kyla had never seen any of these 'friends and family benefits' noted on the computer. And she knew the blue BMW was not sold because it had only come in that morning and Joe had only just entered the registration number on the system. But she returned to her desk without further argument. He was the boss.

When Joe headed out for a smoke she sought out the paperwork for the coupé. The previous owner's contact details were all intact. She might just give him a call, later on when Joe went for lunch, just to satisfy her own interest, that was all.

25

JUDITH AND Constance were sitting next to each other at a table in one of the meeting rooms at Constance's office. Judith had given up a room at any barrister's chambers when she retired some years earlier.

'So, Connie. You have my undivided attention. What's the latest?'

Constance poured Judith a cup of black coffee.

'We don't have decaf. Gives you an excuse to have the real thing, just this once.'

Judith grinned and took a large gulp.

'Not bad at all,' she mumbled before sitting back in her chair and taking out her notebook and pen.

'We're still waiting for the CPS decision but I'm fairly sure they'll prosecute Ahmad,' Constance said.

'What evidence do they think they have?'

'The DNA.'

'What DNA?'

'His hair on her clothing.'

'But we know he was in her room.'

'Yes. But it's unlikely it happened just from cleaning her room and he hasn't offered any other explanation. And the fingerprints.'

'Remind me?'

'All around Mrs Hennessy's room. Yes, I know he cleans in there. And all around the staff room, including on the door leading out onto the balcony.'

'And the jewellery you mentioned?'

'Yes, two very distinctive rings. But he could have taken them any time she was asleep or in the bathroom. He didn't have to kill her for them. Dawson is working on the theory that Ahmad stole the rings on the Wednesday, after Tracy, the daughter, visited, or when she was having her operation on the Thursday. She noticed and confronted him. That's why he killed her.'

'Did anyone see or hear this apparent "confrontation"?'

'No, but some of the patients have been discharged. They're trying to track them down to speak to them.'

'What about the time he left?'

'His security card shows him swiping out downstairs at 8:12.'

'It's such a weak case, Connie. Will they really pursue it?'

'It could go either way. But there's public interest in this one – the "brother" article in the *Standard*. We'll need to ask him about that.'

'Yes. Let's do that together, watch his reaction, but not leave it too long. Either it's false, in which case we give them merry hell and force an apology on the front page, or it's true and we have a monumental PR problem. And before you say it, I completely get the "I am not my brother's keeper" phenomenon. Thank God, I'm not, in my case.'

Constance sat quietly bemused.

'What? What's silenced you this time?'

'You have a brother?' Constance asked tentatively.

'I was speaking metaphorically. Well, a sister actually. Clare. A globetrotter. A nightmare, more like. Always jolly. Ghastly. Don't ask. You?'

'A brother, Jermain. But we'll need a lot of alcohol before I talk about him.'

'So there you are then; my point exactly.'

Constance remained silent, her fingers resting on her keyboard.

'I can see I haven't quite satisfied you. Come on, spit it out,' Judith said.

'Let's say it isn't his brother. Let's say that Ahmad himself has some, well, connections with terrorism. Would you still defend him?'

'I don't like to deal in hypotheticals. It gets you all tied up in knots. Do you know something you haven't told me?'

'No. It's just, what if we find it's worse than the article, and he was involved. How can we defend him?'

'Like I said, we should check our facts first. But it's not up to us to make moral decisions about how deserving or otherwise our clients may be. This isn't like you. You're not giving up already are you? Over one article?'

'I was just asking what you thought,' Constance replied. 'No. I'm not giving up at all.'

'Good. Tell me about his family.'

'I haven't found any parents or evidence of any siblings whatsoever, including the "brother", or any previous employment record. But I can't be certain that the office I'm emailing in Syria even exists any more.'

'When Ahmad came here and sought sanctuary he must have submitted documents to the authorities?'

'He did but they can't find them. There was a fire at the records office and they were destroyed. And I've asked him and he won't speak about it. Says "that life is over" and stares out into the distance. But he is educated. I mean, his English is very good.'

'And his family over here? You said his wife is a recluse.'

'Thin, pale, very sad. She doesn't speak and she doesn't leave the house, and he obviously worries, as he hardly ever leaves the little girl, their daughter, alone with her.'

'Hmm. I wonder what happened to them in Syria? So many people carrying so much trauma around with them these days.'

'You would think the press would give them a break.'

'It's such a fine line. An old lady is dead, too, remember that. A frail old bird who has suddenly become Primrose Hill's most famous artist, posthumously of course. Anyone who's anyone will be turning up some scribble done on a napkin and claiming it as a "Hennessy original". And he's a big strapping man, isn't he?'

'He is physically big, yes. But not rough. You need to meet him. He is very…poised, I suppose.'

'Like you.'

'Maybe.' Constance laughed. Judith was the only one who complimented her so directly, but she didn't find it embarrassing.

'And there's always a tendency to believe the accused is guilty, otherwise what are the police up to? What about the post-mortem?'

'The Home Office pathologist says there was unlikely to have been any trauma before the fall. He is fairly certain now that she fell from the balcony. Apart from anything else, her fingerprints were out there on the rail. Cause of death is the blow to the head, which caused massive brain injuries, but her neck also broke on impact.'

'The operation had been a success?'

'Apparently.'

'Other suspects?'

'Mrs Hennessy's son, Joseph, "Joe", aged forty-one, lives with a woman, Janice Cooper, no children. He claims in his statement given shortly after her death that he hadn't seen his mother in six months. Works at BMW in Mill Hill as a salesman, recently promoted to head up a team. Was arrested for theft when he was a teenager. Stole some TVs from his employer but got off with a warning as he was young and he had letters of support from important people. Got an apprenticeship with BMW, worked his way up. Fifteen years on, things are looking up.'

'If it was so long ago, why is his conviction still on file?'

'I asked that too. It's not. There's still some police around from that time and they are keeping an eye on him. They think he's dodgy so they made sure Dawson knew about it too.'

'OK. Her other child?'

'Tracy Jones, a primary school teacher, aged forty-five. Her husband, Peter, is unemployed. Had his own business. They used to have a big house in Ealing. Fallen on harder times now. He had an accident and injured his back. Couldn't work, so the business went under. Moved to Brentford. Two sons, Luke and Taylor. They started at the local school in September.'

'Hmm.'

'Both have alibis from partners. Both were at home that evening.'

'Dawson shared all that with you?'

'Yes.'

'Gosh. He must be very taken with you. And more willing to share glory than his father ever was.'

'I'm not sure of his motives. He sent me round to Ahmad's when he knew he had the warrant to search for the rings. He didn't do that for Ahmad's good or to enhance my career. Far more likely he wanted to make sure we couldn't challenge the warrant afterwards, argue Ahmad didn't understand, or something like that.'

'No. You're right. Dawson tells us what he wants us to know. So, clearly, he wants us to dig around Mr Hennessy and Mrs Jones more, and he doesn't have the time, the manpower or the energy. That's my takeaway from all that. OK. Anyone else?'

'The ex-husband. Miles Hennessy. The police have only just got hold of him in LA, apparently. He is wealthy and hadn't seen Barbara for some years. Seems unlikely.'

'Other men in her life? A best friend hoping for a windfall? Illegitimate children?'

'I haven't had time to investigate any of those yet.'

'You could try talking to the children, well, the daughter, to start with. If Dawson is not trying too hard, he may not have asked her all the right questions. I'm a bit more wary of the son, given his history.'

'All right. I understand.'

'Then closer to home, did she leave a will, and if so, who is in and who is out? And find out more about our client, if you can. Did he tell his story to anyone when he applied for asylum here? And the other patients. I don't care if they're all paraplegics. Do any of them have criminal records?'

'Anything else?'

'Yes. Do we know when the funeral is?'

'They released the body today.'

'So it could be any day? Good. I love a good funeral. We must go along. You never know who will come out of the woodwork. God, this one is difficult as we've got so little to go on. We're defending air. Those cases are the worst for juries; they've got nothing to get their teeth into. They tend to convict just to be shot of it all.'

'Are you ever optimistic?' Constance asked, as she saved her ever-lengthening 'to do' list.

'Oh, you know I only like to make it sound bad so that I can crow when we win.'

'That's good. For a minute there, you had me a bit worried.'

26

JOE ARRIVED bright and early at Brian's office the next morning with Janice. She was wearing a low-cut flowery blouse with ruffles, and her hair was still wet from the shower. This time, Joe was dressed in a polo shirt and jeans.

Brian ushered them into his office and sat down behind his desk with a brief greeting. He had not forgotten how his last meeting with Joe had ended.

'And you are?' he forced his face into a neutral expression as he addressed Janice.

'Janice Cooper.' Joe answered for her as Brian took her hand nervously.

'So nice to meet you, Janice, nice to see you again, Joseph. Let's get down to business, shall we?' He used that line a lot on new clients. He had heard it in a James Bond film and he thought it imparted the correct measure of professionalism, tempered with edginess.

'Joseph, thank you, your message said that Janice is prepared to corroborate the details of the last time you saw your late mother.'

'Yeah. It was the 8th of March.'

Brian turned to his computer, moved across a few screens and waited for a document to load.

'It'll just take a second,' he explained.

Janice sat with her hands on her lap, her cheeks pink, one ear red where she had inserted her earring with difficulty that morning. Joe stood behind her, his fingers kneading the back of her chair.

'I have prepared a document which I will show you in a moment. Your full name is Janice Cooper?'

'Yes.'

'And you are Mr Hennessy's partner?'

'Yes.'

'For how long have you been together?'

'Almost eight years.'

'And your address is the same as that of Mr Hennessy.'

'Yes. 41, Grant Lane.'

'Thank you. And the date on which Mr Hennessy visited his mother was what?'

'The 8th of March.'

'Did you go too?'

'No. He went on his own.'

'And how do you know what the date was?'

'It was a Wednesday night. He called me to say he would be home late as he was going to see his mum.'

'And how do you know it was that particular Wednesday?'

'I watch *Silent Witness* and it was the last episode of the series. I double-checked. I had to record it so Joe could watch it later.'

'Mr Hennessy. I have to ask you as a formality. You did go to visit your mother that night?'

'Yeah.'

'And did you go out? Did you stay in?'

'I just went to the flat.'

'Did you eat together?'

'Mum had made some soup – tomato. I had a bit. We chatted. I arrived around 6:30, left around eight.'

'Oh so you caught *Silent Witness* in the end then?'

'Eh?'

'If you left at eight, you would have caught most of the show. Doesn't it usually start around nine?'

'No. Traffic was bad, I got petrol. Maybe I stayed later. I didn't get to see it.'

'Ah. That's a shame. It was a really good twist in the last episode. Thank you. I'll just print this off for you both and you can sign, and that's it, really.'

'What happens next?'

'This is early days. It'll take time to get all the paperwork sorted and then a little time to liquidate the investments, if that's what you want to do.'

Brian presented a page to Janice, and showed her where to sign. Joe, still scowling, signed below her.

'That's it then?' Joe snarled, tapping Janice on the shoulder so that she rose hesitantly. 'Come on.'

'Yes, thank you both.'

'Waste of bloody time,' he muttered as he headed for the door.

Janice was now the colour of a pickled beetroot. Without saying another word, she followed Joe out of the office.

Brian read through the statement signed by Joe and Janice. Then he consulted his desktop diary. A smile played across his lips, which, as he read, spread across his entire face. He had tried to make arrangements to visit Barbara on the 1st of March, he could see. They usually had lunch or coffee around this time, on the anniversary of their first meeting.

But last March she had postponed things. She had taken an early break in Spain as she was having a new boiler fitted and she couldn't bear the noise of the workmen. Now he remembered. He reviewed his emails from that time. She had returned on the 9th of March, and they had picked up the following Monday.

He hovered by the window, where he spied Joe and Janice crossing the road to a sporty convertible BMW. Joe was striding ahead, talking loudly into his phone. Janice was hobbling along behind and, as he watched, she removed her shoes half way across the road, massaging one foot then the other, before Joe shouted at her to hurry up.

Brian called up the text of the will again, although he knew the wording virtually off by heart. He thought about Barbara and what she would want him to do, now that he knew her son had lied to him. Of course, he could ignore the deception but how would that sit with his professional duties, including to the other beneficiaries? He resolved not to act rashly. There was plenty of time to select one of a number of options, after a period of calm reflection.

27.

HANI MAHMOOD sat in the cramped consulting room waiting for the others to arrive. It was not an ideal location for their monthly review meeting, but he no longer had an office; none of the consultants did. For the past four years, he had been relegated to the nomadic lifestyle, travelling into work, rucksack full of papers on his back, trekking down from some far-off car park, as the hospital space was frequently full, anxiously trying to retrieve confidential patient data on his laptop with antiquated email systems.

He had raised the valid point (on three separate occasions, including in writing to the CEO of the Trust) that he would have more time and energy to devote to his work were he not endlessly heaving large and weighty documentation around, but the only response had been a gentle but pointed enquiry after his own health and stamina. And today, when he required a bigger room so they could have a sensible dialogue and exchange of ideas for their monthly review meeting, his secretary had told him there was nowhere to go. At least he still had a secretary, but under the latest plans, she was to be axed by Christmas.

First to arrive was Steven King, the junior doctor, just one-year post-qualification, followed by Jane Bridges, the consultant anaesthetist, David Wolf and Lottie Li, the nurse. Lucy Farmer, the Risk Management Officer, arrived last of all, and, as all the seats were taken, including the ones dragged in from the waiting area, she perched herself on the end of the bed.

'Thanks all for coming,' Hani began, standing to assert his chairmanship of the meeting, in the cramped, airless room. 'We'll begin with Mrs Barbara Hennessy. I know it may seem unusual that we are including Mrs Hennessy this month, as there is nothing to suggest that her treatment fell short of our usual high standards.'

Hani paused for a moment, 'But, as head of this team, and I know Lucy echoes this sentiment, I felt it important we ensure we record accurately the treatment she had here up until her sad death. Jane, can you take us briefly through the operation?'

'Thank you, Hani. I will make sure we include a full report from all the monitors of the procedures which were followed both during and after the operation, including the drugs administered. As you know, this was a metatarsal osteotomy carried out without complications under general anaesthetic. The operation took an hour and a half. The bunion was successfully removed, Mrs Hennessy was closed up and pain relief prescribed.'

'Thank you, Jane.'

'Wait a moment.' Lucy had raised her hand. 'I understood there was some problem part way through the operation.'

Jane sat up straight in her chair.

'I think "problem" is putting it too highly,' she replied. 'Some of the monitors recorded an issue with the depth of the anaesthesia about thirty minutes in, but it was easily corrected.'

'You know that first-hand, do you?'

'Well, I know that because she stabilised. All her signs returned to normal.'

'But you weren't in the theatre all the time during the operation? I saw from the log that the ODA called you out.'

Steven coughed and fidgeted. Hani raised one eyebrow.

'Quite right,' Jane said. I had to attend an emergency call. The ODA came in to get me. It had to take priority. I was only out for around ten minutes but when I returned I saw everything had stabilised.'

'Lucy. If the ODA comes, then Dr Bridges has to attend,' Hani explained benignly.

'OK,' Lucy replied. 'But during that time, when Dr Bridges was out, she can't say first-hand what happened 'cos she wasn't there. That's when there were the problems you mentioned, isn't it?'

Jane glanced up at Steven. She had been confident he would manage without her: 'Nothing will happen, Steve,' she had reassured him as she had hurried out to provide her expertise elsewhere.

'Yes. It was,' she replied. 'But she stabilised quickly and the operation was perfectly successful.'

'I just want to make sure our report is full as well as accurate,' Lucy replied. 'There is a police enquiry going on.'

'I don't see that any criticism can be levelled at the anaesthesia,' Hani declared, with a scowl at Lucy. 'Let's move on to the next patient.'

***

'Jane. Can you wait outside for a few minutes please?' Hani called out to her to stay behind as the others filed out, apart from Lucy, who had indicated she wanted a few private words. Jane deliberately ignored the lingering look her husband was throwing in her direction, as she obeyed Hani's instructions. After five minutes or so, Lucy left with a casual nod, and she entered the room and closed the door behind her.

Hani was still standing behind the desk, shuffling papers around. He waited until Jane had sat down and taken out her notebook. Then he sat down himself.

'Sorry to delay you any further. I wanted to say that I feel awful about how things went there with Lucy, in the meeting. It wasn't appropriate for her to speak to you in that way in front of the others and I have made that clear to her. But you can see that we have no choice but to report fully on the operation, to protect ourselves. All the police need is one little inconsistency and they'll become interested. I asked how she knew about you leaving theatre. She checked the ODA records. She's quite a little Sherlock Holmes.'

'It's OK,' Jane replied. 'I understand.'

'With the police enquiry, I have agreed with Lucy that your brief absence should be noted in the report.'

'I would have done the same in your position,' Jane remarked coolly.

'Good,' Hani replied. 'I would hate to think this would come between us. You know I trust your judgement.'

'Was that all?' She closed her notebook and tucked it under her arm.

'Well, no. Not exactly.'

Jane waited. Hani leaned his elbows on the desk, interlaced the fingers of each hand and tapped his thumbs together a few times.

'Your interview for head of department is coming up soon, isn't it?'

'Two weeks.'

Jane thought of her husband and of his warning about Hani, but he didn't appreciate how alike she and Hani were.

'I'm sure you'll get excellent feedback, from everyone.'

'Thank you. Is that all, Hani?'

'No. There's just one more small thing I need to ask from you.'

28

'HAVE YOU READ the front pages today?' Constance and Judith were set for a day's preparation of Ahmad's defence, but Constance had insisted on buying a copy of every daily newspaper and was trawling their contents.

'No. Come on then. Lay it on me.'

'OK, prepare yourself. The *Times* majors on "Man arrested for artist's murder is foreign refugee. Questions are being raised about who let him in and what checks were carried out." Fairly anodyne I suppose.'

'And anodynely fair,' Judith quipped. Constance ignored her.

'The *Daily Mail*? "Syrian cleaner on trial for brutal murder of renowned elderly artist – is no one safe in hospital?" You can't approve of that one.'

'No. How do they suggest our unsafe hospitals improve things?'

'Various ideas like prison-style security and closer vetting processes for staff.'

'Because this member of staff has slipped through the net and is guilty?'

'Yes. And the *Guardian*. Listen to this: "The unnamed man the police have arrested is a Syrian national who came here three years ago and was re-housed at the tax payers' expense. But his past is a mystery, as there is no cooperation with Syria or its law-enforcement agencies.'"

'The implication being that he may well be a serial killer and we wouldn't know it.'

'Yes.'

'This one, the *Mirror*, has a photo of his wife, Aisha, taken through the window. Talked to a named neighbour who says she is not allowed out alone.'

'Ah, so they haven't named Ahmad but they might as well have. Is that permitted? And now the world believes that Ahmad is a domestic abuser too. That's a good angle. Let's try that one on a few agoraphobics I know and see how they like it.'

'At least the theft hasn't leaked out yet.'

'It will though, most likely before trial. Can we not persuade him to give that one up?'

'I've tried. Maybe you should speak to him about it?'

'Yes. I must go to see Ahmad. I know I've hesitated, which isn't like me; bull in a china shop usually. Don't look so surprised. I've been listening to these podcasts on self-awareness – Greg's idea. I just really want our meeting to count, Connie. Do you understand? You've done a fabulous amount of spadework but I want to get something from him which you haven't managed to extract so far. Perhaps even something he saw but he didn't appreciate its significance.'

Constance was staring vacantly at her screen and didn't respond.

'Connie. Can I say something?'

'Yes.' Constance focused on Judith. 'You don't usually ask permission.'

'Well this is something personal.'

'Oh dear. Did I forget to put on deodorant this morning?' Constance shifted in her seat.

'Is everything OK, at home?'

'Wow. That's a bit left field for you.'

'I'm sorry. You don't want to tell me.'

'No. I, well, no, I don't want to tell you. Am I not performing, have I let something slip through the net? Is that it?'

'It was just friendly concern. But it's none of my business. You're right. Let's move on.'

'I'm tired, not sleeping so well.'

'Oh?'

'Mike's gone.'

Judith laid down her pen. 'Gone where?'

'To his brother. For a while.'

'Ah. Better than his mother, I suppose.'

'He says what I…what we're doing, is useless. Worse than that, he says we are defending people who don't deserve a defence, that we shouldn't defend someone with links to terrorism.'

'Is that where it all came from yesterday, then?'

'He asked me to stop representing Ahmad. Did he really think I would?'

'Well not this minute anyway.' Judith smiled weakly.

'I can't believe you're not being more supportive.'

'I told you once how I lost my husband; in reality, some years before he died, it seems. I still question if things would have ended differently if I had been more flexible.'

'If he'd asked you, like Mike did – given you an ultimatum – you wouldn't have budged.'

'No, you're right. But perhaps he means well, he's trying to protect you?'

'That's what he said, but I'm not so sure.'

Judith sighed. This was why she didn't usually get too close to the people she worked with. So much time was wasted on chit chat and sympathetic comments.

'Well if you can't make it work with Mike then at least you're much younger than I was, and you have a chance to start again with someone more in tune with your priorities.'

'You make dating sound like buying a musical instrument.'

They both giggled.

'For now, it means I have no distractions and that's what Ahmad needs. Once it's all over I can think again about Mike. But if you think I'm failing...'

'No. I don't think that at all. Let's spend the next hour taking stock of where we are, and then let's head over to Ahmad. I'm sure he'll be delighted to see us.'

'SHADYA, LET'S PLAY Bananagrams.

'Oh come on. Is it because I always win?

'No I don't. And crybaby is a word. I checked last time.

'We can. I found all the pieces and counted them. They're all here.'

Shaza squatted down on the floor next to her bed and pulled the banana-shaped case out, spilling the letters on to the floor. Then she picked up her Barbie doll and sat her opposite, legs splayed.

'Barbie'll play if you won't.

'No. She's not. This one's Clever Barbie. She wants to be a doctor when she grows up. The other one is Beach Barbie. Suzy says she's an "airhead". But we need to play quietly.

'I know. I put my music on earlier and Mama came in and turned it off.

'Yes I heard her last night too. Do you think Baba's coming back?

'Me too. I don't want to be a single parent family. If you're from a single parent family you have to sit at the front in assembly and talk about stuff with everyone watching. And you have to eat your breakfast at school. Yuch. I don't want two breakfasts.

'Will you read to me tonight instead of Baba?

'No you don't have to do the voices. You can't do them like him anyway.

'All right. I'll read by myself but I think you're being mean.

'Suzy said not to worry when she came over. She said "they'll soon come to their senses and know your dad wasn't involved".

'I asked her "involved in what?" and she didn't say, and Mama came in, and she gave me one of those looks grown-ups sometimes give, that says we shouldn't tell other people what we've been talking about.

'Maybe Contents will tell me when she comes back. She said she would. What d'you think?'

30

DAVID WOLF was bothered when he found himself awake at 8:02 on a Sunday morning. He was more indisposed when he reached out his arm and found that Jane was no longer lying next to him.

'Hello darling. Did I wake you? Sorry,' she apologised, seated at the kitchen table with her laptop open. David crossed the room in his pyjamas and poured himself some coffee from the pot. 'I was just trying to catch up on a few things.'

'No. I couldn't sleep any longer,' he replied. 'This bloody court case is still on my mind. They asked if I "would be prepared" to be a witness now. Not that I know anything useful. I keep thinking we had a murderer working on the wards for two years and we didn't know. He might have killed other patients.'

'I doubt that.'

'Who knows?'

'Well we haven't had any other patients fall out of windows, have we?'

'He might have killed them in different ways; lethal injection, suffocation. I've been researching online. There's loads of them at it, especially in Germany.'

'I think you're being overly dramatic,' Jane mocked him, lightly.

'The police might reopen all suspicious deaths at the hospital. Hani will have a coronary.'

Jane's fingers moved away from her mouse.

'You're assuming the cleaner's guilty,' she said.

'The police seem confident. They keep coming and questioning people. And there were lawyers in asking questions the other day. At least they gave us the room back after a week when I said we would have more dead people if we couldn't use it.'

Jane returned to her laptop.

'Oh, before I forget. I was having trouble logging on this morning, so I used your log-in. Just to tidy some things up,' she said.

'What was wrong?'

'Sometimes my laptop just doesn't like the morning, I think. But it's fine now.'

'Sure, no problem. You must have been up early then? I can't remember when you were last up so early on a Sunday.'

'Well, Hani has asked me to produce the notes from the review meeting and Lucy was keen to see the first draft so I need to bash it out today.'

David paused.

'When he asked you to stay back, after the meeting, he didn't try to...well...make you say something which didn't happen, with Mrs Hennessy?'

'No, of course not. I've told you, he's always very encouraging.'

'Well, who told Lucy that you took a call in theatre?'

'Hani said Lucy checked the log. It's not as if I went off to get my nails done. We've agreed to mention it in the notes.'

David sat down next to her and sipped his coffee.

'What else will go in the report?'

'All the medication she was on, pre- and post-op, brief summary of the operation, like I said at our meeting, prescribed drugs, details of the physio visit. That's all. There's nothing there. Nothing to explain why she fell off the building hours later.'

'Good. Let's hope that satisfies the police and Hani is happy I've done my bit. Do you think the man will ever retire?'

'He's not so old but he's not so bad either. Let me get on with this now and, if I can finish without interruptions, we can go out for some lunch.'

31

BRIAN SAT in a café opposite his office leafing through the *Daily Mail*. He allowed himself to glance down at the holdall tucked neatly beneath his chair and wound the toe of his right foot through the handle possessively as he checked his watch; it was 10:25. Usually he breakfasted at home on a lightly-boiled egg (three-and-a-half minutes precisely from the time the water began to steam) and a glass of orange juice, arrived at 9:30, took a short break to stretch his legs at lunchtime and finished up promptly at five, setting the phone to voicemail as he left.

But today he had departed from routine. The will-reading session with Barbara's children, and its consequences, were playing on his mind. Neither of them had been particularly appreciative of his role in assisting their mother over the years and advising her, wisely, to salt her money away. If it hadn't been for him, one of those many man friends of hers, who appeared as often as the letter 'd' in the days of the week, would have taken it and blown it on a sports car or a long holiday. He was the one who had safeguarded their assets, and a fat lot of thanks he had received for it.

And he had genuinely thought that the conditions in her will were sensible when he had proposed them, given Barbara's expressed concerns about her offspring. Barbara had told him years ago, albeit after gentle persuasion, that she thought Tracy and Peter were 'overstretching themselves' and that it would end in tears, but Tracy wouldn't listen to her and said she was jealous.

Equally, Barbara had confided in him, after some insightful encouragement, her concern that Joseph would 'come to no good' but, rather than disinherit him, which had been her threat for some time, Brian had recommended that, as long as Joseph stayed out of trouble, he should receive his share too.

Brian took a sip of his breakfast tea and checked his watch again. He reminded himself that there were valid reasons for being late this morning and foregoing his egg, and that he had no appointment till 11:30. First, he had felt compelled to instruct a 'search and location' agent, to dig around, quietly, into both of Barbara's children, just to see what could be uncovered, and he had not wanted to risk making the call from the office. And second, very early, he had visited Barbara's apartment; she had given him a key when she signed the will – 'just in case,' she'd said. Both these activities were born from his desire to conduct his executor duties thoroughly and responsibly, he told himself.

It had been strange to wander around the flat without Barbara, and he had felt her presence everywhere; in the choice of the crimson oven splashback, the purple and orange scatter cushions, the black velvet lampshade. 'Are there any colours you wouldn't put together?' he had asked her once. And she had laughed excessively and shaken her head wildly, too overcome by the hilarity of his suggestion for words.

He had not entered her bedroom or the makeshift studio she maintained. He had never been in those rooms when she was alive, so it seemed wrong to sneak into them now she was gone. But in the kitchen he had found (and removed) the calendar to which Joe had directed him on their first meeting and, in the drawers next to the sink, he had found Barbara's diaries. It was these books which were now sitting patiently awaiting his attention in the bag at his feet.

Part of him balked at the thought of scrutinising such private memoirs but, having seen her children up close, Brian persuaded himself that he would gain more from them than either Tracy or Joe would, and also that he might receive some useful guidance on how to proceed. There was also a chance Barbara might have written something about her time in Spain in March, which would help if he chose, after further consideration, to challenge the date of Joe's last visit. Of course, if the diaries he had borrowed were innocuous and boring, he could simply return them quickly to her apartment and no one would be any the wiser.

His hands trembling suddenly, he fished for his wallet. Inside the flap he kept a colour snap taken with Barbara's Instamatic, the one time they met up in Spain, their Sangria-fuelled tryst. Barbara had walked with him to the end of the drive. 'It's such a beautiful evening, it's a shame to stay inside,' she had said, and her gardener had been passing and had captured them beautifully in the evening light. Barbara was wearing a red, intricately-patterned dress, and it was the only time he had ever worn a polo shirt; she had complimented him on it in her casual way. And their heads were so close that they might have been lovers to anyone who had cared to notice.

It was now 10:28 and a two-minute walk to his office. Brian drained his tea. One hour should be sufficient to make a good inroad into Barbara's diaries. But as he closed the newspaper and folded it neatly on the table, he became aware, for the first time, of the leading article on the front page. Reading it from beginning to end, his jaw clenched tight and his heart pounded fast in his chest. He would add one further task to the list for the agent he had instructed that morning; finding the Syrian cleaner couldn't be all that difficult.

32

AHMAD WAS sitting by the window when Constance and Judith entered. Constance had asked Dawson specially if they would bring him above ground for the interview. She hoped that seeing a little of the outside world would cheer him up. He had been so despondent since his arrival, she worried for his health. And he would not allow his wife or daughter to visit; he was adamant about that.

'Mr Qabbani? I'm Judith Burton, your barrister.' Judith remained standing, and waited for an acknowledgement. After a while it came with a turn of the head in her direction. She sat down and edged her chair towards him.

'Am I going home yet?' he asked quietly. Judith and Constance exchanged glances.

'Not yet, no.'

Ahmad stared out of the window again.

'Constance has done a pretty good job of filling me in on all the things you've discussed,' Judith began. 'There are probably other things we should be talking about.'

Ahmad blinked. Perhaps he had expected something more from Judith.

'Mr Qabbani, I won't pretend to you. This is not an easy case for us to defend. It's a paradox. The very fact that there's so little evidence against you makes it harder. I will do my utmost to have the case thrown out, because the evidence is so tenuous, but people have gone to jail for less. I need you to tell us about your family, your friends, even your hobbies. It may help people connect with you more.'

'People connect with me?' Ahmad spat the words back at Judith.

'I know. It sounds strange but the story is all over the newspapers and they're not saying good things about you. We need something from you that will help redress the balance. Something to show that you and your wife are good solid members of British society.'

Ahmad replied slowly and deliberately. 'So, you mean, if I can tell you some stories about having afternoon tea with my neighbours or playing cricket, that will help me? I don't think so, Miss Burton. And I don't have those stories.'

'Oh come on, Ahmad. Stop feeling sorry for yourself. We need you to give us something. If you don't want to talk about now, and I understand that – you want to shield your family from all this – then talk to us about what you did in Syria, your journey here, the people you left behind. Something positive. Anything.'

'I told Miss Lamb. I won't talk about Syria. And it won't help, really it won't. It will only make things worse. You need to know that. And whatever happens, you have to keep my family out of this.'

Judith stood up and paced the room, arms folded, speaking as she moved.

'OK, we'll start with the evidence; a very good place to start. I'll recap on what I know and you correct me if I get anything wrong. You clean at St Mark's Hospital. You cleaned Mrs Hennessy's room on the Tuesday, the day she arrived, and on the Thursday, the day she died. Correct so far?'

'Yes.'

'And you talked to her on those occasions?'

'Yes.'

'What did you talk to her about?'

Ahmad shrugged.

'I was just friendly, that's all. Usual things.'

'Did you talk to her about the weather?'

'Maybe.'

'About her family?'

'I'm not sure. I think so.'

'About art?'

'No.'

'How about the book she was reading?'

Ahmad opened his mouth and then closed it. Judith stopped walking and sat down again.

'Mrs Hennessy was reading *The Arabian Nights*?'

'Yes.'

'Did she talk to you about her book?'

'Yes. No. Well…'

'She was using the receipt as a bookmark. It shows it was bought around the corner from the hospital, on the Tuesday afternoon. She couldn't have bought it herself. I suppose one of those lady friends of hers who visited might have brought it, or her daughter. What do you think?'

Ahmad was silent.

'But the police will check with each of them and the shopkeeper.'

'She asked me,' he said. Constance stopped typing on her laptop and looked up at Ahmad.

'Can you explain what you mean?' Judith continued.

'Mrs Hennessy asked me to buy the book for her.'

'Really? How many other patients at the hospital have you given books to?'

'Just Mrs Hennessy. And I didn't give it to her.'

'So, you went in to clean her room and she asked you for a recommendation on what she should be reading. Your summer reading top ten?' Constance flashed Judith an annoyed glance which Judith studiously ignored.

'No. It's hard to remember now.'

'Try.'

'She asked me what I was reading. I think I didn't answer. I don't have time for reading you see, except for the newspapers, to make my English better. Then she asked if I knew the story of Aladdin.'

'Aladdin?'

'Yes. I didn't understand the name so well when she said it the first time. We pronounce it like this: "Al-a-ddin." But, of course I know this story. So I told her "yes" and I read it to my daughter. And I said it's one of the *Alaef Leila wa Leila*, the thousand and one nights.'

'And what did Mrs Hennessy say?'

'She said she wanted to read it, not the children's one but all the stories. She called it "The Arabian Nights", like you said.'

Ahmad frowned.

'What is it?'

'Nothing. Something which happened later but it's not important.'

'What happened later?'

What had happened? It was the next day or even the one after, when Mrs Hennessy's door had been open and she had two friends with her. They were laughing and joking and Ahmad had heard her say 'Yes, my Syrian friend recommended this. Bit heavy going. But always good to get something from the natives; that's what Miles used to say.'

'I heard her with her friends and I think she didn't like the book,' Ahmad told Judith.

Judith paused and regarded Ahmad carefully.

'Well, she asked you to buy it, so you're not to blame if she didn't enjoy it.'

'I don't understand why the book is important,' Ahmad added quickly.

'Neither do I. But the prosecution has expressly mentioned it and that means they will make something of it. I need to be able to rebut what they say. Constance, have you read *The Arabian Nights*?'

'No.'

'Well, I suggest you purchase two copies straight away, one for each of us and we get reading. We need to be ready for whatever they throw at us. How did you have time to get the book?'

'She asked me in the morning. I bought it in my lunch hour. The lady didn't think they had it. She had to look in the store room.'

Ahmad closed his eyes. It had been a beautiful day, the sun had warmed his back as he walked. He hadn't returned immediately to the hospital but had strolled up to the first of the nearby ponds, the book in one hand and his packed lunch in the other. But once he had finished his food, he made the mistake of staring out over the water. That's when the shaking had started and the cold, the snarling, biting, won't-ever-leave-you-alone cold had returned.

He had tried the breathing exercises but only half-heartedly. Somehow, deep down, he wanted it to happen. He wanted the cold to envelop him. And so he allowed it to seep and crawl right up to his waist. That was the highest he had ever permitted it to go.

Then, while his teeth chattered in his head, he saw the book next to him, one corner of its glossy cover peeking out of the top of the paper bag, and he thought about his daughter, Shaza, and how she had laughed with delight when Aladdin had rubbed the magic lamp and the djinn had appeared to grant his wishes.

And he fought the cold with all his might, the focus on his breathing all-encompassing, ignoring the stares of passers-by, till he felt his fingers again, and eventually his legs. Before his feet were under control he felt a tremendous lurch in his chest. He knew he would not reach the bushes and was only able to turn his head over the back of the bench before throwing up the contents of his stomach into the long grass below. After, once it was over, he grasped the book and held it tightly to his chest, like the life-saver it was.

'I bought the book. I gave it to her. That's all,' he said to Judith.

Judith studied his face closely.

'Did she pay you for it?'

'Yes. She gave me £10. It was £12.99. She gave me the extra money when she saw the price.'

'And that's all?'

'Yes.'

'So let's move on then. Your fingerprints, in the staff room?'

'I have my locker there. I eat my lunch there. So do all the nurses.'

'But your prints were on the door, going out onto the balcony.'

'Sometimes I go out there.'

'Do you smoke?'

'No.'

'Does anyone go out with you?'

'No. I just…well… Sometimes I just want to see the light, breathe the air, that's all.'

'Did you go out there the day Mrs Hennessy died?'

'I am not sure.' Ahmad shifted listlessly in his seat.

'Do you mean you don't remember?' Judith barked at him.

'OK. Sometimes I tip the water out. I must take it down to the ground floor, but if I finish on the eleventh floor I tip my water out.'

'And on Thursday night you finished up on the eleventh floor?'

'No. Well I had already cleaned upstairs before but I got confused, 'cos I came up to talk to Mrs Hennessy. So, in the end I had my water left.'

'I think that answer was "yes". Thankfully you're not on trial for the standard of your cleaning…'

'I'm a good cleaner…'

'Or complying with hospital hygiene rules… Let's talk about the other DNA evidence – your hair on Mrs Hennessy's nightdress.'

'I clean in her room.'

'All right. But so did another cleaner on the Wednesday, and the nurses come in to treat Mrs Hennessy, as do the doctors. But no one else's hair was tangled up in her nightgown; just yours. Any idea how that might have happened? Were you, for example, teaching her the tango?'

'I helped her out of bed, to go to the bathroom.' Ahmad opened his arms wide and then allowed them to drop to his knees.

'You didn't say that before.' Constance suppressed a shiver.

Ahmad sighed again. 'I'm not supposed to.'

'What?'

'I'm not supposed to help her to walk. In case she falls. Because I am the cleaner. But she said she really needed the bathroom.' He remembered Barbara's expression now. *Don't let me humiliate myself. Help me keep my dignity.* 'She held onto me when she stood up. That's all.'

'Why didn't you tell the Inspector that, when we were at the police station?' Constance asked.

'I told you. It's against the rules.'

'Ahmad. This is a murder investigation. If there are other things you haven't told me or the police I suggest you do so now.'

Ahmad bit his lip and Constance made another note on her laptop.

'All right. Next problem area,' Judith announced, 'Mrs Hennessy's rings?'

Ahmad's tongue clicked noisily against the roof of his mouth.

'Two beautiful and very large and bulky rings were found at your house on Monday. Do you know how they got there?'

Ahmad shook his head.

'Can you even hazard a guess?'

'I didn't take them. I told Mrs Hennessy to give them to her daughter, but she didn't want.'

Constance shifted in her seat abruptly and almost dropped her laptop. Judith sighed.

'You knew about the rings?'

'She left them in the bathroom.'

Judith snorted. 'You really expect me to believe that she left two valuable rings lying around in a hospital bathroom?'

'It was a private bathroom, and she did. They were on the

washbasin.'

'How did they get to your house then? On a magic carpet?'

'I don't know. Maybe the police put them there.'

'And why on earth would they do that?'

'I don't know. You work it out. You are my lawyers. I didn't take the rings.'

Judith marched to the far corner of the room, closing her eyes tightly before returning.

'OK, Ahmad. I believe you, I think, although as Constance has told you, it may be hard to persuade the court you didn't take them. But let's leave that topic for now. There was a newspaper report a couple of days ago which claimed that you had a brother who was an ISIL fighter, a commander.'

Judith waited for Ahmad's response, which didn't come.

'Ahmad?' Constance spoke gently. 'Is there any truth in the newspaper report?'

Ahmad clenched his fists tight against his thighs.

'I saw it, the newspaper story. The policemen, they saw it too.'

'Did they do anything to you?' Constance sat forward in her seat.

'It's not what they did.'

He turned to Judith.

'I do not have a brother. Qabbani is a good family name in Syria. I do not have family who fight for ISIL.'

'Can you think of any reason why the people who wrote the newspaper article might think you do?'

'No.'

Judith consulted her notes for the first time since she had entered the interview room, putting them away again after a quick review.

'I have been warned this is not a popular theme with you but, if we advise that it would help your defence – and at the moment you do need a little help – will you allow your wife to give evidence on your behalf?'

'That is a very easy one, Miss Burton. As Miss Lamb can tell you, my wife does not leave the house and she does not speak. She would be of little assistance, even if I were prepared to agree to this. Instead you could you check the Oyster, like I asked.'

'Were you a lawyer when you lived in Syria or in some former life?' Judith couldn't help the sarcasm which crept into her tone.

'No.'

'Or a judge perhaps?'

'No.'

'Now I finally know that you have answered two questions straight for me this morning. May I suggest you leave the investigation to me, please, and you focus on answering my questions. But, as you have asked, yes. They are still running through the Oyster records. And Inspector Dawson is locating the CCTV at your railway station and at Hampstead. It will help if we can show you just walking home, as usual, without a care in the world, but it won't save you.'

Ahmad looked to Constance for reassurance.

'Who can we ask to give evidence for you at trial, Ahmad? Who are your friends, at home, at the hospital?' Constance was keen to defuse the prickly atmosphere.

'I speak to some of the nurses. Lottie is the one I know the best. Lottie Li. We talk a bit. She will tell everyone she likes me. And Maia, she is the other cleaner, from Romania. She will say nice things about me too.'

'The admin staff? Or HR? The person who employed you?'

'No. She is not a good idea. I once lost an apron. She told me about how much people like me cost the health service each year.'

'We'll follow up those two witnesses for you, then,' Judith confirmed. 'I think that's probably all for now. Is there anything you need?'

'Please tell my wife that I am OK. And my daughter.'

'Yes, of course,' Constance chipped in. 'Your neighbour, Suzy Douglas, she is taking Shaza to school each day with her daughter. You don't need to worry. Would you like me to arrange a visit? We might be able to organise a home visit for you, in the circumstances?'

'No.' Ahmad stood up and knocked his chair over. He picked it up hurriedly and stood leaning heavily against it.

'I don't go home till I am a free man.'

Judith rolled her eyes and headed for the door.

'OK,' Constance replied. 'Anything else?'

'I like to read the newspapers. I particularly like the *Times*. Can you let me have some more to read please?'

Judith and Constance exchanged glances.

'Yes of course. Let's see what we can do,' Judith replied.

***

'You were a bit hard on him, weren't you?'

Judith and Constance sat upstairs at the police station, pondering how the interview had gone.

'You think?'

'He was only trying to help when he reminded me about his Oyster. It might be really useful.'

'I don't like my clients to give me advice. Call me old-fashioned.

But I shouldn't have lost my cool, you're right. We got some interesting stuff though, didn't we?'

'Yes. How did you think of the book?'

'It was easy. The other questions, although he was glib, he had no difficulty answering them. That one, he hesitated. And I was on to a winner given that we knew Mrs Hennessy couldn't have bought it herself.'

'Is it bad?'

'What? That he bought her the book? Not in itself, but it suggests a relationship developing between them. It will be easier for the prosecution to concoct some kind of hypothetical motive.'

'I told you he wouldn't own up to stealing the rings?'

'Agh! The rings. Do you believe she left them sitting around and he honourably advised her to give them away for safekeeping?'

'Yes I do, actually. She was an old forgetful lady, and just because he's poor doesn't make him a thief.'

'Yesterday you thought he was a terrorist.'

'That's not fair. That's not what I said.'

'All right. I'll have a quiet word with Dawson about whether they could possibly have been planted. Better me than you. He won't like it.'

'And the prints on the door?'

'Yes. That's OK, I think, and authentic. It perhaps even makes Ahmad more human, that he wouldn't trek down eleven floors to throw away his dirty water. But he hasn't volunteered any of this, Connie, that's worries me too. He waits till we already know and then he owns up. It's really damaging. He didn't offer that he used to go out on the balcony or that he helped her to the bathroom. How much more stuff is there that we don't yet know about that could bury him?'

'You don't believe him?'

'I'm not sure. He seems earnest and sincere and I tend to think I'm an excellent judge of veracity, as you know. But at this moment, I'm not sure.'

'There is one other thing I should mention.'

'Go on.'

'It's probably nothing but he asked for a lawyer, when the police questioned him, right at the beginning.'

'You think he had a guilty conscience?'

'Dawson did, and I think that's coloured everything he's done since then. But I asked Ahmad.'

'And what did he say?'

'Implied that nasty things can happen to people in police custody. Maybe he had a bad experience and he wanted me as protection, I suppose.'

Judith sighed. 'Or, assuming he's telling the truth, he knew he was exposed, with the book and the rings and being more friendly than he should be. He's no fool.'

'Do you still want to defend him?'

'Oh don't panic, Connie. I will keep an open mind for now and it won't stop me doing all I can to unravel this mess. But do share things with me, especially if you get a bad feeling about them. Trust your instincts.'

'What do you want to do about the "terrorist" article?'

'We have to ask them to retract, to apologise, in clear terms. I have a friend, I'll give you his details. He will prepare a suitable communication. He won't charge for it.'

'What about other defence witnesses?'

'Yes. We have very little, unless the nurse can help, or the other cleaner. It's worth a try. But I won't hold my breath.'

33

JANICE CALLED Tracy early on Monday morning. Tracy cursed loudly as she rummaged through a pile of washing to find the phone. Who on earth would call at 7:42 on a Monday? It couldn't possibly be anyone with children of their own.

'Hello Tracy, it's Janice. Is this a bad time?'

'Oh, hi Jan! Mondays are always a bit hectic and I'm still catching up from my time off but I have a second. It's nice to hear from you.'

'I…well, Joe says he hasn't told you yet, so I thought I would. And I wanted to catch you before you left for work.'

'Told me what? Is it another promotion?'

'No. Much better than that. Can't you guess?'

'Hmm. Well no, I can't.'

'We're getting married.'

'Oh.' Tracy elongated the vowel sounds as long as she could, to enable her face to get around the concept of Joe and Janice's impending wedding. Janice misinterpreted the exclamation as a congratulatory one.

'Thanks. It is exciting, I know. I had given up thinking he would ever ask. You know your brother. Keeps things to himself. Anyway, we're going to have a celebration on Saturday, at the local. Hope you can come. Around eight. Do bring Pete. It was a shame he was ill over Christmas. Joe loves to see him and you know how they spend hours talking about football.'

'Gosh. Janice. I must go. I'm half way out of the door, but that is really great news. I'm so pleased for you, and for Joe, of course. We'll make sure we're there on Saturday night. Any idea when the wedding will be?'

'Joe says we should do it straight away; no time like the present. Be nice to have a summer wedding. And, I mean, I am getting on a bit. I did say to Joe, did he want to wait, because of your mum. I mean, it's so soon. But he said she wouldn't have minded. We'll keep you posted.'

'Great. Make sure you do.'

Tracy put down the phone and shook her head slowly.

Perhaps the news should not have surprised her; like the true gambler Joe was, he was simply hedging his bets.

34

HANI MAHMOOD heaved his bag onto his back and locked his car. He had waited almost fifteen minutes for a parking space in the public car park; all this because he had been delayed by a morning conference in Barnet on diversity in the profession. As he began to snake his way out, carefully avoiding the puddles and mud from last night's heavy rain, he noticed a young man on a moped, its front wheel on the pavement, talking animatedly on his phone.

He tutted to himself; the boy had no helmet. Did the youth of today have a death wish or something? Helmets could be purchased so reasonably these days, he failed to understand how anyone would put himself so at risk. He walked on a few paces, then stopped, smiling gently as he contemplated the beneficent act he was about to undertake, and retraced his steps.

The boy was rifling through a plastic bag when Hani approached but he stopped, squeezed the bag possessively and glared at Hani.

'Did you want something, grandpa?'

'I couldn't help but notice that you are riding your motorcycle without a helmet,' Hani began. 'I am a doctor and I see people who fall all the time. You should purchase a helmet.'

The boy laughed nastily in the back of his throat.

'Are you serious?'

Hani swallowed and took a step backwards.

'I… Yes. I am serious, but I can see you are busy. I am sorry to have disturbed you. Do please consider what I have said, about the helmet.'

The boy leaned over to the roadside and lifted up an object which had been obscured by the kerb. Hani flinched, fearing the boy was about to pick up a stone and throw it at him. Instead he waved a battered helmet in Hani's direction.

'Why don't you keep your nose out of other people's business, rag head?' the boy shouted.

Hani started to walk away along the pavement, muttering his continued apology under his breath.

'Is that what you tell your guys to do, wear helmets, before they blow people up?' the boy shouted louder. Hani walked faster, keen to put some distance between the two of them and hoping no one he knew from the hospital was within earshot. His wife was always telling him to keep his thoughts to himself in public, fearful of incidents like this one. She would have advised him against approaching the teenager in the first place.

He had reached the pedestrian crossing opposite the shops in double-quick time and was about to step forward when he heard the monstrous roar of a nearby engine. There was a large puddle of water, which had collected by the blocked drain, partly obscuring the zebra's stripes at the road's edge, and although Hani leaped back at the noise, the bike sent the muddy water high into the air, soaking his shoes and much of the front of his trousers. The boy did not stop but Hani saw him checking his rear-view mirror and crowing to himself as he accelerated away around the corner and out of sight.

Hani sighed deeply and took two steps back from the crossing to lean against a nearby wall. Then he extracted a newly-laundered handkerchief from his pocket and held it to his face before attempting half-heartedly to dry his trousers. When he realised it was hopeless, he stood, paralysed, unable to decide what to do next, torn between his strong desire not to appear before his fellow doctors and students in this dirty, dishevelled state and his wish to begin his already delayed work.

After another sigh he thrust the handkerchief back in his pocket and stared up at the looming hospital building across the road. He suddenly felt the weight of the backpack digging into his shoulders. Checking carefully this time before he stepped forward, he crossed the road and headed in to work.

35

CONSTANCE was lying in bed fast asleep when her phone rang. She had spent the day working her way through her long list of matters to investigate, and had been exhausted when she got home.

She grabbed for her bag, lying on the floor next to the bed, and fumbled around till the phone's blue glow caught her eye. She prised it out and held it to her ear.

'Hello,' she mumbled, squinting at her clock to see that it was a little after midnight.

There was silence at the other end of the line.

'Hello,' she repeated. 'Who is it?'

She sat herself up in bed. Now she was cross. This was the first time for days she had fallen asleep without difficulty and had slept soundly. She was about to hang up when she thought she heard a low sob down the phone. She turned the screen face up and saw the number and she slowly registered who was calling.

'Aisha. Is that you? Is everything OK?'

Another low sob, almost a moan.

'OK,' Constance replied firmly. 'It's OK. I'm coming. I'll be there in around half an hour.'

***

Constance took a taxi to Braham Terrace this time, the driver dropping her without a word. As she stood outside the Qabbanis' house she could see a gaping hole in the front bay window, close to the door. It was the size of a melon and the shape of Africa, with cracks radiating outwards across the pane. She checked behind her in both directions to make sure no one was hanging around and then knocked lightly on the front door.

Aisha opened it almost instantly and stood back to let Constance in. She was hunched over and trembling. Constance crept past her and switched on the light in the lounge. A large rock was lying on the blackened carpet. Aisha entered behind her, sat down quietly and tucked her knees up to her chest. Constance noticed the front of one of her slippers was burned right through, her toe peeping out of the hole.

'Are you OK? Here, let me see,' she said.

Aisha wiggled her foot and shuddered. Constance removed the slipper very gently.

'Do you have something I can put on this?' she asked, 'A first-aid kit?'

Aisha's eyes skimmed Constance's face, then she rose and hobbled towards the kitchen where she opened a sparsely-stocked cupboard and produced a plastic case. Constance found some dressings inside which she applied to Aisha's foot without any response of any kind, although it must have been painful.

'Did you see who it was?' A rough shake of the head.

'Any idea who it might have been?' A light shrug, followed by a muted sob.

Constance put her arm around the woman and drew her towards her, surprised that she didn't resist.

'It's OK,' she said. 'I'll get someone to fix it tomorrow. It's going to be OK.'

As the two women sat together in the kitchen, Constance heard light footsteps in the hallway and Shaza appeared, fuzzy with sleep. When she saw Constance, she blinked heavily.

'Hello Contents. Is Daddy with you?' she asked.

'No. He's going to be away a bit longer.'

Shaza blinked at her mother, who hid her damaged foot underneath the other.

'I heard a noise?' she said, yawning widely.

'Oh, it was just me and your mum chattering, nothing to worry about. Sorry we disturbed you.'

'There's no one to read to me,' Shaza said, already heading out of the room towards the stairs.

Constance smiled enquiringly at Aisha, who gestured to her to go ahead.

'I'll come and read to you, if you like,' Constance said. 'But then you need to go straight back to sleep.'

36

TRACY VISITED the hairdresser first thing on Saturday morning. She had always sported a salon-assisted hairdo for important events in the past, and her brother's engagement party was certainly a suitable contender. At the same time, she was determined not to be upstaged by her soon-to-be sister-in-law, who would undoubtedly pull out all the stops on the personal grooming front. She knew the £22 would be missed but it was months since her hair had seen any refined hair products. While she was enjoying a rare moment alone with *Hello!* magazine, the manicure girl popped in, and she couldn't resist. In the end the make-over set her back a cool £40 but it was a successful investment, she told herself, as she felt a million dollars walking through the front door of the house.

'Is that all in aid of your brother?' Pete commented as she bustled in with some croissants that had been half-price in the local bakery.

'So what if it is?'

'You're right. You look gorgeous.' He kissed her cheek. 'They'll all be jealous of me, all your brother's friends will.'

'I'm not sure how many people are going.'

'Oh.' Pete's face fell. He had hoped there would be a big crowd to reduce the contact he might otherwise have with Joe.

'I mean, she only invited us on Monday. Some people may have other plans.'

'Why's he done it now? Do you think she's pregnant?' Pete grabbed a croissant, cupping his hand underneath to catch any stray crumbs.

'Stop it. Of course not. She's...' Tracy stopped herself. It was likely, she supposed, given Joe's agenda. 'You might have a point. Let's see if she drinks anything. That'll be a sign.'

'Maybe it's not too late for us to have another? A little sister for Luke and Taylor.' He cuddled her tightly and deposited another kiss, this time on her neck.

Tracy wasn't sure if Pete was serious.

'Ooh. I think I'm a bit old to start all that again.'

'Well. Not with that haircut. Just like the first day I met you.'

Tracy detached herself from him and arranged the remaining croissants on a plate.

'I'm going to Mum's flat this afternoon, just to go through her things. Will you be OK dropping the kids at karate? You don't have to get out of the car.'

'That's fine,' Pete said. 'You go and sort things out. Do you want me to come with you? You don't know what you might find.'

***

Tracy faltered outside the door of her mother's flat before forcing herself to go in. She had kept a key for almost ten years but had never once used it. Even now, she preferred to take out her mother's own key from her personal effects, returned by Inspector Dawson. Somehow that felt less intrusive.

Barbara had left the curtains open and the light streamed in to the deserted flat. She had chosen it in the first place because of its triple aspect, extolling the virtues of 'buckets of natural light' to all newcomers. And she had been right; it was hard to feel dull or bored when so much of the outside world was being channelled into your living room.

Tracy wandered from the kitchen to the lounge area to check that all was intact, and then deposited the post she had collected downstairs on the bar in the kitchen. She balked at checking out the bedrooms; she would do that later.

She opened the fridge. It contained the usual staples: milk, eggs, butter and a few hardy vegetables. Their reliability and ordinariness surprised her. She had imagined finding frivolous items there; stuffed olives, bruschetta, tiramisu; the kind of things her mum randomly offered when she came over. She would collect them up when she left and throw them in the dustbin at the back.

She searched for the calendar Joe had mentioned but she couldn't see it anywhere in the kitchen, although there was a bulldog clip attached to the side of the fridge where it used to hang.

One of Barbara's pastels was on the kitchen wall, a rich orange number. It depicted a clump of nasturtiums, drawn from the many clusters which had adorned their window boxes in summers gone by, dangling lazily into the street below.

A notepad and pencil sat by the phone, and Tracy turned the pages, running her fingers over the many doodles and sketches which adorned them.

Barbara had embellished each name with a drawing of some kind, and how endearing they were. The note to herself to pick up a cake for tea with a friend was embroidered with both a towering birthday cake oozing icing and a portrait of a woman regarding it with delight; the word 'BILLS' was written centrally with a sketch of a man behind a desk leaning his head on his hands, and the reminder 'Tesco delivery Monday' was almost obliterated by a neatly-outlined Tesco van with the words 'you shop, we drop' written on the side in stylised letters.

Tracy had to hand it to her mother. She certainly knew how to draw.

Tracy picked up the pencil herself and began to sketch the corner of the room; the edge of the sofa with the magazine sitting open, propped up on a cushion. Then, her tongue between her teeth, she worked hard for a few more minutes until she had added a reasonable likeness of her mother, in customary reclining pose, head thrown back as if in the middle of a laugh, one hand raised in a friendly salute.

She still had it then, her artistic flair. Tracy had considered taking a Fine Art degree nearly thirty years ago, but she was a practical girl and she didn't want to end up scrimping like her mum (or so she had thought). She had satisfied herself with the odd art project at school instead. 'We're lucky we have you,' the head had said once, when she spearheaded a wall of tiles for the school garden, each decorated by a year 6 pupil. And once Pete had given her financial security it had been too late.

Tracy's foray into Barbara's life hadn't progressed any further when the doorbell rang and Constance was standing on the threshold.

'Hello, Mrs Jones. Thanks so much for agreeing to this. I'm sure

I won't be long but, like I said on the phone, I thought I might find something here which would provide a clue to help with the investigation.'

'I haven't been here long myself, and I've only got as far as the kitchen,' Tracy confessed, 'but why don't you go ahead? There's Mum's studio and bedroom. Please let me know if you find anything or you have any questions.'

Constance headed first into Barbara's studio. The floor was covered in the kind of sheeting decorators use, although it was spotlessly clean and there were two easels in the centre of the room, together with an assortment of paints and brushes. Canvases were stacked up against two walls, each around one metre square, but everything was covered in a thick layer of dust and the room itself smelled musty.

Constance knelt down and leafed through the pictures one by one. They were a real mix; some were of flowers like the one she had seen on the wall as she entered, a few were landscapes, but the best, in Constance's view were the portraits. She quickly found a wonderful likeness of Tracy, sitting at the kitchen bar with a mug encased in both hands. Barbara had captured her perfectly, including the air of capability she exuded. Then there were others, all of people unknown.

She paused to view another portrait, this time on a red background, of a dark-skinned young man with a shock of black hair, brooding eyebrows and a cruel face. She took a photo of it on her phone before extracting it from the pile and leaning it against the wall, next to the one of Tracy.

At the very bottom of the pile she found a head and shoulders watercolour of a middle-aged man with receding hair, and glasses balanced at the end of his nose. He was wearing a shirt with a breast pocket and he was squinting off into the distance. She laid this one next to the one of Joe; they made a curious triptych. She shuffled them around so Tracy was in the middle and took another two photos.

Tracy had advanced to Barbara's bedroom and was folding up clothes one by one when Constance entered.

'She had lovely things, Mum did,' Tracy spoke wistfully.

'Will you keep them?' Constance asked.

'Mum was tiny, five foot three and a size eight. And it would make me too sad.'

'A scarf?'

'Yes. I might manage that. She wasn't extravagant. She used to pick them up second-hand or get castaways from her famous friends. Sometimes she would paint someone and they would pay her with a favourite dress or pair of earrings. That's what I remember anyway.'

'How funny to be so unmaterialistic.'

'It wasn't so funny when we needed shoes or food and she needed cash to pay for it.'

'I'm sorry. I didn't want to intrude. Would you like me to leave you to get on with things?'

'Oh no. To be honest it's easier with someone else here. I was dreading even coming into the room. I don't know what I expected. Did you find anything useful?'

'Nothing so far. But if it isn't too much trouble, I'd like you to identify a couple of people your mum painted. One of them may be your father,' Constance said. Tracy nodded obligingly and followed Constance next door.

'Oh how funny,' Tracy let out a loud shriek when she saw the pictures. Then she knelt down and examined them one by one.

'Well this one is obviously me, and a few years back. The one on the left is my brother Joe, but not his best side, let's say, and is that the one you thought was Miles?'

'Yes.'

'Well, I wouldn't have known – not before a couple of weeks back. No, it's not my father. His name is Brian Bateman. He's Mum's solicitor.'

'Well she must have thought very highly of him. What a lovely image.'

'Yes,' Tracy replied, shaking her head in disbelief.

'What is it?'

'Well you're right. It's gorgeous, isn't it? And if you met him in the flesh you might be a bit disappointed.'

'You mean he's not so charming in person?'

Tracy laughed. 'I'm being unfair but he seemed very dull to me, and pedantic, and the will…' She stopped herself in mid-flow. 'Well, you don't want to hear about that.'

'Was it terribly long-winded?' Constance asked casually.

'Oh yes, there is that. No, lots of conditions. Quite complicated. I've had to get another lawyer to explain it to me. I'm not sure I'm allowed to talk about it.'

'I understand. I can always recommend someone to take a look for you. It's not my field, but if you're not sure how to claim your money, for example.'

'No. It's not that. Just complicated, like I said.'

'The paintings are very dusty. Had your mother stopped painting?' Constance changed the subject.

'Yes. She said she was having pains in her hands, especially when she tried to grip the brush.'

'Had she seen a doctor?'

'I don't think so. I gave Inspector Dawson the name of her GP. But she didn't like doctors, generally. That's why she held on for so long before she saw anyone about her feet. She waited till she was desperate.'

'Was she upset she couldn't paint any more?'

'No.' Tracy shook her head confidently but then stopped. 'Well…she never said. I'm really not going to be much help. I know I was her daughter but we were not that close and, going through her things, I feel like a stranger.

'There is something I noticed when I arrived, though. Could you tell the inspector? Two things, really. Mum used to keep a calendar on the fridge with all her appointments. It's not there anymore. And I know she also kept a diary, off and on, over the years. She had quite a few small red books. I think she did it mostly to keep track of all the famous people she met. She used to stuff photographs in there too, and autographs, receipts, newspaper articles.'

'Yes.'

'Well, I have only just started to look around, but there's nothing in the usual places she kept them, either the kitchen drawer or in her bedside cabinet.'

'Oh.'

'It's a while since I saw her with one. Maybe she just got tired of writing. It does seem a bit less cluttered in here than I remember,' Tracy continued.

'Does anyone else have a key to this flat?' Constance asked.

Tracy shrugged. 'I'll ask a couple of Mum's friends and I think Miles always kept one. They were on good terms even though… well, he left us.'

'I would change the locks. Your mother might have given the

key to a workman. Some people are very trusting. And now the place is empty.'

Tracy chewed her lip. She hadn't thought of that.

'I'm sure the police have asked you this, but can you think of anyone who might have wanted to harm your mother?'

'No. I've told the police everything I know. They still think it's your man, don't they? The Syrian cleaner.'

'Yes.'

'Do you know why they think it was him?'

'I can't disclose that.'

'Has anything here helped you?'

'Maybe. It's too early to say.'

'If it was him, the cleaner, then I hope he goes to prison for a very long time.'

'I'll be heading off now,' Constance said. 'Thanks again. I am very sorry for your loss.'

When Tracy was alone once more she carried the portraits of herself, Joe and Brian through to the living room one by one and propped them up on the sofa. At first, she hadn't been sure if she liked the one of herself; her hair was untidy and she was wearing an old striped shirt. But there was a real warmth behind the eyes of the Tracy in the image, and however she contemplated it she found herself smiling.

The picture of Brian was, without doubt, the best of the three. Although he appeared a little younger than today, the depth of colour, the definition, the smoothness of the brush strokes were incredible. And Barbara had painted him with such a forceful and determined expression. Brian in that picture might have been a prime minister or a king. Her mother had been a strange old bird.

Sitting at the bar, in almost the exact position in which her mother had captured her in her portrait, Tracy called Brian.

***

'Hello Brian, this is Tracy Jones, Barbara's daughter.'

'Hello Tracy.' He noted and adopted her deliberate use of his first name.

'I was calling about Mum's will. Do you have a few minutes please?'

Brian picked up his pen in case Tracy asked him anything of importance, but he was pleased, so far, with the tone of the conversation, given the abrupt end of their last meeting.

'I wanted to ask about the debt clause,' she explained.

'I can't advise you. I am the executor. You should get your own advice.'

'This is kind of general stuff, interpreting the provisions.'

'All right. Go on.'

'The will gives examples of what it means by debt. I just wondered whether, if someone gave a personal guarantee, that was included.'

'I see. A personal guarantee is not a debt until someone calls in the debt you have guaranteed.'

'And if the guaranteed debts are called in?'

'The underlying debt would need to be paid off before distribution.'

'Is there any alternative?'

'I can't think of one.'

Tracy sighed. Brian's comments echoed the advice she had received the previous day.

'Except, well, if it was the *spouse* who had the debt, the person receiving the gift could always get divorced, I suppose, before the distribution. But that's a little drastic. And divorces take some time now anyway,' he added.

Tracy tapped her fingers on the worktop.

'Thanks, Brian. What do you need from me then to show you we aren't in debt?'

'Bank statements, credit card statements and credit rating.'

'And the criminal offence? I have a DBS from school.'

'That will be sufficient but I will need a copy.'

'What about when I last visited Mum?'

'If you visited your mother at the hospital then would one of the nurses or doctors be willing to confirm that?' Brian enquired, keen to be able to put forward a practical suggestion.

'Oh gosh. I couldn't ask any of them. What about Pete?'

'Your husband. Did he visit with you?'

'No. He watched the kids while I went.'

Brian paused.

'I'll need to think about that then. Normally that would be fine. But I am afraid your brother has taken advantage of my good nature, so I might need to be more careful in future.'

'What do you mean?'

'He came with his partner, Miss Cooper, and she confirmed, just like you want your husband to do, that Joseph visited your mother on March the eighth this year.'

'Oh. OK? Well that's good isn't it?'

'No, Tracy. Because both he and Miss Cooper lied to me. Your mother was in Spain when your brother says he was – what was it? – "sharing a bowl of homemade tomato soup", with your mother at her apartment.'

'Ah.'

'So now you can see why I am hesitant when you want to use the same method of corroboration.'

'What will you do?'

'About Joseph?'

'Yes.'

'I am considering that myself.'

'He probably just got the day wrong. I'm sure if you ask him again he'll find the right day.'

'That's very generous of you.'

'Well, not really.'

'It is. Given the consequences if your brother can't show conclusively that he visited your mum within the last six months.'

'Brian. I don't think Mum would have wanted all this stuff coming between me and Joe. Are you sure she understood what she was signing?'

'I am sure she understood, and it's not for me to second-guess what she would have wanted. I have to try to follow her instructions. Your brother's conduct has put me in a very difficult position. Very difficult.'

Tracy opened her mouth and closed it again. She had spent the last twenty-four hours cogitating on whether Brian was open to a bribe; a share of the money, perhaps five per cent, in return for turning a blind eye to her and Joe's difficulties. That might end up cheaper than a fight in the courts over who was due what. But she didn't have his measure and now he was angry about Joe, it was certainly not the time to bring it up.

'Was there anything else you wanted, Tracy?' Brian asked.

'No. No thanks Brian. That's all for now.'

Tracy lowered her phone and turned it face down on the

worktop. Then she grabbed the drawing she had made when she arrived, tore it off the pad and scrunched it into a tight ball. Finally, she crossed the room to gaze once more at the portrait of Joe. It was truly horrid, Joe appearing cruel and nasty and vindictive. She turned it to face the wall and then returned to Barbara's room to continue sifting through her clothes.

37

CONSTANCE returned to the hospital that evening to locate Lottie, the nurse whom Ahmad had indicated would vouch for him. They met during her lunch break and headed out of the ward to the coffee shop on the ground floor. Constance bought them each a hot chocolate and asked Lottie to talk about Ahmad.

'I know him about two years,' she said. 'He's a friendly guy. He works hard and he helps out when we ask him.'

'How do you mean "helps out"?'

'He is the cleaner but he sorts out loads of other stuff. When things break he fixes them – even the chair in the staff room and the microwave.'

'And how often do you see him?'

'Very often. He works hard. Never takes time off. But he is quite a sad person I think.'

'Sad?'

'Something happen I think when he is young.'

'What was it?'

'I don't like to ask and he don't like to tell. He likes to talk to me about the news. He is always interested in the news, in what is happening all over the world. I talk to him about my family too. He is a good listener.'

'Do you think he is the kind of man who could hurt someone?'

'No.' Lottie shook her head violently from side to side. 'Absolutely no. He is always thoughtful and helps people. He is a big man, and strong, but, no, never.'

'Did you ever see him with Mrs Hennessy?'

'Yes. I saw him cleaning in the room. They were talking and laughing. Only one time I saw them together.'

'Do you know which day that was?'

'I think on the Tuesday, the day Mrs Hennessy arrived, but I'm not sure.'

'Did you see anyone else with Mrs Hennessy, her daughter, maybe?'

'Yes I see her when she arrived. That's all.'

'Are there any new nurses on the ward?'

'We have new nurses all the time. You can ask the HR and they will give you all the names.'

'Was there anyone here who left suddenly?'

'We have so many agency staff,' Lottie said. 'We never know who will be here.' She shrugged her apology.

'Did you see anything unusual on the night Mrs Hennessy died?'

'No. I worked till ten. I went home. In the morning I hear Mrs Hennessy is dead.'

'Did you see her before you left?'

'No. Her door was closed so I didn't disturb.'

'What's Dr Wolf like?'

Lottie shook her head. 'I don't know.'

'He's been here a long time?'

'Yes, but he's always in a hurry. He doesn't talk to the nurses much.'

'How is he with the patients?'

'Very nice, I think.'

'Is he a good doctor?'

'Oh yes. He is a consultant.'

'Is there a doctor more senior than Dr Wolf?'

'You mean Dr Mahmood?'

'Maybe. What is he like?'

'He's the senior consultant.'

Constance sensed she would obtain very little from Lottie in terms of a view on the character or expertise of any of the doctors so, with regret, she halted that line of questioning.

'Thank you, Lottie. Here is my card. If you think of anything which might be helpful to Ahmad, or if you remember seeing anyone different around the ward, will you contact me?'

'Yes. I will.'

'Otherwise, if the case does go to trial, would you be prepared to come to the court and tell everyone what you just said – you know, that he was a friend, helped people out, that kind of thing?'

'Yes, of course. They must have the wrong person. Of course I will help Ahmad.'

Constance found Maia on the third floor. She burst into tears when she found out Constance's identity and kissed her on both cheeks.

'Tell him I miss him,' she wailed. 'They give me other cleaner to help but not like Ahmad. He does no work, he leaves the buckets all dirty, I don't know where to find them. Oh, I miss him.'

Twenty minutes of questions did not yield anything useful but Maia also promised to be there for Ahmad if needed. She asked Constance for some paper and then drew him a large round sad face with tears coming from each eye. Then she added kisses to the bottom. 'You give him this,' she requested. 'I hope it will make him laugh.'

***

Judith stood in a narrow alleyway across the street from the BMW showroom in Mill Hill. She had been there for around half an hour, just quietly watching. She saw Joe come out, smoke a cigarette, kick a stone around the yard, talk loudly on his mobile phone, gesticulate a lot, collect a plastic bag from somewhere inside, check its contents, then speed off in his car with his music blaring.

She thought hard about whether to wait for his return; he had told the police he hadn't seen his mother for months before her death and had no idea who might have killed her. She reasoned that it was highly unlikely he would change his story now and, from what she had heard of him so far, she didn't relish the prospect of an encounter on a potentially explosive topic.

She could also go inside, look around, ask some casual questions on the pretext of buying a car, just to 'sniff the air'. But the site was far removed from the murder scene and all the pertinent questions she wanted to ask – *Was Joe Hennessy here all day on Thursday 11th of May? Did Joe Hennessy ever talk about his mother? What had happened to make them so estranged?* – would immediately raise the alarm.

As a large black cloud came overhead and the rain began to fall, she checked each way, up and down the street, slung a lingering look at the showroom, then opened her umbrella and walked casually away.

38

Tracy and Pete could hear the party noise filtering out before they opened the door of the pub. Pete swallowed and gripped Tracy's arm. He was sure they hadn't been followed; they had hopped in a taxi from right outside the house and he had been keeping watch periodically through the window. On top of that, Pete had made certain he had grabbed his back and grimaced theatrically as they exited the cab. That should be sufficient if anyone was watching. He had never claimed to be paralysed or anything.

'Pete, please relax. We don't have to stay too long if you don't want to,' Tracy pleaded.

'I'm fine. Let's go do some celebrating. We haven't been out for a while. Do you think Joe's paying?'

'Must be joking,' Tracy replied as they joined the throng.

She could see Joe immediately as they entered, at the other side of the room, propping up the bar, talking loudly and gesticulating wildly. She caught his eye and he nodded once in her direction, before laughing at someone else's joke and turning away. She was disappointed that he was wary of her; she wouldn't do anything to spoil his night. He must know that. Then Janice flew over, kissed her on both cheeks, handing her a large gin and tonic, and she began to relax.

Despite her misgivings, Tracy found she was enjoying seeing old friends and acquaintances. Janice had invited half their street, and Aunty Mae, an old friend of Barbara's, who kept a menagerie of household pets, popped in, trailing cat hair of all colours, to give Janice a hug and tell her that Barbara would have loved to be there. Tracy thought how untrue that was; Barbara hated noisy pubs and stale odours but it was a lovely thing for her to say and Janice beamed for the next half hour.

***

Kyla and Simon were both there too, Kyla had brought along a tall and well-toned boyfriend named Craig, replete with elaborate tattoos on both arms. Simon had come alone but looked up optimistically each time the door opened.

'Can I have a word, Joe?' Kyla was on her third glass of white wine before she had a chance to speak to Joe alone, and she draped one arm around his neck before a sideways glance from Janice forced Joe to take a step backwards and detach himself.

'Sure. What's up?'

'I brought my boyfriend, Craig, along tonight. He's over there talking to Si and he's happy to come over, if you're interested. I just have to ask him.'

Joe swallowed. He had seen Kyla arrive with Craig but hoped against hope that he was just some casual acquaintance of hers.

As he moved his head to the right, he realised he could see down the front of her blouse. He swallowed and tried to catch his breath.

'Interested in what?' he mumbled.

Kyla leaned in close and whispered in his ear, and for a second, he thought she might be about to suggest some kind of nefarious sexual practice, which, given the occasion and his recent attempts to remain faithful to Janice, he would be forced to decline but would regret forever. Instead she said, 'The IT security at the garage is crap.'

'What?'

'How long do you think it took me to find out exactly who the previous owner was of the 6 series we sold to Mr Carter, what you paid him and what the mileage was when it arrived?'

'What?' He repeated, staring at her in disbelief, and with more than a touch of disappointment.

'And he's not the only one.'

'Kyla, can we not talk about this here? It's my engagement party.'

'You're right. I just thought it was an opportunity not to be missed. Craig's a very busy man. I'm not going to shop you, by the way. That would really spoil your party, wouldn't it? I was thinking more of a business proposition. See, Craig won't work with just anyone; he's very particular. He has to like you before he'll work with you. He's a wizard on the computer, can put data beyond the reach of everyone official but, at the same time, you can find it whenever you need. Would you like to meet him?'

★★★

Tracy was re-doing her lipstick in the ladies when Janice tottered in.

'Hi Trace. Are you enjoying yourself?'

Tracy turned and gave Janice an air kiss. It was unlike her to be so giddy but she had drunk three gin and tonics in close succession and she was feeling decidedly light-headed.

'Lovely party, Janice, and you look fabulous.'

Janice smoothed her hair in front of the mirror.

'Thanks. Listen, I'm sorry. I still feel awful about having the party now. We should have waited till after the funeral. I did say to Joe but he was so keen. He said it didn't matter. It's OK with you, isn't it?'

'Sure. Mum would have been delighted with your news. And you've got so many people here, at such short notice. My lot are always booked up weeks ahead.'

Janice hovered next to Tracy and picked at a cotton on the front of her dress.

'As you've mentioned it, and I don't want you to hear from anyone else first…'

'What? Hear what?'

Tracy wound the cotton around her finger and pulled it off with a sharp tug.

'It wasn't so long before, but we invited some people around ten days back, as soon as Joe proposed. I wanted to invite you then, but Joe wouldn't let me.'

'Oh.'

'It isn't that he didn't want you here. He said you didn't know people so you wouldn't enjoy it, but you would feel you had to come. So, I'm just so pleased you are here, and you and Pete are enjoying yourself.'

Tracy felt sick. Her only brother had got engaged and he hadn't intended to invite her to the party. After all the times she had saved his arse over the years.

'The bloody sod,' she muttered and Janice spread her hands over her face with a wail.

'Oh, I'm sorry, Trace. Don't tell him I told you, please. I just would have died if someone else had said they knew first. You've always been a lovely person to have around, like having a real sister.'

Tracy bit her lip. Janice was a good sort. It was Joe who didn't know how to behave. She sighed and put her arms around Janice, who wept into her shoulder.

'It's not his fault I suppose,' she muttered to the stricken Janice. 'The crazy will's got him all messed up.'

Janice straightened up and began to dab at her eyes with a paper towel.

'How d'ya mean?' she asked, tugging herself out of Tracy's embrace.

Tracy applied some powder around her nose and then packed away her make-up into her bag.

'Well, you know – all the conditions that Mum stuck in the will. It wasn't her – most likely Brian, the solicitor chap.'

Janice was perplexed.

'But we sorted it out. I went with Joe to see Mr Bateman. I told him when Joe had been to see Barbara. March the 8th.'

'Yeah, sure. He saw Mum then.'

'What do you mean, Trace? It's all done, isn't it? Mr Bateman said we had done all we needed to do. I signed the paper.'

'Joe didn't see Mum that night. According to Brian, she was away in Spain. I know you wouldn't lie, not on purpose.' As she

189

said the words, Tracy wondered if that was true. If Pete had asked her for that kind of 'support' she may well have provided it without too many questions.

'What's Mr Bateman going to do?' Janice was gripping the tissue tightly in her hand.

'I've no idea. I've got more important things to worry about, myself. But I thought that was why…why you'd decided to get married now.'

'What d'ya mean? What should us getting married have to do with your mum's will?'

Tracy tucked her compact in her bag and headed for the door. Her brother was a nasty piece of work to treat Janice in this way.

'Ignore me. I've got confused. Too many G&Ts. Let's get back to the party.'

Janice's hand thumped the door above Tracy's head. Tracy had forgotten quite what a big girl Janice was, with a long reach.

'You're no good at lying, Trace. I was straight with you. Now tell me. If it's about Joe, I've got a right to know.'

'I can't tell you,' she said. 'It wouldn't be right. It's about Mum's will and if Joe didn't want to tell you then I shouldn't. I haven't even told Pete all the details.'

'Your brother made it my business when he dragged me to that lawyer's office and made me sign something. He said that was all I had to do. And now you're telling me it wasn't true and I swore it was. For God's sake, if you don't tell me I'm going to go out there now with everyone here and ask him.'

'Please don't,' Tracy implored her. She had been angry with Joe and she'd opened her mouth. Poor Janice. She didn't deserve all this.

'I'll do it!'

Janice tried to push past Tracy and open the door but now Tracy barred her way. Fuming, Janice raised her hand but, as she did, she caught sight of her newly-purchased engagement ring glinting under the strip light. It was a beauty; a pear-shaped diamond on a white gold setting. Then her face creased into a wretched scowl. She began to ease the ring off her finger – no easy task now her blood was up.

'Stop it!' Tracy cautioned but Janice continued to struggle with the ring, her tears falling fast to the floor.

Janice finally succeeded in displacing the ring and held it aloft. 'I'll bloody throw it back in his face, I will, if you don't tell me.' Her chest heaved up and down.

'OK,' Tracy answered, realising she had few choices. 'OK, calm down. If Joe can't get his share of Mum's money, because he didn't visit her like he says, then the only way he can get the money is if he has children but he has to be married first.'

For a second Janice was motionless, then her head fell forward and it might have hit the wash basin if Tracy hadn't caught and steadied her. The ring went up in the air, landed on the floor and began to roll across it. Just at that moment, there was a light tap on the door. Pete's voice was channelled to them through a small crack.

'Trace, love. You've been ages. Is everything OK?'

Tracy stretched one foot out to block the door, whilst still supporting Janice and searching around frantically on the floor for the ring.

'Just helping Janice with her make-up. We'll be out in a tick,' she called. She located the ring, picked it up and held it out to Janice who was staring at her reflection in the mirror, both hands pressed flat against her stomach.

'I knew about the girl, you know, Debi, who he worked with. But he sent her away and he came back to me.'

'He loves you, Janice. I know he does,' Tracy said softly, trying to repair some of the damage she had inflicted. 'It's not about the money.'

'Why didn't he tell me then? About the will?' she asked, placing the ring back on her finger and pushing it firmly into place. 'I would've still said yes. There's no one else for me, he knows that.'

'With Mum dying and the way she died, we've both been pretty upset. And then the will stuff just complicated things. I think that because of Mum it made Joe re-evaluate, you know, think about what he really wanted in life. And that's you.'

'He didn't get home till late the night your mum died.' Janice held her head high as she revealed Joe's secret.

'You mean...'

'Yes, I lied for him – twice now, I can see. He was probably with some new bit on the side then as well – maybe that Kyla he invited along this evening.'

'I don't think so. She's brought her boyfriend and he's got fifteen years on my brother. And Joe's been working pretty hard recently.'

Janice stared at her reflection in the mirror.

'Don't worry, I won't tell him I know about the will. Not tonight, anyway. But this is his last chance, Trace. It doesn't matter how I feel, I do have some self-respect. If he lies to me again, about anything, I'll leave.'

Tracy smiled encouragingly at Janice, although the revelation that her brother had not been at home on the night her mother died was nagging at her conscience. And despite what she had said to Janice, she knew he found it almost impossible to resist the allure of a pretty girl.

'Make sure you smile when you go out there,' she said to Janice. 'It's your party.'

'If they ask I'll just say my feet were killing me. But the solicitor – Mr Bateman – what's he going to do about what we signed?'

'I don't know. He said he'll call me next week. And when he does, I'll let you know.'

39

WHEN PEOPLE started to arrive at the church for Barbara's funeral, Tracy was pleased that she'd ordered sandwiches and sausage rolls and reserved some tea urns. She had feared it might be just her and Joe and their families. Instead, there was a steady stream of people of all ages; neighbours from Barbara's block, old artist contacts, Tracy and Joe's own friends and at least one or two journalists.

Barbara had shown little interest in religion, other than to wax lyrical about Eastern spirituality from time to time, usually after meeting someone foreign in a café or bar or in the park, so it had been difficult to know quite how to mark her passing. Fortunately, they had discovered a vicar who didn't mind presiding over a service for a murdered lady he had never met and who, if she had been asked, would probably have said she didn't believe in God. And Joe had agreed to pay upfront, muttering about how it would soon be repaid ten times over, when Tracy tried to thank him.

Tracy sat next to Pete, followed by Luke and Taylor in the front row, and then Joe and Janice took up the remaining seats. Joe was quiet, for once, accepting condolences with a nod and a grimace, Janice stepping in to thank well-wishers in his stead.

Brian was also there, sitting near the back of the church, his expression solemn. He had received two messages from Tracy since their telephone conversation, one on his work answerphone and the other on his mobile, politely enquiring if Barbara had left any instructions with her will about how she would have liked her service to be conducted. He had not replied.

He focused on the coffin resting on a pedestal in the aisle, and tried to imagine Barbara lying placidly inside, arms folded across her chest, eyes closed, but it was impossible. The Barbara he knew was always bustling around, forever active, her hands constantly moving, her mouth not far behind.

But Brian was not only unsettled because he was here at Barbara's last send-off and was being forced to confront the reality that the brightly coloured whirlwind of a woman she had been was now contained within a wooden box, his reading of her diaries had left him confounded and shattered. It wasn't what Barbara had written which had troubled him, it was what she had omitted to write.

For all his years of devoted service, all the hours he had attended Barbara, both professionally and personally, all the days of work where he had 'gone the extra mile' to provide her with the best, without charging for it of course, and all the hours he had spent just sitting at home and thinking about her face, her smile, her laugh, she had written next to nothing. It was as if he had never existed.

He had found only two entries, both short. On 2 March 2014 she had written 'BB 2pm' and on 2 April 2016 he had seen

'Meeting 4.30 café BB'. Even the inclusion of the second 'B' left him cold. She hadn't felt able to write 'Brian' or 'B' to illustrate the closeness of their relationship, she had needed his second initial to remind her of who he was.

He had tried to be fair to Barbara, he prided himself on being an even-handed person, and he recognised that she was more of an artist with a paintbrush than a pen, the diaries were not packed with salacious stories or deep, angst-ridden confessions or poetic turns of phrase, but there were anecdotes there, spread across the years, entries with circles around them or exclamation marks to illustrate their importance and pencil sketches of countless people, pieces of fabric, newspaper snippets, lists, and he had found himself included, reduced to two initials, only twice. If he could have had some sign from Barbara that she had appreciated him even a little, he would have been satisfied.

On top of that, his plans to return the diaries, without them being missed, had been frustrated. He had revisited Barbara's flat yesterday evening with the books neatly repacked in his bag, only to find himself unable to unlock the door. At first, he thought he might have brought the wrong keys, but Barbara's key ring with its weighty glass bauble filled with multi-coloured strands was impossible to confuse with his own. After several attempts he resigned himself to the fact that the locks were new and he was stuck with the offensive items, at least for now. And so he sat in the church and brooded, and a new bitterness against Barbara and her family took root.

David Wolf sat on the third row with Jane and Hani. Buoyed up by Hani's original advice to be more in control of the fallout from Barbara's death, he had suggested attending the funeral, but Hani thought it a great idea and decided he should attend too, as head of the department. David had hoped that a few choice words would dissuade him. 'Hani. Just so that you know, it is in a church. I am sure people would understand if you felt unable to attend,' and 'If we send too many people don't you think it might appear as if we are worried about something?' But Hani had brushed away all objections with a brusque 'we are going to pay our respects, nothing more,' so now all three of them had come.

Judith and Constance sat in the row behind Brian, and Constance quietly pointed him out to Judith. From their vantage point they could see everyone entering and leaving. Constance had felt forced to leave behind her trusty laptop, but Judith had a small notepad on her knee in case anything of importance came up.

Tracy had chosen a poem by Christina Rossetti to read, not because it had been a favourite of Barbara's, but because it was one she knew and it seemed appropriate, and she managed to walk stiffly to the front of the church and address the fifty or so people, some of whom she did not recognise, with the poet's words.

'"Remember", by Christina Rossetti,' she announced regally.

'Remember me when I am gone away,
Gone far away into the silent land;
When you can no more hold me by the hand,
Nor I half turn to go yet turning stay.
Remember me when no more day by day
You tell me of our future that you planned:
Only remember me; you understand
It will be late to counsel then or pray.
Yet if you should forget me for a while
And afterwards remember, do not grieve:

For if the darkness and corruption leave
A vestige of the thoughts that once I had,
Better by far you should forget and smile
Than that you should remember and be sad.'

But as Tracy read out the words, she realised they were not appropriate for Barbara at all, as she would almost certainly have wanted them all to think of her, and often. She might not want them to weep and wail, that was true – she had once attended the funeral of a friend in a crimson trouser suit with enormous heart-shaped earrings swinging in the wind – but she would have wanted fuss and noise and memories to be shared. And that made Tracy sad, as she had contemplated something more celebratory, had suggested to Joe that they fill the church with Barbara's paintings (although she knew she would not include the portrait of Joe they had discovered) but he had scoffed and she hadn't had the courage to take the idea forward alone.

As she finished her reading and headed back down the steps to rejoin her family, the door of the church opened and a man leaning heavily on a stick entered. He was smartly dressed, wearing a camel-coloured overcoat and white silk cravat and he sported a shock of black hair. He had a small suitcase in his hand, which he deposited behind the back seats. Then he began to walk slowly down the aisle and, as everyone watched, he hovered by the coffin and rested his hand on the top, lowering his head in prayer or contemplation.

Tracy nudged Pete. It was Miles. 'Oh Lord,' Pete said.

Everyone, including the vicar, waited patiently; Miles' shoulders heaved once, he wiped his eyes and sighed, then he took his mobile phone out of his pocket and appeared to be checking through his messages. Joe's eyes rolled in his head and Janice caught his wrist as he began to rise out of his seat. Tracy saw him mouthing words out of place in a church and she nudged Pete to intervene, although she wasn't sure what Pete could do, if Joe chose to confront his father.

Miles lay the phone on top of the coffin and shuffled his way into the closest pew. Suddenly music started to play, and a song, recognised by some of the mourners, reverberated out for all to hear.

'What's the song?' Constance asked Judith, whose foot had started tapping out the rhythm.

'Oh what a scoundrel,' Judith muttered. 'That must be Miles Hennessy. See the hair and the clothes, oozing Californ-i-a. He's playing Dionne Warwick, one of my mum's favourites. It's called "Say a Little Prayer". It's better than some of her other songs he could have chosen, I'll give him that, and the sentiment is there.'

Tracy wanted to be cross with her father, but now she heard this song, she remembered how much her mother had liked it, and it upset her that Miles had remembered when she hadn't and that he had had the courage to act so spontaneously. But Joe's hands were balled up into tight fists and Janice was gripping his sleeve, and Luke and Taylor were both giggling.

The song came to an end and Miles retrieved his phone, kissed his fingers and touched the top of the coffin and then trundled forward to take his place in the front row. Tracy moved up one space to accommodate him and allowed herself to be kissed; Joe turned his head away but at least his fingers were now hanging loosely at his sides.

'It's just like the best Agatha Christie,' Judith muttered to Constance gleefully.

'How do you mean?'

'Everyone is here. All the suspects in this one place. All we need now is some natural disaster, a snowstorm, to force us all to remain here for a few hours to allow you and me to solve the murder. If no one else gets bumped off before then, that is.'

'I'm pleased it's summer then,' Constance replied with a shudder. She found the image of spending hours closeted together with these people distinctly unappealing.

After the ceremony, Joe, Pete and four other men shouldered the coffin and the mourners followed it outside and lowered it into the ground. Brian kept his distance. He was already formulating in his head the letters he would write as soon as he returned home. His appointed agent, whom he had met in a pub in Neasden only the previous day for a debrief, had 'come up trumps' in terms of results. Granted, Brian had spent most of their furtive conversation reflecting ruefully that he should perhaps have given the agent more guidance at the outset, on all aspects of the parameters of his instruction including its methodology, but there was no point in lamenting that now. And the man was so pleased with his achievements (and so heavily-muscled), that Brian did not have the heart to admonish him.

The first letter was easy; Trading Standards would receive an anonymous tip-off regarding all the illicit practices which went on at Joe's showroom. He would lay it on thick, pretending to write on behalf of the relative of a 'wronged customer.' The agent had found three such people who had bought cars from Joe where the mileage was clearly too good to be true and had followed it up. The information had been obtained in a fairly unorthodox way, but Trading Standards didn't have to know that.

The second was more difficult, and he bore less animosity towards Tracy, although the very fact that she had so little insight into the kind of woman her mother had been that she had had to ask him for ideas for the funeral disgusted him. And she had allowed herself to be led into penury by her frivolous husband; he now knew the extent of her financial woes. All in all, she was a woman of little substance.

And as Brian watched the men taking turns to shift the piles of earth and depositing them on the coffin, the initial rattle of dry fragments on waxed wood slowly becoming a dull thud, he knew how he could spoil things for Tracy too.

***

Tracy saw Brian for the first time, hovering near the door of the church. She waved her hand to beckon him over. She would give him the painting, his portrait, she had decided. At first, she had made the decision because she wanted to keep Brian sweet but, as the days had passed, she realised she wanted him to have it. And more than that, when she had been sifting through her mum's drawers, she had found a sealed letter addressed to him which she would also hand over. Had Brian known her mum better than she suspected?

***

Brian noticed Tracy gesturing to him from near the grave and toyed with going over. But his bitterness was rising up inside him and he worried that he may say something untoward which would be overheard. And then he saw Miles, the impostor husband, put his arms around Tracy and whisper in her ear and he turned and walked smartly away from them all.

***

'He was in rather a hurry to leave, our friendly neighbourhood solicitor,' Judith remarked to Constance.

'Yes. I noticed that too.'

'Overcome with affection for the deceased, or something else, I wonder? Do you think we should pay him a visit, purely for completeness?'

Constance considered Brian's departing figure. 'I'm not sure. Tracy said he was very particular, so he might be the sort to put in a complaint, whatever we say or do.'

'Only if he has something to hide, surely?'

'Shall we go?' Constance shivered, although the day was warm.

'Oh no. I'm sure there's so much we might overhear that would benefit our client's case,' Judith replied. 'Frankly, we could do with some new leads.' People were gradually filing back into the church, towards the food, and Judith stepped back to allow them to pass before also re-entering. 'Why don't you hover near Tracy and her husband and also target Joe. I'm going to mingle with some of the other guests.'

And before Constance could object, Judith had marched off and left her alone.

Judith positioned herself close to an older lady, with whom she could have an innocuous conversation, who happened to be standing almost back to back with Miles, who was himself leaning heavily on Janice and eating a sausage roll at the same time.

'So Janice, how's my son doing? I know better than to ask him myself,' Miles was saying.

'He's fine, promoted to head of the Mill Hill branch,' Janice replied.

'Chip off the old block then. And sales are good?'

'I think so.'

'Is that his beamer I saw outside, the convertible?'

'The red one, yes. Have you just flown in?'

'Yes, night flight and I came straight from the airport. I don't have anywhere to stay yet. Left my bags at the back. Actually, I do need to ask a favour.' Miles bent in even closer to Janice.

Janice was silent, the colour draining from her lips.

'I have found someone, a soulmate, after all these years. Amazing it didn't happen sooner but, well, when the time's right… I'll tell Tracy, but I don't want to tell Joe myself, especially with the timing. You will all be invited out for the wedding, to LA. Maybe in a few days, when things have calmed down, you could tell him for me?'

Janice breathed again. She had worried that Miles wanted a bed for the night, and had anticipated the response that might invoke from Joe.

'How nice. Who is she?'

'Name's Kim. She's a gym instructor and yoga teacher. That's how we met. I took one of her classes. It's done wonders for my posture.'

'She sounds very nice. I'm happy for you.'

'So you'll tell him, but not till I'm gone?'

'Sure. Did Barbara know?'

'I had mentioned it to her when we last spoke but sounds like she chose not to share it.'

'We have something to tell you too, me and Joe,' Janice said.

'Oh. What is it? Am I going to be a grandfather again?'

Janice detached herself suddenly from her almost father-in-law.

'No, not that. But please keep it quiet and don't tell Joe I told you. It is Barbara's funeral after all.'

Miles bowed gravely and Janice waved her ring finger in front of his face.

'Me and Joe. We're getting married too,' she said.

Miles beamed widely and gave Janice a big squeeze.

'I'm so pleased, my girl,' he whispered, pressing his finger to his lips. 'In other circumstances I would suggest a double celebration but I think not in our case. Congratulations to you too.'

★★★

Pete and Tracy were standing together at one end of the table laid out with food, which was quickly being consumed. Pete was tucking into the sandwiches and their boys were hoovering up the sausage rolls. Tracy held only a glass of water in her shaking hand. Constance couldn't immediately see Joe, so she stationed herself near them for now, taking out her phone and pretending to be preoccupied with her messages.

'It's nice that Miss Thompson came,' Pete said to Tracy.

'I would've been cross if she hadn't.'

'Really?'

'Oh come on. I've worked in that school ten years, all right, off and on. But I've worked hard.'

'Fair enough. Have you told her you're leaving yet?'

'No.'

'She'll be devastated to lose you.'

'Maybe. They prefer young teachers these days. No other responsibilities, they don't answer back and they're cheaper. She'll make a fuss though. Make me feel I've betrayed her; I know what she's like. You should've heard what she said behind the music teacher's back when she left.'

'When are you going to tell her?'

'You could tell her for me, drop it into the conversation. I mean, she won't make a scene here in front of everyone.'

'I can't believe you.' Pete spoke through clenched teeth. 'This is your mother's funeral, Trace. Not here.'

Tracy's eyes welled up.

'OK then. I'll speak to her on Monday. But you'll probably hear the screams from home.'

'I'll go and talk to her anyway, say how touched you are that she came, butter her up a bit, OK?'

Joe entered the church through the side door, and any rumour that he might have been spending the last five minutes sharing a last few words with his mother was dispelled by him tucking his cigarettes back in his pocket. He headed for the table to pour himself a cup of tea.

'Maybe we should've had a bottle of whisky?' he muttered to Tracy, who smiled obligingly. 'Not sure tea is strong enough. Did you see Brian came? What on earth was that all about?'

'I think it was nice he came. I would've liked him to stay,' she replied.

'What, so he can gloat again? At least he had the sense to make himself scarce.'

'Ooh dear,' Pete grinned. 'What's this Brian guy done then?'

Tracy glared at Joe to warn him to choose his words carefully. 'He's Mum's lawyer, the one I mentioned. He gave us a bit of a hard time when he read us the will,' she said.

Joe grinned now, revelling in his sudden understanding that Pete may have been kept in the dark about aspects of Barbara's will and the value of her estate. He was pleased he wasn't the only one to keep secrets. 'Where's Janice?' he asked before spotting her across the church, waving her ring finger at Miles. 'What's she doing with Miles? I told her not to speak to him.'

'He probably collared her, and he is our father. And he's come a long way.'

'I'm going to find out what she's telling him.'

Tracy laid her hand on Joe's sleeve. 'I think that's pretty obvious as she's waving her ring around. Listen, there are a lot of people here, including journalists. Go easy, OK?'

'Don't tell me what to do, Trace. I don't want him here and I told her not to talk to him.'

'Oops, I'll make myself scarce,' Pete quipped. 'I'll go talk to Miss Thompson. Excuse me, brother,' and he left Tracy and Joe together.

Tracy stood with her back to Constance and pulled her brother into a close embrace.

'Janice told me you were late home the night Mum died,' she whispered, clutching his arm. Joe stiffened. 'Don't go off on one, Joe. Standing behind me is the lawyer for the man they think killed Mum.'

'What's she doing here?'

'I imagine she's waiting for an opportunity for one of us to make a fool of him or herself and it's not going to be me. So, if you know what's good for you, you'll go and shake hands with our father and make your peace. And you'll thank your lucky stars that you've got Janice in your corner. OK?'

Joe released himself from her grip, scowled at Constance and headed hesitantly over towards his father. Tracy turned towards Constance and pretended to notice her for the first time. She smiled, not only to appear friendly but also because Constance's presence had helped her appreciate that, in her relationship with her brother at the very least, she may now hold all the cards.

***

'Hello, Mrs Jones. I'm Dr Bridges, Jane Bridges from St Marks. This is Dr Wolf.' Jane strode towards Tracy with her hand outstretched.

'Gosh. How nice of you both to come.'

'Not at all. We wanted to say how sorry we are. Dr Mahmood is here too, the head of our team.'

Jane gestured over towards Hani, who, having removed his glasses, was preoccupied examining the main window of the church closely.

'Dr Wolf. You operated on Mum. And we heard it was all successful. I do appreciate what you did for her, even though it's all ended up in this awful mess.'

'That's very kind. Yes, what a terrible thing to happen.'

'Was she happy, at least, once it was all over?'

'Yes. I think she'd been nervous beforehand. She was very relieved and looking forward to returning home.'

'Can I ask, would she have felt anything, with what happened?'

'No. It would have been instantaneous.'

Tracy choked back her tears, nodded sadly and then made her way over to join her brother with Miles.

'I feel a bit of a fraud, accepting credit for a wonderful operation,' David muttered to Jane.

'Don't say that. It comforted her. It was the right thing to say.'

'Can we grab Hani and leave now?'

'Sure. He's more interested in the architecture than talking to anyone anyway.'

'Let's go then,' David said. 'It's cold in here and I feel like God is judging us from every angle.'

40

IT WAS THE NIGHT before Ahmad's trial was due to start, and he lay on his bed gazing up at the ceiling. He couldn't sleep. Whenever he closed his eyes he saw Aisha's face staring at him accusingly. He had failed her, and in the worst way possible. He had brought her thousands of miles to a new life and now their family faced disgrace and disaster.

He sat up in the semi-darkness and began to leaf through the newspaper the prison officer had left in his cell. Most of it was depressing news; another London stabbing (a boy of fifteen), a cyclist under a lorry (a thirty-six-year-old mother of three), more homeless on the streets, London on the highest level of security alert, the impossibility of buying a first home, the uncertainty of post-Brexit Britain. And then he saw it. 'Syrian cleaner on trial; is this the face of a callous murderer?'

He had skipped over it deliberately first time around, as Constance had entreated him to do. Now, alone and distracted, he indulged himself by devouring the article, lashing himself with each word. At first, he was so preoccupied by his reading that he failed to notice the cold stealing up on him; it was licking his calves before he realised it was back. Of course, he possessed the tools to defeat it, to fight back. He simply had to focus on the face of the ones he loved and slow his breathing down but, on this occasion, Aisha's face did not appear warm and welcoming; it was instead harsh and judgemental.

And now he discovered something interesting about his own psyche. If he immersed himself totally in the newspaper, the cold would leap upwards unchecked. And those words he was reading – 'plunge', 'catastrophic', 'calculating', 'ingrate', 'loner', 'defenceless' – each one invigorated his attacker, fuelling its spread through his body, freezing his organs in its wake.

By the time he had the wisdom to fling the newspaper to the floor and fight back, the biting frostiness had gripped him by the throat, threatening to shut down his airways and relaxation was the antithesis of his instinct, which was to battle hard. He collapsed on his bed, his body convulsing.

Through a fog of pounding in his head, Ahmad heard the noise of bolts being drawn back and heavy footsteps. The prison guard entered the cell and flooded it with light. Within seconds he had rung the emergency bell and had wrapped his arms around the stricken man, bringing him to a sitting position.

'So cold,' Ahmad mumbled.

'You don't feel cold,' the guard replied. 'You're sweating like a pig.' He took Ahmad's pulse. 'You need to slow down, mate.'

He grabbed the newspaper off the floor, drew the four corners of one sheet together and held it up against Ahmad's lips.

'I want you to breathe really slowly into this. Watch it inflate. Nice and slow.'

Ahmad's heart was racing but his breathing was shallow, almost non-existent.

'Come on. You're not trying,' the guard roared. 'I want to see the bag inflate. Here. You feel cold? I've put the blanket around you. Now breathe.'

Ahmad tried really hard. The contact from the guard seemed to fend off the choking hold on his windpipe and, for the first time since the guard had entered, he filled his lungs with air.

'Good. Now do it again.'

Ahmad breathed a second time and then a third, his heart finally starting to reduce its breakneck speed. The guard took a step away from Ahmad and watched his back heave up and down.

When Ahmad felt warm again and his breathing had returned to normal, he murmured 'so tired' before closing his eyes, lying down on the narrow bed and finally going off to sleep.

The guard stood outside Ahmad's cell with the senior prison warder.

'What happened?'

'I don't know. I just checked on him. He was lying on the bed, shaking all over. He said he felt cold but he was boiling hot. Should we call a doctor? He wasn't good.'

The senior warder drew back the shutter and viewed Ahmad. He was now lying peacefully on his side, his body rising and falling rhythmically. Then he thought about the poor woman they said he had murdered, with the splintered head, and how his own mother would be seventy-one next month.

'He'll be all right now,' he replied. 'And he needs the sleep so he can be bright tomorrow morning. No point getting someone in to prod him around. I don't think anyone else needs to know about this. We wouldn't want them accusing us of not looking after the star of the show, would we?'

The guard shrugged in capitulation, but every hour through the night he checked on Ahmad until he went off duty and, on two occasions, he crept into the room. The first time he had the excuse of removing the newspaper, the second he entered blatantly, just to ensure that Ahmad was still alive.

41

CONSTANCE and Judith sat together once more at Constance's work, keen to finalise their trial preparation for the following day. Constance had already commented extensively on Judith's opening statement and Judith was poring over the changes.

'Why have you put a question mark next to the whole of the first page?' Judith asked indignantly.

Constance gulped. She knew this was coming.

'We have no evidence it was suicide,' she said. 'Isn't it a risk to assert that right at the start?'

'We have no evidence it was murder, but that hasn't stopped the entire British public believing it was.'

'I'm just trying to explain why I put the question mark. At the funeral, you seemed pretty sure it was murder.'

'Well, I was hoping we would find out something definitive by keeping our eyes and ears open. Instead, we got morsels and scraps, insufficient to lay the blame at anyone else's door.'

Judith circled the question mark Constance had drawn and

then lay her papers down on the table.

'Bear with me for now. If we major on an accidental death, then what hurdles do we have?'

'I suppose we don't have a reason for her to be in the staff room. I mean, if it was an accident, why on earth was she there in the first place?'

'Yes. She hadn't confided in anyone that she felt cooped up, wanted fresh air, that kind of thing?'

'Tracy didn't say when we met. Although I had to tread carefully with her, so I stuck to the key questions. We can ask her in the box. Ask about Barbara's love of nature; she painted lots of flowers. Maybe she wanted to look at some?'

'At night time? We could suggest she was restless, fed up with being in hospital, went in for one day, ended up staying three. But that would be pure supposition.'

'And it was hard for her to walk.'

'Yes. It will be difficult to get the jury to swallow her choosing to stroll down the corridor for pleasure. But you're right, too, that the suicide track is risky. First there was no note, although they don't always leave them. We know about the pain in her hands, well done for getting that from Tracy and, of course, we heard from Miles Hennessy that she wasn't happy he was getting remarried, although I suppose he might have been mistaken. Men of that age can sometimes overvalue their worth, I think.'

'We only have his word for it.'

'Any areas we can usefully probe further?'

'The will.'

'Yes, I have that. And Tracy's reference to its complications. I'm not sure how much leeway the judge will give me, that's all. It sounds as if she may have left Tracy something, given she's giving up her job and taking her own legal advice. But, again, if we are majoring on an accident or a suicide then that's all immaterial.'

'Can we try to hint that it might have been Joseph? They were estranged and he was cross about something at the funeral.'

'Dawson interviewed him and didn't get anywhere, did he? And I can't see his fiancée, who is happily flashing her ring around, withdrawing her cast-iron alibi. I know they've tried CCTV to track his car that evening, but it was all inconclusive. We could put him in the box and see if he cracks, but I doubt it. Casting him as the villain won't have any legs unless we do. And we have nothing on him, apart from a love of fast cars and bad taste in music, which is unlikely to be sufficient to convict him of anything, sadly. And it cuts across our 'accident/suicide' theme, which may be our best hope of an acquittal.'

'She might have written something in her diaries.'

'What diaries?'

'Tracy said she used to keep diaries, but she couldn't find them in the flat.'

'Hmm. That doesn't really help us either, does it? I mean, a murderer might take them to hide any clues to his identity but if it was suicide there would be no need.'

'They might show she was depressed?'

'Yes. But we don't have them, do we? And only Tracy's word that they ever existed.'

'Maybe we should stick with the accident theme then?'

'Let's see how things go. If I do well with the forensic man we may be onto a winner. I'm going to push him hard. You remember what we planned?'

'Sure. I remember.'

'OK, problem areas?'

215

'The rings.'

'Yes. I will leave to your imagination what Dawson's response was to my enquiry about his officers' integrity. We have to run with the denial for the time being. And the video of Ahmad's little episode. Ugh! Amazing, isn't it? There's no film in the camera at the hospital, but there's plenty at Acton Central station, retrievable at the flick of a switch. Do you think they keep the crown jewels there in an underground bunker or something?'

Constance managed a smile. 'Dr Atkins' report is largely helpful.' She was trying to be optimistic.

'I agree, on the face of it. But my opponent could do a lot with that in cross-examination. And PTSD, it makes Ahmad sound like Rambo, which isn't the image we want to portray.'

'Rambo?'

'Oh. It's another of my ancient references. Don't even bother to Google it.'

'Should we not call Dr Atkins then?'

'We don't have a choice. We have no other explanation of Ahmad's behaviour. Without Atkins, the jury will think he's mad and probably dangerous. What about the distinguished Dr Wolf, what's his Achilles' heel?'

'I don't know why you dislike him so much.'

'Have you got all day? And what was he doing at the funeral? And the other two doctors?'

'Maybe they were told to go. I wish I could've heard more of what they were saying. I had to back off because Tracy kept staring at me. I heard her thanking Dr Wolf for the operation and he seemed embarrassed.'

'Understandable, I suppose. Pity they didn't stay for longer so we could find out some more.'

Judith returned to her papers.

'Do we know if Ahmad's OK?' she asked after a few minutes.

'I called earlier and they told me he was sleeping.'

'Good. A sign of a clear conscience, I think. I'll be heading off myself soon too.'

PART THREE

42

JUDITH had bought a new suit for Ahmad's trial. It had set her back almost £400 but she was not prepared to wear the old ones any more. Not only was she slimmer now, but she associated them with her previous life and with Martin, her deceased husband. She had bought two shirts also and had surprised herself by asking Greg which he preferred her to wear on the first day.

Constance noticed that Judith was exceptionally smart but said nothing. She, herself, had bought one new white shirt for the occasion, although she felt the guilt of its price tag weighing heavily upon her when she collected Ahmad's aged suit from his house the previous night. Then, quick-thinking as ever, she made a short diversion. She had a friend, who was a sharp dresser and of very similar build to Ahmad, and he owed her a favour; she had written him a glowing reference for his accountancy job two years ago and her senior partner had agreed to sign it. She told Ahmad that his own suit had been eaten by moths during its time in the wardrobe, and glowed when she saw his transformation.

But no clothes could cover the deep rings around his eyes.

'Constance.' Now, after much cajoling, he had finally begun to call her by her first name. 'I have a bad feeling about this. I have read the newspapers. Already they think I am guilty, all of them, like Miss Burton was saying.'

'They're just trying to sell a story. Once they hear what we've got to say they'll change their tune.'

'I'm not sure,' he had replied. 'They don't like to admit they are wrong. You know that. Maybe it's not so different here from Syria?'

'You mustn't give up just because of the newspapers. In a few days' time they'll be onto the next story. I need you to be strong in there. I have asked them to give you a pen and paper. Anything you think of while the judge is speaking, or the other lawyer, or any of the witnesses, you make a note. Anything, however small. And don't react to things they say, even if you think they aren't true. Just calm and cool and relaxed.'

'My wife?'

'I saw her last night and she was fine. And a police officer went over this morning to check on things. I spoke to her a few minutes ago and your wife was having a cup of tea. Your daughter is at school, as normal.' Constance hesitated. She hadn't told Ahmad about the broken window. She had arranged for it to be repaired and had asked Dawson for some extra patrols on the street. He wouldn't promise her anything, she understood that Aisha was not a police priority, but he had reluctantly agreed to send someone today for an hour, to provide support for his wife, as the trial opened.

Ahmad thought that his wife didn't drink tea – not the English kind – and she didn't like strangers in the house, however well-meaning. She would sit with the mug on the table and stare at it. A sob formed in his throat.

'Don't think about them now. Think about yourself,' Constance said.

When they brought Ahmad up from the cells, Constance walked next to him. As he settled himself in the dock and his handcuffs were removed, she leaned in close and whispered 'Remember what I said' in his ear. He gave a cautious half smile before sitting back in his seat and then raising his head to take in his surroundings. Constance took her seat behind Judith.

'What's up?' Judith muttered behind her hand.

'All good.'

Judith's youthful opponent leaned over to shake hands.

'Hello, Judith. Andy Chambers. We met once a few months back, at the Lord Chancellor's Garden Party.'

'Really? I meet so many people, but I'm sure you're right.'

Chambers ignored the brush-off. 'All ready for the fight then?'

Judith eyed him carefully.

'We're ready, yes,' she replied.

Mr Justice Seymour entered on time. He was known as a forthright judge with a quick temper. But Constance's meticulous research had revealed that he had come to the attention of the public recently. In his last murder case, in the spring, he had delivered a lengthy lecture on the importance of sticking to the point in cross-examination. Unfortunately, there had been at least three occasions when he, himself, had wavered from the subject in hand. There was a rumour (strenuously denied) that a liquid lunch might have contributed to his lack of coherence. In any event, a stand-up comedian, related to one of the witnesses, had been in court, and the result was a parody of the cruellest kind.

Judge Seymour had achieved celebrity status (briefly) with snippets of his speech being played on a fictional form of the radio show, Just a Minute, where he received penalty points throughout for repetition and deviation.

'He's no nonsense. He'll be good for us,' Judith had ventured to Constance that morning, hoping to convince herself as she spoke.

Judge Seymour sat down and scowled at all assembled. Not a good start. Then he took his glasses from their case, which he snapped shut, put them on, and squinted with greater clarity across his courtroom. Judith gripped the bench with both hands. The beginning was always the hardest part.

'Mr Chambers, you appear for the prosecution. Shall we start?'

When Ahmad's name was called, he rose to his feet. He threw back his shoulders and made eye contact with the judge, and then he allowed his eyes to wander towards the jury, as Constance had suggested. And when he replied, 'I am not guilty of the charges you have brought,' in perfect, hardly accented English (he had practised this over and over) when a simple 'not guilty' would have sufficed, surprise rippled through the courtroom.

Even Mr Justice Seymour seemed taken aback. The media had portrayed Ahmad as an impoverished cleaner, uneducated but physically strong, a true Goliath. Although he stood tall and imposing before the world, his voice was soft, controlled, even gentlemanly. And Judith had to hand it to Constance, the suit was a triumph. She even worried they might have overplayed their hand this time. If anyone had been au fait with their labels they would have questioned how a hospital cleaner could afford to wear an Armani suit. She witnessed the raised-eyebrow exchange between Chambers and his solicitor. Touché, Judith thought to herself. Two could play at this game.

Mr Chambers stood up with an encouraging air which rapidly morphed into a more solemn demeanour as he leaned forwards onto his lectern. Judith could not help but stifle a giggle. When she was first admitted to the Bar, one of her colleagues had written a piece about the indispensability of the lectern, focusing on the curious poses some of their more celebrated peers adopted when addressing the court.

She remembered some of the names – 'the hugger' and 'the prop' were the most obvious but Chambers' stance was more like that of 'the mistress', which had caused the most hilarity. 'The mistress' stance involved resting on one elbow, the fingers lightly touching the forehead, the other hand caressing the worn surface of the lectern. The writer had explained that this position indicated considerable attraction but not total commitment to the lectern; this had been the analogy which had earned him a serious rebuke, even in the non-PC days of the late 1980s.

First, Chambers regarded Ahmad, his gaze long and searching, before turning his attention to the jury.

'Members of the jury. This is a terrible crime of which Mr Ahmad Qabbani is accused.' He stretched Ahmad's name out into its composite syllables, Qa-bba-ni, making it as long and disjointed as a freight train. 'The murder of a woman; not just any woman – a lonely woman, an elderly defenceless woman – in a place where she thought she was safe, a place of sanctuary and recovery, in one of our best-loved flagship hospitals.

'You will hear from Dr David Wolf, her dedicated consultant, that she had a routine operation and was preparing herself to return home, when she was callously and cruelly thrown from the eleventh floor of the building, breaking her neck in two, just like that.' He snapped his fingers. Two members of the jury flinched.

Judith rolled her eyes and cleared her throat.

'The defence will say there was no motive for the killing, but there was, ladies and gentlemen; greed and jealousy. Mr Qabbani stole two precious rings belonging to Mrs Hennessy, one given to her by her late mother, the other by her husband, each of considerable sentimental as well as monetary value. He does not deny he knew of those rings, both their existence and their location, and they were found in his house three days after Mrs Hennessy's death.' Ahmad remained still, his eyes directed towards the floor.

'It is true we don't have anyone who saw what Mr Qabbani did to Mrs Hennessy, no eye witnesses. Because Mr Qabbani made sure of that. Because he waited for his chance, till it was night, till the ward was deserted. And then he flung her to her death, calmly left the building and caught the train home. He might have even sat next to one of you on his way, just cold and calm, as if nothing had happened. How do we know this? Miss Burton will say it's all conjecture, but no, we have evidence. That is what cases are based upon; hard, irrefutable evidence.

'You will hear forensic evidence from Dr Jason Lewis, who will tell you that Mr Qabbani's hair was found wrapped around the buttons of poor Mrs Hennessy's nightdress, no doubt when she wrestled with him in a desperate attempt to save herself.'

'Objection.' Judith sprang to her feet.

'Yes, Ms Burton?' Judge Seymour's voice was loud and challenging.

'That's pure speculation, your honour. There is no evidence, including from forensics, as to how my client's hair found its way onto Mrs Hennessy's nightgown. My client, of course, will give his own account of events at the appropriate time.'

Judge Seymour sighed impatiently.

'There is nothing wrong with Mr Chambers expanding upon the forensic evidence to explain how the prosecution will put its case but, Mr Chambers, do stick to the facts please; not too much embellishment.'

'Yes, your honour.'

'And Ms Burton, I understand your enthusiasm but let's try to keep the interruptions to a minimum, shall we? Mr Chambers is putting the prosecution case forward. You will have your opportunity to speak shortly.'

Chambers smirked at Judith good-humouredly and resumed his 'mistress' position.

'As I was saying, Mr Qabbani's hair was wrapped around the buttons of Mrs Hennessy's nightgown. And, unusually – and we will come back to this later on, so I ask you now, just to hold that thought...' Chambers held his right hand up in a claw-like motion to indicate seizing something.

Judith swallowed. Chambers was good. This was going to be more difficult than she had anticipated.

'...there is more forensic evidence. Mr Qabbani's fingerprints were all over Mrs Hennessy's medical notes.' He paused and his eyes bored into Ahmad, as did those of every other person in the courtroom. Ahmad remained motionless at the start but then he tucked one hand inside the other and shifted in his seat. 'Not just on one page; on the cover and on each and every page.' Judith made a note herself to talk to Ahmad about this privately. 'Why should Mr Qabbani have read through Mrs Hennessy's notes unless he was plotting his moment to strike, waiting until she was at her most helpless?

'And, more importantly, his fingerprints were found all around the staff room, including the door which opened out onto the fire escape from which she fell. I will repeat that, members of the jury, the door which opened out onto the fire escape from which she fell, and this is not disputed by the defence.

'In addition, the day following Mrs Hennessy's heartless murder, after Mr Qabbani had been questioned by police, the day he failed to mention "helping her to the bathroom", we have CCTV from the platform of Acton Central mainline station which I will play to the court; disturbing footage of Mr Qabbani behaving in an erratic manner.

'And Mr Qabbani's Oyster card was swiped at Hampstead Heath station at 8:45pm when his shift finished at eight. He could walk to the station in less than ten minutes. What was he doing in those extra thirty-five minutes? Simple but terrifying – he was murdering Mrs Hennessy.' Judith's throat went dry. This hiccup in the timeline was problematic and Ahmad would have to deal with it convincingly in court.

'And finally, and we shall get on to this also in more detail later, just to give an insight into the kind of person Mr Qabbani is – a runaway from Syria, a person to whom we gave a home, a job and sanctuary from his own war-torn land – he thought he was above his role as a cleaner. He gave Mrs Hennessy a book, but no ordinary book, The Arabian Nights.' Chambers coughed out the name of the book so raucously that the judge grunted under his breath. 'A book full of misogynistic imagery, of magical misdeeds and violence.'

Judith muttered 'what a load of nonsense' as loudly as she dared as she gestured in Chambers' direction, the microphones picking it up and provoking a low chuckle from one or two quarters. But Chambers was enjoying himself and continued without drawing breath.

'Why should he have given her any gift? I'll tell you. It was to ingratiate himself into Mrs Hennessy's affections. He could see she was alone and he wanted to take advantage of her. Perhaps he was hoping that she would give him something in return.'

Ahmad's eyes closed, his eyelids flickering, a low moan came from his lips. Chambers halted once more and waited for a response. Ahmad opened his eyes and raised his head to meet the challenge of Chambers' words.

Judith was struck by the fact that in different circumstances the two men might have been a match for each other. Not just physically, at either ends of a rope in a tug of war, but also in terms of their presence. Chambers was better-looking in a public-school boy kind of way, but his dancing eyes were without depth. He was eloquent and convincing but he provoked the impression that life had been easy for him. Everything from his naturally curling hair, to his flawless complexion, to his manicured nails, to his black, highly-shined shoes oozed easy wealth.

When you perused Ahmad's face you saw the experiences of the world etched across it. Judith imagined each line representing a challenge he had faced and overcome: poverty, starvation, war, death. In an endurance test, she knew whom she would back. But of course, they were not in those different circumstances, they were not competing on a TV survival show. Instead, Ahmad was forced to sit mute and listen to these accusations, completely at the mercy of Andy Chambers. And smooth, articulate words and clever arguments were worth more in this courtroom than inner strength and stamina.

And Judith had remembered Chambers; she never forgot a face. She had met him, shortly after her return to work on the

Maynard case. He had congratulated her warmly on her victory, had encouraged his friends to lift a glass in her direction, but she had felt their tribute insincere; it might have been her sensitivity about Martin, her former husband, raising its head again. In any event she had acknowledged them politely and moved swiftly away.

Chambers was now sitting down and tidying his papers on his desk, his opening statement at an end. She glanced over her shoulder at Constance, hoping she was keeping notes as her own wandering thoughts had obliterated the last two minutes of Chambers' speech. Constance was tapping away at her keyboard, and Judith composed herself with a quick 'nothing to it' inside her own head.

'Your honour, members of the jury,' Judith began. 'There is no evidence linking my client to Mrs Hennessy's death, and no reason why he would have wished to kill her, no what we often refer to in legal parlance as "motive". Ahmad Qabbani was a hard-working cleaner at the hospital. He finished his shift, his security card records him leaving the building promptly and he knew nothing of Mrs Hennessy's tragic demise until the following day, when her body was found, in the undergrowth at the back of the hospital.

'In fact, there is no evidence whatsoever that Mrs Hennessy was even killed. Dr Lewis, the pathologist from whom you will hear, has propounded some unusual theories as well as more well-recognised ideas, but none of them is conclusive. What is undisputed, however, is that Mrs Hennessy was unsteady on her feet after her operation and that she fell to her death from a fire escape with a low barrier. It is perfectly possible that no one pushed her; tragic as it may be, Mrs Hennessy might simply have fallen.

'There is a camera opposite the entrance to the ward, a ward into which members of the public are free to enter and leave at any time of the day or night. But sadly, it was not operational on the evening of Mrs Hennessy's death. A recent report by NHS England recounts that it is no longer able to afford the upkeep of the cameras in any of its hospitals, not even in one of our "flagships".

She smiled at Chambers, who returned the compliment. 'Understandably, there are no cameras on the wards, either. And, tellingly, no one saw Ahmad Qabbani push Mrs Hennessy off the balcony, or accompany her from her room, the long trek down the corridor to the place from which she fell, past six other rooms, three each side of the corridor with glass doors, each one occupied. Or force her against her will from her room. No one saw it, members of the jury, because it didn't happen.

'My client was seen leaving the hospital at the end of his shift. His security card confirms his time of exit from the ground floor as 8:12pm, his Oyster Card was used at Hampstead Heath station at 8:45pm and shortly after that he caught a train home. Of course, it is not impossible that he returned to the hospital later on in the evening, after having dinner with his wife, reading to his daughter and pretending to go to sleep, although there is no evidence of any kind that he did. No, members of the jury, the facts I have set out are much more consistent with a man who calmly leaves his place of work to return home; calm, not because he wears a mask to hide the face of a ruthless killer but simply because this day is no different from any other. After he left, Mrs Hennessy died. A calamity but not of my client's making.

'True, a single hair from my client's head was found attached to Mrs Hennessy's clothing. A single hair. Yes, "DNA evidence", as we like to call it. It sounds so snappy, doesn't it? "DNA evidence" is invaluable in many cases. It's particularly helpful when it links a person who may otherwise be completely unconnected with the deceased, to the case – a passing lorry driver, a hitch hiker – either of whom might be identified and linked to a person they had never previously met, by a stray thread from clothing or saliva residue; it is next to useless when we know that Ahmad Qabbani was already acquainted with Mrs Hennessy and was with her on the day she died.

'As to the evidence that Ahmad's fingerprints were in the staff room; well it would have been surprising if they were not. This was a room used by all staff, of which Ahmad was one. He had a locker in that room, he ate his lunch there and, from time to time, he went out onto the balcony for some fresh air, as did other members of staff, whose fingerprints were also found at the scene.

'My client accepts that he helped Mrs Hennessy out of her bed on the morning of the day she died, as she needed to go to the bathroom. The prosecution will make much of the fact that he did not tell the police about this when he was first interviewed, at a time when he was not a suspect. I say it was foolish but understandable that he kept this to himself. He was not supposed to help the patients. It was against the rules. His natural desire to help Mrs Hennessy, so she would not lose her dignity, has been twisted into the only piece of tangible evidence against him. And that is cruel and unjust. And in this country, we are neither of those things.

'Yes, it's true that my client was born somewhere else, in Syria, a country gripped by civil war since 2011, from which more than five million civilians have fled. On arrival in the UK, he could have sat back and received benefits as others do. Instead, he chose to go out to work, taking home just above the minimum wage for nine- or ten-hour shifts, both day and night, sometimes seven days a week. His foreign nationality alone is not a reason to suspect Ahmad Qabbani of involvement in this crime.'

'What about the rings?' Chambers muttered in a loud but muffled voice. Judith paused and glowered at him.

Judge Seymour dropped his pen onto the desk top with annoyance.

'Mr Chambers, be quiet please. Miss Burton, you probably asked for that, given your intervention earlier. Can that now be an end to your games, please? Continue.'

'Members of the jury, you have to be sure beyond reasonable doubt that Ahmad Qabbani killed Barbara Hennessy, that he lured her to the fire escape and pushed her off. Once you have heard from the witnesses and seen the meagre and paltry evidence, I don't believe you will have that certainty and I urge you to acquit my client and let him return home to his wife and daughter.'

Judith sat down disgruntled. She vastly preferred clinical factual opening statements to the 'wearing your heart on a sleeve' kind of advocacy with which she had just concluded things. And she suspected the judge didn't like it either. But she and Constance had discussed it at length. The public was involved on an emotional level in this case and if they failed to engage in the same manner, they ran the risk of losing the jury's (and the public's) interest. Sadly, Judith had little to serve up in terms of Ahmad's story to engender support; she could only negate the story Chambers put forward. That troubled her.

43

FIRST UP FOR THE prosecution was Tracy, red-faced and carrying an extra three kilos since her mother's death. The stress of recent events had rendered her unable to stick to any healthy eating regime. She was wearing the same navy suit she had donned for the reading of the will, and a cream-coloured blouse with a flamingo motif, which was pulled taut across her chest, like a sail straining against a northerly wind. She shifted uncomfortably in her chair to draw her jacket closed.

'Mrs Jones. This must be very hard for you, having lost your mother so recently,' Chambers cooed, and, right on cue, Mr Justice Seymour remembered to peer over his glasses and release an insipid smile. Judith coughed noisily.

'But I am going to take you briefly through your evidence and then Ms Burton here will ask you some questions.'

Tracy spoke sensibly about her mother's health and stay in hospital and her last visit. She was the epitome of a grief-stricken daughter who was holding it together, wiping away the occasional tear, hands shaking, lips trembling, eyes and voice low. Judith watched her every move. She was keen to challenge Tracy a little, to shake the impression of devotion, but not too much or she would risk coming over as harsh.

'Tell us a little about your mother's art.' Chambers spoke encouragingly.

'She loved to paint,' Tracy replied. 'She had a studio when we were kids, and in her flat – she'd been there the last ten years or so – she turned the second bedroom into a studio.'

'And did she have any plans for future paintings?'

Again, Tracy was thankful for the prompt.

'When I saw her at the hospital, on the Wednesday, she asked if I would sit for her, with Pete, my husband, and my boys, for a painting.'

'So, she was enthusiastic about the future?'

'Yes.'

'And what did you say?'

'I said "yes" of course.'

'Mrs Jones, given what you have just said, do you think there is any chance your mother would have wished to take her own life?'

'Absolutely not. Mum was always cheerful.'

'Previously? I know she brought you and your brother up on her own. Did she ever suggest she was unhappy or show signs of depression?'

'No. Never. She wanted to get her feet sorted and get home again; that's all.'

'And outside of her painting, what else did your mother do?'

'Well, she liked to help with local charities, giving out food and clothes, especially to refugees.' Judith groaned inwardly. She could tell what was coming.

'Did she ever mention Mr Qabbani, the defendant, to you?'

'No.'

'But Mr Qabbani will say that he and your mother were friends. Is that possible?'

'Mum loved to chat, and probably, with his background, with him being from Syria, she would have wanted to help him, in any way she could. She couldn't have known what he would do in return.'

There, it was said. Barbara Hennessy had chatted to Ahmad because she wanted to help him in a benevolent, open-handed, generous way, and he had repaid her by flinging her off a fire escape on a dark night.

'Mrs Jones, do you need a moment to compose yourself or are you able to continue?' Judith began, once Chambers had completed his perfunctory examination.

Tracy raised her head and took in Judith. Joe had advised her only that morning that Judith would try to trip her up in any way possible.

'Thank you. I'm fine to continue.'

A grimace from the judge followed, forced and brittle, unable to keep up his earlier façade of empathy. He disliked sentiment as much as Judith and was already anticipating ditching the relatives and moving on to the forensic evidence.

'How often did you visit your mother in hospital?'

'I went once.'

'Not every day then.'

'No. I work full-time and I have two children and I couldn't leave them.'

'Visiting is any time though, for private patients.'

'Yes, I know.'

'Your husband is not working?'

'No.'

'So he could have helped out?'

Silence.

'Is that a question, Ms Burton?' Mr Justice Seymour twitched and lay down his pen.

'I will rephrase that. Did your husband visit your mother with you?'

'No.'

'Or your children, they could have gone to see her?'

'I didn't want them to see Mum in hospital.'

'Ms Burton, where is this all going?' Judge Seymour was pouting at Judith.

'I am just trying to ascertain from Mrs Jones the frequency of her visits; that's all. But after the operation, once she was better?'

'She's told us that. She went to the hospital once. Move on.'

'Thank you, your honour. And remind me, which day did you visit?'

'On the Wednesday. Mum was upset because her operation was postponed twice. I was supposed to pick her up on Thursday but I...'

Now, after being on the verge for most of her testimony, Tracy finally collapsed into a fit of sobbing, simultaneously searching for Pete in the public gallery. He rose stiffly to his feet, grumbling under his breath and holding his back, and nodded reassuringly at Tracy. Tracy's bottom lip stopped quivering.

'No, I'm all right,' she waved away the usher offering a cup of water. 'It's just that if I had gone on the Thursday, Mum would still be alive now.'

'I see. Take your time, Mrs Jones. Is there a particular reason you didn't pick her up on the Thursday?'

Now Tracy sat very still.

'I had an appointment,' she said.

'An appointment?'

'Yes.'

'Which you had to attend?'

'Yes. They said Mum couldn't be discharged after 6, you see.'

'I understand. You are a busy person. We will hear from Dr Wolf, your mother's surgeon, later, but had your mother suffered from any serious illnesses or health issues in the past?'

'No. Not that I know about. And this time, she didn't tell me all her details. She was a bit forgetful in the months before... before this happened – missed meals. I thought it might be the beginning of some kind of dementia.'

'Can you remember anything in particular which concerned you, other than the missed meals?'

'We used to speak to each other about once a week. Suddenly she began to call more often, forgetting she had already called and telling me the same things.'

'I see. And did you do anything about this?'

'I don't know what you mean.'

'Did you tell your mother you were worried about her memory, suggest she go to her GP or discuss this with your brother?'

'No. It wasn't so bad. It sounds worse now you're asking me.'

'How often did you see your mother before she went into hospital?'

'About once a month.' Tracy's lip shuddered. She knew that sounded pretty awful, although some of her friends only saw their parents at Christmas.

'And how far is it from your house to where your mother lived? Google Maps says twenty-six minutes, but we all know that can be a little optimistic.'

'It is only about a half hour in the evening, I suppose, but during the day more like an hour. Like I say, in the week I have work, and at the weekend the boys have football and karate. And I have marking and lesson plans.'

'We've heard your mother was an artist?'

'Yes.'

'She sold her paintings?'

'When we were younger. Not recently. She hadn't painted for at least two years.'

'And why was that?'

'She had pain in her fingers. She said it hurt to hold the paint brush.'

'Just the paint brush or was she having difficulty with her grip generally?'

'I'm not sure. I told her to go and see her GP but she wasn't keen.'

'Mrs Jones, would you say painting was important to your mother?'

'Yes, vital. She was an artist; that's what she did.'

'So the prospect of not painting again would cause her considerable distress?'

'I can see what you're trying to get me to say but it's not true. At the hospital she said she wanted to paint me and Pete when she came home.'

'But if her hands were painful, that may not have been possible.' Judith paused to allow her words to produce maximum impact. 'How mobile was she?'

Tracy sniffed back her tears and wiped her eyes with a paper tissue.

'Before the operation? Well, she was a funny one. Not into fitness but still active, if you know what I mean. But I knew her feet were painful. She couldn't get shoes to fit any more. And she did love shoes.'

'You didn't see her after the operation?'

'No.'

'You mentioned to Mr Chambers that you didn't know Ahmad Qabbani. Can I check, have you ever seen my client before today?'

Tracy glared at Ahmad, pulling her shoulders back as she did, as if distancing herself as far as she could from him. He raised his head on cue, allowing her to examine him closely without challenge.

'Only in the newspapers,' she replied quietly.

'Quite,' Judith mumbled. 'Mrs Jones, we're nearly finished, you'll be pleased to hear. Mr Chambers has made much of a book which my client gave your mother to read while she was in the hospital. We've heard it was a copy of *The Arabian Nights*. Did you see that book on her bedside table?'

'No I didn't.'

'So you've no idea when your mother received it?'

'No.'

'Do you know anything about your mother's reading habits, the kind of books she liked to read?'

'I've never seen my mother read a book. Magazines, yes.'

'Did your mother mention my client to you at all?'

'No.'

'Any other hospital staff?'

'She mentioned Dr Mahmood.'

239

'Do you remember what she said about Dr Mahmood?'

'Not really. I think, just that he had been to see her.'

'Who else visited your mother in hospital?'

'I didn't know this at the time but two of her friends did visit. The police told me. But that was on the Wednesday, I think – after me.'

'Your brother, Joe?'

'No.'

'Why didn't your brother visit?'

Tracy faltered, trying but failing to find Joe among the sea of faces in the public gallery.

'They weren't close,' she said.

'Was your mother a wealthy woman?'

'That's not an easy question to answer.'

'I accept "wealthy" can mean different things to different people. But can you give me some idea of her lifestyle?'

'Joe and me, we had always assumed not. She had a nice flat in Primrose Hill, two bedrooms, with a small terrace, but that was bought years ago, before the prices went crazy. And she went on holiday to Spain each year. But she lived quite simply, ate in a lot.'

'But?'

'Sorry?'

'Well you said you had *assumed not*. That suggests something else was the case.'

'Yes. Well, I am not sure if I'm allowed to talk about it, my mum's will.' Tracy peered out into the public gallery again, and this time, in the second row, she located a man with grey hair and hexagonal glasses perched far down his nose. It was Brian, his lips set tight, and he leaned forward and gave Tracy a reassuring smile.

'I wasn't sure if it was private, that's all – the will, what it says.'

Mr Justice Seymour put on his glasses and coughed. 'I'm not sure Ms Burton is asking for precise details of what the will says, in terms of who is to receive what money; she's asking about the extent of your mother's estate.'

'Do I have to answer?'

'Yes you do.'

'All right. She left just under two million pounds.'

There was a sudden crescendo of noise, followed by a low babble in the courtroom, which faded quickly under the blistering scowl of Judge Seymour. Suddenly, Mrs Hennessy was not such a 'poor' defenceless woman. Judith worked hard to maintain her composure; she had anticipated something substantial, given their intelligence that Tracy was planning to leave her job, but nothing had prepared her for this bombshell.

'And when did you and your brother discover that your mother was wealthier than you had expected?'

'Mum's solicitor, Mr Bateman, told us when he read the will a few days after her death. He said she'd sold some paintings when she was younger, and invested the money.'

'And you and your brother are the beneficiaries of the will?'

'Yes.'

'Are you telling us that you had no idea, before then, that your mother had any savings?'

'Well…'

'How did you think she supported herself?'

'I don't know. I thought Miles supported her.'

'How long ago is it that your father, Miles Hennessy, and your mother were divorced?'

'About forty years.'

'And you thought he supported her financially still? Really, Mrs Jones?'

Tracy coloured and remained silent.

'And you intend to leave your teaching position now you have this large inheritance from your mother? One million pounds is a lot of money.'

'Your honour, we object to this line of questioning.' Chambers was on his feet, this time strumming his fingers against the edges of his lectern (the 'guitar' position). 'We are now certainly straying into personal details of no relevance whatsoever, if we were not before.'

'Ms Burton, move on please.' Judge Seymour was annoyed again.

'I just wanted to say, your honour, that I am taking another job,' Tracy answered the question in any event. 'I have a promotion to head of Key Stage 2 at another school.' She raised her chin indignantly, and Judith chastised herself for having asked one question too many.

'Am I right that your father, Miles Hennessy, is getting remarried?'

Tracy's eyes narrowed. How could Judith possibly know that? 'Yes, he is.'

'Did your mother know about this?'

'Janice, my brother's fiancée, she told me that Mum knew. But Mum hadn't mentioned it to me.'

'In your view, would this information have made your mother happy for your father?'

'I think she would have tried to be happy for him. But, no, it would have made her sad.'

'Your honour, those are all the questions I have for Mrs Jones.'

Mr Chambers shook his head rapidly, indicating he had no intention of standing up again with this witness.

'Very well. Thank you, Mrs Jones, you are excused.'

44

THE SECOND prosecution witness on the first day was David Wolf.

He crossed the room in short steps, seated himself in the witness box and ran his fingers through his receding hair. His statement was short; his colleague, Dr Mahmood, had seen Mrs Hennessy in February and recommended the operation, but he had been her surgeon. The operation had been a success and she was lined up to head home the following day. Mr Chambers asked him to describe an incident which had led to Ahmad being given a written warning the previous year.

'I don't remember the incident very well,' he replied, in clipped tones, 'but I think there had been an emergency on the ward and there was a suggestion that Mr Qabbani, the defendant, had interfered in some way with the process.'

'Interfered in some way?' Chambers was incredulous, his eyes bulging.

'The patient had gone into cardiac arrest. I attended and administered CPR and he stabilised. But an investigation by the

Trust found that Mr Qabbani had been in the patient's room for some minutes before I entered and he was standing over him when I arrived. It…'

Mr Chambers held up his hand to stem David's flow.

'One moment, Dr Wolf. You say Mr Qabbani, the hospital cleaner, was found standing over a patient who went into cardiac arrest on the ward?' Chambers moved his head deliberately from David Wolf to glare at Ahmad. Ahmad ignored him.

'Yes.'

'Go on.'

'Well…it was…the Trust felt it was necessary to write to the defendant to remind him that while he should always do what he could to assist patients, as any normal, caring person would, his obligation was simply to raise the alarm as quickly as possible and leave things to the professionals.'

'I see. Very sensible. Did you know Mr Qabbani well?'

'Not really. He was one of a number of hospital cleaners. I would see him around the hospital. One other time he was a bit shirty with me, but I, well, I just ignored him.'

'In what way, shirty?'

'I, well, I think I walked where he was cleaning. I was in a hurry, an emergency. He appeared rather cross – angry, even.'

'So your previous interactions with Mr Qabbani had left you with a negative impression of him?'

'Well…I'm not sure.'

'I will rephrase the question. Before this tragic incident, generally speaking, did you think of Mr Qabbani in a positive or a negative light?'

'Negative, I suppose, but I am trying not to be unfair to the man, you see.'

Judge Seymour raised his hand to stop Mr Chambers mid-flow.

'Dr Wolf. That is not your job in this courtroom. Your job today, in this courtroom, is simply to tell the truth, that's all. Questions of fairness and judgement are left to other people, like me. Do you understand?'

'Yes, I apologise. I understand.'

'Thank you, Dr Wolf, your honour. No more questions. Please wait for Ms Burton.'

Judith rose to her feet slowly, shortly after the judge's public rapping of David's knuckles, savouring her opening words in her mouth before serving them up.

'Hello, Dr Wolf. Thank you for coming here today. We know the life of a doctor is a hectic one. All those patients to see, lives to save.' She smiled and he smiled back. Constance groaned inwardly. She knew Judith didn't like David from their night-time encounter at the hospital, neither did she, but she hoped Judith would remember the job they had to do and not get side-tracked into useless point-scoring.

'You mentioned that it was your colleague, Dr Mahmood, the senior orthopaedic surgeon at St Marks, who saw Mrs Hennessy before she was admitted.'

'Yes. And when she came into hospital.'

'So why did she come under your care?'

'Dr Mahmood had a full schedule, so he asked me if I would oblige.'

'Oblige?'

'Operate on Mrs Hennessy.'

'And you agreed?'

'Yes. It's very much my kind of operation. I've done at least fifty very similar procedures. I was glad to assist where I could.'

'Can you tell us, in layman's terms if possible, what is involved in the operation.'

'Yes. I'll try not to be too graphic. Bunions are caused by a thickening of the bone on the inside of the big toe. We don't know what causes them. Sometimes, it's wearing the wrong shoes, but not always. The treatment Mrs Hennessy had is called metatarsal osteotomy. It involves shaving the bone and then realigning the big toe. It takes around an hour under general anaesthetic. But in Mrs Hennessy's case it was also necessary to realign some ligaments and reposition the first metatarsal, putting some pins in. It was at the more complicated end of the bunion operations.'

'But not life-threatening?'

'There's always risk whenever a general anaesthetic is used but Mrs Hennessy was a non-smoker and in good health.'

'And why did she not have her operation till Thursday the 11th of May? She was admitted on the Tuesday. Why the delay?'

'Like I said, Dr Mahmood brought Mrs Hennessy in, but he had some emergencies which took priority on Tuesday and Wednesday. When he knew he was also going to be too busy on the Thursday as well, that's when I was asked to take over.'

'Is that usual?'

'Not usual but it does happen.'

'Dr Mahmood is the senior consultant at St Marks?'

'Yes, he's the head of our team but we work together, as I said, sharing responsibility.'

'Was Mrs Hennessy taking any medication, before her operation?'

'Not as far as I am aware.'

'And is it correct that on the day she was admitted, she was asked to fast?'

'Yes. That was in case we operated that afternoon.'

'But you didn't?'

'No.'

'This happened again, the following day.'

'Yes.'

'And on the Thursday.'

'Yes, when the operation took place. Look, the delay was far from ideal, but she would have eaten in the evenings, once we knew the operation couldn't take place, and we constantly monitored her blood pressure.'

'The nurses checked her blood pressure?'

'Yes, many times; it's recorded in her notes.'

'And the operation was successful?'

'As far as we could tell immediately afterwards. You have to wait till the swelling goes down to be certain. I would have seen her again two weeks later for a follow-up.'

'Was she in pain?'

'Standard painkillers were prescribed for her.'

'Did you know Mrs Hennessy lived alone?'

'Yes. She said she was divorced and lived alone.'

'Is it unusual for patients in their seventies to come in to hospital alone?'

'Fairly, but it does happen, yes.'

'Did you suggest to her that she contact someone else, her son or daughter to take her home?'

'No. I'm not a social worker. I was interested in what was wrong with Mrs Hennessy medically, and how to fix it.'

'Of course you were.'

Judith decided to try a different tack. She wasn't getting anywhere with this line of questions.

'When did you see Mrs Hennessy next?'

'The afternoon of the operation, Thursday. Well it was probably evening, around seven o'clock.'

'And how was she?'

'She was recovering. Said she was a bit sore. But that was to be expected.'

'And that was the last time you saw her?'

'Yes.'

'Dr Wolf, would all the treatment given to Mrs Hennessy be recorded in the log book by her bed?'

'Yes.'

'You still use a handwritten copy?'

'We write the medication by hand into a book and then, at the end of each shift, it gets recorded on the digital file.'

'Ah. So you would ensure there was also a soft copy record for each patient?'

'Well, the nurses do this, at the end of each day, but yes.'

'Was Mrs Hennessy able to walk after the operation?'

'Yes she was, although she would have been in pain. The notes record that she was attended by our physiotherapist and that she walked around the ward with him.'

'Unaided?'

'The notes mention crutches. It's important not to put weight on the foot at the beginning.'

'She needed crutches to walk?'

'Yes.'

'Is it possible for Mrs Hennessy to have walked the length of the corridor, from her bedroom to the staff room, from which she fell, with the aid of her crutches?'

'Yes. That's why the physio would have attended, to make sure she could get around. But the crutches were found in her room.'

Judith swallowed hard. She had allowed herself to be led into that one.

'Can we stick to my questions, please. I am interested in what Mrs Hennessy could have achieved, physically, post-operation, and you have confirmed that she would have been able to walk along the corridor with her crutches?'

'Yes.'

'Could she have walked without the crutches?'

Dr Wolf considered the question carefully before replying.

'She could have. Maybe if she held on to things as she walked, for support. But there is no reason for her to walk down the corridor. If she needed a nurse she could simply have rung the bell next to her bed.'

Judith thought about a further admonishment to Dr Wolf for embellishment but she held herself back.

'I just want to pick up on your description of an interaction you had with Ahmad which you provided to Mr Chambers. You said he "got shirty" with you?'

'Yes.'

'I want to try to visualise the scenario. Ahmad was cleaning the floor?'

'Yes.'

'Mopping the floor?'

'Yes.' David's second 'yes' was louder than the first, and tinged with irritation.

'Does he put up one of those signs when he cleans – you know, a plastic one, warning people that it's slippery?'

'Yes I think he does, probably.'

'But you were in a hurry?'

'Yes. I don't remember precisely why.'

'You don't remember precisely why, but you said, in your evidence earlier, that you were on your way to an emergency?'

'Well, I –'

'Are you disputing that you said that? I can have the transcript read back to you, just to be certain.'

'No, I…I –'

'Would you like to clarify your evidence?'

'I don't precisely remember why I was hurrying but I do remember I was in a hurry.'

'Thank you. And my client was in the way?'

'Yes.'

'So you ignored his sign to take care, which was placed there to warn people. Why do you think Ahmad puts that sign out when he is cleaning?'

David's upper lip twitched a few times, then he fingered the end of his moustache with his right hand.

'To make sure they know the floor is wet.'

'Yes. So that they don't fall?'

'Yes.'

'Or at least, if they do, they have been warned?'

'I suppose so.'

'So you ignored the warning, because you were in a hurry and you walked through the clean floor as my client was mopping it. Did you leave footprints on the floor?'

'I probably did.'

'And, think hard, what did Ahmad say or do, as a result of this?'

'He, well, he just sort of looked rather annoyed.'

'Did he say anything to you?'

'No.'

'Did he do anything threatening at all?'

'No.'

'So, you charged on through his cleaning zone and left dirty footprints and he looked "rather annoyed"?'

'Yes.'

'Dr Wolf, do you think of yourself as a patient man?'

'Yes I do, actually.'

'Thoughtful, calm, collected?'

'Yes.'

'Do you do the cleaning at home?'

'Sometimes.'

'If your wife were to barge through your cleaning area in a hurry, without warning, do you think you might look "rather annoyed"? Or perhaps you might actually say something?'

David stood and twirled his moustache.

'Ms Burton, I think we have got your point. Move on please,' Judge Seymour sighed loudly.

'Thank you, your honour, much appreciated. Can we speak, just briefly, about this warning you mentioned that the Trust, I think you said, administered to my client a year ago.'

'Yes.'

'And by the Trust, just so we are clear, you mean the hospital authorities, rather than yourself or any of the other doctors.'

'Yes, that's right.'

'Something that you didn't remember when you were first interviewed, or in your second interview. It was only when you provided a written statement, some four weeks later, that you recalled this incident.'

'As I said, I don't know Mr Qabbani well and I hadn't connected the two.'

'I see. So, on this previous occasion, which you remembered four weeks after you were first questioned, an alarm went off, you went running into a patient's room and there was my client "interfering" with the patient. Are you suggesting that my client did something which caused the patient's emergency?'

'No,' David replied nervously. 'Absolutely not. If I or any of my colleagues had thought that, then Mr Qabbani would have been dismissed and the police called, not just a warning. No, if the decision had been mine then there would have been no further action taken. I mean the fellow is only a cleaner.'

'I see. It didn't appear serious to you at the time?'

'No.'

'But it remains serious enough to mention now at my client's trial.'

David shuffled around and twisted his moustache in his fingers again.

'I remember a little more now. The Trust felt that your client could have done more. The emergency button rings through to the nurses' room and a light goes on outside the room too, or he could have run for help himself. All those things might have been more effective in bringing help sooner, instead of just standing there.'

'You're not suggesting, then, that he should have assisted the patient in any way himself – sort of good Samaritan, that kind of thing.'

'No, not at all. Quite the opposite. The letter he was sent reminded him that he must not touch the patients but should seek help in future.'

'It…put him in his place, so to speak.'

'I suppose so, yes.'

'And if he had, notwithstanding this warning, "touched" patients – I mean, had physical contact with patients in future – would his job have been in jeopardy?'

'Yes. But quite rightly. I mean. We can't have cleaners playing doctors.'

'No further questions, Dr Wolf.'

'Thank you. We will break for lunch,' Judge Seymour announced loudly. 'See you back at 2:15 prompt.'

45

THE NEXT witness was Lottie Li, the staff nurse on duty the night Mrs Hennessy died. Since Constance's chat, when she had agreed to assist the defence, she had ignored their calls and emails, and here she was now on the other side. And Maia had disappeared completely. A letter sent to her had been returned, and a call to the hospital administration revealed she no longer worked at St Marks.

Somehow, out of uniform, Lottie seemed even more tiny and gossamer-like than in the hospital setting.

'Nurse Li. How long have you been working at St Marks?' Chambers began.

'Two years.'

'And before that you were a nurse in the Philippines?'

'Yes. For five years.'

'How did you make the transition to nursing over here?'

'Some people came over to my country to employ nurses. They came to our hospital, they tested us and then they offered us positions in the hospital.'

'And you live locally?'

'Yes, there is accommodation provided close by.'

'Nurse Li, how well do you know the defendant, Ahmad Qabbani?'

Lottie glanced at Ahmad, who was sitting head down, rolling one thumb around the other.

'He started when I did, about two years ago.'

'How often did you see each other at work?'

'Yes, often. He kept his cleaning things on the private ward so he was there always at the beginning and end of his shift.'

'Was he hardworking?'

'Very, yes. And strong. So, we used to ask him to help out if things needed doing.'

'You're saying he's strong? Is he the kind of person who would help if something needed lifting or carrying, that kind of thing?'

Judith coughed. She did not want Lottie dwelling on Ahmad's physical strength, even if he used it historically for chivalrous acts.

'Yes, but he was also good at fixing things, too.'

'How was your relationship? Would you say you were friends?'

'We were colleagues. We work in same place, but we do separate things; that's all,' she said a little too quickly.

Judith studied Lottie's face closely. What had happened to the glowing testimony she had been prepared to provide some weeks earlier? Constance's jaw hardened behind her as she, too, noted Lottie's lacklustre performance.

'You didn't socialise outside work?' Chambers continued, delighted so far with his muted, understated witness.

'No. He went home quickly when he finished work.'

'Did Ahmad like to talk to the patients?'

'Sometimes.'

'What kinds of things would they talk about?'

'I don't know, just chatting.'

'Did you ever see Ahmad in Mrs Hennessy's room?'

'I have been thinking about this very hard as it is so difficult to remember. I think he may have been cleaning once in Mrs Hennessy's room when I was there. But I'm not sure. I definitely saw him outside her room, cleaning in the corridor.'

'On the night Mrs Hennessy died, you were on duty?'

'Yes.'

'Did you see anything unusual, any new people on the ward?'

'No.'

'What time did you go off duty?'

'Around ten.'

'When did you last see Mrs Hennessy?'

'I am not sure. But I saw Ahmad leave at about eight o'clock. Mrs Hennessy's door was closed.'

'Do you think Ahmad liked Mrs Hennessy?'

Judith was only half way out of her seat, when Judge Seymour intervened.

'Mr Chambers, you know you can't ask that question.'

'Apologies, your honour. Did you see anything, or hear anything, which indicated to you that Ahmad and Mrs Hennessy were friends?'

'Like I said, I never saw him in Mrs Hennessy's room for definite but…' She paused now and stared at Ahmad, her face crumpling inwards.

'Go on?'

'I saw Ahmad, it was, I think, on the Wednesday, and he was cross, and I think it was because of Mrs Hennessy.'

'Can you explain what you mean?'

'She had some friends in her room. They were two ladies and they were talking a lot, loudly. Later on, I saw Ahmad when he was putting things in his locker and he seemed angry. I asked him if he was OK and he just shook his head. Then he told me that the ladies in Mrs Hennessy's room had been laughing about something and it had upset him.'

'Do you know what it was?'

'No. I just told him not to be upset, that I was sure they didn't mean anything.'

'Did that satisfy him?'

'He was upset for a little while, I think. We didn't talk about it again.'

'Thank you. Did you ever get the impression that Ahmad thought being a cleaner was beneath him?'

'I don't know. I...'

'Mr Chambers, I don't want to tell you again. What Nurse Li thinks Mr Qabbani thought is not evidence and you know it,' the Judge reminded him.

'Yes, your honour. I was carried away momentarily. Thank you, Nurse Li. No further questions.'

Judith was worried about Lottie Li's evidence. Before she had appeared, she had questioned why the prosecution had even bothered with her. She now maintained she wasn't certain if she had ever seen Ahmad in Barbara's room (that may or may not be helpful), she had worked successfully with him for two years and, even if they weren't friends, they had built up a working relationship, and she had confirmed that he was hardworking and reliable.

But it was the subtleties of Lottie's evidence which lent

credence to the prosecution storyline, and she could not help but admire Chambers for his manufacture of this. The overall impression Lottie had given, so far, was that Ahmad was easily capable physically of throwing Mrs Hennessy from a building, that, at best, he was sensitive and took offence easily, and at worst, Mrs Hennessy or her friends had mortally offended him in some obscure way, giving him a possible albeit unusual motive. She had also implied that he was a loner, preferring to do his work and go straight home rather than building up friendships with his peers. Coming after David Wolf with his story of Ahmad's tetchiness about his clean floor, despite Judith's masterful unpicking, it began to paint a disquieting picture.

'Tell us about Mrs Hennessy,' Judith began benignly enough.

'She was admitted on Tuesday the 9th of May. She had her operation on Thursday and I looked after her.'

'Did you talk to her?'

'Yes. She talked about her daughter and her grandsons.'

'And her son?'

'I don't remember her talking about her son.'

'What did she say about them?'

'That she missed them, her grandchildren. And she told me she was a painter.'

'Did you meet any of her family?'

'Her daughter came to visit on one day when I was checking her.'

'How did they seem together?'

'I don't know.'

'Well, was Mrs Hennessy happy to see her daughter?'

'Yes. I think so.'

'Did they kiss or hug each other?'

'I didn't see that.'

'The evidence you just gave to Mr Chambers was that you don't have any particular memory of seeing Ahmad in Mrs Hennessy's room.'

'No.'

'In the evidence you gave immediately after Mrs Hennessy's death you said you had seen him in her room.'

'I know. Now I'm not so sure.'

'What's made you change your mind?'

'I…I just can't be sure now and I want to get things right.'

Judith sneaked a quick glance at Constance for a prompt on any line of questioning she might have missed. Constance would not usually try to influence Judith mid-examination of any witness. She feared a tongue-lashing of gladiatorial proportions. But then Constance's face took on that far-away expression and she began to scribble something on her notepad. Judith took the note from Constance with interest.

'Ask about A's family,' it said. 'Will help sympathy vote.'

Judith's shoulders sagged. She very much doubted that. But she could at least get corroboration from Lottie of the time Ahmad went home. She turned the note face down.

'You said you remember seeing my client outside Mrs Hennessy's room, in the corridor?'

'Yes.'

'Do you remember which day that was?'

'It was more than one day, I think, but definitely on the day Mrs Hennessy died.'

'What time was that?'

'It was when he was going home, around eight o'clock. He had his bag.'

'After you saw my client outside Mrs Hennessy's room, what happened?'

'He went out of the ward.'

'You saw Ahmad Qabbani leave the hospital, then?'

'I saw him leave the ward. It doesn't mean he didn't come back later.'

'No. It doesn't.' Judith allowed that one through with a gentle inclination of the head.

Judith's fingers brushed the edges of Constance's missive. It was too risky. Even though Lottie was a little more malleable now. Judith might ask 'tell me about Ahmad's family' and receive a diatribe about his agoraphobic wife. Much safer to get Ahmad to talk about them, if he could only be persuaded to do so.

'Did Ahmad work hard?'

'Yes.'

'Did he have days off for illness?'

'Once he had to go home when his daughter was sick but otherwise he was always there.'

'Was he punctual?'

'I think so.'

'Polite?'

'Yes.'

'Some people have said that, because Ahmad is physically strong, like you said, that he might be a violent person. Did you ever see any evidence of Ahmad being angry or violent?'

'No. It's all about what's inside,' Lottie answered innocently, 'isn't it?'

Judith crushed Constance's note within her right hand and dropped it into her pocket.

'No further questions, your honour.'

'Thank you, Nurse Li, you are excused. Mr Chambers, who is your next witness?'

'I move to forensics now, no more witnesses of fact.'

'Because there aren't any facts,' Judith spoke quietly, behind her hand, but into the microphone.

'Ms Burton. I hope I won't need to remind you again that you are in a courtroom and not gossiping in a bar. Save your opinions for later. This the last time I will say it.'

Judith stood tall to accept her admonishment. But she was secretly pleased. The judge's rebuke drew attention to her words and a number of people in the court were now asking their neighbours what she had said to draw his ire.

'Let's begin tomorrow then, 9am please. Court adjourned.'

***

'Why didn't you ask Lottie about Ahmad's family?' Constance was seething but maintained her self-control. Judith opened her mouth to explain but Constance had already turned away and was collecting her things. She wasn't interested in an answer.

46

'DON'T BE CROSS with me Connie. I couldn't risk it,' Judith protested later. 'She wasn't our witness and someone had definitely got to her.'

Constance and Judith were back at Constance's office, preparing for the following day.

'And Ahmad can do that stuff, talk about his wife.'

'If he will. He asked us not even to mention her, don't you remember?'

'Defendants on trial for murder don't always know what's best, wouldn't you agree?'

'Yes, but...'

'Presumably that's why you instructed me. You thought I might do a marginally better job than Ahmad would do on his own.'

'Oh, of course. Don't be so prickly. I just meant he does have rights too. If he specifically asked us to keep his family out of things, we should respect that.'

'Hang on. A minute ago, you wanted me to ask Lottie to spill the beans.'

'Well, she wouldn't have said anything really personal, just that he had a wife and daughter. That is better than giving Ahmad the third degree in public.'

'Connie. Stand back for a moment. We have no real defence here, do you agree? I mean, there is no real hard evidence against Ahmad, but he was there, at the time, so theoretically, he could have committed the crime.'

'Yes.'

'So we're never going to be able to show that he *couldn't* have done it – he was sighted a hundred miles away, he wasn't physically capable – any of that stuff we love to uncover if we can.'

'Unless we find the real murderer.'

'OK. Yes. Unless we stumble upon someone else, which we and the police have not managed to do after two months' investigation.'

'What's your point?'

'The best we will be able to manage, I fear, is to find some explanation for the rings that doesn't involve murder and to tell the jury that one hair is not enough to condemn a man to fifteen years in prison. And if that is all we have, appealing to their judgement, I want them to know he has a wife and child who love him and depend upon him. Now, leaving aside all your sensibilities of what you may or may not have promised Ahmad in a rash moment of empathy, you must agree with me?'

Constance huffed and sat down on the bench.

'How did you think it went today?' she asked, happy to change the subject.

'Not great. Tracy Jones was slightly in our favour but more because of what she didn't see or hear than anything else.'

'I think your cross-examination about the will was useful.'

'Marginally. I mean, who would have thought it? Two million pounds. Far more than I ever imagined. Mrs Hennessy with a small fortune doesn't seem quite so helpless, but that could give Ahmad more of a motive. Who knows what Chambers will try when we put Ahmad on the stand? He might say Ahmad was jealous; Mrs Hennessy had all the things Ahmad didn't have; that kind of thing. With the theft of the rings it all falls into place.'

'Why didn't you ask her where she went on the Thursday?'

'I just didn't want to chance it; I had no idea what she was going to say. I mean, she might have said "I have terminal cancer and I had to see a doctor". Unlikely, but you get my point. Better to leave it that she had what she professed to be an "appointment" which was clearly more important to her than visiting her sick, aged mother, and let everyone else join the dots. And the stuff about Barbara's hands worked too. I'll use that in closing to emphasise that she may have been so distressed about her inability to paint that she wanted to end her life.'

'And if she slipped on the fire escape she might not have been able to hold on.'

'Yes, that too. But even so, there's something fishy going on, isn't there?'

'What do you mean?'

'Well, if you had just inherited one million pounds, would you be starting a new full-time job in Ealing primary school in September?'

'Perhaps she loves teaching?'

'Or perhaps those "complications" she told you about are keeping her away from her money. And her brother's engagement news which I overheard at the funeral. You know I'm not big on coincidences.'

'Maybe when his mother died it put things in perspective for him.'

'Hmm. Joseph Hennessy does not strike me as the sentimental type. Maybe she said he had to be married to get his share.'

'Well his partner, Janice, seemed pretty happy anyway.'

'Yes she did. It would be cruel of me to suggest that's because she's marrying a millionaire. What else? Yes, Barbara's forgetfulness may be useful, too, if we can show she might have become confused, disorientated, that kind of thing. Perhaps with the combination of the drugs she was on and the aftermath of the anaesthetic.'

'What about Dr Wolf?'

'Ah, *that* sanctimonious prig.'

'You still like him, then.'

'Oh come on. First, he accuses Ahmad of anger management issues because he dares to look askance when Wolf's brogues make dirty great marks on his clean floor, then he maintains Ahmad has "interfered" with a patient, pejorative enough to make the jury think he's been harming patients all along and has only now been caught. But when I tackle him he realises, 'cos he's not stupid, that he has to renege. If Ahmad had been caught doing something naughty, how could he or the Trust have kept him on, to go on and kill Mrs Hennessy? Ahmad gets convicted and the Trust is faced with a corporate manslaughter charge too. And he doesn't like Mahmood either.'

'Why do you say that?'

'Mahmood has been head of the unit since before Wolf qualified. But he puts the two of them on a par. Oh yes, he is glad to help out by taking Mahmood's patients and they have the same expertise.'

'Maybe Wolf wants his job.'

'I don't doubt that for a second. But this case isn't helping his prospects. I think he's slippery and self-serving and there's more we could find out from him.'

'You don't think he killed Mrs Hennessy?'

'No motive. Unless something went wrong in the operation and she knew about it, threatened to tell. Seems very unlikely. Especially with a bunion operation. It's not like removing the wrong kidney! And the mortality rate of his patients is average, well, better than average actually. He appears, from the statistics to be a very good doctor. But he certainly had ample opportunity, hanging around till the small hours. Did we ever find the physiotherapist?'

'No. He was Italian and he left back in May some time. The police couldn't find him, although I'm not sure how hard they tried. I could do some digging if you think it's important.'

'Never mind. You have lots to do and we have enough from Wolf confirming she could have walked unaided, which is all I would ask him. That was useful too.'

'There's one thing I want to investigate further. I didn't get much of a chance yesterday when I first saw it. If I find something we can re-call him, can't we?'

'As long as old Seymour lets us, but I'm sure I can manage that one. What is it?'

'I'd rather complete what I'm doing and then tell you, if that's OK.'

Judith shrugged. 'What's Ahmad's answer on the Oyster card?' she asked.

'You mean the timing?'

'Yes. It doesn't take twenty-five minutes to get from the ward to the station, even if the lifts are busy.'

'You won't like it.'

'Lay it on me, Connie.'

Constance giggled. Judith was so larger than life.

'He had forgotten...'

'Again?'

'But his wife's birthday was coming up, so he had made a short diversion to the shops, on the way to the station.'

'The shops, which were all closed.'

'Yes. He said he went window-shopping.'

'Which windows?'

'I didn't ask.'

'OK, so this will come up when he takes the stand and we need to be ready. Ask him which shops, what items specifically he remembers seeing in those shops and take photos, although the windows may well have changed now. We need support for what he says from the shop owners.'

'How can I do that if we're in court?'

'Ring them or send someone from your office. Don't you have any junior staff?'

'OK. I'll sort it.'

'And while they're at it they should time how long it takes to walk from the hospital to those shops to the station.'

'All right. I can do that.'

'Good. Did you get hold of Dr Atkins, remind him of the timing of his evidence, tomorrow or Wednesday?'

'Yes.'

'His report is OK, as far as it goes on the PTSD, but you've spoken to him; what's his take on Ahmad?'

'He is willing to say that the behaviour exhibited in the station is consistent with an episode suffered by people with PTSD, a kind of flashback. But that is it. I think he was cross when Ahmad wouldn't open up to him, felt his time was being wasted.'

'OK. Not great but I've been forewarned. I suppose most of the time he knows what the trauma is before he has to diagnose the related stress.'

It was two hours later that Inspector Dawson called from outside in the street. All the staff had gone home and Constance let him in and led him through the deserted corridor to their makeshift research hub. Judith sat at the head of the largest meeting room, her third coffee of the evening between her hands.

'Hello, Charlie.'

'Judith.' Dawson deliberately avoided eye contact with Judith and did not shake hands.

'Were you in court today?'

'No time. Out catching criminals. PC Brown was there and filled me in on the best bits, without picking anyone's pocket – that may surprise you. How're you doing?'

Judith shrugged. She would let Dawson's challenge remain undefended. She understood his anger, directed obliquely at her suggestion the last time they had spoken, that one of his officers might have tried to frame Ahmad. The fact he had come this evening when Constance had called was evidence, at least, that he would still work with her.

'Could be worse,' she replied.

'So, what've you found, then? What's so pressing I have to miss the cricket highlights?'

'I'll let Constance tell you. We're hoping to ask Dr Wolf what it means, in court.'

Constance scrolled through a couple of screens on her laptop.

'These are the hospital forms for Mrs Hennessy,' she said.

'OK.' Dawson sat down and unbuttoned his coat. Judith rose and came to stand behind him.

'If you scroll through the admissions forms, they are all numbered, but page 7 is missing. It's been removed.'

'Yes, I can see that.'

'I asked Dr Wolf's secretary when I noticed it, last week, but she said she couldn't remember what the form was. She thought it must have been something routine, but she hadn't removed it.'

'OK. So, what's the importance of this missing page?' Dawson asked casually.

'These are the forms for another patient, Mr Wilson, also private, seventy-five years old, discharged the day before Mrs Hennessy died.'

'How did you get these?'

'Dr Wolf's secretary gave them to me.'

Dawson raised his eyebrows but remained silent. Constance scrolled forwards then reached the screen she wanted. With finger and thumb she enlarged it so it could be read more easily.

'Page 7 for Mr Wilson is a form giving consent to a particular treatment, signed by Dr Wolf and Mr Wilson.'

'What's the treatment?'

'It's not very clear. If you see at the bottom, it says "Aladdin Trial". And also, "I, the undersigned, confirm that I give my doctors permission to use the Aladdin process currently being trialled, in addition to or in place of conventional processes, at their absolute discretion".'

'And what the hell is that?'

'I don't know. But it's clearly important enough that it's been removed for Mrs Hennessy who is now dead.'

'Any idea who removed it?' Dawson was interested now but wishing he wasn't.

'The metadata shows the last person to work on the document.' She pointed Dawson towards the name on the screen.

'Ah, surprise, surprise, Charlie, it's our friend Dr David Wolf,' Judith chimed in.

'And there's something else, too, which I have only just discovered,' Constance added. 'It may mean nothing, but just in case.'

'What?'

'The anaesthetist, Dr Jane Bridges, is Dr Wolf's wife. She practises in her maiden name.'

'Lots of doctors marry each other. So do lots of lawyers I'm told. Not many coppers though.'

'He didn't tell us when we asked him. He just talks about "Dr Bridges" as if they are not connected to each other. I think he and his wife are involved in something they are trying to hide and that may give us the answer to Mrs Hennessy's death.'

Dawson sat and mused over Constance's words. Judith began to pace, arms folded.

'Clearly, we must recall Dr Wolf tomorrow and ask him about this, but only after forensics, I think,' she said.

Dawson looked from Constance to Judith and back again.

'Can you send me these documents?' he asked.

'Yes of course. Share and share alike,' Judith replied sarcastically.

'What will you ask Wolf about all this in court?'

'I suppose I just have to ask him what it all means. I haven't quite decided yet. It will need careful thought – and at least one more cup of coffee.'

***

Judith slipped into bed late but couldn't break the habits of a lifetime; at least two files accompanied her and she propped herself up with a glass of Chardonnay, her blue notebook on her lap. Often she had her best thoughts at night, lying quietly surrounded by the darkness.

Greg moaned and turned over noisily to make space for her.

'What time is it?' he asked.

Judith patted his arm lightly. She had neglected him the last few days with all the preparation for the trial, she mused. Then she paused in abject horror. The thought which had just entered her head was so alien to her that she feared she had lapsed into unconsciousness without noticing. Martin, her late husband, had always given her so much space; either he wasn't around or, if he was, he had so much of his own to divert him, she would never have contemplated how much attention she was paying Martin, because it would never have concerned him.

Judith and Martin had spent time together – restaurants, opera, theatre – most of it divine and decadent, but had they really been together? When she thought back to those joint experiences, she wondered if they had truly been shared? They had so infrequently talked about them afterwards or mentioned them to anyone else. True, Martin had often called her when he was travelling, for a download, especially if she was working on a big case, but they hardly ever really chatted when they were together.

Greg expected so much more. If they were out somewhere, he wanted to laugh and joke and hold her hand and drag her over to read things or view the world from a particular angle. And if they were at home, he wanted to talk about his day and hear about hers. When he took a phone call, always accompanied by an apology if it was 'after hours', he wanted to lament it, or imitate the person on the phone or swear, each time anticipating a reaction from her. This need to be responsive, to participate in his life, to allow him entry into hers, was unfamiliar. So she had taken things very slowly with Greg; it was a month before they kissed and now, almost a year into their time together, they were trying out a period of him staying over. Neither of them had articulated how long it was intended to last.

Judith thought about Ahmad and the kind of husband he was; which of the men she knew he most closely resembled, if any. Constance said his wife didn't speak at all. And Constance was getting involved again with the family and she mustn't. It wasn't that Judith was uncaring. She had to remain aloof in order to make sensible judgements about the case. She didn't have the luxury of forming attachments with clients. She hoped Constance understood that and didn't think her cold and totally unfeeling.

Judith focused back on the present. When the trial was over she would do some rearranging. Having Greg living in, even temporarily, required a re-think of how to use her limited living space. The gap between the dressing table and the curtains, on the opposite wall, for starters, bothered her.

For a moment she couldn't remember why there was a gap there at all; then she recalled that Martin's trouser press had sat there until recently. It was the only personal item of his she had retained from their former life. She hadn't burned his possessions on the lawn, as Greg had admitted he had done with those of his adulterous wife. She had, instead, found a nice 'clearance' lady and asked her to find suitable homes for everything which had been Martin's – shirts, shoes, briefcases and stationery. And had agreed to leave most of the furniture behind.

But the trouser press had come with her. It wasn't sentiment; quite the opposite. In the immediate aftermath of his death and her discovery of his serial infidelity, she had wanted to inflict pain on Martin, even if it was posthumously. Martin had always timed the pressing of his trousers to the last second to have the creases perfect, so she had taken his suits from the wardrobe and pressed the trousers over and over until they started to singe and wrinkle; this had been her revenge.

But when Greg expressed a desire to spend more time with Judith and they agreed this trial arrangement, she no longer felt any need for this last remnant of their cohabitation. The trouser press had been driven to the dump and unceremoniously tossed into a large skip. And now only the space where it had stood remained.

She allowed her eyes to travel around the room, taking in the chair, dressing table with mirror, wardrobe, bedside cabinet and wastepaper basket, and thought about Mrs Hennessy's room at the hospital. Then she extracted the envelope of photographs Constance had taken and leafed through them again. Eventually, she stopped. Now she knew what had bothered her about the furniture in Mrs Hennessy's room.

Barbara Hennessy's bed clothes were thrown back on the side facing the door, as if she had climbed out of that side of the bed. But her crutches were over by the bathroom door, propped against the chair for visitors. If she was to use the crutches to help steady herself and walk, Judith would have expected them to be next to the bed. Had someone other than Mrs Hennessy moved the crutches out of her reach, and if so, why? That lent support to a third person being involved in her death after all.

'What time is it?' Greg muttered again. 'Why don't you turn off the light and go to sleep?'

Martin would have slept through her scribblings and would never have dared to tell her to stop working. But Martin wasn't here any more, and although she was still sad he was gone, she was pleased not to be alone.

She exited her bed slowly and entered the bathroom, ran some cold water into the basin and soaked her left hand for some minutes. Then, with the aid of a bar of soap, she eased her wedding and engagement rings off her finger and lay them on the edge next to the tap. She thought of the dressing-down she had given Ahmad when he had dared to explain that Mrs Hennessy had placed her rings in a similar place.

She stretched her left hand out and examined closely the space where the rings had sat. It felt strangely naked; she tried dropping it to her side and glancing at it casually. That was better. Then she dried the rings and her hand and slipped them back on. 'Not yet,' she whispered to herself. 'Not yet.'

Scrambling into bed, she switched off the bedside light, turned on her side, wrapped one arm around Greg and went to sleep.

***

Constance returned to her empty flat. There was no point even trying the fridge for food. She knew there wasn't any. Judith had a strong constitution, she thought. After a whole day in court she was still full of vigour at 11pm, but Constance was desperate to sleep.

She could hear Judith's endorsement ringing in her ears after she had discovered the missing hospital form. 'Well done, Connie.

You did it again.' But she wasn't entirely sure what she had done or where it would lead. She hadn't particularly warmed to Dr Wolf but she had been the one who tried to rein Judith in from her early suspicions that he was hiding something. Now she wished she had supported Judith more at the time.

She knew she should shower, undress, prepare her bag for the following morning, but somehow all those activities seemed like things which could be done just a little later. Before long she was fast asleep, fully-clothed on top of her bed.

The musical chime of her mobile woke her and a shaft of light, squeezing through a chink in the curtains, struck her temple as she reached for her phone. As Constance muttered 'hello' she noticed the time on her clock by the bed. It was already 7:10 – much later than she had expected to rise.

'Is this Miss Constance Lamb?'

'Yes. Who's calling please?'

'My name is Dr Al-azma. I am calling you from Damascus. In Syria. You have been trying to speak to me.'

'I MISS BABA.

'I know. Suzy said he would be home soon but I'm not sure. They think I don't know what's happening.

'I went to Mrs Crane and I asked her just before break. I asked "what's a murderer?" and she said it's someone who kills other people and asked who had been talking to me about things like that. And her face got this red mark, well, on her neck, really.

'No, she is nice but she has this red thing when people ask her things she doesn't want to answer or, like the time when Mr Ingles sat at the back of the class to watch her. He said "just ignore me, children; pretend I'm not here" but then he kept coughing and writing notes on a piece of paper, and poor Mrs Crane had these red spots everywhere by the time he left.

'So then I told her. I said "Mikey Ingram says my dad's a murderer".

'She went all funny. She crouched down and put her arm around me and said "it'll be all right" and then her eyes went all blurry. Then she said "you shouldn't always listen to Mikey".

'No. I asked Suzy this afternoon on the way home. She said that Daddy had been taken away by the police to Hampstead. So I said "I know that. I saw the car. And the police messed up my room." But that was months ago. I asked her if he had a new job with the police. Was that why he couldn't come home? She said "no". So I asked if he still had his old job and she said "I think so". Then she said that if I didn't tell Mum she would show me Daddy on the television.

'Yes. It's like he's really famous. He's in this great big room with lots of important people. He was on the news, just for a second. Baba always liked watching the news. I know because he liked to talk about it. He must be excited now that he's on it. He didn't do any talking though. There was a man sitting at the front with funny white curly hair. Suzy says he's the judge. Says he will decide if Baba can come home or not.

'Baba looked really sad though. I went up and touched the television screen. He couldn't see me of course. No, silly.

'She said if he's on the news tomorrow, I can see him again but I mustn't tell Mum.

'No. I don't know. I just wish he could come home.'

48

THE PROSECUTION called Dr Jason Lewis, consultant pathologist, to opine on Mrs Hennessy's death. He confirmed the cause of death was catastrophic head injuries sustained on impact with the ground, although Mrs Hennessy had also sustained a broken neck and three broken ribs. The nature of the injuries and the position of the body were also consistent with a fall from the eleventh-floor fire escape. And, tellingly, her fingerprints had been found on the railing on the eleventh floor too.

He mentioned the wound to Mrs Hennessy's foot from the operation, which had been neatly closed, he commented that she was light, around seven-and-a-half stone, and that there were very few reported cases of people surviving a drop of such magnitude. He would expect most people to die from such a fall.

Dr Lewis accepted he had originally given the police a window for time of death of between 7pm and midnight on Thursday the 11th of May, but he was adamant that this was very much 'finger in the air'; the conventional wisdom of measuring changes in body temperature had been largely discredited recently. It was much better to find other corroborating evidence to assist with time of death.

Andy Chambers began with the fingerprint evidence and continued with the small but crucial matter of Ahmad's hair on Mrs Hennessy's nightdress.

'As I've set out in my report, a single hair from the head of Mr Qabbani was found attached to the second button of Mrs Hennessy's nightgown,' Dr Lewis confirmed.

'When you say second button, can you indicate where that was on her person?'

Dr Lewis pointed to an area just below his neck. 'Her buttons began at the neck so around here.'

'And how was it attached?'

'It was wound around the button twice.'

'If Mr Qabbani had simply been cleaning in Mrs Hennessy's room and had not approached her, is there any way the hair could have attached itself to her nightgown?'

'No. He would have had to interact with her, touch her, come very close to her at least.'

'Were there any other hairs attached to any of the other buttons?'

'No.'

'Any DNA of any other person found on Mrs Hennessy's nightgown?'

'No.'

'Thank you. That's very clear. Let's move on to the part of your expert report which comments on Mrs Hennessy's body as it was found, outside the hospital. Tell us what you determined from the position of Mrs Hennessy's body on the ground?'

'Mrs Hennessy was lying on her stomach. Although she had landed on soft ground on top of leaves which had cushioned her fall to a significant degree, her head had struck a large and jagged tree-stump, resulting in a very serious head and brain injury.'

'She would have died instantly.'

'Yes. And in terms of her position, she was lying traverse to the building at a distance of 8.5 metres from the base.'

'And can you glean anything useful from her position?'

'It's extremely unlikely that she jumped.'

'Why do you say that?'

'If she had jumped she would almost certainly have been twelve or thirteen metres from the building.'

'I see. And can you say anything about how she fell?'

'In my view, it's more likely than not that she was pushed from behind or from the side, rather than falling backwards, say, overbalancing, over the railing.'

'Can you explain that please, doctor?'

'Yes. When a person falls backwards, the body is bent in an unnatural way, and it resists and, even in mid-air, tries to correct it by leaning forwards. That tends to mean the body landing far closer to the building. I would have expected around six to seven metres away from the building only. I should add that if a person were flung off a building of that height – I mean picked up by their wrists and ankles and swung off – then we would be back at the twelve or thirteen metre mark.'

'So, to summarise, Ahmad Qabbani's fingerprints were on the door leading out onto the fire escape, Mrs Hennessy's prints were on the railing, which is the place from which she almost certainly fell, there must have been some kind of physical interaction, most likely, contact, between Mrs Hennessy and Mr Qabbani for his hair to have attached to her nightgown, Mrs Hennessy most likely fell forwards or sideways over the railing (that is, was pushed from behind or from the side) and it is unlikely she jumped?'

'That's a fair summary of my evidence, yes.'

'Thank you. No further questions.'

'Dr Lewis. Can you tell the members of the jury what qualifications you hold please?' Judith showed her teeth in the breadth of her smile.

'Yes, certainly. I am MBBChir (that's my medical and surgery degree), I have an MA, then MRCP (that's membership of the Royal College of Physicians), MD, DMJ, FFFLM (that is the faculty of forensic and legal medicine), MCB, FFSoc, FRC (Path) which is my fellowship of the Royal College of Pathology.'

'And how many years have you been a pathologist?'

'Twenty-one.'

'And in how many cases have you appeared as an expert?'

'Too numerous to count. Because I'm a home office pathologist, I've been in court at least once a week almost every week for the last eighteen years.'

Chambers frowned. He was confused as to why Judith would want to celebrate Dr Lewis' qualifications.

'Very impressive credentials. I imagine that's more than anyone else in this courtroom bar his honour. Your evidence in your report is that there were no marks on Mrs Hennessy's body other than those from impact.'

'Yes, but I need to qualify that statement, as I did in my report. Mrs Hennessy's head injury was very significant, the skull was smashed and she suffered broken ribs. My view is that the damage to her head and brain and the bruising on her abdomen was caused on landing, but I can't absolutely rule out the small possibility of Mrs Hennessy having sustained either a head injury or a chest injury before she fell.'

'Because the injuries caused by the fall were so substantial, you mean?'

'Yes, they would mask anything less severe suffered before the fall.'

'But there is no specific evidence of Mrs Hennessy having been injured before she fell?'

'No. So there was no blood in her room, on the railing or in the corridor and there was no implement recovered at the scene which might have been used to inflict any injuries on her.'

'Which is why you feel confident in your analysis that her death was caused by the impact from the fall?'

'As confident as I can be, yes.'

'You have mentioned in your report that her limbs were largely intact?'

'Yes. I was initially surprised, but after further consideration I believe that was because of the softness of the ground she fell upon – earth and leaves – although she had some very light marks on her left forearm. Very tiny, reminiscent of fingertip pressure.'

'All right. We'll come on to those later. Isn't the absence of more substantial evidence of force on Mrs Hennessy's limbs rather strange?'

'Well, how strange?'

'If my client had, for example, manhandled Mrs Hennessy, dragged her along the corridor, or carried her roughly, would this have been reflected somehow on her limbs? Might there have been more significant marks around her arms?'

Dr Lewis paused.

'I am merely commenting on the cause of death but, to assist the court, if a violent struggle of some kind had taken place between your client and Mrs Hennessy then I would have expected more and different marks on her arms, yes.'

'Heavier marks than the ones you have noted?'

'Yes.'

'What kind of heavier marks?'

'Bruising on her arms, as you say, from Mr Qabbani's fingers, if he had, indeed, dragged her or carried her, consistent with a hand being closed around the arm or the wrist. But that may not have happened. She might have gone with your client willingly.'

'If she did not, so if Mrs Hennessy were trying to resist my client leading her along the corridor in some way, would you be surprised to see no further marks on her limbs?'

'If you put it that way, yes. The absence of marks on Mrs Hennessy's limbs, of any evidence of bruising, apart from the very tiny spots I identified, is inconsistent with Mrs Hennessy being forced against her will to accompany your client down the corridor. But if you read later on in my report – I believe it's page twenty-one – I mention, like I said, those faint marks on Mrs Hennessy's left forearm.'

Chambers grinned smugly. Judith had almost escaped earlier, but with her persistence now, she had fallen right into that one.

'All right. Tell me about those marks,' Judith said.

'They are faint and, as I explained in my report, they would be consistent with someone facing Mrs Hennessy and pushing her with his or her right hand, but not with great force.'

'That's very interesting. Perhaps if your honour would permit, I could ask my instructing solicitor, Miss Lamb, to approach you and you could demonstrate.'

'Certainly.'

Constance rose slowly and her hand went immediately to her hair. Judith had warned her of this line of cross-examination and her potential role but, even so, she felt the heat of the attention of so many people. She saved her document on her laptop, half-closed it and stepped out from behind the low table. She walked up to Dr Lewis, who descended from the witness box. First, he gripped Constance around her wrists and then moved his hands to her arms just above the elbow.

'There were no marks consistent with Mrs Hennessy being held like this or like this. And if she had been held around the waist like so,' – thankfully, he simply made as if to circle Constance's waist with his arms – 'then I would have expected some bruising to the waist. But there were the prints of three fingers here, on Mrs Hennessy's forearm.' He pressed the fingers of his right hand up against Constance's left arm, near the top. 'If Mrs Hennessy had been facing your client, those might have been sustained from pressure. A push for example.'

'Dr Lewis, is it correct that older people bruise more easily than younger people?'

'On the whole, yes. Older skin is thinner and has less collagen, which keeps skin supple. And the blood vessels of older people tend to be weaker, so a bump can lead to it leaking out into surrounding tissue. That's what causes a bruise.'

'I see,' Judith murmured sagely, pretending that Dr Lewis was educating her, too. 'And what kind of pressure might have left this sort of light, faint mark?'

'I accept that a very small amount of pressure could have caused this level of bruising in a person of Mrs Hennessy's age. The marks were very faint.'

'Dr Lewis, do you know how blood pressure is routinely

measured?'

'Yes, of course.'

'Dr Wolf testified earlier that Mrs Hennessy's blood pressure was taken a number of times during her stay. She was right-handed. Her notes record that her left arm was used for the tests.'

'Yes.'

'Can I hand up a blood pressure kit, please your honour? And Miss Lamb, please can you remain there for a moment?'

Constance's mouth was set fast.

'Dr Lewis, can you wrap the rubber tourniquet around Miss Lamb's arm, please? Slowly. There's no need to inflate it.'

Dr Lewis shrugged. He understood already where this was leading.

'Now, as you place the cuff on Miss Lamb's arm, do you apply pressure?'

'Yes.'

'With your fingers, around the place where you saw the marks on Mrs Hennessy's arm?'

'Yes.'

'Would you say, given Mrs Hennessy's age and the condition of her skin, that those faint marks you mentioned could have been caused by any one of her blood pressure tests, rather than by someone pushing her over the fire escape?'

'I have to accept that's possible, yes.'

'Thank you. Miss Lamb. I don't need your assistance any further.'

Constance shuffled back to her seat, unwrapping the rubberised sleeve as she went.

'Dr Lewis. My learned friend asked you about time of death and you talked about other "corroborating factors" assisting you, rather than things you can measure, like body temperature. Can you explain what you mean by that?'

'Yes, simple things really. I had given a very provisional earliest time of death as 7pm. But Dr Wolf, I understand, said he visited Mrs Hennessy around seven. So clearly she was still alive then.'

'I see.'

'Also fingerprint evidence. Mrs Hennessy's fingerprints were found in one place only, on the eleventh-floor railing. Now you would expect fingerprints to be washed away by rain. It had rained that day in the afternoon and the railing might well have stayed wet until around six or 7pm. So, again, that gives us an indication that she was there after 7pm. We can't be certain but it's likely.'

'What about this theory you propound in your report about the position of Mrs Hennessy's body being evidence of what happened before she fell? You helpfully cited the research you used in your bibliography.'

'Mrs Hennessy was found 8.5 metres from the foot of the building. Research has been undertaken in Japan – I cited the paper in my report – which lends support for the fact that the distance and position of the body reveals a lot about whether a person fell or jumped. Based on the Japanese research, Mrs Hennessy definitely didn't jump from the railings.'

'And why is that?'

'As I told Mr Chambers, when most people jump, their bodies are carried forwards, away from the building. A jump from this height would have most likely left her body at twelve to thirteen metres away.'

'Can you show us with your hand, please, how high the railing is on that eleventh floor?'

'Yes, up to around here.' Dr Lewis indicated a height around mid-thigh.

'That is a fairly low railing, wouldn't you say?'

'Yes, for that height off the ground, but I have seen similar in other large buildings.'

'Sort of fingertip height?'

'Yes.'

'Now, let's leave to one side for now the possibility of Mrs Hennessy having climbed up onto the top of that low railing and leaped off, which, you say, would have left her body, probably twelve or thirteen metres away.'

'Yes.'

'And she had had the surgery on her foot, of course. If, instead, she stood behind the railing and allowed herself to fall forwards, then, do you accept that 8.5 metres would be within the range of where she would fall?'

'Yes. I accept that I can't distinguish from the position of the body whether she was pushed over the railing or fell over herself, but, like I said, I am almost certain she did not stand up on the railing and actively jump.'

'Thank you. And you also said that a person falling backwards,' – at this point Judith turned her back on Dr Lewis and leaned back over her lectern – 'like so, tries to counter the fall and so ends up closer. You estimated six to seven metres I think.'

'Yes.'

'Were the people who carried out this research professors?'

'No. They were research students, but they already had undergraduate qualifications and they were following on from other research by more senior professors.'

'But it's fair to say that they, themselves, were inexperienced?'

'Yes. Although the description they give of the way they set up their experiments is sound.'

'Hmm. How many subjects did they use?'

'Ten.'

'Men and women?'

'Yes.'

'And the research involved those subjects either jumping, falling or being pushed off a building which was nearly four metres high, I read. That's around thirteen feet. And then they extrapolated those results to make assumptions about higher buildings?'

'Yes. They filmed the subjects falling so they could make projections about the trajectory.'

'And the subjects were recorded jumping with one and two feet, falling and being pushed forwards and backwards in different ways?'

'Yes.'

'How old were the subjects?'

'They were all aged between nineteen and twenty-two.'

'Ah. The eagerness of the young. Even so, I understand some of them refused to undertake some of the exercises.'

'Yes that's right.'

'Why was that?'

'They were frightened.'

'Understandably so. But, Dr Lewis, this is all very interesting as an academic exercise, but you have so many other factors to consider, don't you? Height, weight, the prevailing wind – and fear, as you just accepted? Are you telling us that in your expert view, many qualifications, twenty-one years of experience, hundreds of court appearances, based on one survey conducted in Japan, by students, on ten young adults, Mrs Hennessy could not possibly have jumped?'

Dr Lewis paused. He had a fantastic reputation, and it probably wasn't worth jeopardising it over this interesting, but largely unaccepted, academic paper. Citing the paper alone would, in any event, give it credence.

'No. I wouldn't go as far as that,' he replied, 'but I would say highly unlikely.'

'Highly unlikely – so, ninety-ten, eighty-twenty?'

Dr Lewis paused again. 'I'd say more like seventy-five percent.'

'Thank you. And is it your expert view, also, that Mrs Hennessy could not possibly have slipped and fallen?'

'No. That I can't say with any certainty. A person falling by accident is more likely, as I said, to try to stop themselves, to resist. In Mrs Hennessy's case if she had overbalanced backwards I would have expected her to be one to two metres closer to the building. But if she had fallen forwards, the position would have been much the same.'

'Thank you. The fingerprints you mentioned – you said only one set of prints on the railing. That's odd, isn't it? If there had been a prolonged struggle on that stairwell, wouldn't you have expected more fingerprints of Mrs Hennessy, gripping on in different places, clinging on for dear life?'

'If there had been a prolonged struggle, there might have been more prints, but we don't know how long any struggle lasted. And I said that the railings had been wet. They were dry when we took the fingerprints but that was ten hours later.'

'So, you found one set of prints, which establishes that Mrs Hennessy was there, but more prints might have been obscured or washed away, so there's really no way of knowing now?'

'Yes.'

'Did you find any prints belonging to Mr Qabbani on the

railings?'

'No.'

'On the door handle leading out onto the fire escape?'

'No.'

'On the door frame or any part of the door leading out onto the fire escape?'

'Yes, his fingerprints were on the panel of the door in various places.'

'As if he had pushed the door open with his hand, rather than turning the handle?'

'Yes. But they were on top of the prints of other people, indicating he had used the door more recently than others.'

'Were attempts made to identify the prints of these other people?'

'I don't know. You would have to ask the police.'

'The DNA evidence. One hair only from my client's head was attached to a button at the front of Mrs Hennessy's nightgown. Is that correct?'

'Yes.'

'Now you told Mr Chambers it could not simply have fallen there from a distance?'

'I am not sure what you mean.'

'If you and I are having a conversation and we are standing close together, would you expect a hair from my head to become attached to your clothing, without us interacting in any way?'

'No, that is unlikely.'

'Thank you. Why do you think that?'

'Well, buttons are generally not very exposed. If a hair were to fall from Mr Qabbani's head I would expect it simply to fall to the ground.'

'Quite. And if there was a tussle of some kind? Both parties moving around, pushing, shoving?'

'Again, it would not be impossible for the hair to have found itself on Mrs Hennessy's nightgown but it is very unlikely.'

'This very unlikely; seventy-five percent again?'

'No, in this case more like your ninety-ten.'

'That's clear. In your expert opinion – twenty-one years, eighteen years of expert testimony, week in week out, all those impressive letters after your name – how might the hair have ended up attached to Mrs Hennessy's nightgown?'

'Well, this is certainly opinion rather than fact.'

'Yes, we all understand that.'

Dr Lewis allowed himself a peek across at Mr Chambers before he answered.

'Mrs Hennessy could have dislodged a hair from Mr Qabbani's head, for example, by gripping onto him, onto the back of his head or neck or onto his shoulder. Then, if shortly afterwards, she touched the buttons on her own nightgown, for example to open them or close them, she might have transferred the hair to the buttons.'

'So if Mr Qabbani had helped her to the bathroom, for example, and she had then taken a shower?'

'It's feasible, yes. I'm not saying that's what happened.'

'If there had been some kind of struggle between the two of them, as the prosecution alleges – although we have already heard that, despite her age it was not sufficient to leave any marks on her arms or legs – if there had been some kind of violent struggle, is it your view that any stray hairs from his head would most likely have fallen to the ground?'

'That's my view, yes.'

Chambers' mouth was open. For a moment he wanted to ask Dr Lewis in court if he was serious in his evidence, given the journey he had embarked upon from the starting point of his expert report. Instead, he composed himself.

'Your honour. We are now approaching the lunchtime break,' he mumbled half-sitting, half-standing. 'I should like a few moments to consult with my instructing solicitor. Would it be possible for us to adjourn now but ask Dr Lewis to be on hand to return after the break if necessary?'

'Dr Lewis. Is that convenient for you?'

'Yes, your honour. I have another engagement at five but otherwise I am happy to assist.'

***

Over the lunchtime break Judith communicated with Chambers and the judge that she wanted to recall Dr Wolf, but he had a full schedule of operations that afternoon, and would not be free till the following day. Chambers confirmed he did not wish to recall Dr Lewis, meaning that it was now the defence's turn to put forward their evidence.

'Miss Burton. You don't appear to have many witnesses. Am I wrong?' the judge asked blandly.

'Your honour. Apart from Dr Wolf's re-examination, I have Dr Atkins, the consultant psychiatrist, and the defendant. I propose to call Dr Atkins next. But only if your honour will permit me to bring in Dr Wolf tomorrow when he is available. That may mean my client's evidence being interrupted to interpose Dr Wolf.'

'That's a bit irregular,' Andy Chambers chimed in.

'I should prefer Miss Burton to complete the cross-examination of Dr Wolf now, too, but we should not interfere with Dr Wolf's operating schedule for a second day and it would be unsatisfactory to waste court time. Go ahead Miss Burton. We'll hear from Dr Atkins, then your client, and interpose Dr Wolf when you can.'

***

Brian Bateman was also busy that lunchtime. He had relinquished his place in court for an hour or so to stand a safe distance away from the Mill Hill BMW garage over which Joe Hennessy presided. He saw three men arrive in a black Audi and march in. He waited for the shouting.

On his way there, he posted a carefully worded letter addressed to Indis insurance company. In it, he described the wide range of physical activities he had seen Peter Jones performing recently, without any apparent discomfort, including carrying his mother-in-law's coffin and digging the earth around his mother-in-law's grave. He did feel a momentary pang of guilt about ruining things for Tracy, but then he fortified himself by the memory of how she had urged him to forgive her errant brother, despite his obvious deception. And the impression she had given of her mother when she gave her evidence yesterday, of some confused and dependent old woman, was demeaning to Barbara's memory.

49

DR ATKINS had made it clear to Judith that his giving evidence at the trial would be conditional on the video of Ahmad's 'episode' at the railway station being shown in full before he spoke. Judith and Constance had discussed this at some length; the film was awful, for a start. Ahmad appeared to go into a trance, and at various stages he quivered, muttered, stamped and clenched and unclenched his fists. It was not easy watching and, at best, it made Ahmad appear strange and confused.

'My duty is to the court,' Dr Atkins had pontificated, 'not to your client. But his behaviour is not extreme and is easily explicable. And if you don't show the whole of the film, your opponent will.'

Judith accepted that the latter was a valid point. They would not be able to stop the video being shown; *why on earth had Ahmad chosen such a public place for his show of emotion?* And better to be open about it, than allow the inference to be drawn that he had something to hide. Even so, when blown up large on the screens in the courtroom, it made for uncomfortable viewing.

'Dr Atkins. Given your extensive experience as a psychiatrist specialising in trauma, can you tell the court your observations when you watch the video we have just seen, please?' Judith began slowly.

'Yes, thank you. I see Ahmad Qabbani step off the train at 5:52pm. I note he appears distracted, he walks stiffly, checks around him as if he is disorientated and then, when he sits down on the bench, it's as if he finds it there for the first time. So my first conclusion – tentative – is that whatever is going on in Mr Qabbani's mind, the process has begun on the train. Something is bothering him before he pulls in to his home station. He is sufficiently in control to recognise his station, exit the train, but then he becomes confused, overwhelmed by other thoughts – most likely traumatic memories – and his vision of what is actually going on outside recedes.'

'You mean he starts to see a memory and not what is actually around him?'

'Yes. Then, at first, he sits very still on the bench. This is common in a person who is starting to regress, to go back to that memory. He is allowing himself to be immersed in the memory.'

'What do you mean by "allowing himself"?'

'People who have suffered trauma in the past, sometimes they can't prevent the thoughts coming into their head but sometimes they can. It's rather like if you have a very sweet tooth and you stand in front of a kiosk selling chocolate. You can tell yourself that you don't like chocolate, you don't need it, you shouldn't have it, or you can just allow the craving to take over – you don't fight it, you succumb.'

'So Ahmad succumbs to a traumatic memory and becomes very still?'

'Yes. The first stage is the stillness, and if you note, he's not just still, his whole body stiffens, becomes rigid; he's like a statue. Then we see his lips move and hear a sound. I understand the police tried very hard to work out what he was saying by slowing things down, but they came up only with the sound 'Sh' or 'Sha.'

'Could it be his wife's name, Aisha?'

Ahmad inhaled loudly on hearing his wife's name being called out.

'It could be, yes,' Dr Atkins continued. 'Then we see Ahmad stamp his feet, apparently with some difficulty, the feet appear heavy, he moves his fingers, then his hands, then his arms and finally he loosens up his shoulders and neck.'

'And what is happening there, in your expert opinion?'

'It is hard to say but I believe he has made a conscious decision to extract himself from the memory, or it is beginning to fade. Either way, he is returning to the present, and his movements are to stimulate himself to start to move and to begin to live in the present again.'

'What would be happening to Ahmad, physiologically, during this time?'

'Interestingly, although he appears still, his pulse is likely to be racing. He would be feeling panicky, the kind of feeling you get in a time of extreme anxiety. We can't see from the film but he would probably perspire and this episode was relatively short. If it had continued, we might have seen his body start to shake.'

'Dr Atkins. This behaviour appears strange, even frightening to some people. Should we be scared?'

'Not necessarily. I have seen many patients who have suffered, and who experience these kinds of episodes from time to time. I don't often have the opportunity of watching them on camera, but what we see here is usually just what they describe. It's fairly normal for someone with PTSD.'

'In your opinion, does this behaviour mean that my client is dangerous in any way?'

'No. The fact that he has suffered this episode, in itself, is not an indication that he is a dangerous person.'

Andy Chambers raised his left eyebrow in Judith's direction as he prepared to cross-examine Dr Atkins. Judith linked her fingers beneath her gown and told herself that, however badly the next half an hour went, things could still be resurrected.

'Dr Atkins. How many patients with PTSD have you examined?' Chambers asked.

'Probably around a hundred and fifty.'

'You visit soldiers in the main?'

'Yes I do, those still serving and those who have been released because of PTSD or similar. I do also see some civilians.'

'I've heard your evidence that having these kind of flashbacks does not necessarily make a person dangerous but isn't it often the case that the very reason people have these horrific memories is because they have been exposed to awful, terrible things?'

'That is generalising; for some people a single life event, the death of a parent, for example, can prove as a catalyst, for others, it might be months of living in a war zone. But, essentially, yes.'

'So the person suffering from PTSD is necessarily hardened to horrible events, has probably witnessed a lot of death and suffering?'

'I would say possibly rather than probably.'

'And when a person gets hardened to horrible events, they start to lose perspective and find it hard to know what is right and what is wrong?'

'Sometimes.'

'And rather than the memories express themselves in the way

we saw with the defendant on this occasion, where he was wrapped up in his thoughts, can sufferers strike out at other people?'

'Again, it can happen.'

'What brings on these episodes?'

'Usually, there's a trigger. So, the sufferer is reminded by a noise or a smell or a flash of light of whatever the traumatic event was. Alternatively, simply being under pressure, more generally, being anxious for an unconnected reason can light the fuse.'

'Would throwing someone off a building be a potential trigger for an episode like this?'

'Objection, your honour.' Judith was pink with indignation. 'How can Dr Atkins possibly answer that question?'

'I don't agree, Ms Burton,' Judge Seymour interrupted. 'That's just the question he needs to answer. Dr Atkins?'

Dr Atkins stared at Ahmad who raised his head slowly, his eyes large and mournful.

'I need to answer this question carefully, as I appreciate its significance,' he began. 'Yes, a violent, physical act, like the one you describe, could trigger this kind of episode. However, lots of other activities or activators – as I said, familiar smells, sounds – could have the same impact. Or the stress of being questioned by the police.'

'How often do sufferers have these flashbacks?'

'It varies from person to person. I can't generalise.'

'You asked the defendant about this?'

'Yes, I did.'

'And what did he say?'

'He said he had no memory of it happening or of what the trigger was, which is quite normal, I have to say.'

'In your opinion, is the defendant suffering from PTSD?'

Dr Atkins laughed amiably. 'Normally, I could answer that question with confidence, as I would know what trauma the patient had suffered. He or she would be willing to tell me or we would try a route like hypnosis to find the underlying cause.'

'But you have been unable to do this with the defendant?'

'No. He refuses to talk about his previous history and he also refused to undergo hypnosis. I am not allowed to force him.'

'Is it possible that the reason he refused is because this PTSD diagnosis is convenient and, in his case, there is no trauma at all? He's worried that if you hypnotise him you'll find that out?'

'Yes. But he didn't know anyone was watching in the station, I assume, so it would be an unusual thing to do, to fake an attack like that.'

'I note you said "unusual" rather than "impossible". A person who had read about PTSD or even been with other sufferers could mimic the symptoms?'

'Yes. I suppose they could.'

'And then wouldn't it be rather convenient to say that you've blacked out? Mr Qabbani could say that, if he killed Mrs Hennessy, it was in this trance-like condition and that he had no memory of it.'

Judith half rose but Judge Seymour was on the ball.

'Dr Atkins you don't have to answer that. Mr Chambers, the defendant is not pleading any kind of diminished responsibility, and you know that. If he changes his plea later on I will allow this line of questioning, but not now.'

'Yes, your honour. Again, you told Ms Burton that Mr Qabbani was not necessarily a dangerous person, just because he may, if we believe this behaviour caught on video to be genuine, suffer flashbacks.'

'Yes, that's right.'

'But some people do commit crimes while in these detached states, don't they?'

'Yes, they do.'

'Might Mr Qabbani, an otherwise courteous person, have committed a violent act, that is, dragged Mrs Hennessy along the corridor and flung her over the railing, while in a trance like this and had no memory of it afterwards?'

'It is not impossible,' Dr Atkins began, 'but what I see when I watch the video is Mr Qabbani's body become stiff and rigid. While he is reliving his experience, whatever it may be, he appears unable to move. It is only as he is revived and returns to the real world that he can move freely again.'

Judith congratulated herself. Chambers had gone too far. The impression he had created when he conjured up an image of Ahmad being battle-hardened had been his high point. Now he had confused things by bringing forward other possibilities. Chambers knew this himself, knew he had asked one question too many. But he had more tricks up his sleeve.

'Last question, Dr Atkins. We have heard that Mr Qabbani has a young daughter, aged nine. Do you think it is safe to leave his daughter in his care, given these flashbacks? Surely Social Services should be alerted immediately.'

Ahmad sprang up in the dock and banged his fists down loudly against the wood.

'No,' he yelled angrily. 'No one is taking my daughter away.'

By the time Ahmad had calmed himself and sat down, Dr Atkins' response had become irrelevant. Now Chambers smirked sideways at Judith.

'No further questions, thank you.'

50

AHMAD QABBANI took the stand at 2:30pm, blinking heavily. His chest heaved up and down as he struggled to maintain his composure. Constance peered out from behind Judith to give him reassurance but, even so, she could see how anxious he was.

'Ahmad. Your first language is not English.'

'No. I speak Arabic first.'

'Do you feel able to speak to this court without an interpreter?'

'Yes. I understand you. I may not be able to choose my words so beautifully, but I think that you all will be able to understand me too.'

'Thank you.'

'How old are you?'

'Thirty-two years old.'

'And you have a wife and family?'

'I have a wife and daughter yes.'

'And where are you from?'

'From Syria.'

'How long have you been in England?'

'Three years.'

'And why did you come to England?'

'Our home was destroyed. We were lucky to escape.'

'And your job is cleaning at St Marks Hospital?'

'I've been there two years.'

'Do you enjoy it?'

'I like the people. I work hard.'

'Tell us about Mrs Hennessy.'

'I met Mrs Hennessy the first day she came in. It was a Tuesday. She had been told there might be some delay in her operation.'

'And was Mrs Hennessy unhappy about that?'

Ahmad thought back. He could see Barbara's face vividly before him.

'Hello,' Mrs Hennessy had called out tunefully, perched on the corner of the bed, her feet dangling limply, her hair glaringly orange, a lime green shawl draped around her shoulders. 'Who are you?'

'I'm Ahmad,' he had replied, closing the door behind him. 'I come to clean your room.'

'Well, Ahmad, you're going to need to entertain me, I'm afraid. I can't have my operation today and they've just told me that I may not have my operation tomorrow. They're going to starve me, just in case, of course. But then I'll have to wait and see. What do you think to all that?'

'It's not so bad here,' he had ventured, and she had glanced left and right, taking in the limited capacity for fun presented by the sparsely furnished room.

'Do you know, I didn't even bring a magazine. Thought I'd just be in and out. No time even to make a shopping list.'

Then he had realised he was just standing there with his bucket and mop.

'It looks quite clean in here,' she had said to him. 'Perhaps we could just have a chat instead. I mean. I wouldn't want to keep you from another job but, I won't tell if you won't.'

'She was cross she had to wait. She hadn't brought anything to read,' Ahmad told the hushed court.

'That's how *The Arabian Nights* ended up next to her bed?'

Ahmad opened his mouth and closed it. That bit was also not straightforward, as Judith knew.

'I'm Barbara,' she had said next and stuck out her hand. Ahmad had never had any patient shake his hand on a first encounter; only one or two on leaving.

'What does Ahmad mean?' she had continued, tilting her head to one side.

'It means "much praise",' Ahmad had replied.

'That's it!' Barbara had declared excitedly, as if it had been on the tip of her tongue all along. 'I'll make sure I remember next time. So lovely these names with old and deep meanings. Barbara means "traveller from a foreign land" which clearly I'm not, having lived most of my life within five miles of here. And I doubt my parents had a clue about that when they christened me. There were two other Barbaras in my class at school. But that was OK. I didn't want to be unusual, then. And later on, well I couldn't cope with taking on a new name – you know, a stage name – as some artistes do.'

Ahmad had agreed, although he knew nothing of celebrities adopting new names.

'I've never been a great one for reading,' she confessed. 'I get bored so easily. And when I'm at home there are so many other things to do. Do you have a garden?'

'Yes, I have.'

Ahmad thought of the bare scrubland at the back of his house which could pass for a garden, if only he or Aisha would tend to it.

'And do you grow lots of lovely fruit and veg, or is it all flowers?'

Ahmad gulped. He opened his hands wide, dropped his mop which fell with a clatter and picked it up hurriedly. 'I don't have time.'

'No, of course you don't. How silly of me. It's just that I so miss a garden. When I was married we had a lovely garden. Now, I do have a little terrace, so that keeps me happy pottering around. But it is so very time-consuming. Have you read anything interesting recently?'

'I…I read to my daughter when I get home sometimes.' Ahmad felt the need to say something to show that he was not entirely ignorant.

'That's nice. How old is she?'

'She's nine.'

'Have you read "Aladdin"?' Barbara had suddenly asked.

Ahmad looked straight at the jury.

'She, Mrs Hennessy. She asked me if I knew the story "Aladdin",' he said. 'And she said she wanted the book with the story of Aladdin and the other stories. The one thousand nights and one night.'

'She asked you to buy it for her, the book?'

'Yes, I told you, Miss Burton. I went in my lunch break. She paid me £12.99.'

'So it wasn't your book, that you gave to her?'

'No.' Ahmad was confused. 'Who said it was?'

Judith allowed Ahmad's comments to sink in.

'We'll come back to the book soon. I want to get an overview first, if possible, of your relationship with Mrs Hennessy.'

'Yes.'

'So, you first met on Tuesday the 9th of May, the day she was admitted to the hospital?'

'Yes.'

'And on that day, you had a chat?'

'Yes.'

'Did you clean her room the next day, Wednesday?'

'No. Maia, the other cleaner, she cleaned, but I did in the corridor. They called me up because someone spilled on the floor.'

'And the Thursday?'

'Yes. She had her operation that day. I cleaned on Thursday.'

'What time of day was it?'

'I saw Mrs Hennessy in the morning, before her operation.'

'Did you speak then?'

It was such a silly question, given Mrs Hennessy's garrulous nature. Mrs Hennessy had knocked on the window pane as he cleaned in the corridor.

'I hope you are not thinking of just passing me by without wishing me luck,' she had said as he opened the door. 'I saw you yesterday and you never came in.' And then she had stumbled and grabbed the door handle.

'Are you all right, Mrs Hennessy?' he had asked with concern.

'Oh yes. I just didn't eat. Third day in a row. And call me Barbara, I told you. Let's hope they do my operation this time or I'll fade away.'

She had hobbled back into her room and got back into bed. Ahmad had followed her.

'Were you planning to clean my room this morning or when I was out?'

'I was going to finish in the corridor, but I can clean now if you

like.'

'I do like. You can cheer me up. My daughter came yesterday but that wasn't much fun. She has money trouble. She thinks I don't know it. And the girl came to clean yesterday, from Romania. Terrible place. Remember Ceausescu. All those orphans.'

Ahmad had shaken his head. 'Maia?'

'Yes. That was her name. You must say goodbye to her for me if I don't see her again.'

'When you go, remember to take all your things with you,' Ahmad had advised her. 'Don't leave anything behind.'

'No, you're so right. And Tracy says I am getting forgetful. Now where did I leave my rings? Oh you know what. I left them in the bathroom again. Can you bring them for me please? It saves me hoisting myself in and out of this wretched bed.'

Ahmad had rested his mop against the wall and entered the bathroom. As Barbara had remembered, two large, gaudy rings had been left lying on the edge of the wash basin. One was gold in colour with a large green stone, the size of an olive. The other was also gold, made up of many strands wound into a gigantic knot, with tiny glittering chips. She accepted the rings with a nostalgic grin and held the green one up to the light.

'It's real you know,' Barbara had declared knowledgeably. 'My husband, my ex-husband I should say, bought it for me for our engagement, from Zimbabwe. I didn't wear it much then. You can't when you're busy with children, can you? But now I rather like to; it shines so gloriously and I didn't want to leave it at home, you see. In case I got burgled.'

Ahmad remembered now how he had cautioned her.

'You should give it to your daughter when she comes. It could become lost in here.'

'Tracy? Yes, she said that too. But I'm not letting her have my ring. She'd have it down the pawn shop before I was even halfway home. But anyway, she's not coming till I go home now so I don't have any choice.'

Ahmad hadn't understood the term 'pawn shop' but he had a fair idea what Mrs Hennessy meant.

'And this one was from my mother.' She surveyed the second ring with pride, turning it over and over on the palm of her hand. 'She told me that my father bought it for her when I was born. But I'm not sure that's true. I think she told me that because she thought I would like the story. It's funny, isn't it? When you're very young and when you're very old, people tell you things they think you want to hear.'

Ahmad had nodded non-committally. He liked Mrs Hennessy but he couldn't contribute much to this sentimental conversation.

'No. I should put them away, though where I'm not sure. I can't remember where I had them before. Perhaps in my wash bag. Oh yes. I could try my purse, I suppose. It's as good a place as any. Just pass it to me, Ahmad. It's down in that cabinet.'

Ahmad had walked around the bed and fished around among Mrs Hennessy's things in the bedside cabinet before locating a sparkling, beaded wallet.

'Yes, that's it. Fabulous isn't it? Nothing boring or black or leather for me, eh? Although I'll let you into a secret, it's completely worthless. It's a trick a very attractive actress friend of mine taught me years ago. If you have style you can carry anything off, even the cheapest accessories. Are you married, Ahmad?'

'Yes I am.'

'Oh yes. I know I've asked you that before. And you told me. Your wife is called Aisha. Did I remember right?'

'Yes. That's correct.'

'But, damn. You told me what her name meant and I've forgotten. Don't tell me. Just give me a second. No. It's gone.'

Ahmad had crouched down and picked up a discarded tissue in his gloved hand.

'Where was I, before I started rambling about names? Oh yes. So, make sure if you do nothing else that you buy your wife one really special piece of jewellery, like Miles did for me. You see, he left me almost forty years ago and I still have the ring. I'm not saying it has to be something quite as elaborate as this,' she waved the green ring around in the air, 'but something stylish, something really dazzling. Everyone likes to be dazzled once in a while.'

And she beamed so broadly at Ahmad he thought her face would crack in two. He thought for a moment of Aisha sitting quietly at home staring into nothing, her hands devoid of rings, folded neatly on her lap. They had sold everything in order to fund their journey to England, and when they had reached the streets paved with gold, there had been far higher priorities for their limited income than jewellery, however special it might make Aisha feel.

But as he gritted his teeth and entered the bathroom, grabbing the toilet brush and moving it in a clockwise motion around the toilet bowl, he decided Mrs Hennessy had a point, even though she had made it in a thoughtless way. Everyone, however impoverished, needed something bright and shiny to gaze at and treasure. It would be Aisha's birthday next week. He always remembered but it had been impossible to take pleasure in anything for so long. Perhaps now it was time to have a celebration, just a small one. And to treat his wife to something special, as Mrs Hennessy had said.

'Yes, we spoke. She asked me to bring her rings from the bathroom where she had left them,' Ahmad told Judith in the voice of someone recounting a distant memory.

'Those are the rings which you are accused of stealing?' Judith asked.

'Yes.'

'What did you do with the rings?'

'She had a purse with all bright colours. I put the rings away for her in the purse.'

'Why did you do that?'

'So she wouldn't lose them.'

Chambers snorted under his breath.

'Your honour. We have those two rings here today. Can they be shown to the members of the jury?'

'Yes, thank you Miss Burton.'

'Did you steal Mrs Hennessy's rings?'

'No. Of course not. It would be a terrible thing to steal from anyone, but to steal from someone in a hospital when they are old and sick…' Ahmad's eyes were wide and Judith marvelled at his indignation. He was on trial for murder and he was offended that people thought him guilty of theft.

'Did you see Mrs Hennessy again that day?' Judith asked.

'Listen. Will you drop in and see me later?' Mrs Hennessy had said, as he was packing up to leave. My daughter's not coming today, you see. It'll be nice for me to think of a friendly face for when I wake up.'

Ahmad remembered how confused and bemused he had been. Mrs Hennessy had only met him once two days before and now she was relying on him for support.

'She asked me to return later. She said it would be nice to have someone to talk to, after her operation. But I was busy all day and when I came back in the evening her door was closed.'

'Did you enter her room?'

'No. I thought she was sleeping. And I thought I see her on Friday before she goes home.'

'Let's return, just for a moment, to the book you bought at Mrs Hennessy's direction. *The Arabian Nights*, or as you called it, The Thousand and One Nights, the tales which Scheherazade recounted to King Shahryar night after night to prevent herself from being killed.'

'Yes.'

'Are you familiar with the stories in the book?'

'Well they are magical stories, folk stories, very old. More than a thousand years.'

'Mr Chambers, standing next to me, talked about them being violent stories, with crimes against women in them. Can you comment on that?'

'I didn't read the book, this book. But I know the stories like Aladdin and Ali Baba from when I was a child. They make them into Disney films.'

Judith was momentarily stumped by the answer Ahmad had given. She could not have provided a better illustration of the monstrous nature of this line of attack if she had planned it for a week.

'Your honour, members of the jury, I will accept that some aspects of some of the stories in this version (and there are many different versions) are unpleasant if they are rationalised and scrutinised with a twenty-first century lens. It's certainly not politically correct to take a virgin to your bed every night, deflower her and behead her at dawn. But we gloss over those parts, don't we, and focus instead on magic carpets and genies? We adopt that technique with all great but outdated literature.

'As Ahmad has kindly reminded me, Disney, the paragon of virtue and the purveyor of the 'U' certificate, tells these stories from this book with their drama and colour and noise, tales of bazaars and spices and sea monsters, but without the disembowelling or beheading, so how can we criticise my client for buying a copy for a lady who asked him to do so?

'Moving on, can you tell me any reason why a strand of your hair might have been on Mrs Hennessy's clothes? You heard testimony from Dr Lewis before the break.'

'I am not sure. Maybe when I cleaned in her room.'

Judith paused. Ahmad had just sat through her triumphant and resourceful dismantling of the expert DNA evidence, and this was his response? She tried a new approach to encourage him to expand his answer.

'Was there any time that you touched Mrs Hennessy when you were in her room?'

Ahmad hesitated for a moment before answering. 'On the Thursday morning when I went in to clean.'

'Yes?'

Ahmad remembered Mrs Hennessy perfectly in that moment, the slant of her head, the tremble in her sweet voice. He had finished cleaning in the bathroom after he had put her rings away for her and she was still sitting in bed but her eyes were closed. As he tiptoed towards the door she had woken with a start.

'Hello Ahmad,' she said. And then 'Oh damn. I need the bathroom.'

Ahmad had stood nonplussed. 'I will call the nurse for you.'

'I don't think there's time. They take so long. You can help me. I feel so giddy.'

He had remained still, knees slightly bent, undecided about his next move.

'Oh come along, Ahmad. Can't you help an old lady to the bathroom? Otherwise there's going to be an awful mess. I won't tell if you don't.'

And before he could make any decision she had placed her foot on the ground and let out a sharp gasp of pain.

'I won't tell if you don't,' Ahmad mumbled the words to the packed courtroom. Judith coughed to bring him back to the present.

'She asked me to help her to the bathroom,' Ahmad said. 'She said she couldn't wait for the nurse.'

'Did Mrs Hennessy put her arms around your neck when you helped her to the bathroom?'

Ahmad thought hard. He could see Mrs Hennessy trying to put weight on her foot and falling forwards. He had caught her and propped her up and her hands had been around his neck.

'Yes. She fell and I catched her,' he said. 'Then I helped her walk to the bathroom.'

'And what happened then?'

'She said not to wait. So I went back to my work.'

'Did you say goodbye?'

'No.'

'Why not?'

'She was in the bathroom. It was not polite. And I thought I would see her the next day.'

'Did you ever touch Mrs Hennessy's medical notes?'

'Yes. They were in a book by the wash basin. I would clean there.'

'Do you remember moving the notes?'

'Yes. But I often move them – not just for Mrs Hennessy – so I can clean. I put them back afterwards.'

'Do you accept that your fingerprints were found on more than one page of her notes?'

'Yes. She was in the hospital three days. I cleaned two times.'

'Mr Qabbani. What did you do in Syria?'

Silence.

'You weren't a cleaner in Syria?'

'No.'

'Can you tell the court please?'

'It's not important.'

Mr Chambers sprang to his feet.

'For once, your honour, I am agreeing with the defendant. This is completely irrelevant.'

Judith studied Chambers, the angle of his head, the colour of his cheek, the slight breathlessness on delivery. *Did he know?* she wondered.

'Your honour, some latitude for a moment, please. Ahmad. What was your job in Syria?'

Ahmad's face crumpled and his shoulders sagged. He shook his head from side to side and clamped his mouth shut.

Constance very deliberately tapped Judith on the shoulder and handed her some papers. Judith read through them, raising her eyebrows and held one out at arm's length.

'Your honour, I have a letter before me from a Dr Faisal Al-azma from Damascus University Hospital. It was sent to my instructing solicitor Miss Lamb late last night. Ahmad, tell us all what you did when you lived in Syria.'

Ahmad drew himself up tall, rolled back his shoulders and spoke in a half whisper.

'I was a doctor,' he said.

For the second time in the trial, a loud muttering filled the court, gradually petering out as Judith began to speak again.

'What kind of doctor?'

'I specialised in spinal injuries, paralysis, paraplegics, quadraplegics. I treated a lot of soldiers and others, victims of the war.'

'Your honour, I will need an opportunity to review the letter Ms Burton is waving around,' Chambers said quietly.

'You'll have one, my learned friend. Miss Lamb will provide you with a copy. Your honour, if I may continue, where did you train?'

'I trained in USA for two years, then returned to Damascus where I practised from 2007 to 2014, when I left Syria.'

'Why did you leave?'

'Our house was destroyed. We were lucky to survive. Our quarter was just piles of bricks. Then two of my colleagues were killed at the hospital. I decided I was better use to people if I could stay alive.'

'Did you try to obtain work as a doctor in the UK?'

'Yes.'

'But you couldn't?'

'There were problems. First, they wouldn't accept my qualifications. They said I had to take some tests. Then they said they needed the original certificates. I received them from Damascus after some months. I sent them and they were lost.'

Judge Seymour took note and cleared his throat.

'Mr Qabbani, the government office to which you sent your certificates lost them?'

'Yes, your honour. They had a fire. I was not the only one to lose important documents.'

'So, are they lost for ever?'

'Before they lost the documents I kept saying "I am a doctor. I don't need to do more exams." Then, after they lost them I said "Just let me do the exams". About three months ago I had a letter. They said that because they "could not locate" the documents they were "prepared to accept" that I was a doctor in Syria and they offered me the chance to enrol on a course in London to take the exams. The exams cost £1,100. We don't have £1,100.'

'Would you like to practise as a doctor again?' Judith asked.

Ahmad cleared his throat.

'Being a doctor is not easy. You work hard. You see terrible things, especially in Syria, at the end. But you can help. And when you help there is no better thing on earth to be.'

He wiped his hand across his eyes.

'Would you like a moment to compose yourself?'

'No thank you. I can continue.'

Brian, recently returned from his outing to North West London, shifted awkwardly in his seat at the back.

'When you moved Mrs Hennessy's medical notes, did you ever read them?'

'I did move them to clean, like I said. But sometimes I would read the patients' notes to see what drugs they were prescribed.'

'Did you read Mrs Hennessy's notes?'

'Yes.'

'Why?'

'I was interested to see if British medical practices were the same as ours. And I didn't want to forget things, just in case…'

'And the caution you received in May last year, which Dr Wolf mentioned. Can you tell us about that, please?'

'There was a patient on the private ward. Can I say his name?'

'Yes.'

'He was called Timothy Morrison. He was young, twenty-five years of age. One day I came in to clean his room and he was rolling on the bed from one side to the other side. He was very breathless. I went to him and he held tight to my arm. Then suddenly he let go, his heart stopped, all the monitors stopped. I pressed the emergency button but no one came.'

'What did you do?'

'I pulled away some tubes and I did CPR. No one came for so long. So I carried on. It took two or three minutes but then it was OK. He coughed and he started to breathe.'

'And then what?'

'A nurse came in and said *what should she do?* so I said she must get Dr Wolf. But when Dr Wolf arrived he pushed me away. He said I had "interfered with his patient". He was very angry. Asked me how I knew CPR. I didn't want to say I was a doctor. I didn't want to lose my job. I said I had seen how to do it on an American TV show. I am not sure he believed me. But he told me that this would go on my record, but we had to say *he* saved Mr Morrison in the case report. He said it would stop me from getting into any more trouble.'

Mr Chambers rose with less verve than he had exhibited yesterday.

'Can anyone confirm what you've just told us. Any of it?'

'When he left, Mr Morrison told me he knew I had saved him. I'm sure with the great power of the media you can find him today and ask him. Timothy was his first name.'

Chambers retreated into his seat. Judith glanced theatrically up at the clock, which was showing nearly 3pm.

'Your honour, can we take a break now, please? I understand it may be possible to hear from Dr Wolf again today if we do, rather than tomorrow. He has now finished his schedule for the day. I hope to be quick with him so that we can finish in good time this evening.'

51

DAVID WOLF climbed the steps into the witness box a second time, his forehead a mass of perspiration.

'Dr Wolf, were you in court just before the break?' Judith asked.

'No. I arrived about twenty minutes ago and I waited outside.'

'Thank you. Has Mr Chambers acquainted you with the evidence my client gave just before we adjourned?'

He played with his moustache before answering.

'I know that the defendant says he was a doctor in Syria, if that's what you mean.'

'Yes. Thank you. Did Mr Chambers tell you what Dr Qabbani said about the incident with Timothy Morrison, the cardiac arrest? You told us yesterday that he received a reprimand?'

'Yes he did.'

'Is there anything you would like to add to your evidence of yesterday, by way of clarification?'

'It was some time ago but it is true that your client told me at the time that he had administered CPR. But he wasn't a doctor, I mean, I thought he was a cleaner.'

'You didn't believe him?'

'My priority was to ensure the patient, Mr Morrison, was stabilised. I wasn't focusing too much on what Mr Qabbani may or may not have done.'

'So you did believe him?'

'I was called by a nurse, I came running, I saw Mr Qabbani standing over a patient with lots of his tubes removed, some of his monitors were fine, some were not. I had no idea what had happened.'

'Do you believe now, given that you now know that Ahmad was a qualified doctor in Syria, do you now believe that he saved Mr Morrison's life by administering CPR?'

'I can't say whether he saved the patient's life, but I believe that he may have administered CPR correctly and the man lived, yes.'

'Thank you. There are some documents we located since you gave your evidence yesterday. If you view the screen to your right, you should see the documents to which I am referring.'

'Yes. I will try to be of assistance.'

Judith put up the admission form for Mrs Hennessy, blown up extra-large and took Dr Wolf through the information on the form.

'Can you see that the pages are numbered one to nine at the bottom of each page, but there appears to be no page 7?'

'Yes. You're right. Perhaps it was on the back of page 6 and did not copy.'

'Perhaps.'

Judith brought up the next document.

'This second document is important. This document appears to be a consent form. Can you see that, at the top, it says "consent form"?'

David remained silent, rigid as stone. Constance shuffled noisily behind Judith's back.

'This isn't a trick question, Dr Wolf. Do you agree that this is some kind of consent form?'

'Yes... Yes, you're right... It is,' he stammered.

'Now this form is part of the standard admissions pack at St Marks, which your secretary helpfully provided. You can take my word that when you count through the pages – the various things which the incoming patient must read and sign – this consent form appears at page 7.'

'Yes.' David frowned.

'But, if you recall, Mrs Hennessy didn't have page 7 among her forms.'

'No, she didn't.'

'Can you read out the words in the bottom line of this form?'

'Yes, it says "Aladdin Trial".'

'And now the words in the penultimate line of this consent form, for everyone in court, please.'

'Yes. It says, *I, the undersigned, confirm that I give my doctors permission to use the Aladdin process currently being trialled in addition to or in place of conventional processes, at their absolute discretion.*'

'It seems we have a bit of an *Arabian Nights* theme here, too. What is the "Aladdin process", or the "Aladdin Trial"? Do speak up so we can all hear please.'

David cleared his throat.

'I was confused momentarily when you said there was a missing form. I wouldn't have seen Mrs Hennessy's admissions forms because Dr Mahmood admitted her. But this consent form, page 7, is standard. It allows us either to operate ourselves or to use robotic help. The patient, technically, has to agree to this on admission.'

'Robotic help?' Judith enunciated the words slowly, like a spider playing with its helpless prey.

'Yes. The Trust invested in a machine last year which can help with most surgical procedures.'

'That sounds a little *Brave New World.*'

'Not at all. The technology has been around since 2001, and used in tens of thousands of operations. It has many benefits.'

'Tell me about them.'

'Well, in some cases, it means we can go into a patient through a very small incision, leading to quicker recovery time. Also, in long operations surgeons do suffer from fatigue. The robotic hand is very steady and doesn't tire. Prostate removal is one area where it has been used extensively. It is a very inaccessible part of the body but using a robot we can make much smaller incisions and manipulate the instruments with more ease.'

'What about how quickly the operation is completed?'

David reddened.

'Yes, that too.'

Judith sensed his reticence.

'Are operations performed more quickly with the robot?'

'Usually, yes.'

'And why the name "Aladdin"?'

'That's its name. The first model was called Da Vinci, after the man, because of his knowledge of the human anatomy, I believe.'

'But St Marks doesn't have a Da Vinci?'

'It's very expensive. The latest Da Vinci model costs around £1.5 million. The version we are trialling is from China, more cost-effective and even more advanced.'

'Ah. Hence the name, so nothing to do with magic lamps, then?'

'No, well, some people might think it makes their wishes come true, I suppose.' He attempted a smile which Judith ignored.

'Can you describe for us what this robot looks like?'

'Certainly. It's a big piece of kit in a number of sections. You have one part which holds the instruments. It has a number of arms around a central spine and you can attach the instruments to each of those. There is also a separate…I suppose you would call it a "console". It's the place from which the surgeon can direct Aladdin what to do. But one extra feature which sets Aladdin apart is its ability to constantly monitor the patient during the operation and adjust quantities of various drugs if needed.'

'Do you use Aladdin?'

'Yes.'

'Did you use Aladdin on Mrs Hennessy?'

'Aladdin was used on Mrs Hennessy to manipulate the instruments.'

'Is there any other feature which makes Aladdin more advanced than the previous robot models?'

David paused.

'Can you answer my question, please? I can certainly adjourn to find an expert on your Aladdin machine if you are having difficulty explaining things for me.'

'Aladdin can operate autonomously.'

Judith's eyes widened. 'Autonomously?'

'Yes.'

'You mean, on its own?'

'Yes. Aladdin can be programmed to carry out the operation

with the surgeon on hand, to intervene only if necessary.'

'You say "on hand", so, theoretically, the surgeon could even leave the room and the operation would continue.'

'Yes, that's right.'

'What about other staff?'

'The other theatre staff may be there; clearly it's less crucial, and, in time, their involvement will almost certainly be reduced as well.'

'So with Aladdin you can potentially carry out many more operations with fewer staff?'

'Yes, and as you know, Ms Burton, we are under pressure to cut through our backlog.'

'Is it explained to patients that a robot will do their surgery?'

'Yes. We give them the forms to sign, like the one you asked me to read out. And we explain it's a trial.'

'And are patients happy with that?'

'Almost all patients I have talked to have indicated they are happy to participate. And the results have been extremely favourable. We have patients with quicker recovery times because the surgery is so much less intrusive, leaving same day rather than needing a two or three night stay in hospital and almost always less surrounding tissue or nerve damage, so, essentially, a much better result.'

'Does everyone share your love of the new technology?'

'No.'

'Who doesn't like it?'

'Some doctors are a little reticent; it tends to be the older doctors.'

'Why is that?'

Chambers was half standing to object but Judge Seymour

waved to him to sit down.

'No, Mr Chambers, I want to hear this. Dr Wolf, please answer Ms Burton's question.'

'Some people see Aladdin as usurping the surgeon's expertise. You know, you spend years honing your skills only to find a machine can do things better. But it must be better for patients if that's the case, and that's what's most important.'

'Isn't there a risk that if, for some reason, the equipment malfunctions on a particular day, the surgeon who has relied on it for so long is then on his own, without sufficient practice?'

'It's a risk, but no more than the risk of a human making an error, which does happen from time to time.'

'Can you think of any reason why that form, the form consenting to the use of robotic surgery, the Aladdin Trial form, should have been removed from Mrs Hennessy's files?'

'No. I can't explain that. Sometimes copies of papers do go astray. We're all human.'

'If I told you that the metadata, the trail left on the hospital computer regarding Mrs Hennessy's admission forms, shows you, using your log-in, as the last person to access the forms, one week after Mrs Hennessy died, can you explain that?'

Dr Wolf froze. He stared out blankly across the courtroom. Then he composed himself.

'No, I can't explain that. I can only confirm that I personally had no involvement in deleting the consent form.'

'Just recapping on the evidence you gave yesterday regarding Mrs Hennessy's mobility after her operation…'

'Yes.'

'Given you used Aladdin, is it possible that she had less pain than other patients and conversely was more mobile than those who had the traditional operation?'

'It is possible. I didn't discuss with the physiotherapist how easily she coped with walking when he attended. But every patient is different in terms of pain relief and recovery times, so it's hard to say.'

'But, given your comments about smaller incisions and the like, it is possible?'

'Yes. It is possible that she had less pain than she might have had if Aladdin had not been deployed, and that might have enabled her to walk more freely. That's the best I can say.'

'I see. Thank you, Dr Wolf. No further questions.'

'Ms Burton, given the time, I think we should adjourn now and your client can continue his testimony tomorrow.' Judge Seymour gave his direction with his spectacles clasped in one hand and left the room more quietly than usual, leaving their case behind on the desk.

Andy Chambers leaned over towards Judith as she tidied her papers.

'God, they told me you were the queen of the red herring,' he said, 'but I didn't realise quite how many hours of irrelevant rubbish I was going to have to endure.'

'You're just cross you didn't know about it first.'

'Oh come on, Judith. Unless you are going to find some evidence from China of Aladdin, the robot, going berserk and flinging a dissatisfied patient off a building, this has all been a fascinating but pointless diversion. When we get to the rings, which you have studiously ignored so far, that's when the fun will start. What's your client going to say about those, then?'

'I couldn't possibly divulge.'

'Can I give you a small piece of advice?'

'I suspect you intend to do so with or without my consent.'

'For Mr Qabbani's own good. He should plead guilty to the theft. Otherwise I will turn him into toast on that part of his testimony alone and, once I've done that, the jury are unlikely to see the uncharred version of your client again.'

52

'AM I HOPELESSLY out of date, having concerns about robots conducting surgery, Connie?' Constance and Judith had taken some time to reflect in one of the court break-out rooms.

'He's an experienced doctor and he says it's very good.'

'But it must assume that all patients, all bodies, are the same. And if there's an emergency, time is of the essence, and if the surgeon is elsewhere, it must be more risky.'

'But you balance that against three times as many operations, and a consistently steady hand, even after operating back-to-back. And all those other things he talked about.'

'Yes, you do. Can we use it to our advantage? I don't see how the fact that a robotic arm helped with Mrs Hennessy's operation has any connection with her falling off a building.'

'Is that what Chambers was saying to you at the end?'

'Hmm. Well, essentially, yes. And he's not wrong.'

'Well, there's what you said to Dr Wolf, about her improved mobility?'

'Yes, there is that. It's not my best argument but I can feed it into the mix. Remind me what happened to the physiotherapist?'

'He was Italian; gone back to Italy. The police have tried letters and emails. You told me to prioritise other things.'

'You're right; I did. His departure is a little convenient, perhaps.'

'We did get Wolf's acceptance that Ahmad probably saved Timothy Morrison's life.'

'Yes. That's true. That was good. I'll use that in closing.'

'Although you let him off the hook,' Constance said. Judith raised an eyebrow. 'I'm sorry. I know why you did it, but he lied, didn't he? Not only at the time, but again, in court when it was really important. Or maybe you think you should protect him because he's a doctor?'

'I gave him enough of a hard time with the missing document. And our focus has to be on Ahmad and his defence and how best to conduct it, not totally annihilating Dr Wolf.'

'Do you think Dr Wolf really didn't know who erased the consent form?'

'I have no idea. He appeared genuinely surprised but, as you say, he has not been a wholly candid witness.'

'Were you happy with how it went with Dr Lewis?'

'Yes, on balance I was. I think his evidence supports the possibility of Barbara falling rather than being pushed and we might get the jury to accept the argument about Ahmad's hair. But I think that largely depends on Ahmad and how he stands up to the scrutiny, the pressure and Chambers' no-doubt Rottweiler-like cross-examination.'

'You think Chambers will go in hard?'

'Definitely. Look at how he baited Ahmad about his daughter. He did it on purpose, you know. I could have warned Ahmad it might happen.' Judith bit her lip. 'Ah. Too late now. There is one thing that bothers me though, about Dr Lewis' evidence, but I think it's unhelpful to Ahmad to raise it.'

'What's that?'

'He said there was no blood. Do you remember that?'

'Yes.'

'No blood on the railing, in the staff room, in the corridor.'

'Yes.'

'I don't know how they would have bound up Barbara's foot after her operation, but I can't help thinking that if she had walked down the corridor, leaning on that foot, there would have been some traces of blood, however small. Oh, who knows? They might have cleaned again first thing, before the body was found.'

'Listen, Judith, I want to suggest something you won't like but, well, just hear me out.'

'Ah, I sense a heartfelt emotional plea.'

'Stop it! You think this has all been wrong too, from the very beginning. Can't we do something to redress the balance for Ahmad, not just get him some measly acquittal?'

'Measly acquittal? You mean save him from a life sentence and his family from a life of penury?'

'It's not enough.'

'We're not out of the woods yet. We've had one good day. Seymour is notoriously perverse and...'

'I thought you said he was straightforward.'

'I was trying to be optimistic. And Chambers is clever. I don't want him cross-examining Ahmad. It will be a disaster. It's bad enough me taking him through things.'

'How do you mean?'

'Oh, Connie. You play back today's transcript. He's so earnest, so keen to explain everything. Chambers will chop him up into tiny pieces. We need to stop things before then, if we have enough material to use.'

'Ahmad deserves more,' Constance protested. 'If you won't do it because it's the right thing to do, then just think about Chambers' face.'

'That's a comment unbecoming of you; please retract it.'

'OK, I'm sorry if I suggested that you were motivated by anything other than the desire to help our client. I am, really.'

Judith closed her notepad.

'What are you suggesting we do?'

'We tell the Qabbanis' story in court.'

'We don't even know their story. What if we don't like it once we hear it?'

'We know now Ahmad was a doctor and he had to leave Syria. We put Aisha on the stand. She tells the rest.'

'She can't speak.'

'She can. She just chooses not to. When I was over there the other night I heard her speak; only whispering, but definitely talking. And Shaza let slip that her mother talks to her, sometimes.'

'Ahmad will go berserk. He hyperventilated when her name was mentioned and he would have garrotted Chambers if he could have, when he talked about Social Services.'

'I think you're underestimating Ahmad. He coped when you told everyone he was a doctor. More than that; he rose to the occasion.'

'It's a massive risk. And I'm not sure it's admissible evidence.'

'You can get anything in, Judith, you know you can. And Seymour is interested. You saw his face at the end today. He loved the Aladdin stuff. That's why he let you ask about the forms and about Morrison. He wants to know their story, why Ahmad is the way he is. And I've been doing some research; he's a good judge for defendants. He hates trumped-up cases. He'll help us.'

Judith opened her note book once more.

'I can't do it. It's too risky. We don't know what she'll say or how Ahmad will respond. We stick to the rules and we go for the acquittal.'

'Will you at least think about it, please? I need to head off somewhere for the next hour or so. I'll meet you back at my office at 6:30.'

'Where are you going?'

'I want to talk to Lottie Li again. She's on duty this evening but she says she will see me just before her shift starts.'

'You're wasting your time.'

'I don't think so.'

'OK. Message me if you find anything useful. I'll head downstairs now, before they take Ahmad away for the night.'

53

Tracy had seen Brian leave court just before lunch and return during the afternoon session. She was determined to get his attention this time. She caught him on the steps of the court house at the end of the day.

'Brian! Brian! Wait a minute.'

Brian halted. It would be rude to ignore Tracy, even though he knew it was safer to keep his distance, now he had put various negative events in motion.

'Hello Tracy.'

'Brian. I've left you messages. Didn't you get them?'

'Oh, my damned secretary. She's forgetful sometimes. Funny how the case is going, isn't it?'

'I don't think it's very funny, especially not what we heard today. I just want it to be finished and that man in prison. I don't want to talk about it till that's done. Listen, do you have an hour to spare? I want to take you to Mum's. There's something there you need to see. We could get a taxi now, if you have time.'

Brian was going to refuse but then his curiosity got the better of him. And, at worst, he would get some intelligence on the new lock situation. If only he had brought the diaries with him, he could have tried to return them surreptitiously now.

***

Twenty-five minutes later, Tracy unlocked the door to Barbara's flat.

'There's a surprise here for you,' she said. 'I hope you like it. Come in and see.'

They entered the flat and she led Brian through to the lounge area. There, propped up on the sofa was the portrait Barbara had painted of him. Brian stopped dead in his tracks, then his knees went weak. If the sofa had not been close at hand to prop him up, he might have fallen.

'Pick it up if you like. It is good, isn't it? I've been through the whole lot and I think it's probably her best. You could hang it in your office.'

Brian reached out and stroked the edge of the canvas. The portrait was truly magnificent. He loved it; he loved it almost as much as he had loved Barbara.

'How long do you think it took Barbara to paint?' he asked shakily.

'Days,' Tracy replied, hoping that was the right answer (in reality she had no idea how long her mother had spent on these things, but she suspected they were painted hurriedly, like most things in Barbara's life). 'Or even weeks,' she added.

'Do you really like it?' Brian asked.

'Yes, I really do,' Tracy replied. 'It's a perfect tribute to you and to Mum's skill. She loved to paint with real feeling. She must have felt truly indebted to you for all your hard work. Joe and I, we want you to have it. Barbara would have wanted you to have it. Like I said, it will look lovely in your office. But there's something else too. Wait a minute.'

She rummaged around in the top drawer of the desk and then handed Brian the letter she had found in a shoe box in Barbara's wardrobe.

'This is for you, from Mum. I'll just do some tidying in the bedroom, let you read it on your own,' she said kindly.

Brian held the letter with trembling fingers. He was overwhelmed. Barbara had not only thought about him, she had spent many hours painting him. She might have prepared drafts, sketches in pencil, pen and ink or charcoal, and this was the culmination of hundreds of hours of effort. He had heard it had taken Michelangelo four years of constant work to paint the ceiling of the Sistine Chapel. No one had ever paid him such a compliment.

The letter was short and written in Barbara's erratic, spidery hand.

Dear Brian

> *You have always been such a good friend and I know you might have wanted to be more. I'm not great with men. All the ones I tried to love found me too stifling or inattentive or frivolous or loud. You stayed constant all these years and for that I am eternally grateful. I know that you will look after the interests of my children and grandchildren in the same loyal and unselfish way you have looked after me.*

Take care always

Love
Barbara

When Tracy returned from the bedroom a respectful amount of time later, she found Brian, the portrait and the letter had gone.

54

'LOTTIE. You were so great in court. A real professional,' Constance began, knowing this was how Judith would have done things to butter up a witness, even though she was privately seething at Lottie's change of allegiance.

'Thanks.' Lottie was appreciative in her response, oblivious to the offence she had caused Constance.

'Can I get you a coffee? You must get tired working so late.'

'No. It's OK. I am used to it. I have just a few minutes before I start work.'

'Yes, of course. This will be quick. Shall we sit down over here?'

Lottie and Constance were in the café on the ground floor. It had closed earlier but a machine could be operated manually to buy tea or coffee after hours, in desperate straits.

'Lottie, did someone tell you not to return my calls? I had asked you to be a witness for Ahmad. Do you remember?'

Lottie lowered her eyes.

'I feel very ashamed,' she said, 'but Dr Mahmood, he told me that I should not help Ahmad.'

'Dr Mahmood?'

'Yes. He said not to be a witness for him and not to say we were friends.'

'Is that why Maia, the other cleaner, isn't here too?'

'I don't know. One day she was cleaning, the next day she was gone.'

'Did he explain to you why you shouldn't help Ahmad?'

'He said Ahmad was on trial for murder and the hospital shouldn't get involved in defending him. We should let the police investigate and they would find out what happened.'

'I see.'

'I am sorry but I am not sure I could help so much anyway. Will you tell Ahmad I am sorry?'

'Yes, I will. Listen, one more thing. Judith didn't ask you about Ahmad's family. Of course, it isn't relevant really, but I wanted to know. Did he ever talk about his family?'

'No.'

'He didn't talk to you about parents or brothers and sisters or about his wife, Aisha, not ever?'

'No.' Lottie answered. Then, as if she had suddenly made a decision, she said, 'But his daughter did.'

'You've met his daughter, Shaza?'

'Oh yes. Lots of times.'

Constance swallowed hard.

'But how?'

'He used to bring her, if there was no one to care for her at home.'

'To the hospital?'

'Yes. Maybe seven or eight times. She would come and sit in

the room, you know, the one Mrs Hennessy…the staff room, and do colouring and I braided her hair in my break. She liked that. She said her mum did that too.'

'Why do you think he brought her those times?'

'It could be school holidays, I don't know.'

'Did you ask Shaza why she came?'

'Yes, so she would say *Mum's not well today* and *Suzy* – that's the lady who looks after her – *has to go to work*.'

'Was it allowed?'

'No, but no one said anything. She was a sweet girl.'

'She stayed inside all those hours?'

'Yes. I did say I will take her for a walk in my lunch hour but Ahmad said "no". He was worried she would get lost.'

'When was the last time she was at the hospital?'

'It was around the time Mrs Hennessy died.'

'Would you be able to check exactly which day it was?'

Lottie thought for a moment.

'It was the Thursday, the day of Mrs Hennessy's operation, because I had to do a double shift. I was there early and I didn't finish till late – even later than Ahmad – around ten. But she only stayed a couple of hours. The neighbour, Suzy, came and collected her in the afternoon.'

***

When Judith spoke to Ahmad after the day had ended she found him quiet and sad.

'Did you have anything to tell me, any observations from the day?'

Ahmad did not answer.

'Oh come on. Nothing? I think we had a pretty good day.'

He swallowed noisily.

'OK. I'm sorry I sprung the doctor stuff on you. I should've told you before that we knew. Why did you keep it hidden that you were a doctor anyway?'

'I would have lost my job. No doctor wants another doctor washing their floors, watching what they're doing.'

'They might have helped you get on the course?'

'You've seen them. You really believe that? Listen Miss Burton, I…' Ahmad's eyes filled with tears and his voice quivered.

'What?' Judith was on her guard.

Ahmad's shoulders began to jerk and he lay his head in his beautiful, willowy hands.

'What is it?'

'I was thinking maybe I did it?' he whispered, trying to catch his breath.

'No!' Judith replied, horrified at Ahmad's words.

'No, listen. I don't remember the stuff in the train station, but I know it's happened to me before. I get this cold feeling and time passes and I don't know what I do in that time. But then, like Dr Atkins said, afterwards I'm not cold, I'm hot and sweating and my heart is beating so fast. Maybe I didn't leave the hospital but instead I killed Mrs Hennessy. Or at least took her rings. I don't remember but it's possible, isn't it? That's what Dr Atkins said.'

'No. I don't think it's possible. You took the train home.'

'But I had time. How long would it take to walk down the corridor?'

'Without anyone seeing you? Nurse Li was sitting in there when you left. No.'

'I am thinking, Miss Burton, that I should just say I am guilty and then this will all stop. You, in court, you are just doing your job. I think you enjoy it, the talking and arguing and telling the other lawyer he is mistaken. And Constance is listening and writing and staring at me in case I do something wrong. For me, every word is like a knife. I want it to stop. This could be what I should do.'

Judith's phone rang in her pocket and she rose stiffly to take Constance's hurried call, all the time keeping a close eye on Ahmad, and horrified by the sentiments he had just expressed. When she returned to Ahmad she could not suppress the excitement in her voice.

'That was Connie,' she began, touching his shoulder lightly so that he raised his head and wiped his eyes.

'Yes.' He was calmer now.

'She has been talking to Lottie, Nurse Li. Lottie wanted you to know she was sorry she couldn't help you more.'

Ahmad shrugged. Judith took a deep breath.

'I apologise if I have not appreciated before now how hard this is for you. You are right; this is my job and I sometimes forget how alien a place a courtroom can be for other people. I even enjoy making them feel uncomfortable, if it's going to help my case, well, your case.

'I can't be absolutely certain that you didn't kill Mrs Hennessy but my instinct and all the facts I have before me tell me that you waved goodbye to her that evening and went quietly home. I am not telling the court that because it's my job. I am doing it because it's what I believe. Now, what Lottie just told us, I think it is going to help sort this mess out. So don't even think of repeating what you said to me to anyone else, OK? Now please listen to me carefully, and answer carefully. Why didn't you tell us you took

Shaza to the hospital sometimes?'

Ahmad's eyes widened.

'You didn't ask me.'

Judith tutted loudly and rolled her eyes. Then she reined back the sarcastic comments which were forming in her mouth.

'Lottie says Shaza was with you on the Thursday Mrs Hennessy died. Is that right?'

'Yes. She came in the morning. Aisha was ill. I couldn't leave her. They had some teacher's day off. Then Suzy was nearby. She collected her early in the afternoon.'

'When Shaza was at the hospital, that day, do you think she might have gone wandering around, into any of the patients' rooms, into Mrs Hennessy's room?'

Ahmad was quiet again, but this time he was focused, dredging back into his memory to find the right images. After a full minute he made a choking noise at the back of his throat.

'Yes,' he said. 'I mean, of course she had many chances and I would not know. But on that day, she had her school bag full of colouring and some homework, and now I remember, when Suzy arrived it was hard to find Shaza. She wasn't in the staff room. Lottie found her on the ward. And when I got home much later, she had her schoolbag up in her bedroom and I thought that was strange because she usually leaves it in the hallway. Oh no. She must have…you mustn't blame Shaza. She is only nine years old. I don't want you to blame her. Please, Miss Burton. I will say it was me.'

Judith patted Ahmad on the shoulder gently. She wanted to tell him that everything would be all right but she couldn't find the words.

55

One hour later Constance and Judith were standing outside the Qabbanis' house. Constance knocked lightly and Mrs Qabbani answered the door.

'Sorry to come by so late,' Constance began. 'This is Judith. She's the lawyer representing Ahmad in court. Can we talk to Shaza please? It's important. You can be with us all the time. I promise we won't frighten her.'

Mrs Qabbani glided up the stairs, tapped on Shaza's bedroom door and beckoned her daughter to come down. Shaza stood before them in the lounge, twisting her hands. Her hair was neatly plaited down her back.

'Wow, your hair is beautiful,' Constance started. 'Do you do that yourself?'

'Mum does it,' she replied, touching it lightly with the fingers of one hand.

'And sometimes Lottie does it for you at the hospital, but probably not as good as Mum, eh?'

Shaza nodded her agreement. Aisha took a step forward but Judith deliberately moved between her and her daughter and blocked her way.

'Do you like it when you go to the hospital with your father?'

'It's OK. Sometimes it's a very long time and I get tired.'

'But you take things with you to do?'

'I take colouring and books, and sometimes Lottie gives me chocolate when Dad isn't there.'

'Are you not supposed to have chocolate?'

'Dad says it's a "luxury",' she drew the word out into three long syllables, 'and that English children eat too much chocolate.'

'I see. He's a wise man, your father. Do you ever go to talk to some of the patients?'

'Not really.'

'So, just one or two of them?'

'I'm not supposed to.'

'Not supposed to talk to them?'

'Lottie lets me go with her sometimes, but said not to tell Daddy.'

'Why does she let you go with her?'

'When it gets dark I don't like being on my own in that room.'

'Quite right. I'm not big on the dark either. And do you remember a lady called Mrs Hennessy, Barbara, with orange hair? You met her on your last visit to the hospital. I can show you her photo if you like.'

Shaza stiffened. She looked away.

'Do you think you spoke to this lady?' Constance removed the photo of Barbara Hennessy from her pocket and showed it to Shaza.

'I'm not sure,' she replied.

'What kind of things did you talk to the patients about?'

'About school and home and pictures.'

'Pictures? Did she ask you about pictures?'

'Yes, she asked if I liked painting.'

'Who did?'

A pause.

'The lady in the photo.'

'So, you do remember her?'

'I think so.'

'Do you like pretty things?'

The girl's face lit up.

'I love pretty things.'

'Like flowers?'

'I like flowers.'

'What's your favourite colour?'

'Pink and purple.'

'Those are really lovely vibrant colours. You know when the police came here – it was a few weeks ago – I was here that day too. Do you remember?'

'Hmm,' Shaza mumbled.

'They found something in your bedroom?'

Now Shaza shook her head very slowly from side to side but it was clear she did remember.

'It was a pink purse with beads and sequins. It was very beautiful.'

'I remember the purse.'

'Ah, great. Clever girl.'

'Did you see that purse in one of the rooms at the hospital?'

Shaza's cheeks flushed and she puffed them out wide. Then she folded her arms in front of her and lowered her head. Her mother moved sideways but Judith barred her way a second time.

'Mrs Qabbani, please. This is so important. One more minute.'

'Did you take the purse from the hospital and bring it home?' Constance asked.

'It was so pretty and the lady said I could have it. She showed it to me when she asked me about painting.'

'She said you could have it?'

'I said it was pretty and she smiled and said "it was only a cheap purse".' Shaza imitated Barbara. 'She said she found it in a market and if I liked it I could have it.'

'Was there anything inside the purse?'

'I thought it was just a purse but when I was back in the staff room I opened it.'

'What did you find?'

'I found two big rings. Magic ones. Like in Aladdin.'

'What did you do then?'

'I ran back to the lady's room to give them back but she wasn't there any more.'

'So what happened then?'

Shaza hung her head. 'I was going to ask Lottie what to do, if she could give the rings back to the lady, but she suddenly came running and said that *Suzy was here* and *she was in a hurry* and *where had I been* and I had to go straight away.'

'You didn't tell her?'

'Daddy was there too, and he was cross I wasn't in the staff room. I didn't want to say. I thought the next time I went to the hospital I could give them back to the lady.'

'What did you do with the purse when you got home?'

'I put it in my drawer. To keep it safe.'

'Did you tell mum or dad about it?'

'No.'

'Thank you so much, Shaza. You are a very grown up and brave girl telling me all these things. No one is cross with you. Do you understand?'

Shaza brightened up.

'Where's Daddy? Is he in Hampstead?' she said.

'Yes. He is.'

'Can we see Daddy now?'

'I hope very soon.'

'Is Daddy coming home then?' she asked. 'Is he still famous?'

'Famous?'

'Yes, on the television.'

Aisha gasped.

'Well done, you,' Judith whispered to Constance, as she stood back and allowed Aisha to run to her daughter and clasp her to her chest.

'Mrs Qabbani.' Judith spoke after allowing mother and daughter a brief moment together. 'Can I talk to you now please, alone? Constance will stay with Shaza.'

Aisha stroked her daughter's hair, then released her with a further squeeze and led Judith into the kitchen.

'The trial is going well, as I said, but we still have some way to go and there have been some difficult questions. I know you want to help your husband,' Judith explained.

Aisha did not respond and Judith wondered if she should ask Constance to come and join them; Aisha clearly trusted her more. But there was so little time, she decided to plough on.

'So here's what we need to do,' she advised. 'First, Constance is going to type up a statement of what your daughter just told us. She took the rings, and not your husband. We are going to send it to the police and the people prosecuting your husband and the judge. If they won't accept it is true, we will ask for your daughter to be allowed to give her evidence in person.'

Judith heard Aisha's sharp intake of breath.

'Don't panic. We will record a session – a bit like the one we just did with Shaza – and we will blur out her face. We can ask for the court to be cleared, so just the jury and the judge will hear. Do you understand? But we're worried that won't be enough, not with the huge media interest. The case has made it onto national news. We need you to come to court tomorrow.'

Aisha shook her head over and over and began to moan low in her throat.

'We know something bad happened to you in the past. Ahmad won't tell us what it was. It must have been something terrible; I'm so sorry. I can't imagine what it was, because I'm lucky enough never to have been exposed to some of the things you must have seen. But Constance says you can speak; you just prefer to be silent.'

Aisha turned her head away.

'Ahmad needs you to do this for him. I'm worried that we don't have enough yet to convince the jury that he's innocent. That he may go to jail for a long time. And that he'll never be a doctor again.'

Aisha covered her face with both hands.

'I won't pretend. He is desperate. He is even thinking of saying he's guilty so this will all end now. I think it would really help if you came to court tomorrow to give evidence on your husband's behalf. It might save him. We will be with you all the time. Do you think you can do it?'

Aisha lowered her hands and gazed out of the window at the

play kitchen which had blown over in the wind. She folded her arms around her body. Then she turned back towards Judith and straightened up.

'Yes,' she said softly.

'Thank you,' Judith replied. Then she shuddered. Some of Constance's influence must be rubbing off; she wasn't usually so soft-hearted.

'And are you able to tell me why you and Ahmad are so sad, what happened to you? Then I can decide how best to use it tomorrow,' she added.

Aisha stood in silence for a full minute before heading for a drawer to the right of the sink. She took out a faded photograph and handed it to Judith. Judith studied the photograph carefully.

'I understand,' she said. 'Let's talk about tomorrow.'

***

Neither Constance nor Judith had much sleep that night. Constance typed up Shaza's statement and sent it to Inspector Dawson, Andy Chambers and the judge. Dawson agreed to send a female officer to the Qabbanis' home with strict instructions to bring Aisha to court at 9:30. Arrangements were made for Shaza to be brought to the court building and cared for by Suzy Douglas pending a decision on her evidence.

Judith went to see Ahmad in the holding cells before court. He was very quiet and unkempt.

'Don't you have a clean shirt?'

He turned his head away.

'You think I care about how I look in the courtroom?'

Judith was annoyed to find him still so despondent despite her pep talk of the previous night. 'We have to counter the picture the prosecution wants to paint of you, the false picture. That you're a rough character, with no morals, who will throw an old lady out of a window for a bit of stolen jewellery.'

'I am wearing the suit, and you made me tell everyone I was a doctor.'

'OK, forget the shirt. We have more important things to talk about.'

'You talked to Shaza?'

'Yes. She took the rings. She says Mrs Hennessy gave her the purse and she only found the rings inside later on. She went back to the room and Mrs Hennessy had gone, presumably for her operation.'

He raised his eyes towards Judith, thoughtful and still.

'You believe me now. I told you I am not a thief.'

'Yes. I believe you.'

'But I am not sure you did before. Why did Mrs Hennessy give her the purse if it had the rings inside?'

'Maybe she just forgot. Her daughter has said she was confused. You said she hadn't been eating for days.'

'Yes, that's right. Because they thought she would have the operation each day. And I put the rings in the purse.'

'What do you mean?'

'When I found them in the bathroom, she asked me to put them in the purse, but I'm not sure that is the place where she usually kept them. Maybe she didn't see, or maybe, like you say, she forgot. What will happen now?'

'We are trying to get the prosecution to accept it and drop the theft charge against you without pursuing Shaza or making her give evidence.'

'But you *must* do that, you *must*. She's just a child. If you don't I will say I did it.'

'I am trying very hard. But I may have to deal with it, with all of this phoney case against you, in an unexpected way.'

'What do you mean?'

'I'm not going to tell you now. You have to trust me on this one.'

Ahmad's eye narrowed.

'What are you going to do, Judith?'

It was the first time he had used her first name and she understood why; he was asking her to trust him too.

'I have thought long and hard, most of the night in fact, about whether it's better for me to tell you. And I've decided not to tell you now. What you need to know and remember – promise me – is that whatever you think, if you are angry about what happens, you remain calm in court. Can you do that for me? I'm going to see the judge now in his room, so we may be a little delayed this morning.'

'It's hard for me to promise when I don't know what you are going to do.'

'I understand. But I want you to draw on that strength I know you have, the strength that has kept you going through darker times, and use it today.'

'So I will try too. But so many things are still not clear.'

'You're right. But the only thing you need to remain clear on, the only thing the jury needs to know, is that you didn't kill Mrs Hennessy. They don't need the whole story, the whole *One Thousand and One Nights*.'

'We know now, at least, why she asked me for that book,' Ahmad added, almost smiling.

'Yes,' Judith replied. 'Now we know.'

56

DAVID WOLF and Jane Bridges parked in the bays opposite Hampstead police station. Dawson had asked them to come in as early as they could manage, and to come together. Suddenly Hani Mahmood's distinctive Jaguar pulled out of the space two cars behind them, leaving in a hurry. He didn't see them.

'Shit!' Jane sat down low in her seat, even though Hani had already disappeared down the hill.

'What's the matter, Jane? You said there was nothing to tell, nothing to worry about. Why was Hani here?'

Jane allowed her seat belt to retract noisily and grabbed her handbag. Then she faced her husband.

'I deleted the form,' she said. 'The Aladdin Trial consent form. I'll tell the police if that's what you want.'

'What? It was you?'

'Oh for God's sake, David. It's hardly a crime.'

'I thought it was just a mistake, a photocopying error. How could you think I would want you to take the blame? I've been trying to protect you, especially with the promotion coming up.'

'I don't need you to protect me. Christ! This is so like you. I don't need you to tell me how to do my job, or how to make sure the notes I prepare are accurate, either. I have done my job for eleven years now and I am good at it. Your brand of chivalry would have been sweet in the eighteenth century but frankly now it's stifling and insulting.'

She got out of the car and slammed the door. David followed her.

'How could you delete the form, when we were in the middle of a hospital investigation and a murder enquiry?'

'I just did, OK. That's all.'

'And how could you think that I'm trying to trip you up? Look. I'll say it was me and I forgot. No need for you to get into any trouble.'

'Don't you listen to anything I say? I don't need you to lie for me. I will tell them I did it.'

'But why? Please tell me. I think I deserve an explanation.'

'Hani asked me to.' She walked two car lengths down to locate a safe place to cross the road.

'What? Why?' David stepped out into the road then retreated as a passing Range Rover hooted.

'When Lucy stayed on at the end of the review meeting she told Hani that the Trust didn't want any discussion of Aladdin in the public eye. She said it was "sensitive information" and that it was a legal minefield if the robot was to blame in any way. Apparently, there are law suits involving Da Vinci all over the USA and Aladdin is a cheaper version. You can imagine the headlines, especially when everyone's already saying we're a second-rate country and the NHS is in crisis.'

'I still don't see the connection to Mrs Hennessy.'

'Lucy asked Hani to make sure there was no mention of Aladdin in the report into Mrs Hennessy's treatment. She said that the Trust wanted another year of positive results from the trial before going fully public. Hani asked me to ensure the Aladdin consent forms disappeared from the hospital records for Mrs Hennessy.'

'Well that's all messed up now, isn't it, now I've blabbed about it all in court. Why didn't you tell me before?'

'Oh come on, David! This is hardly the time to start worrying about what you said in court, given the lies you told in there willingly, to protect yourself.'

'That's not fair.'

'Anyway, Hani asked me not to. And you couldn't avoid answering the questions about Aladdin, once that lawyer got started. They can't blame you for that.'

'But why did Hani agree to any of this? He hates Aladdin, says he likes to "feel his way" inside the patients. And, for his faults, he hates capitulation.'

'They bullied him. They reminded him that he's not meeting his targets for number of operations completed. Lucy said she would give him another chance to catch up if he helped the Trust out this time around, kept quiet about Aladdin. There's no reason to think Mrs Hennessy's death was anything to do with her operation – we both know that – so I didn't feel I was doing anything wrong.'

Dr Wolf stared out across the road at the doors of the police station.

'Oh God. What a mess.'

'David. I will do whatever needs to be done to get you off the hook. Anyway, you're a terrible liar so there's no point trying to pretend to the police that it was you.'

David nodded resignedly.

'We don't know what Hani told them, that's the only problem,' Jane lamented as a break in the traffic finally allowed them to cross the road.

'We just tell it as it is,' David replied. 'Come on, let's get it done.'

57

'Your honour, I provided you and my learned friend with some new evidence last night in the form of a witness statement from a child, the defendant's daughter. It's not signed but it's verified by my instructing solicitor. And the nurse on the ward, Nurse Li, will corroborate that the child was at the hospital that day. Can you confirm you received it?' Judith and Andy Chambers sat opposite Mr Justice Seymour in his room.

'Yes, thank you, Ms Burton. And I have read it. Mr Chambers, what do you have to say about it all?'

'It's most unfortunate that this has only come to light now,' he said.

'I hope you're not trying to suggest it's the defence's fault,' Judith replied angrily. 'The police found the rings in the little girl's room and jumped to conclusions. They could easily have discovered this at the outset and saved us all from this farce.'

'You could have asked your client or his wife or his daughter who took the rings. He chose not to say anything. That's perjury or at least perverting the course of justice.'

'You are seriously suggesting that now you know my client is innocent of the theft, you are going to prosecute him for something else? And who in their right mind would shop their own daughter when they could not possibly have any confidence in the English legal system?'

'Well, you wouldn't know the answer to that first-hand, would you?'

'Stop it, both of you!' Judge Seymour rose to his feet and banged the palm of his hand on the table. 'Remember who and where you are. Mr Chambers, you say the Crown accepts that Mr Qabbani did not steal the rings. So that charge against him will be dropped. Are you intending to prosecute the nine-year-old girl? I suggest you think very hard before you answer that question.'

'No, your honour. We don't see it as in the public interest.'

'Thank you. A sensible decision, I might say. Where does that leave Mr Qabbani?'

'We have the forensic evidence and the defendant's curious behaviour in the railway station...'

'Which the psychiatrist has explained.' Judith could not hold her tongue. Judge Seymour silenced her with a swift and piercing glare.

'Clearly he's capable of violence,' Chambers continued, 'we have no idea what "trauma" he has suffered, if any, and his relationship with Mrs Hennessy was not normal, befriending her, giving her gifts. We want to take it to the jury.'

Judge Seymour hesitated. Every day in court cost in excess of £3,000, and this was a high-profile case. He didn't want to be criticised for prolonging things unnecessarily if a 'not guilty' verdict was returned quickly.

'Ms Burton?'

Judith wavered. He was encouraging her to move now for the acquittal. She smelt it. They could do the deal now in here quietly and Ahmad would be released and led out of a back door to go home. Constance would be invited to issue a short statement afterwards 'on behalf of the family thanking friends for their support.' But there was an alternative; the one Constance was urging on her. She thought of Mrs Qabbani sitting alone in the house with the peeling wallpaper while her husband was out cleaning each day.

'Your honour, the defence is happy for the case to continue and go to the jury, if the theft charge is dropped and the prosecution agrees that no action will be taken against any member of the Qabbani family in relation to the rings. But we want to interpose a new witness, the defendant's wife, this morning.'

Judge Seymour muttered under his breath and wrinkled his nose. Then he tapped his pen on the desk.

'Are you sure this is what you want?'

'Yes.'

'Mr Chambers?'

'Yes, we want to go ahead. But we had no notice of the wife coming.'

'I'm telling you now.'

'All right, Ms Burton. If you are sure and you are both in agreement. I shall be interested to see what Mrs Qabbani has to say, as, I think, will the jury. But this is a court of law and we have no other mistress or agenda. Is that clear?

'Yes, your honour.'

58

AHMAD STOOD quietly in the dock. Judith had told Constance, as succinctly as she could, what had transpired in the judge's room and what they needed to do next. Judith stood up and thought, fleetingly, of her own technique of lectern leaning. Sometimes she adopted the 'praying mantis'; she found that lent her an air of piety and false reverence.

But that was unacceptable for this next witness. She needed something foreign to her every breath, she needed to appear empathetic. And so she alighted upon a stance with her fingers splayed on the top of the lectern, elbows bent, chest slightly forward and her head gently inclined to one side. 'The budgerigar,' she whispered to herself triumphantly. That would do.

'Your honour. As agreed with my learned friend, Mr Chambers, and with your permission, I now call Mrs Aisha Qabbani.'

Gasps of surprise filled the courtroom and heads turned in anticipation of viewing the reclusive, down-trodden wife. But Ahmad leaped up, his eyes blazing.

'No!' he shouted. 'No, please, no! I forbid this.'

The two police officers on either side were quick off their feet and restrained him, or he might have jumped from the dock. Even so, they wrestled with him until he was knocked to the floor. A third officer joined them to hold him down. The judge banged his gavel to restore order and Ahmad was raised to his knees, with his arms twisted behind his back.

'Oh God, Connie. What a mess,' Judith muttered. 'We should have taken the deal.'

'No,' Constance replied. 'This is good. Keep going.'

Mr Justice Seymour glowered at Judith before turning his icy stare on Ahmad.

'Mr Qabbani, I can see this is difficult for you but this is not a public house or a Syrian bazaar. This is a court of law, my court, and you will sit quietly and listen to the evidence, whether you like it or not. Do you understand?'

Ahmad pouted, desperation etched across his face as the officers lifted him up slowly and pushed him back down in his seat.

'I don't like doing this but I am going to ask the police officers to replace your handcuffs just to ensure we won't have any more disturbances,' he continued.

'Your honour, I am sure that won't be necessary,' Judith pleaded for Ahmad.

'This is my courtroom and I am sure it will be. This is the second time Mr Qabbani has interrupted inappropriately and it will allow us all to be more relaxed for the next few minutes. If it happens again, he will be removed. Go ahead, please.'

Ahmad closed his eyes tightly as the handcuffs were placed on his wrists and snapped shut. *How could his wife see him like this?*

'I understand that your next witness is the defendant's wife, is it, Ms Burton?'

'Yes, your honour.'

'Let's get on with it then.'

Aisha Qabbani entered from a door at the back of the court, with Constance at her side. She was dressed in navy trousers and a turquoise blouse and she wore a brightly coloured head scarf.

'Mrs Qabbani,' Judge Seymour began. 'Ms Burton will ask you some questions which you must answer truthfully and fully. Usher, please give Mrs Qabbani some water.'

'Mrs Qabbani, tell us about your husband's daily routine – when he goes to work, what time he comes home,' Judith began.

Aisha gazed around the room, allowing everyone to see her from every angle before she spoke.

'My husband, Ahmad…'

Ahmad let out a gasp at hearing his name come from his wife's lips after so long, but then lowered his head and clasped his hands together. Despite Judith's treachery, he had promised he would try to stay calm. Judith wondered if he were praying.

'My husband, Ahmad, works six days a week at St Mark's Hospital in Hampstead. Sometimes he begins at eight in the morning and finishes at five or six. Other times he begins at five and works until very late, four or five in the morning, sometimes he finishes at eight o'clock.'

'And his job?'

'Cleaning; that's all.'

'On the night Mrs Hennessy died, Thursday the 11th of May, what time did your husband arrive home?'

'It was about 9:30.'

'Do you live close to the station?'

'Yes. It is just a few minutes to walk.'

'Did he go out again that evening?'

'No. He stayed at home.'

'Did you notice anything unusual about how he looked or his behaviour?'

'No. All was like usual. He ate dinner. Sometimes he reads to Shaza, our daughter, but she was already asleep.'

'Does your husband like his job?'

'Before we came to England, we had lots of plans. Ahmad thought he would be a doctor here, too.'

'And what happened?'

'They didn't accept his qualification. They said he would have to do more studying. We had no money for studying.'

'So he took the cleaning job?'

'Yes.'

'Did he talk to you about his work?'

'Sometimes.'

'What did he tell you?'

'That he liked talking to the patients. I think it made the job easier for him.'

'Does your husband ever take anyone to work with him?'

'Yes.'

'Who is that?'

'Our daughter, Shaza.'

'How old is Shaza?'

'She is nine, will be ten years old soon.'

'Why does your husband take Shaza to work with him sometimes?'

'He worries.'

'What does he worry about?'

'That I can't look after her.'

'Why does he worry about that? Take your time.'

Aisha's lip trembled. She took a sip of water, peered forlornly over at Ahmad and then faced the court. Finally, she turned towards the judge.

'We had a beautiful house in Damascus, Barza neighbourhood.' She spoke softly, as if she were recounting a dream. 'And a villa in Al-hama. It had four bedrooms, a big courtyard and we had a pomegranate tree. Sometimes, in the summer I would reach my hand out of the window and pick pomegranates. Ahmad worked at the hospital in Damascus and I taught English at the University.

'Then things got bad. Even before 2011. It was my fault. We had friends in the USA. That is why Ahmad was able to study there. But they would send me things and I posted them online. It was stupid. The police took Ahmad in for questioning. He was away for three days and nights without any messages. When he returned he was very quiet. I don't know what they did to him or what he saw there; he never said. One other of our friends was taken away and he never came back.

'But then they bombed near our house and two of his doctors were killed. I told him. If we stay we will die. All of us. You are a doctor. We will go somewhere else, somewhere safe. You can be a doctor again there and help people. That must be better, I said, better than a pointless death. And this time he agreed.'

'What happened on your journey here?'

'Objection, your honour.' Mr Chambers spoke this time with only a fraction of his usual volume and fervour. 'This is not relevant to the defence's case.'

'Your honour, this is a trumped-up case in any event. It is based on hypotheticals and conjecture. There isn't even any evidence that Mrs Hennessy was murdered. Yet my client and his family have endured trial by media. The evidence Mrs Qabbani will give is relevant to understanding the trauma my client experienced in the past, which will, in turn, help explain his "curious behaviour" in the railway station, evidence of which Mr Chambers has led. In my submission, your honour, not only is this testimony highly relevant so that the jury can assess the credibility of the accused, the criminal justice system owes my client the opportunity to have this evidence heard.'

'Continue, Ms Burton, with less fuss. I would have let you continue anyway. Mr Chambers, sit down.'

'Mrs Qabbani. Take your time. What happened on your journey here?'

Aisha took a deep breath and closed her eyes and she was there, standing on the shore, gawking at the vast expanse of water.

The dinghy in front of them was bobbing up and down. It seemed tiny and insignificant against the massive spread of the sea. Ahmad was staring too and he held his hand out to her.

'Is it safe?' she had asked him, knowing the answer herself but wanting some reassurance from him. His grip on her hand had tightened. They had stood together on the shore, agonising over what to do next. What was for the best.

But they both knew the moment they saw the boat that they had been duped. How could a dinghy, twenty-foot long, transport their busload of men, women and children (and let's not forget old Abdul's wheelchair) across miles of unforgiving ocean?

Yet not one of them spoke up. How could they? There was no alternative, no way back, homes abandoned, goods sold or given away and money handed over. At least the man who had taken their money had the good sense not to wave them off; Ahmad might have given him a piece of his mind. Some of the other men might have given him something more. There seemed no point rising up against the simpleton he had sent in his place; a man who could only gesture and point at the boat before limping back to the bus and driving off, leaving them all standing there on the shore.

Aisha had clung to Ahmad briefly, touching her hand to his neck, before striding out; she wouldn't make this his decision. After all, she had been the one who had insisted they leave.

'We took a boat,' she said in a small voice to the attentive court, 'from near Bodrum in Turkey. We wanted to reach Sicily but we thought Greece if not. But our boat was too small and too old.'

It was only thirty minutes into their journey that the engine had cut out. Khalil, an engineer from Basra had tried to re-start it without success. Abdul had muttered under his breath. His son asked Ahmad what was going wrong. What could he do to help. They had two paddles and took it in turns to drive the vessel forward; thankfully the waters were calm and the children settled down to sleep with the lapping of the water.

'How far is it?' Aisha had asked quietly, out of earshot of the children.

'One or two hours,' Ahmad had replied, his voice cracking, and Aisha had allowed her eyes to hover over his face for a second longer than usual to test his reply for weight, before turning her attention to the horizon.

After another hour, one of the men had called out excitedly that he could see land. And he was right. A great land mass appeared to their right, but the wind was now starting to blow and no matter how hard they paddled, they began to travel left, to the west and away from their longed-for destination. And then the water began to seep in; Ahmad felt it first as a chill around his toes and those seated on the bottom of the boat began to moan and shuffle uncomfortably. It was that chill, the rising water, which returned to him over and over in times of stress. At first, he was reassured; they bailed out with teacups (Abdul's wife had brought a tea service with her which had been part of her dowry) but within a few minutes the water was back with more friends, and he knew then that they were going to sink.

'We used the paddles for a bit, then the water started to come in,' Aisha told the silent court. Ahmad sobbed audibly into his hands.

As the little craft bobbed and weaved, they began to distribute the life vests and, finding them short – there were only twenty – they gave them to the women and children. Abdul refused his over and over again, until his wife screamed that she would drop hers in the sea if he rejected it one more time.

The boat sank lower and Shaza's eyes grew wide. She, alone of the children, was awake. She trailed her arm in the water and Aisha reprimanded her, calling out that she would get her new coat wet. They tossed and turned and lurched their way onward, Aisha fearing at every bump that they would capsize. She could hardly draw breath for fear of unbalancing the boat. And then Ahmad had spied a faraway dot and nudged Aisha to look too. She had tried to appear encouraged but her face wouldn't obey.

Ahmad had shouted to Khalil to search for flares and one was located. The men were arguing now. They wanted to throw the wheelchair overboard to lighten the load. Abdul's wife was weeping, they had saved for two years to buy it. Two years of living on bread and milk. How would her husband get around in the new world without it? 'If we don't throw it overboard there won't be any new world, don't you see?' Khalil had remonstrated with them.

'We started to throw things over that we didn't need. We had hardly anything anyway,' Aisha explained.

Ahmad had manoeuvred his way between the bodies on the boat, had spoken to Abdul's tearful wife calmly and, after a fashion, detached her from the wheelchair, which the younger men flung overboard with drama and passion. The dot on the horizon was now clearly a ship.

Shaza was trailing her hand in the sea again, defiantly, staring down into the depths. 'Are there sharks, Mama?' she had asked.

'Ahmad had the gun, the flare gun,' Aisha told the court. 'There was a ship. But then the water came so fast.'

A colossal wave had washed over them and thrown them into the freezing, icy water, the boat upended and bobbing like a cotton reel. Shaza, close to her mother, was flung towards her.

Aisha, in the courtroom, drank her water down.

'Take your time. Who from your family was in the boat with you?'

'In the boat was Ahmad, Shaza and...' – she turned her sad eyes from the judge to the jury – 'Shadya.'

'Shadya was who?'

'Our other daughter. Shaza's twin sister.'

'And what happened to Shadya?'

'The boat turned over. One minute she was in my hand, then she was gone.'

'Your daughter went into the sea?'

'Yes. And then the ship arrived. A big ship. British. And they picked us up. But not Shadya. Ahmad tried to find her. He tried for so long, but we didn't succeed. After, the captain told us that some of the life vests were full of cardboard, it made her sink not float. And I put it on her.'

Ahmad had shrieked and yelled and dived under the water,

searching desperately for his daughter. Even when he had been pulled aboard the rescue ship he had wrestled with the men and dived back into the sea. The man in the boat had asked, 'What the hell does he think he's doing? Doesn't he want to be saved?'

'Our daughter,' Aisha had mumbled to him, her eyes entreating him to understand. 'Ah jeez,' he had exclaimed. 'He won't find her.' But they had waited patiently while Ahmad had plunged below the waves and screamed and shouted till, exhausted, he had been dragged onto the rowing boat and the medic had stuck a needle in his side to sedate him.

'What happened then?'

'We came to England. We were lucky. Some of the others had to go back to Turkey. Ahmad got the job at the hospital.'

'Why does Ahmad worry about leaving Shaza with you, Mrs Qabbani?'

'Shadya couldn't swim. She was a quiet girl, well-behaved. Not so physical. Shaza could. She was always more…active. When the boat tipped I reached for Shadya but Shaza grabbed me instead and Shadya was gone. I told Ahmad that night what had happened. He thought I blamed Shaza for Shadya's death. I couldn't believe he would think that of me. I stopped speaking or going out. Most of the time I am OK. I can care for Shaza. Some days the blackness comes and I need to be alone.'

'You say the blackness comes. Does your husband also suffer from what happened?'

'Yes. When we arrived in London, the captain on the ship was very nice. He wanted to help us. My husband had such terrible nightmares and shaking; he couldn't control it. The captain paid for my husband to see a psychiatrist. He gave Ahmad some breathing exercises and he carries a photo with him, a photo of me and Shaza. It is supposed to help him, to bring him back to the present. There are pills but he won't take them. It never goes away.'

'Why did your husband hide from people here the fact that he was a doctor in Syria?'

'He is a proud man, even after all that has happened to us. And he didn't want pity from people, I think. Much better to just be doing the job he has and doing it properly.'

'What do you say to the people in this country who have accused you and your husband of being parasites, of biting the hand that feeds you?'

'My country Syria was a beautiful country. It is a beautiful country; it's just that the beauty is covered up with a big, grey blanket and I'm not sure when we will see it again. We had a beautiful life there. We didn't want to leave. We had to leave. We will never forget that England has given us a home. Ahmad and I, we can't contribute so much; it's always this way for refugees. Everything is so different from our way. But our daughter and the sons and daughters of all who came with us, they will always remember the kindness of the people, their humanity. I hope my daughter will be a doctor like her father. Then she can help people here too.'

'Thank you, Mrs Qabbani. No more questions.'

'Mr Chambers?'

Andy Chambers shook his head to indicate he would not question Aisha, all the time staring hard at Ahmad.

Aisha rose slowly and descended from the witness box. She had only taken three steps across the floor of the court when the back doors opened and Shaza came barrelling towards her with a police officer in pursuit. She raced towards her mother but then, on seeing the judge and all the other people, she skidded to a halt. The police officer stopped too, and Aisha put out her hand to rein her daughter in.

The public gallery erupted and Judge Seymour was forced to bang his gavel, but to little effect.

'Your honour, can my learned friend and I approach the bench?' Judith fought to be heard over the noise.

'Yes. Good idea,' Judge Seymour replied.

'Your honour. There is now no evidence against my client other than a single hair from his head and he has explained how it might have found its way onto Mrs Hennessy's clothing. And this has been endorsed by none other than the expert for the prosecution. There is nothing else to link my client to the murders any more than any other person working in the hospital. The rings, the "curious behaviour", as my learned friend liked to call it, we now know its tragic origin; the misogynistic literature, all found to be nonsense or easily explained. There is only one course open to your honour.'

'Mr Chambers?'

'I will have to take instructions but I suspect the prosecution will withdraw the case.'

'You suspect?'

'I will need to take instructions overnight.'

'Oh no!' Judith's hackles were raised. 'You can't possibly let this family go through one more night of hell because of your desire to control the fallout from this ridiculous circus.' She allowed her voice to rise loud enough for the microphones to pick it up. A hush fell over the courtroom.

Mr Justice Seymour chewed the end of his pen. Judith had drawn herself up to her full height, nostrils flaring wildly before him. In contrast, Mr Chambers was red-faced and shrunken. But Judith had rejected the deal he had offered first thing this morning, and now everything would be so much more public.

He mused things over again. He wasn't stupid. This is what Judith had wanted for her client. A very public acquittal – and before her client was cross-examined by Andy Chambers. And he didn't like that; he didn't like being manipulated. But he also disliked the very public humiliation he himself had endured after his last murder trial, and it was clear where the public's sympathies would lie once the court journalists had had their say.

He turned his attention to Ahmad, who was standing in the dock, tears pouring down his cheeks, Shaza calling to him from the floor of the court, unable to extract herself from the vice-like grip of her mother and the police officer.

'Dr Qabbani.' The judge was firm but not unkind.

'Officers, please take the handcuffs off Dr Qabbani. I am sure he is quieter now.

'Dr Qabbani, I rule that there is insufficient evidence against you for this trial to continue. In fact, the evidence was so flimsy in the first place that I venture to suggest it should never have been brought. Members of the jury, thank you for your patience but you will not need to rule on this case today or, indeed, at all. You are discharged. Dr Qabbani, you are free to go.'

And he banged his gavel once, stood up and left the court.

The police officers uncuffed Ahmad slowly and Aisha and Shaza ran to him and embraced, Shaza repeatedly kissing his cheek.

'We could walk out the front if you like,' Constance was at Ahmad's side asking him what he wanted to do next, 'give a formal statement to the press?' Ahmad stroked Shaza's hair, hugged Aisha close, then he shook his head.

'We go quietly,' he said, 'please, Constance. We just want to go home.'

PART FOUR

PART FOUR

59

INSPECTOR Dawson sat in his office with the blinds down. Constance and Judith sat opposite him. He had invited them in without giving any reason.

'Thank you both for coming. You know, Judith, I didn't think your guy did it. But there were no other suspects.'

Judith and Constance waited. They knew Dawson would get to the point eventually and Judith didn't want to embark on a conversation based on recriminations.

'The mayor has asked for a formal apology to be made to your client,' he said.

'I see.'

'He wants me, as the officer leading the investigation, to make a statement on television. I have written something out. Would you take a shufty at what I prepared?'

He handed a piece of paper to Judith who read it quickly and handed it back.

'Make whatever statement you like. I'm sure you know what

to say. Are you any closer to finding out what really happened?'

'I can't say.'

Judith leaned forward. 'Charlie. This investigation was flawed from the start. We helped you save an innocent man from a grave miscarriage of justice. Now, we do want to feel reassured that the investigation is progressing expeditiously and along the right lines.'

'Dr Mahmood, Dr Wolf and Dr Bridges have fully cooperated with the police.'

'Oh come on, spill the beans Charlie.'

'All right. Just high level. Wolf didn't erase the consent form. Dr Bridges did. The Trust didn't want it to come out that St Marks was trialling the robot.'

'Why?'

'They were worried about a law suit and how complicated it might be if it involved new technology.'

'Ha! Hilarious!' Judith quipped. 'They don't mind throwing their human employees to the lions but they want to protect their robots. That's loyalty for you.'

'But why did Dr Bridges do it?' Constance asked.

'She says she was instructed to ensure that any evidence mentioning Aladdin should disappear. She felt comfortable that Aladdin was nothing to do with Mrs Hennessy's death, so she did as she was told. Her log-in was down so she used her husband's.'

'Hmm. All this anonymous 'Trust' stuff is very convenient,' Judith complained.

'And Dr Mahmood?' Constance asked.

'He is the one who asked Dr Bridges to delete the form. A Ms Lucy Farmer in the Risk team instructed him as head of the team. He then instructed Dr Bridges. Dr Wolf didn't know about it, which I am told is what he said in court. The evidence of the three doctors ties up.'

'And...'

'And what?'

Constance pouted. 'So we know why the consent form was deleted. To hide the fact that Aladdin was involved in Mrs Hennessy's operation. Big deal. Dr Wolf told us in court that it was involved. I thought you were going to say you knew who killed Mrs Hennessy. The killer may still be out there.'

'We have all we need, Connie,' Judith said. 'We had it the moment Ahmad walked free. We can't help everyone. She was probably depressed; lived alone, couldn't paint any more, husband getting remarried to a younger woman, estranged from her son. Maybe, like Charlie said to you at the beginning, she decided to end it all. Let me know when you're going to be broadcasting the apology, Charlie, so we can make sure everyone sees it.'

TRACY WAS sitting in her kitchen, with a mug of coffee in her hand. Before her, on the worktop, were two official letters. On the left, was the long-awaited formal letter from Ealing Primary, confirming 'with great pleasure' the offer of the position of Head of Key Stage 2, starting in September, together with responsibility for child protection. The new salary was an extra £5,000. If she and Pete were very careful with money, she could probably pay off her personal debts by next spring.

She still felt keenly the guilt of having attended the interview on the afternoon of Thursday the 11th of May, the day her mother died. But she had been up against a male competitor and she had feared that cancelling at the last minute would count against her. It has to be said that her remorse was not sufficient to make her contemplate turning down the job.

On the right, was a curt letter from Indis Insurance, advising that Pete had been seen undertaking a whole range of strenuous physical activities at Barbara's funeral, and that, as a result, no further sums would be due from his insurance policy. They had the right to sue or go to the Insurance Ombudsman if they were dissatisfied with the decision.

While she had cried when she first opened the Indis letter, now she was being philosophical. Pete's histrionics over the last year had worn her down. She thought they should accept the decision and move on with their lives. She wanted to be able to walk down the street with Pete, without him glancing over his shoulder every five paces. And if he wasn't worried about surveillance, he could take another job too.

She knew now that if she wanted to inherit her cool one million pounds she could either put off the distribution as long as possible, in the hope they could pay off the debt in time, or the only other real alternative was a divorce; Brian's throwaway line had been endorsed by her own lawyer. If it came to the crunch – and she desperately hoped it would not – Pete would understand, she was sure of it. They could get remarried a respectable amount of time afterwards for no one to smell a rat. Elizabeth Taylor had done it. Tracy couldn't give up the life-changing money because of the mess Pete had got into. She just needed to find the right time to bring this up for discussion; that was all.

But then, as she nudged the two letters and shuffled them around the table top, she had a further thought. Clearly, the person who had 'shopped' Pete knew more than a little about their family and had almost certainly attended her mother's funeral. It may well be the same person who had 'tipped off' Trading Standards to raid Joe's showroom. And, as she sat and reflected on the tragic events of the last three months, one person's face came into her mind: Brian.

Tracy shook her head. She was being silly. Brian was a plodding, nit-picking lawyer and he had no reason to wish her or Joe ill, although he had been cross with Joe for lying to him, she knew that. And the nature of his relationship with her mother was also unclear. She wondered if she should call Inspector Dawson and mention Brian, although the police had proved singularly unimpressive so far, and decidedly absent since the end of the trial. But as she sat there, evaluating and pondering and sipping at her steaming drink, she realised that there was someone else who might be interested in her predicament and prepared to help her out. She scrolled through the contacts on her phone until she found Constance's number.

***

Brian was sitting in his office. Every thirty seconds or so, his head would jerk around to check that the portrait, the wondrous portrait, painted with flair by his favourite former client, forever in his thoughts, was truly hanging on the wall behind him. He thought of Barbara often now, and his thoughts were warm, all bitterness vanquished. Barbara sitting opposite him in this same office, Barbara meeting him in the park when her children were still young and tearing around, Barbara in that red dress in Spain.

He was contemplating retiring in the next couple of months. In fact, he had asked his accountant to check over the figures and do some projections, and his secretary to ensure that she chased all outstanding bills, especially those more than sixty days old. Maybe he would try Spain; the climate was so warm and the people friendly and he had picked up a few words from his previous trip.

He heard a light step on the stairs and stood at the knock of his latest client. Perhaps he shouldn't have accepted her request; he had almost decided not to take on anyone new. But this woman had sounded interesting, and her reference to 'foreign investments' had piqued his interest.

Judith entered Brian's room, replete with headscarf and dark glasses. Once she was seated, she removed both smartly. Brian gulped. He had no idea why Judith had come, but he sensed it was not to ask him for legal advice.

'Hello, Mr Bateman. Or can I call you Brian?'

'Brian, please.'

'I'm Judith Burton. You may remember me from the Qabbani trial.'

'Yes. Yes, I do.'

'Oh good. That makes things a lot easier. I'm sorry I didn't give my real name when I rang. I was worried you wouldn't want to see me and I do have something important to talk about. Oh!' Judith's shriek disconcerted Brian, until he realised that she was staring at his picture.

'What a fabulous portrait!' she cooed.

'Thank you,' he said.

'Was it painted by anyone famous?'

'Barbara Hennessy painted it,' he muttered. Judith beamed at him.

'Could be quite valuable then, in the circumstances. I'll get straight to the point, should I?' she said. 'Let's begin with your Cayman Islands trust.'

'Ah!'

'It's the ultimate beneficiary in Mrs Hennessy's will and in a number of other wills prepared by you for your clients.'

'How do you know what's in Barbara's will?'

'Tracy Jones sent me a copy, via Miss Lamb, my instructing solicitor. You may remember her from the trial too. Tracy is in rather a pickle working out how to comply with all those conditions you put in the will. Poor woman, not only has she lost her mother, she's even contemplating losing her husband now. After I read it, I thought we really needed to speak.'

'It's a confidential document, the will. She shouldn't have shared it.'

'She also told Miss Lamb that someone, who had attended Barbara's funeral, had written to the insurance company handling her husband's personal injury claim, insisting that her husband is fit and sprightly and that, as a result, his policy won't pay up. Any idea who that might have been?'

Brian was silent, but Judith detected a trace of a smile; he couldn't hide his pride at that part of his scheme bearing fruit.

'And that Trading Standards raided her brother Joseph's car showroom recently, on the basis of an anonymous tip off. She is wondering, as am I, if it was someone close to the family who was responsible for both those unusual occurrences.'

'What is it precisely that you want?'

'Well, that isn't the extent of your involvement, is it, this whistle-blowing activity? I would never have thought of you as a violent man, but do you want to tell me how it happened or should I ask Inspector Dawson to come and join us?'

Brian said nothing but he ground his teeth.

'Why don't you make things better and explain things, from your side?'

Brian's glasses slipped off and fell onto his lap and then to the floor. He picked them up and placed them on the table.

'I'm sure you'll feel better once you've got things off your chest.'

'All right,' he replied angrily. 'I asked an enquiry agent to do some digging around Tracy and Joseph. I accept that I shouldn't have trusted a man I had never met before with such sensitive tasks but I did not tell him to take the law into his own hands and damage that man's property. I just gave him the article and asked him to find out where Mr Qabbani lived. Naturally, he, like me, was upset by what he read and he unfortunately responded in a very basic way. But no one was hurt. And all I did with Tracy and her ne'er-do-well brother was tell the truth, and no one can criticise me for that.'

'I'm a little confused,' Judith said.

'The window. At the Qabbanis' house. The agent I hired to find where they lived threw a brick through their window. Isn't that what you mean?'

Judith sat back in her chair, slightly off balance as a result of Brian's revelations, but determined not to let it show.

'I'm not here to talk about Mr Qabbani's window.' She recovered her composure. 'This is about your Cayman Islands trust, as I said, before your interesting admission diverted me. Most people can't find out anything at all about Cayman Island entities. But I'm not most people. My late husband had his fingers in lots of pies, including in the Cayman Islands, and I felt the need to resurrect some of his contacts only this week, after reading Mrs Hennessy's Will. They told me an interesting story about the BB Charitable Trust, Brian.'

'Oh,' he muttered. 'That.'

'Sounds like you have a nice little nest egg there – nearly three million pounds, I heard, "off the record", of course. Would you care to comment?'

'No.'

'That's a shame. Because, given that Barbara was likely to be one of your wealthier clients, that suggests a lot more "tailor-made" provisions in other wills you have prepared. I could get a court order now to seize your files and we could examine how many times you have taken money from your clients in this way, and if any others have died in unusual circumstances.'

'I haven't taken anything. It's a charitable trust.'

'Over which you have absolute power. How much do you make each year? Three million pounds is a lot of money; certainly enough to kill for.'

'Hang on. You came here because you think I killed Barbara. For her money. That's the most ridiculous thing I have ever heard! I loved Barbara, I loved her with all my heart.'

He paused to fling a loving glance over his shoulder at his portrait.

'I should have married her,' he told Judith, 'years ago. I had it all planned but that son of hers, Joseph, he wouldn't make himself scarce. He kept trying to get her attention, wanted her to push him on the swing, to help him climb the wall. Somehow I never found the time to ask her again. And no other woman could hold a candle to Barbara, no one.'

'Oh, come on. Why put these provisions in her will if you loved her?'

'I am not just a lawyer, I don't just give legal advice. I spend time with people, often when they are at an all-time low, when they need help. And when you spend time with people and get to know them, it's your duty to explain things to them. Wills are often written in a hurry, and years before a person's death. In the intervening period, families often become estranged and children don't always live up to expectations. My tailor-made offerings helped cover those eventualities. I didn't let my feelings get in the way. I treated Barbara the same as my other clients.'

Judith guffawed. 'Nonsense. You were trying to play God, Brian. This isn't about helping fulfil the testator's wishes, you want these people under your control; you choose whether they inherit or not, you wield tremendous power. And if they don't, your trust pockets the money. You must have loved it.'

'Tell me again why you are here.'

'Your professed love for Barbara is all very convenient now she is dead. Perhaps it gives you a motive, if your passion was not returned. Just because Mr Qabbani was acquitted, you should certainly not consider the investigation closed. And there is one thing of which I am certain. Your sideline in unusual will provisions has to end here. You are taking advantage of people like Barbara Hennessy, who want to pass their hard-earned cash onto the next generation.'

'All the testators – they agreed to the conditions – thought them an excellent idea. They wanted grandchildren. Funny how money makes people suddenly change their minds about procreation.'

'All right. You feel so comfortable with your conduct, you're so happy that you're morally clean, you can explain your philosophy to the solicitors' conduct board.' Judith rose to leave.

'No, Miss Burton, Judith, wait a minute. I'm sure we can work something out which means you don't need to spend your valuable time on this matter. And let's begin by my paying for that broken window. That's the least I can do.'

Judith sat back down as Brian took out his cheque book and pen.

61

CONSTANCE and Judith walked down Braham Terrace with some misgivings. It was Shaza's tenth birthday and they had been invited to a small family party. Constance was carrying a large teddy bear under her arm; the largest the toy shop had to offer. Judith had a plant in a pot, all wrapped up.

As they approached the house the two women were stopped in their tracks. A number of people were congregating outside, one was setting out some cakes on a table, another was busy blowing up pink and purple balloons and a third man was tying the filled balloons onto some string. And all the dumped rubbish which had previously overflowed the pavement had been removed.

'Are you here for the party?' Judith asked them, as casually as she could manage.

One of the people turned around and then Constance recognised her as the woman she had met on her first visit. 'Cath, isn't it? How nice to see you again,' she said.

'Oh, hello. I remember you. Wanted Mrs Qabbani. I sent you

to the café. How was it?'

'Very good thanks. Was this your idea then?'

'We all wanted to do something. To show them they're welcome here after…well, after what happened. My daughter baked the cakes. Mrs Qabbani knows we're here. We're almost ready for Mr Qabbani.'

Constance knocked on the door of the house and was surprised that Aisha opened it.

'We're a little early,' she apologised, 'but it seems you have some company already.'

Shaza bounded down the stairs and hovered at the bottom.

'Hello Contents, hello Judith. Thank you for coming,' she announced. 'Do you want to come upstairs?' she added cheekily. 'You have to see my new bedroom.'

Constance obliged and Judith followed Aisha into the kitchen.

***

Shaza stood at the door of her room and waved Constance ahead of her. Constance placed the teddy bear down on the bed and Shaza made a space for it among her collection. The room was newly painted in a soft shade of pink and the fitted wardrobes were now a deep purple. At the bottom of one of the wardrobe doors someone had painted a whole shoal of mermaids with streaming black hair.

'Wow, Shaza! How beautiful your room looks!'

The little girl beamed.

'Yes it does. Baba painted the walls and Mama painted the mermaids. She said if I was sad about Shadya I could think of her as a mermaid with all her friends, if I wanted.'

'You miss your sister?'

Shaza shrugged. 'We talk a lot, so it's OK I suppose. She loves my new bedroom too.'

'That's good.'

'It was one of my three wishes, you know?'

'Was it? What were the others?'

'Number two was that Mama would be happy again.'

'And how's that one going?'

'It's starting. She still cries a lot, but now she laughs a bit too.'

Shaza sat down on the bed. Constance hesitated but curiosity got the better of her.

'What was your third wish?'

'Oh that,' she said. 'I wished for Dad to become the best doctor in the hospital, saving lots of people with his operations.'

'That's a lovely thing to wish for,' Constance said.

***

Downstairs, Judith gave Aisha her gift.

'It's a pomegranate tree,' she said as Aisha unwrapped it and placed it on the draining board. 'It's probably not as impressive as the ones you had back home, and you need to bring it inside from October till May. But you might be lucky and get some fruit in a couple of years' time.'

'Thank you, Judith. That is a very thoughtful gift,' Aisha replied.

'Oh and I almost forgot.' Judith fished in her pocket and handed Aisha a cheque for £1,100. 'I understand you had a problem with a window a while back. This gentleman, he wanted to make a generous donation to the repair fund.'

Aisha smiled in astonishment, then folded the cheque and

tucked it in her pocket. 'That's very kind. Please tell him we appreciate his donation.'

'How's Ahmad?' Judith asked, spying him sitting in the back yard, at the centre of a group of men, talking loudly and confidently about their plans to make a garden.

'He is better,' she replied. 'He had such good news. The medical course to qualify in the UK. They say he can start next month. But there will be no charge.'

'That's the best news. I'm so pleased.'

'It was Dr Mahmood, from the hospital. He arranged it for Ahmad.'

Constance joined them in the kitchen.

'Gosh,' Judith said. 'People never cease to surprise me.'

'Yes,' Aisha replied. 'He came to see us a few days ago. He said it is all arranged. And that he would make sure Ahmad found a job when he finished the training.'

Ahmad suddenly looked up and noticed Judith and Constance in his kitchen. He made his apologies to his friends and headed inside.

'Constance and Miss Burton. I didn't know you were coming.'

'We won't stay long. We don't want to intrude. We just wanted to see how you were and bring a gift for Shaza.'

'That is so kind. You must stay for tea. Aisha has been preparing.'

'All right, but first, you need to come and see what our neighbours have arranged,' Aisha said, 'if we can tear you away from your friends, that is.'

Aisha led Ahmad to the front of the house. He stood for some moments in silence before going out to each of the neighbours and shaking hands.

'Dear friends, do come inside and celebrate with us. My wife will make you some tea to go with that wonderful cake,' he declared loudly.

As the neighbours filed into the house, Ahmad held back to speak to Constance, clearly with something on his mind.

'You know I still think about Mrs Hennessy, even though she caused me all this trouble,' Ahmad began. 'She was a nice lady. She talked to me like, well, like a real person. She was lonely I believe.'

'Yes. Her daughter only visited once a month. And the son, hardly ever,' Constance replied.

'Ah.' Ahmad held up a finger. 'Now that is what I wanted to tell you, but there was so much going on.'

'What?'

'I saw him. The son, Joseph Hennessy.'

'What? When?'

'After the trial. I saw him on television, on the news, with the daughter, Tracy Jones. And then I knew I had seen him before. The night Mrs Hennessy died. I was just leaving the hospital and he was coming in, with a bunch of red roses.'

Constance leaned back against the wall of the house.

'He lied about visiting her. Oh God, I've been so stupid. Thank you, Ahmad. I won't stay for tea after all. I'd better grab Judith as well.' She stuck her hand out and Ahmad took it in both his hands.

'Goodbye, Constance Lamb. *Bieltoufeek*. I wish you good luck always.'

62

JOE HENNESSY was incensed at being summoned from his early evening barbecue, the gleaming gas monstrosity a little treat he had purchased with his share of his mother's money, together with an apron and some specialised accessories. He didn't have any of the money yet, of course, but in anticipation of the large additional income soon heading his way.

Dawson was grim-faced when he entered the interview room, Constance and Judith this time behind the glass to view the show.

'Mr Hennessy. Thanks for coming in to assist us.'

'We've got friends coming round in an hour. I've had to leave Janice to get on with it. Will this be quick? She's pregnant you know.'

'You had a little visit recently from Trading Standards, I heard.'

'Yeah. Bastards came during the trial. Pretended they didn't know. No respect.'

'But fortunately you were at work?'

'Yeah.'

'And has there been any fallout?'

'I thought this was about Barbara. If you are going to ask me about that, I want my solicitor. But let's say I'm not too worried, Inspector.'

'You lost your foxy lady who was pulling in the punters. Do you think she was the one who spilled the beans?'

Joe scowled at Dawson. 'No one says "foxy" any more,' he said.

'All right. Let's get on with why you're here. Is there a reason why you and your sister have not persisted in trying to find out what happened to your mother?'

'How d'you mean?'

'Well. The man who was prosecuted for her murder was not guilty.'

'Yeah. You made a right hash of that one.'

Dawson's shoulders tightened but he did not rise to the bait.

'Can you explain to me why you and your sister have not been more active in asking us to find her real killer?'

Joe Hennessy grinned nastily. 'That's your job, isn't it? Trace and me, we don't want to interfere. We're just pleased we were finally able to put Mum to rest and grieve.'

'Well. Would you be pleased if I told you we had a new lead? Into your mother's death.'

Joe swallowed and his smile began to unfold at the edges.

'Yeah, 'course I would. But…I mean…it's been months now.'

'Let's cut the crap. Why didn't you tell us you went to see your mother on the evening she died?'

Joe's face instantly drained of all colour but he didn't flinch. He didn't reply either.

'I'll make the question simpler so that you can answer "yes" or "no". Did you visit your mother in hospital on Thursday the 11th of May, the day she died?'

Now Joe placed his hands flat on the table.

'I told you. I hadn't seen her for months. We had an argument.'

'No. That's what you told us when you gave your statement back in May. But that wasn't true, was it? You see, there is a small car park at the back of St Mark's Hospital. It's quite hard to get in there –pretty impossible during normal visiting hours – but after 8pm, when people go home, that's a good time to find a space. And, do you know what else?'

Joe remained silent.

'On the right-hand side of the car park, there's a tiny camera set up to record all the number plates of the vehicles as they enter.'

Now it was Dawson's turn to gloat.

'So your car, licence plate YY66 JOE was in the car park at 8:06pm that evening. I have two officers, as we speak, running through the CCTV. It's only a matter of time until we find a nice mugshot of you. So, it's just the two of us in here. Why don't you tell me what happened?'

Joe Hennessy rested his head on his hands for some time. For a few seconds he broke into a tuneless whistle. Then he sat upright and stared over Dawson's head.

'OK. I went to see Mum that evening. I hadn't seen her for months. We'd had an argument, like I said before. She'd thought I'd been doing stuff she didn't approve of.'

'The conviction at Mackenzies?'

'That? That was years ago. There had been a theft at my new work six months back, just before Christmas. It had nothing to do with me, I swear. But Tracy had said something, and Mum overheard – and the look on her face. I'll never forget it.'

'She thought it was you.'

'Yeah. Pathetic isn't it. It didn't matter what I did, hold down a job for fifteen years, find Janice; we've been together for nearly eight. She still thought it was me – my own mother. Do you know Inspector, when we were kids, she never bothered with us much? Tracy used to make the meals and buy my clothes. She was either "in her studio" or at parties. Sometimes she used to bring people home who pretended they were interested in her art. One of them tried it on with Trace. I thumped him. He threatened me with the police and I told him I'd tell them why I'd thumped him.'

'She never harmed you, your mother?'

'Not in the way you mean, no. But she made me feel like nothing. I used to lie awake at night trying to work out why she loved Tracy and not me. I reminded her too much of Miles, I think. Stupid sod, lauding it about at the funeral. She pretended they were still friends but she never forgave him for leaving. Things were better when Janice and me got together. Although Mum didn't like Janice. Janice is quite a big girl; Mum preferred small and dainty.

'People thought she was easy-going because she was an artist; just the opposite when either of us found someone we liked. She thought Janice was too big and she didn't like Pete either; thought he wasn't clever enough for Trace. Funny how she was so fussy with our partners, whereas the guys she took up with were hardly Mr Universe or rocket scientists.'

He took out a packet of cigarettes and removed one, holding it between thumb and forefinger.

'Janice said I should go and see her – said she must be a bit lonely – so I did.'

'You went to see your mother in the hospital?'

'I bought some roses.'

'Red roses?'

'Yeah.'

'Did she like them?'

'I don't know.'

'What do you mean?'

'She wasn't there.'

'When you arrived?'

'At all. I looked everywhere. She wasn't in her room. I went all around the ward in case she had gone visiting and then I wondered if I had the wrong room, but her name was on the door.'

'So what did you do?'

'After a few minutes I found a nurse – young girl, Asian, maybe Thai or Philippino – the one who spoke at the trial. I asked her where Barbara, my mother, was. She seemed confused first of all and she came to the room with me. She looked at Mum's notes and then she asked me to wait a minute. She disappeared for maybe around fifteen minutes. When she came back she said I shouldn't worry but Mum had gone for a walk with the physiotherapist, she had felt breathless and he had taken her to see one of the doctors. She said I could wait but she couldn't be sure how long it would be before she was brought back up.'

'What did you do?'

'I waited another ten minutes or so, I stuck the roses in water and put them next to her bed.' Joe hesitated. He had snapped the stem off one as he unwrapped them and he had suddenly felt vulnerable. He remembered he had looked across at the bed and imagined Barbara sitting there, brandishing a paintbrush, admonishing him for his carelessness in destroying a work of nature, as she used to do when he was a boy. He had thrust the decapitated bud into his pocket to hide it from further scrutiny.

'When she didn't come back, I left,' he said.

'What time was this?'

'You tell me, as you seem to have all the details. It was around half an hour after I arrived, all told. Look, can I go now please? We're having a barbecue.'

'You aren't going anywhere. Why didn't you tell us any of this first time around?'

'What difference would it have made?'

'Why didn't you tell us?'

'When Mum ended up dead I thought you'd try to pin it on me. Like I said, we didn't get on very well and people know I have a temper. I wanted to say something, like when your officer first came around. Then, when I heard how much money she had, and that she kept me in her will after all, I was even more worried how it would look.

'Even then, I decided I would tell if you asked me again, to "help the enquiry", but you never did. You didn't ask me any more questions, you didn't ask me to give evidence at the trial. So I kept shtum. Thought I'd let you find out where she had gone, but you didn't.

'It wasn't as if I knew what had happened to her anyway. I just knew she wasn't there. I've told you all I know now, so if you're going to keep me here I want to call Janice and I want my solicitor.'

Dawson exited the room smartly and rejoined Judith and Constance.

'What do you think?' he asked.

'What do you think?' Judith replied.

'I think once a scumbag always a scumbag,' Dawson said.

Constance remained glued to the glass, watching Joe. He had lit his cigarette despite the clear 'No Smoking' sign taped to the door, and was leaning back in his chair, blowing his smoke up towards the ceiling.

'He could easily have killed her,' Judith replied. 'Were there any prints of his in the staff room?'

'Not that I know of, but you could open that door with your shoulder and the railing had been wet if you remember.'

'Why didn't we pick up his prints in her room?'

'I don't know. I suppose that if there'd been a print on the door handle it might have been covered up by all the people who opened and closed the door after him. And maybe he just sat down on the bed, so no prints.'

'On the wrapping from the flowers?'

'We tried that at the time, looked at everything in the bin and the vase. We didn't get any prints. It doesn't matter really, now he's admitted he was there.'

Judith began to pace the room, folding her arms and tapping her fingers to her mouth. After a few turns she stopped.

'He says he spoke to Lottie, the nurse. We need to talk to her again. She didn't tell us any of this. She's hiding something. We knew she was a bit flaky but I put it down to nerves and pressure from her superiors to downplay her friendship with Ahmad. But maybe it was much more than that.'

'Yes.'

'And the physiotherapist. You remember we wanted to call him for the trial and you said he had gone back to Italy?'

'Yes. We had a contact number for him at a hospital in Milan. We tried a few times and then we gave up. We also wrote to him but never heard back.'

'What was his name?' Judith asked.

'Filippo Adamo,' Constance replied. 'I found him on Facebook during the trial.'

'Did you contact him?' Judith asked.

'No. I…well, you said we didn't need him then.' She grabbed her phone and scrolled through until she found an image of a smiling young man. 'Here. I'll message him now.'

Within five minutes of sending her message Constance was speaking to the Italian physiotherapist. When she hung up, she was very serious.

'What did he say?'

'He says he never met Mrs Hennessy.'

'What?'

'He says she was on his list of patients to visit post-op that day. He went up to her room and, like Joe, he found it empty. He says he brought her up some crutches so they could practise walking but, as she wasn't there, he just left them leaning on the chair.'

'I knew that was strange,' Judith replied, thumping her fist down hard against her thigh.

'He says he eventually got hold of one of the doctors, a junior doctor. He doesn't remember his name and the doctor assured him that Mrs Hennessy didn't need any physio. He was pretty cross as he had a long list of patients to see and he spent ages looking for her.'

'And his leaving?'

'Yes, that's also suspicious. He says the day after Mrs Hennessy died, he had an email from HR. He says he still has it and he'll forward it to me. But it said that they had been offered another physiotherapist on some new government scheme, free of charge and they had to take him because of the cost saving. Filippo was on a six-month contract with only one month to run. They agreed to pay the extra month so he worked till the end of Sunday and then packed up and left.'

'So Barbara Hennessy wasn't in her room at 8pm, someone wrote in her medical notes that she saw the physiotherapist, which wasn't true and it looks as if the physiotherapist was encouraged to leave pronto so no one could check with him. Did anyone give evidence they saw her in her room after her operation?'

'Only Lottie. No. Dr Wolf did too, didn't he? I am sure he did. He said he saw her at 7pm.'

'Yes, you're right. He talked about prescribing her a painkiller. But, Connie, just focusing on Lottie... When we saw Shaza, do you remember that she said she'd seen Lottie when she was in the hospital on the Thursday morning. She gave the impression that Lottie was around on the ward when she arrived, and later on when she left with Suzy Douglas. That's right, isn't it?'

Constance turned to face Judith. 'Yes. You're wondering how Lottie could have been in Mrs Hennessy's operation if she was back on the eleventh floor.'

Judith nodded. 'There might be a perfectly good explanation for all of this, but we need to find out.'

'So we call in this Lottie for questioning?' Dawson asked.

Judith shook her head. 'No. I think we need to be much more inclusive than that. If there's an issue here, it goes beyond Nurse Li.'

63

JANICE COOPER sat alone in her bedroom with the curtains closed. There was only half an hour till her guests would arrive and she had finished preparing all the salads and desserts. She ran her fingers across her belly and grimaced.

Lying on the bed were the scattered petals of a red rose; she had found it in Joe's jacket pocket a few minutes earlier. She had wanted matches to light some candles in Joe's absence and her fingers had curled themselves around it, dried up and shrivelled but still mostly intact. Joe had never bought her roses so it was obviously meant for – or received from – some admirer of his.

She knew that people said 'once a cheater always a cheater' but she had really believed Joe had changed. He had been so attentive since he proposed, and had seemed genuinely happy with the prospect of them starting a family together.

Janice remembered her words to Tracy at her engagement party and bile rose up in her throat. She had promised that she would leave if Joe deceived her again; now he had, she simply needed to decide if she had the courage to do so.

✦✦✦

Kyla Roberts sipped a lychee Martini on the deck of the cruise ship. She could see Craig splashing around in the pool; she would join him in a few minutes but, for now, she was working on her tan. She was on a seven-day trip around the Mediterranean, courtesy of a one-off 'golden handshake' from Joe for her hard work on recent unspecified projects.

She thought back with delight to the day that the police and Trading Standards had raided their office; the looks on their faces when they realised that all the systems were locked down and that they would not be able to extract any information from the computers. Of course, later on, head office had negotiated via its legal representatives and revealed a small amount of spotless data, after complaining bitterly about the unwarranted investigation.

She was sad to be moving on though. She had liked the set up in Mill Hill. But Craig hadn't appreciated the looks Joe had given her once or twice when he had come to the showroom to work his IT magic, and she appreciated that to lose Craig, a man of many talents, would be very careless indeed.

✦✦✦

Brian Bateman sat in his office cutting and pasting different names and addresses onto the pro forma letter he had prepared. He had not appreciated quite how many different clients, current and former, he would have to contact, and the task was likely to take him the best part of a week, if not a little more. Predictably, he carried out his activities in a regimented way, as agreed with Judith, giving little thought to any potential consequences or fallout.

First of all, he was tackling the next of kin of testators whose funds were sitting in his overseas account, providing them with the name of an independent solicitor to whom they could go for advice on the will he had drafted for their nearest and dearest. He was also making it clear that, if they chose not to take up alternative advice, then they could nominate a charity to which the languishing funds could be donated.

Once that was complete, he had agreed to contact all those, still living, for whom he had provided his special brand of designer-will, offering them a more straightforward alternative, or the charitable option.

Of course, he had been forced to scrap any prospect of retiring this year. But he comforted himself with the realisation that he would almost certainly have become quickly bored, and that they were unlikely to make his breakfast the way he liked it in many Spanish cafés. And he was still young and full of energy, and charged with new ideas for how to ease his clients' difficult path through the vagaries of life and death.

64

DAVID WOLF'S displeasure at the interruption to his evening could not have been clearer if he had written it on a piece of paper and held it in front of Judith's face. Even so, he was polite, if direct.

'Miss Burton, you are not the police and I don't want to see you. Please go. I have to set off shortly on my last round of the day.'

Dawson loomed behind in Judith's shadow.

'Hello, Dr Wolf. Sorry to disturb you. Miss Burton is here with me this time. Miss Lamb has gone to fetch some of your staff with one of my other officers. They'll be here in just a moment.'

David stroked his moustache.

'Can you tell me what this is all about? I have just explained that I have patients to see.'

'No sir. But if you wait a few minutes all will be revealed. Is there a larger room we can use, do you think? There are going to be a fair few of us. And could you call your wife please, and ask her to join us too?'

'Dr Bridges?'

'That's the one.'

David headed out into the reception area. The clinics had finished for the evening and they waited there for the others to arrive. He poured himself a cup of water from the fountain.

Some light footsteps in the corridor heralded the arrival of Constance with Nurse Li. And PC Brown followed shortly afterwards with Steven King and Hani Mahmood. Jane Bridges took another five minutes to arrive. Dawson nodded amiably towards Judith to begin.

'This is outrageous,' Hani fumed. 'We have sick patients to administer to. I demand to know what on earth is going on that you should treat me and my staff in this reprehensible way.'

'Please, everyone, let's sit down,' Judith said. 'I will try to keep this brief but that depends a little on each of you. I am afraid that we are back here talking about Mrs Hennessy's death, and some of you know more than you have let on. I will start with Nurse Li.'

Lottie shivered as her name was called.

'Nurse Li. Can you tell everyone here how you spent the morning of Thursday the 11th of May, the morning Mrs Hennessy had her operation – just in general terms, to start with.'

'She was in the operating theatre, like I told you,' David interrupted.

'Nurse Li?'

Lottie gazed around the room for salvation, which did not materialise.

'I'm sorry, Dr Wolf. I didn't want to lie to you,' she began. 'I took Mrs Hennessy to theatre but then I went back to the ward. I had to do double-shift that day; other nurses were ill. I asked Steven and he said it was all right.'

'I said we would manage without her,' Steven acknowledged with a shrug.

David turned to his wife. 'So who was in theatre for Mrs Hennessy?' he enquired, wide-eyed.

Judith glared at him. 'You mean you weren't there either, Dr Wolf?'

He glanced at Hani, who was staring from one member of his team to the next in astonishment.

'David, what is going on? In the report you said you had the usual team in theatre. Was that not true?' Hani's words rebounded off the walls accusingly.

David sighed but before he could reply his wife took over.

'Hani didn't know about any of this,' she said quickly, standing up and taking centre stage. 'We have new targets from management,' she explained, 'and we decided, David and I, that the only way we could meet them, with our current number of doctors and nursing staff, was by running operations simultaneously with skeleton staff. Aladdin allowed us to do that. David was never in Mrs Hennessy's operation. Steven presided, with my help. When Lottie was stretched, we released her to help on the ward. Aladdin did all the work. We could call David if we needed him.'

'So, David, let me get this straight,' Hani asked, barely controlling his anger. 'You were never in Mrs Hennessy's operation. You left her in the hands of that machine and Steven, a one-year qualified doctor?'

'The operation was simple,' David replied. 'Aladdin could do it blindfold. And Jane was present, a highly experienced anaesthetist. And I thought Nurse Li was there too.'

'But Nurse Li returned to the ward, as we have heard, and then Dr Bridges was called away?' Judith said. 'That's recorded in the report you provided.'

'Yes.'

'So Steven was left alone.'

'Only for ten minutes or so.' All eyes shifted to Steven, who gulped audibly. Then he lowered his head into his hands.

'It's my fault. I shouldn't have left him,' Jane continued, 'but I had another emergency and Mrs Hennessy was routine. I had to prioritise.'

'I should've been able to manage,' Steven cried in exasperation. 'As soon as Jane left, the monitors went haywire. I tried to stabilise her but we'd given Aladdin control of everything. I couldn't stop it in time.'

'What do you mean exactly?'

Jane stepped in again. 'David told you that Aladdin is more sophisticated than the older models; that, if we wanted, we could pretty much hand medical procedures over to Aladdin. What he didn't tell you is that this is what we have been doing, on the simpler operations, for the last six months or so.'

'No!' Hani called out.

'It's no big deal. We tell Aladdin what the plan for the operation is and he performs it. We key in the weight, height, age of the patient, and Aladdin works out all the doses of oxygen, anaesthetic and any other drugs, and monitors and adjusts them throughout the operation. Again, it's just one step on from what we've done before, handing over autonomy to Aladdin to free up nurses and anaesthetists. We can override him but it takes maybe sixty seconds to kick in, and Steven didn't have a lot of practice in how to do this. Lottie or one of the other senior nurses would usually operate the manual override.'

'And the incisions, removing the bone which Dr Wolf so

meticulously described for us in court?'

'All Aladdin. And it was done very neatly.'

'What did you find when you returned to theatre after your emergency call?'

'Mrs Hennessy was dead.'

'Oh my God!' David leaped up and staggered towards his wife. She took two steps backwards but then held her ground.

'So had Aladdin malfunctioned?'

'It was a combination of human error and the machine. Steven had keyed in the figures incorrectly at the start, leading to one hundred times the usual dose of Propofol, the anaesthetic. The instructions are unclear primarily because they have been translated, but the machine should have picked this up straight away and corrected it, as it also monitors the depth of anaesthesia. For some inexplicable reason, it didn't. In Mrs Hennessy's case she was given this huge dose and the machine kept on increasing the dose as she went deeper to sleep.'

'The anaesthetic killed her so quickly?'

'Yes, that dose would have led to toxic levels building up in a matter of minutes, and her heart suddenly stopped. Since the incident, I spoke to the manufacturer and corrections have been made to the Aladdin algorithm to make sure the problem won't occur, or if it does it will be immediately detected and corrected. I did everything I could, with Steven, to revive Mrs Hennessy but we failed.' For the first time Jane's voice cracked mid-sentence. Her husband was staring at her in horror.

'What happened next?' Judith asked.

Jane continued in an unsteady voice.

'Steven was desperate. He had not lost a patient on his watch and he didn't want to be blamed. And I felt I should share responsibility as I had left him alone. But if we told what happened it would expose the flaws in our system, the one David and I had been operating so successfully, treating many more patients, faster, with less staff and far better outcomes. We were saving lives using Aladdin – more than we had anticipated at the outset – and improving quality of life; I didn't want to jeopardise that.'

'And Aladdin?'

'If we shopped Aladdin that would be very costly for the Trust after its investment, each one costs upwards of a million pounds – funds which we can't afford to waste. I didn't want it to be my fault, my misjudging which was the more needy patient, that caused the whole project to be scrapped and patients to die on the waiting list, or from mistakes that surgeons make every day.

'So I persuaded Steven that rather than make a big fuss, we should talk to Aladdin's manufacturer, which we have now done, like I said, to remedy the software issues and quietly issue some guidance to nursing staff on keying in the quantities into Aladdin for future reference. We didn't have to throw the baby out with the bathwater.'

'And what about "the baby", poor Mrs Hennessy?' Judith asked.

'I told Steven that I would find a way of hiding his involvement in Mrs Hennessy's death. It wasn't easy because they were expecting her in recovery. But we had operated in one of two overflow theatres as the others were all full and she was the last operation scheduled in there that day. So I told the recovery nurses that she was a bit slow to come around, and that Steven and I would keep her in theatre and look after her until she did. They had no reason to doubt what I said.'

'Did no one come in?'

'No. Those two theatres are only used when we are really

stretched. But we left her hooked up to a couple of tubes and switched the monitors back to the display mode. If anyone had come in, she would have appeared asleep. We also used some warming devices – they're rather like mini fan heaters – to keep her warm until we could decide what to do next.'

'Did she ever return to the ward?' Dr Wolf asked this time.

'No. Steven went up to the ward and made some notes in her medical log, so that it would look as if she had returned, listing the painkillers you asked about. Around 9:45, we wheeled her back up to the ward. We used the service lift out the back, but we didn't see a soul.'

'Who decided to drop her off the building?'

'I did,' Jane replied, shakily. 'I realised early on that if we just put her back into bed we would be found out, so I had the idea of dropping her body from a height. We were helped by her room being on the top floor so that it would be seen as a suicide or a terrible accident and the trauma of the injuries would cover anything else up. We turned the covers back on one side of the bed so it would look like she just climbed out herself. I never imagined for one moment that the police would think it was a murder.'

'But when Ahmad was arrested, you stayed silent.'

'You can't blame me. I was hardly going to own up then. I decided that if it looked as if he was going to be convicted then I would speak up. But you did your job very competently and he wasn't.'

'That's very convenient for you to say now, after the event.'

'I was in a difficult situation.'

'Of your own making. And I suppose you are a doctor with, what, a decade of training, and my client was only a cleaner! What about when Lottie rang to find out where Mrs Hennessy was?'

'I told her she was with the physiotherapist,' Steven piped up.

'Weren't you suspicious?' Judith asked Lottie, who hung her head. 'And you told us you saw Mrs Hennessy, when that wasn't true.'

'I persuaded Nurse Li to say what she did,' Jane intervened. 'And I pretended it came from Hani. I knew she would accept what he said without questioning. And she knew she should have been in theatre so I was doubly sure she would co-operate. She didn't know what we did though. We waited till she was occupied with another patient to throw Mrs Hennessy off the fire escape.'

Hani Mahmood gasped and shook his head repeatedly from side to side.

'But Dr Wolf, you lied too. I asked you how Mrs Hennessy was after her operation? You said she was "fine". I remember the exchange vividly,' Judith continued.

David remained wide-eyed, standing in the centre of the room. 'Dr Wolf?'

'Jane. How could you do this? If you'd asked me I would've helped you. We would have found another way of dealing with this. Not this.'

'Dr Wolf. Can you answer my question? Why did you lie to me? Why did you lie in court?'

'As far as I knew, Mrs Hennessy was "fine" after her operation. Don't you see? I had no part in her death or cover up. OK, I didn't do the surgery and I asked Steven to go up and see Mrs Hennessy post-op and to up her pain relief if she needed it. He told me he had. I didn't want to admit that I delegated, that's all. A tiny white lie in the scheme of things.'

'You pretended you operated on her when you were never

there. You confirmed the state of her health afterwards when you never even saw her. These were significant events you lied about.'

David continued to stare accusingly at his wife.

'I did it for the best!' Jane shouted at him.

'Best for whom? Hardly for Mrs Hennessy,' Judith replied.

'We couldn't bring her back. We tried. We were trying to salvage something.'

'So when Lucy asked me to persuade you to remove the Aladdin forms, that was all a pretence?' Hani asked. 'You and Lucy had already planned everything together.'

'Lucy didn't know about how Mrs Hennessy died. She was just "risk-averse" and didn't want Aladdin mentioned in court.'

'How did you know I would agree?'

'Lucy didn't give you much choice, from what I remember.'

'Yes. That's true.'

'What did she say to you, Dr Mahmood? That you'd get the sack if you didn't toe the line?' Judith asked.

'Pretty much,' Jane said. 'I didn't mean to deceive you, Hani, but I thought that was the best way to keep you quiet. And it worked. And David. You would never have gone along with it, I knew that. So it was better to keep you in the dark too; I'm sorry. Aladdin is a great addition to our hospital workforce. Its importance cannot be underestimated. We did this for patient care; nothing more. We knew we were risking our own positions.'

'But Lucy challenged you in the review meeting, about taking that call. She embarrassed you. Why did she do that, if you were working together?' Hani needed to understand it all, how he had been taken in so entirely.

'Yes. That was a bit of a surprise, I admit. She wanted to keep me in line too. To make it clear that it would be easy to make me a scapegoat, if the Trust wanted. I don't blame her.'

'Why didn't the high level of anaesthetic get picked up on the post mortem?' Judith asked.

'Probably not enough blood left for any meaningful testing,' Jane said. 'I had hoped that would be the case. And there was no reason to carry out those additional "toxicology"-type tests you would have to do anyway to detect it, given the obvious "cause of death". Our pathologists and laboratories are frantically busy. Why manufacture extra work when things are so clear-cut?'

Judith strode around the room, circling all its inhabitants, finishing next to Inspector Dawson.

'Inspector Dawson, I believe you need to take Dr Bridges and Dr King into custody then. Am I correct?' she asked soberly.

'You are,' he replied. 'And the rest of you need to be available to answer questions at the station tomorrow morning. For tonight, you are free to go. But please don't think of taking any holidays for quite a while.'

65

'That means Joe Hennessy is off the hook then, doesn't it?' Judith and Constance were breathing the evening air with relief as they stood outside the railway station awaiting Judith's taxi.

'I suppose it does. God, I hope Dawson can get him for something though. He's so dodgy.'

'He's going to be a father now. Maybe that will sort him out.'

'I doubt it. What did Dawson say? "Once a scumbag always a scumbag".'

'A very astute assessment from our illustrious partner in solving crime.'

Judith's taxi pulled up at the kerb. 'Are we finished now? Are you satisfied?'

'Yes. I think we're finally done.'

'Do you know what I'm going to do when I get home – after a pot of coffee and a long bath, that is? I'll need all my strength for this one.'

'No?' Constance laughed.

'I'm going to call my mother!'

Judith blew an air kiss in Constance's direction as she clambered into her cab.

'You sure I can't drop you somewhere?'

'No. I'll walk. I could really do with some fresh air after police stations and hospitals. Speak soon.'

'Last time you said that it was three months before we spoke.'

'You were the one who went all reclusive. Your fame went to your head.'

Judith giggled. 'Will you come and have dinner with me and Greg one evening? I promise not to talk about work.'

'That would be lovely, thank you.'

'Greg's idea, not mine,' Judith quipped. 'I hate having company.'

Constance threw back her head and laughed out loud as Judith's taxi sped away.

On a whim, she walked back along the street to the twenty-four-hour newsagent and bought herself an ice cream. Then she strolled up the nearby avenue of trees and sat down on the bench overlooking the pond and ate it greedily, enjoying the cool sensation on her tongue. She allowed herself to savour the last morsel before taking her phone out of her bag, switching it on and waiting to review her messages.

She had a WhatsApp from a number she recognised.

'Hi Sis. I'm in town next week. I'll call you, J.'

Constance shrugged. She wouldn't hold her breath. Sometimes Jermain did what he said, more often not. Next she dialled up her voicemail and heard a familiar voice.

'Hi Con. This is Mike. I miss you. Sometimes I'm really stupid, you know. Well I'm sure you do. And I get stuff wrong. I saw you on the news. You were really great. Can we have a drink some time this week? Tomorrow night, eight o'clock, usual place? I'll have a red carnation in my button hole.'

Constance's eyes filled with tears as she deleted the message. She wiped them away with the back of her hand as she replaced her phone in her bag and walked purposefully towards the Underground station.

ACKNOWLEDGEMENTS

My thanks go to all the team at Lightning Books: to Dan Hiscocks for his continued support and belief in my abilities, to Scott Pack for his incredible editing skills and guidance, to Hugh Brune for his enthusiastic sales campaign, to Simon Edge for his marketing expertise, to Shona Andrew for the fabulous cover design, to Clio Mitchell for copyediting and typesetting, and to Kat Stephen for proofreading.

I must, of course, also acknowledge the enormous contribution of my parents, Jacqie and the late Sidney Fineberg, both inspirational teachers, who encouraged me and my sisters to spend all our waking hours reading.

Particular thanks for their specific input into *The Aladdin Trial*, at various stages of its journey towards the final draft, and for answering my endless medical and forensic questions fully and comprehensively, must go to each of: Dr Liam Brennan, consultant anaesthetist, Dr Suzy Lishman, past president, Royal College of Pathologists, Dr Stuart J Hamilton, Home Office registered forensic pathologist, Professor Naomi A Fineberg, psychiatrist, and Dr Carmel Bergbaum. Thanks for an invaluable contribution on Syrian food, locations, names and language must go to Dr Abduljabbar Murad, and to Louise Lemoine for relevant background to the refugee crisis.

Finally, a huge thank you goes to everyone who has reviewed *The Aladdin Trial* and my first novel, *The Pinocchio Brief*, for taking the time to read my books and share their views in a variety of ways; including in radio broadcasts, space in some of our most prestigious national publications, for hosting me on their blogs and websites and for taking the time to post online reviews. Their support has provided me with the confidence to continue writing and, without their backing, I would not have been able to reach such a wide audience; I am forever indebted.